SECRETS IN THE MIST
PUBLISHED BY BRIGHTSTONE MEDIA, INC.
Copyright © 2016 by Anna Aycock

Cover Design and Interior Format by

SECRETS
IN THE MIST

ANNA LEE HUBER

For my grandmother, Virginia, who taught me the meaning of strength, dedication, resilience, and unconditional love. And whose laugh I shall never forget.

It still rings in my ears whenever I think of her.

Acknowledgements

I have so many people to thank for making this book possible. First and foremost is my husband Shanon, for his unwavering devotion and belief in me, and for pushing me to always strive for my best. Many thanks to my agent, Kevan Lyon, for always supporting and guiding me.

My gratitude to my writing group partners Stacie Roth Miller and Jackie Musser, whose enthusiastic response to this crazy idea helped give me the courage to pursue it. And extra special thanks to Jackie, whose impeccable eye and editing skills helped to shape the story into what it is today.

Thank you to my brainstorming partners Erin Knightley, Hanna Martine, and Heather Snow for their insightful suggestions while I was plotting. Much appreciation to Deb A; and to Kim, Jennifer, Shelly and the entire team at The Killion Group for all of their expertise.

Thank you to Tonya Kappes, Erin Knightley, and Christine Trent for their publishing advice. And last, but certainly not least, many thanks to all of my friends, family, and readers who continue to make my pursuing this career that I love possible; and immeasurable gratitude to God for all of His bountiful gifts.

Chapter 1

England
1812

I KNEW THAT TONIGHT OF ALL nights was not the time to be caught out in the marshes. It was the type of night those of us living amongst the broads and fens of East Anglia had been cautioned about since we were small children. When the mists rose up from the rivers and waterways through the reeds and tall grasses, they obscured the winding marsh paths and blinded us from the danger of the bogs. The shifting banks of fog were as hazy and insubstantial as smoke, and yet impenetrable to the eye, as well as the brightest lantern.

Had I any other choice, I would have remained safely inside, tucked up close to the warmth of the hearth. But tonight Kate needed me. With each passing hour her fever burned hotter, her breathing more labored. I was afraid that if I didn't return with the medicine she so desperately needed she might not last through the night.

So while the mist was still gathering I'd returned home to Penleaf Cottage to fetch what was needed. But before I could set out again, old Mrs. Brittle, our last retainer, had cautioned me about going back out into the marshes in such a fog.

"Be ye daft, lass? Ye canna gey back oot in this."

"I must," I had replied as I filled a basket with sickroom supplies, many of which were Mrs. Brittle's receipts. "Kate's illness is too severe for me to wait until morning."

She hobbled a step closer, leaning her bad hip against the table. "Yer care o' Mistress Rockland be admirable, but she'd no' wish ye to take such a risk."

"What else am I to do?" I demanded of her. "I cannot ask you to undertake such a journey. And Father—" I broke off, finding it difficult to voice the words. I turned away. "Well, he's certainly not able."

Mrs. Brittle pressed her gnarled, bony hand to my arm. "I ken, lass."

Earlier when I'd removed the empty bottle and the tumbler of cut glass from Father's study, where I'd found him insensible in his favorite chair, Mrs. Brittle had only shaken her head. But this was nothing new to either of us and I ruthlessly pushed it aside.

"There's no one but me," I told her in determination as I reached out to wrap the ends of the cloth I'd used to cushion the basket over the top of its precious contents.

Her leathery face crinkled into even deeper lines as she scowled up at me. "The Lantern Men be walkin' tonight. Mark me."

I turned away with a frown, lest she see the genuine apprehension her words had caused me. I was old enough and educated enough to recognize the legend of the Lantern Men for the fiction it likely was—a story meant to convince curious and unruly children to behave, an anecdote to explain the unexplainable. But I had also seen the lights—the will-o'-the-wisps, as they were called—mysterious glowing balls that sometimes hovered over the marshes, seeming to defy all logic or explanation. It wasn't easy to dismiss them or discount them, and so the tales of the Lantern Men had not lost all their power for me.

I had always avoided the marshes at night, particularly when the fog rose up or when the will-o'-the-wisps were seen glowing in the distance, on the chance that the legend was not so fictitious, but tonight I could not. Kate needed me, needed the medicine I carried, and I would never forgive myself if I let a silly fable keep me from my dearest friend. She was all I had.

"I'll be careful," I told Mrs. Brittle. "I promise."

She harrumphed. "So they all say. And then they ne'er come back. Remember Joseph Bexfield."

I scowled, hating how everyone brought up that poor man's name whenever someone was about to do something they deemed foolish. "How could I forget?"

Her beady black eyes hardened like jet. "There's no need to be smart. I s'pose ye'll be takin' yon lantern, as well." She nodded to the lamp I had set on the scarred table by the door. "Ye might as weel sing a ballad fer 'em while ye're at it," she snapped, touting local legend on what was most likely to draw the Lantern Men towards their next victim.

"Mrs. Brittle," I protested.

"Go on, then. Tempt fate if ye wish. But dinna say I didna warn ye." She wagged her finger at me. "And dinna expect me to mourn ye when they find ye face-doon in the marsh like Joseph." Then she had turned away and hobbled across the room to her little bedchamber off the kitchen and slammed the door.

I paused now and stared at the clouds of white swirling about me and wondered if perhaps I should have listened to her. Or at least decided to take the roads instead. Traveling the carriageways would have taken me nearly twice as long to reach Greenlaws House and forced me to pass through the village, but it surely would have been easier to follow a wide lane of packed earth than a meandering trail through over-grown marsh grasses that was difficult for those not native to the Broads to navigate on even the driest and sunniest of days. I had made the conscious decision to sacrifice safety for speed, but now I doubted the wisdom of that choice.

Taking a deep, calming breath, I realized there was nothing for it but to push onward into the cool, eddying mist. Besides, I was familiar with this particular stretch of marsh path, having traversed it often in the past two decades. I knew its course, its twists and turns, like I knew the plot of my favorite novel. Even when the heavy rains of late spring and autumn altered its course, I knew where it would be diverted. I had not become truly lost in the fens since I was a little girl, and our faithful hound, Matilda, had found me then quickly enough.

I wished Matilda were with me now. Perhaps her sharper senses could have picked up on what I was missing. The mist not only disoriented me visually, with its ever-shifting haze of white that swallowed up what little light my lantern cast, but also audibly. It dampened what little sound there was, masking the ripple and flow of the moving water I would have normally used to help guide me in the dark. I could hear nothing but the sound of my own breathing and an airy chorus of marsh grasses brushing together in the night breeze. It unnerved me to think that a person would have to be standing quite near for me to hear them.

More than once I felt the soles of my kid-leather boots sink into the boggy ground at the edge of the path, reminding me how easy it was to stray from the drier ground at the center. Each squishing step set my heart racing. Twice I stumbled to a stop, confused by my surroundings, and was forced to retrace my steps until I figured out where I'd gone wrong. I began to understand how even the most experienced of wherry men could become lost on such a night.

Proceeding cautiously, I weighed every step and calculated each turn with greater concentration, trying to utilize my other senses. I noted the feel of the ground beneath my feet, and the brush of the marsh grasses against the hem of my cloak. The musty stench of the fens, though muted by the wet banks of fog, served as a sort of guide—the sharp odor of decaying vegetation telling me where the more stagnant bogs lay. My ears strained for the slightest sound of moving water, knowing I should be approaching the stretch of path that ran parallel to a wider offshoot of the River Yare for several hundred yards, separated only by the reeds growing along its banks, before it veered left again. Normally I could hear the ripple of its current long before I reached it, but it wasn't until the trail had already straightened out to follow it that I heard the stream's swell.

I breathed a sigh of relief, knowing I was now more than halfway to my destination. I picked up my pace, anxious to be at my dearest friend's side and out of this swirling nothingness. The air was cooler here, and I shivered in my summer cloak, feeling the cold damp of the fog begin to penetrate its thin fabric. My arms were too full with the lantern and the basket to try to wrap the cloak tighter around me, and I didn't know that it would have made me warmer anyway. I told myself I only needed to ignore the discomfort for a little while longer.

That's when I saw them. The lights. The will-o'-the-wisps faintly glowing through the fog on my right, as if they hovered over the stream beyond the reeds.

I stumbled to a stop, suddenly panicked and uncertain what to do. For a moment I tried to convince myself they were nothing but a mirage manipulated by the mist. But then they all seemed to turn as one and move towards me. I glanced down at the lantern in my hands and cursed it. I knew—and if I'd forgotten, Mrs. Brittle had warned me—that carrying a lantern was rumored to be one of the things most likely to attract the Lantern Men.

I shook my head at the ridiculousness of entertaining such

nonsense. I was certain there was a logical explanation for the lights. But either way, the light from my lantern had alerted whoever was out there to my presence.

I lifted the lantern and fumbled to open the glass panel to blow out the flame, but then hesitated. How would I find my way through the marshes without the light? This fog was too thick for the pale light of the moon to penetrate, and without some source of illumination I was sure to become lost in the haze. What good would escape be if I then stumbled into a bog?

I slammed the panel shut, making the flame flicker, and forced my feet into motion. Whoever wielded the lights was gaining on me now, but if I could just get beyond the turn in the path, the marsh grasses would block most of the light from my lantern, and I hoped the fog would do the rest.

My feet slid on the mist-dampened grass, but I kept moving, with one eye on the path before me and the other on the pursuing lights. My heart leapt sharply against my rib cage as I realized that one light had pulled away from the others, moving to intercept me further along the trail. I bit back a whimper and pushed my feet to move faster, now rushing blindly through the fog. I knew it was dangerous, that I was as likely to go careening off the path as to be caught, but I couldn't stop myself.

As I approached the end of the straight stretch, I realized I was moving too slowly, that whoever was moving ahead to cut me off was going to catch me. A bolt of pure terror shot through me, seizing the breath in my lungs. I ducked my head and hastened my speed—praying something would impede him, that somehow I would surge past him—only to crash into something solid and immovable. I opened my mouth to scream, but no sound emerged.

I looked up into a pair of dark eyes. The...man...before me had dropped his light source at our feet in order to wrap his hands around my upper arms, throwing his features into shadow. He was swathed in darkness from head to toe, including a voluminous hood, giving me nothing but a glimpse of his sharp eyes as they bored into mine.

I stumbled backwards, surprised when his grip slackened, though he did not release me. He simply continued to study me with his pitch-black eyes, the corners narrowed like a cat's. His gaze unsettled me, though I could not seem to look away no matter how I tried. It was as if something held me immobile, sending tingles of awareness through me. I watched breathlessly as his eyes searched mine, seeming to brush against my skin with just the power of his gaze. I realized then that my hood had fallen back, giving him a clear view of my face and my auburn hair.

Shaken by the realization that he could see all of me while I could see almost nothing of him, I started to lift my lantern, wanting to know just who I was facing, but he would not let me raise my arm. He arched his eyebrows in faint mockery at my futile effort. And that sardonic expression was enough to rouse my good sense. I needed to escape. Now. Before it was too late.

Fortunately, my chance came when a voice behind me shouted, alerting us both to the approach of whoever carried the other lights. The man turned to watch them, and as he did I twisted from his grasp, dashing down the path to the left. I felt his hands grasp at my cloak and I pushed myself to move faster, heedless of the slick grass beneath my feet.

My heart pounded loudly in my ears, and I felt certain I could feel his fingers reaching for me again, that at any moment he would recapture me, hauling me back against his hard chest. When my foot slipped off the trail into a bog at a sharp turn, soaking my booted foot, I was forced to slow my steps. I risked a glance over my shoulder and was startled to see nothing but the swirling mist.

I inhaled a shaky breath, shocked to find I'd gotten away from them. If the legend was true, no one escaped the Lantern Men. They lured unwary travelers and foolish meddlers alike to their doom in a boggy mire or a watery grave. And yet here I was, alone again in the marsh.

I glanced around me, suddenly afraid they would approach from another direction, but the fens were silent and foggy white.

What did it mean? Why had the cloaked figure let me get away? Was it because he was alone? Would the situation have changed if others had arrived in time to intercept me? I shivered at the thought.

The path I followed continued to lead away from the stream toward Thurlton and Greenlaws House, and I was grateful for the distance it put between me and the Lantern Men. I could think of nothing better to call them. And yet, was that really what they were? He had felt as real and solid to me as any human, and what I could see of his disconcerting dark eyes had not been so different from other men. But, of course, the Lantern Men had always been rumored to be fae-like—ethereal, mischievous spirits akin to humans. Or so Mrs. Brittle believed.

I scowled, irritated at myself. I was being ridiculous. The Lantern Men were a myth, nothing but a bit of superstition. Clearly I had been listening to Mrs. Brittle's stories too often of late if I was actually willing to believe even for a moment that such creatures haunted the marsh.

Of course the figure was human. There was no reasonable alternative. Just because I had not recognized him, even though I knew everyone who lived within five miles of my home, did not mean he was some mythical being. Perhaps he was a relative of one of the townsfolk, a nephew or cousin recruited to help the local smugglers who plied the Broads. But I had never known the villagers to wear disguises as they went about their illicit trade. And if the man had not been familiar to me, then I was almost certainly unknown to him as well. He couldn't have recognized that I already kept their secrets. So why had he allowed me to escape?

My chest tightened at the memory of his eyes searching mine. The intensity of his gaze seemed to have marked me in some way I didn't understand, but felt to the core of me.

I increased my pace, suddenly glad of the thick walls of fog surrounding me, for if I could not see them, then surely they could not see me. At least, I hoped.

I exhaled in relief as I realized I was nearing the end of the marsh path. I made one last turn to bypass Thurlton village and headed straight toward Greenlaws, where Kate lived with her older brother. Perhaps it was wishful thinking, but I thought the fog was less dense here. It certainly seemed easier to breathe.

Seeing the marsh grasses begin to thin around me, I adjusted the basket of supplies on my arm and lengthened my stride, anxious to escape the fens and everything behind me. I welcomed the slope of open ground rising away from the marsh, even though the muscles in my legs burned from the exertion of the climb.

I was halfway up the hill before I realized I wasn't alone, and by then it was too late to react before the hand closed around my arm.

Chapter 2

THIS TIME MY LUNGS WERE not petrified by fear and I screamed. Tugging against the grip, I whirled about to face my attacker, raising my lantern to illuminate him. I tripped over my skirts and slipped on the slick grass, almost going down, but I caught myself in time to stay upright. My assailant shied away from the light, lifting his arm to cover his face.

"Ella, it's me," a familiar deep voice cried.

I lowered the lamp a fraction. "Robert?" I gasped, peering at him more closely. "Is it really you?"

He dropped his arm, still blinking at the brightness, and frowned at me. "Well, who else would it be?"

I bit my lip, unable—or perhaps unwilling—to answer him after my scare earlier out in the marshes. In any case, he didn't seem to expect a response.

"What are you doing here? I thought you'd returned to Penleaf."

"Kate needed this medicine." I lifted the basket looped over my arm in illustration and then turned to stride through the mist toward the house.

Her brother fell in step with me, taking the lantern from my other hand. "And you believed it couldn't wait until morning?" He shook his head. "I appreciate your loyalty to my sister, but wasn't it a bit foolhardy to venture into the marshes in this fog? I can't believe your father allowed it."

I frowned down at my feet where they kicked out the hems of my skirts. "He was indisposed," I replied indirectly, angry that Father had put me in such an awkward position, and irritated that Robert should even mention him.

I hoped he would leave the matter at that, but out of the corner of my eye I saw his gaze soften, and I got the impression he knew exactly what I wasn't saying. I refused to turn my head, lest he read it for certain in my eyes.

To cover my embarrassment, and to keep him from posing any further questions I didn't wish to answer, I asked after Kate.

His face crumpled in concern. "She still has a fever, and her breathing sounds no less ragged than before." He glanced down at the basket on my arm and then back to my face, a sheen of genuine fear in his topaz eyes. "Do you think I should send for Dr. Polk again?"

I lifted my hand and pressed it to his arm in comfort. "There's nothing more the doctor can do," I assured him. At any rate, it would take hours to fetch the physician from Norwich, if he would even come. Upon his departure in the early afternoon, after calling in the local apothecary to bleed Kate what I believed to be a dangerous amount, Dr. Polk had informed us there was nothing to be done but watch and wait. When Kate had worsened, I'd decided it was time to take matters into my own hands. Mrs. Brittle had been dosing my family with her own salves and tinctures since the day she and her late husband joined my parents' household long before I was born, and she'd rarely lost a patient on her watch—in fact, only once that I knew of. But I shook the troubling memory aside. In that case, there was nothing Mrs. Brittle could have done.

"It's up to us now," I informed Robert, infusing my words with as much confidence as I could muster.

My determination must have rung true, for he nodded and grabbed hold of my hand. Despite my preoccupation with Kate, I noted the warmth of his touch. It was a welcome distraction under the circumstances, and I refrained from pulling away from him, as I normally would have done these days. There had been a time when I would have given much for him to touch me like this, but that was a long time ago and things could never be as they once were.

The pale outline of Greenlaws emerged from the fog like a mirage until it took on solid form and substance. Though small compared to the nearby manor houses of Raveningham Hall and Waveney Hall, Greenlaws was still by far the largest home in Thurlton proper. Its pale red brick and pristine white trim stood in stark contrast to the weather-beaten boards of Penleaf Cottage. Not so long ago, our cottage had been as lovingly cared for as Greenlaws, but that was before—before the war, before my brother Erik's death, before Father started drinking.

I allowed Robert to guide me up the steps to the portico, but rather than opening the door as I expected, he turned to look at me as if he wished to say something. Worried it was something I didn't wish to hear, I pulled my hand from his grasp and reached for the door handle myself. He shifted his feet to block me, forcing me to look up into his handsome face.

"Ella, was there…" He hesitated uncomfortably and then took a step closer. "Did you…see anything out in the marshes?"

My heart leapt in my chest, glad this was all he wished to ask me about. However, the memory of those dark eyes staring down at me swiftly banished any relief. I had to resist the urge to turn my head to gaze out over the fens where they stretched out below us, wondering if the light of those lanterns could be seen from here. I already knew the fog, as well as the reeds and marsh grasses, would block anything from my view, but the compulsion was strong.

Not for a second did I consider telling Robert the truth, though I didn't quite understand why. It simply seemed better for him not to know.

"Of course not," I lied, worried my voice sounded higher in pitch than normal.

He studied my face for a tense moment and then nodded in acceptance.

I tilted my head in sudden curiosity. "Why? Did you see something?"

He glanced over his shoulder in the direction of the marshes, rubbing a hand across his forehead and into his caramel-brown hair. "I thought I did. But…it may have just been your lantern." He glanced down at where he still held my lantern in his hand and then smiled sheepishly. "I have to tell you, when I first saw your light coming out of the marshes and up onto the lawn, it startled me."

"And so you went out to investigate?"

"Well, of course," he replied as if that was all the explanation I needed. And perhaps it was. Robert was nothing if not dutiful. He took all of his responsibilities seriously, including protecting his household. It was one of the things I'd always liked about him, even when I didn't.

I turned away before I could say something I would later wish unsaid, and lifted the basket on my arm again. "Kate?"

"Yes." He stepped to the side, opening the door for me.

I hurried past him and up the stairs without another word.

"How is she?" I whispered, touching Nora gently on the

shoulder where she dozed in a chair by Kate's bed.

The maid blinked open her eyes and arched her back forward to stretch it. I set the basket of supplies on the bedside table and turned to examine our patient.

"Not so good, miss," Nora replied, concern tightening her voice. "She won't drink much, though I did try, more than once."

Kate slept fitfully, her eyes moving back and forth beneath their lids and her forehead furrowing with each raspy breath. I pulled my gloves off and laid the back of my wrist against her skin, feeling that it still burned with fever.

"Well, we'll simply have to force her then," I replied, hoping it wouldn't come to that, but determined to get water into her regardless. "Can you heat a kettle of water?" I asked Nora while I dug the tin of dried yarrow, feverfew, and sage from the basket. I handed it to her. "Steep three teaspoons of this in it."

The maid nodded and hurried off to carry out my instructions, closing the door softly behind her. I picked up the cloth resting in a bowl of water on the table and wrung it out, then leaned over Kate's unconscious form and bathed her forehead. She groaned and turned her face toward the coolness, seeming to seek it out, further disturbing her already uneven breaths.

"Shhh, Kate," I crooned. "It's only me. Ella."

She made no sign of having heard me, and I swallowed hard, forbidding myself to give in to a spate of worrying when there were things to be done.

Pulling the blankets back from her shoulders, I could feel the heat radiating beneath. I folded the coverings down to her waist and began to unlace the top of her nightdress. After carefully bathing her there, I dropped the cloth back into the bowl of water with a soft splash and reached for the jar of balm. As I removed the lid, the pungent but not unpleasant odor of peppermint filled my nostrils, accented by the more mellow floral notes of hyssop and yarrow. The smell instantly took me back to the sickrooms of my childhood, and my mother's gentle touch and sweet voice singing me lullabies.

For a moment, I was stunned by the force of the memory. It had been a long time since I'd allowed myself to think about my mother or my brother, and in the space of less than an hour I'd conjured both of their faces. Squeezing my eyes shut tightly, as if that alone would slam closed the lid on painful remembrances, I stuffed the emotions they evoked back deep down inside me where they belonged.

I sat down on the bed next to Kate and dipped my fingers into the balm. Then I leaned forward to rub it across her chest and neck. Kate's throat rattled with congestion as she inhaled, her nostrils flaring at the scent. Careful to disturb her as little as necessary, I rolled her to the side and slathered more of the ointment across the skin on her upper back beneath her nightdress. After settling her back against the feather mattress, I did up the ties of her nightclothes loosely and left the blankets down around her waist.

I sat back to look at her, wondering if she was already breathing better or if it was just wishful thinking on my part. She seemed more comfortable, even if her fair skin appeared just as flushed, her normally shiny brown hair damp and matted with sweat.

I silently urged my friend to open her eyes, even though I knew that for the moment it would be better if she didn't. Her fever-bright eyes would only frighten me, and the icy ball of dread pressing down on my chest was already almost unbearable.

Kate was my closest friend, dearer to me than even a sister could be. She knew me better than anyone in the world. I sometimes thought she was the only one who truly knew me at all. The closeness that had existed between Robert and I had vanished almost four years ago. Father was nearly a stranger to me, and Mrs. Brittle was old and nearing death's door. Kate was all I had. And if she left me too…

The icy ball inside me squeezed, stopping my breath.

I reached out to clutch her hand between my own, running my thumbs over her clammy skin while I prayed that Nora hurried with the feverfew tea.

The clatter of a cup pulled me from my uneasy dozing. I blinked open my eyes and squinted into the muted light of dawn pouring through a crack in the curtains and falling across my face. I leaned forward, and groaned at the soreness in my muscles from sleeping in such an awkward position. Rubbing a hand across my eyes, I turned to watch Kate's fat, orange tabby cat jump down from the bedside table. She'd tipped over a half-full cup of feverfew tea, sending it dribbling over the side of the table to puddle on the floor. I cursed the nosy feline and grabbed a dry cloth to dab at the mess.

The worst of it cleaned up, I turned cautiously toward Kate, worried what I might find. Her chest moved up and down evenly beneath the covers, still crackling with congestion, but much softer than the night before. Her face was smoothed of its lines of pain, and I dared to think her complexion appeared less flushed, more healthy pink than fiery red.

I shifted forward and gently pressed the back of my wrist to her forehead, finding it cool to the touch. Just to be sure I wasn't fooling myself, I slid my hand over her cheeks and down her neck, finding them cool as well. The breath I'd been holding for what felt like days left me in a rush, and I sank back in my chair to bite back tears of relief.

Kate's fever remained broken, but even so I stayed with her through the rest of the morning and late into the afternoon, continuing to dose her with feverfew tea. She slept through most of the day, but stayed awake long enough in the middle of the afternoon for me to spoon half a bowl of beef broth into her. Even her chest congestion seemed to be less than the day before, though I knew that upon nightfall it was likely to worsen again.

Despite these improvements, I had intended to remain another night at Greenlaws to ensure her illness did not return. However, my father it seemed had a different idea.

Having apparently slept off the ill effects of drink the night before, he came looking for me in the early evening, when the bright orange ball of the sun had just begun its descent over the marshes. This was a move I had not anticipated. My father so rarely seemed to care what I did or where I went that I'd long since stopped leaving word of my intentions. In any case, Mrs. Brittle always knew where I could be found.

So when Robert called me down to the front parlor, I expected to be asked to give a report on his sister's progress. When instead I found myself facing my father, I was slightly alarmed.

Father was clean-shaven and dressed in freshly pressed clothes, though they could not hide the pale green cast of his skin or his bloodshot eyes. He appeared uneasy, and I found myself wondering when he had last entered this room. Glancing at Robert's awkward stance I thought it might have been during the reception held a few weeks after Robert's London wedding. None of us wanted to remember the commotion Father had caused then. It was just months after news of Erik's death had reached us. Just months after Father had resumed his drinking.

"Father," I gasped, coming to a stop just inside the door. "Is something wrong?"

"No, no," he replied in a voice made hoarse from disuse and strong spirits. "I've just come to fetch you home."

My gaze slid from him to Robert, who watched our exchange with curiosity, and back again. "I thought I might stay another night with Kate. Her fever only just broke this morning and she's still very weak." I looked to Robert, hoping he would support me in this, but he remained silent.

"Well, Miss Rockland has a maid who can sit with her, does she not?" Father turned for confirmation to Robert, who nodded. "So it sounds like matters are well in hand."

My brow furrowed and I clenched my hands at my sides. "Yes, but I would rather remain here in case she needs me."

Father slapped his gloves lightly against his palm, repeating the action as he'd always done when he was impatient. "You've dosed her with Mrs. Brittle's tea, haven't you?"

"Yes, but—"

"Then you've nothing to worry about. I've never known that brew not to do the trick."

I wasn't certain whether I was supposed to find this statement comforting, but in any case, it didn't work.

"Gather your things and we'll be off," he proclaimed.

"Father, I really think—"

"I'll be waiting for you on the porch. Good to see you, Mr. Rockland," he remarked, crossing the room and disappearing through the door.

I glared at Robert. "Why didn't you correct him?" I demanded.

Robert leveled the same steady, superior gaze at me that used to infuriate me as a child. "Perhaps it's for the best. I'm sure Kate will recover quickly now, thanks to you. But even given the circumstances, you know your staying here isn't strictly proper."

I wanted to snap at him. There was no society about to protect our reputation from, and even had there been, given our recent past I doubted they would have suspected anything untoward. Robert knew this, but I sensed it would be useless to argue. Both men had made up their minds, whatever their true reasons. I sighed and stomped out of the room to return to Kate's bedside.

Had Kate truly still been in danger, nothing could have pulled me from her side, but they were right. The worst was past, though it would be a matter of weeks before she made a full recovery. In the meantime, I could leave instructions with Nora for her care and feel certain they would be carried out. If Kate's condition worsened, I could also trust her to find a way to get a message to me, even if it meant circumventing her master should he deem contacting me unnecessary.

I gathered up my cloak and crossed the entry hall, only to be halted by Robert. I could see Father pacing back and forth across the porch through the window by the front door.

"Ella," he murmured, his eyes saying more things than I could understand. "You will be all right, won't you?"

I narrowed my eyes at him, refusing to be swayed by his show of concern. That he was talking about my father was clear, and I felt the sting of a blush across the crest of my cheeks. I cursed him for making me feel it. "It's none of your concern."

Whatever right he'd had to worry about me had been forfeited when he'd married Olivia. Her passing changed nothing.

I turned away with a swirl of my cloak and pulled open the door to join my father.

Chapter 3

FATHER INSISTED WE TAKE THE road through the village instead of the marsh path. I didn't argue with him, not eager to venture into the fens again so soon after the night before. In any event, I knew Father wanted to stop by the White Horse Inn, and I was too tired to protest, though it left a sick feeling in the pit of my stomach. He left me sitting on the bench outside while he completed his transaction.

Few people ever visited Thurlton, and those who did were usually guests of Greenlaws, so the White Horse Inn was really nothing more than a pub with a few dusty rooms upstairs. Its worn façade, with the last remnants of white paint sticking to the wind-blasted wood like burrs, inspired little confidence in its prominence. But it was the physical and social center of the village, at least for the men. At any time of day, a group of at least three or four men could be found inside arguing about something of no consequence.

In contrast, their wives preferred to cluster in the churchyard across the street diagonal to the inn. Nowhere in England was there a better-tended front walk, bordered by flowering bushes and fragrant blossoms, the maintenance of which the women used to excuse their gathering there to indulge in idle chitchat. Ivy and rose trellises crawled up over the lychgate, inviting the passerby to step inside, a stark contrast to the dull wood and stone and thatch of the rest of the businesses clustered in the center of the village along the single road that ran through town. In one direction the carriageway led to the town of Hales and further on to Norwich; in the other, it meandered deep into the marshes only to end at Penleaf Cottage.

I sat watching the women prune deadheads off the roses growing over the lychgate, wishing I could offer to help. But I knew from experience that while my assistance would be welcomed, it wasn't truly wanted. The women couldn't properly gossip while I was about, so an awkward silence would fall, strained by polite exchanges, the distance between us in blood and tradition simply too great to overcome even though I was far from being the grand lady of any manor.

In all honesty, as much as I wished I could bridge that gap between the village women and myself, I was also grateful for it. It kept them from behaving in too familiar a manner, and from displaying the pity I suspected they felt for me—spinster daughter of a drunkard. I dropped my gaze to the scuffed and worn toes of my boots, a pair one size too big for me that I'd pulled from my mother's closet when my own pair had worn through the soles. Mrs. Brittle had urged me to take them to the cobbler, but I couldn't. Not when I wasn't sure he'd been paid for the last two visits our family had made to his shop.

"Albie told me he saw 'em last night. Movin' through the fens, headed fer the Dawkins place."

I glanced up as Mrs. Turner and her neighbor Mrs. Harper, arms linked and heads tilted toward each other, emerged from the path between the inn and the apothecary and turned toward the church.

"Even through the fog?" Mrs. Harper gasped in awe.

Mrs. Turner nodded her head, her voice grave. "Those lanterns o' theirs are no' normal. They're witch lights. Brighter 'n even a star." She leaned in closer to murmur, "Some say it's 'cuz they're lit wi' the souls o' their victims—those they drained the life from."

A shiver ran down my spine at her words, as I knew precisely what she was talking about—the will-o'-the-wisps, the Lantern Men. Between my concern for Kate, my exhaustion, and my father's uncustomary interference, I'd had little time to contemplate the matter, but I had managed to convince myself the man I'd encountered in the marshes must have been working with the local smugglers. However, hearing Mrs. Turner's and Mrs. Harper's concerns, now I felt less certain.

Everyone in Thurlton knew about the smugglers. People in Norfolk had been smuggling goods in and out of the country for the better part of 150 years. It had begun initially as a solution to the hefty import and export taxes few could afford to pay, but the system had simply become too ingrained in people's lives to stop even when the taxes were lowered or repealed. Much of the village depended on their enterprise, and a large number of the men were employed by them in some capacity, including Mr. Turner and Mr. Harper. We all knew, but no one talked about it. At least, not in public. I assumed their wives and families were aware of far more than the smugglers wished them to know. So to hear Mrs. Turner and Mrs. Harper speak of those lights as if they were still the figures from myth, something to be feared, made my stomach hollow in apprehension.

That the women should notice me at the same moment was bad luck. I somehow managed a wobbly smile as they asked after Kate, hoping the women would attribute the strain in my voice as concern for my friend. I wanted to ask them more about what their husbands had seen the night before, but I knew I couldn't. Not without breaking the unspoken rules we all followed. They were kind, assuring me they were all praying for Kate's recovery, before they hurried off to join their friends, who were now pretending not to watch us from the churchyard.

Thankfully, Father came striding out the door a moment later, his step lighter than before, and a noticeable bulge in the pocket of his greatcoat. I didn't comment, wondering if he actually thought he was hiding the bottle of brandy from me, from any of the villagers, or if he only carried it in his pocket out of propriety. After all, gentlemen simply didn't stroll the streets with bottles of spirits. A discreet silver flask tucked in the inside pocket of a frockcoat, maybe, but not entire bottles. They normally didn't collect it themselves either, but we'd long since lost all of our manservants, being unable to pay them, and Mrs. Brittle refused to procure the devil's brew for him. How he was able to pay for the brandy when he couldn't pay most of the shopkeepers, I never knew, but I had long suspected the steady supply of brandy Mr. Ingles, the proprietor, provided was the local smugglers' bribe for my father's silence.

I hurried away from the center of the village and the churchyard full of watchful women, knowing father's long stride would easily keep up with mine. The sun was at our backs and the marshes stretched before us, the lush green blades of its grasses gently waving back and forth beneath the pale pink-and-gold-streaked sky. I watched my father out of the corner of my eye as we strolled past the last house on the outskirts of the village, wondering if he realized how ironic it was that it had been the French who killed his son, and now they and their cursed brandy were killing him, too. I bit back the urge to tell him so, knowing from bitter experience that nothing I said would make a difference. Father would only become cross and take greater pains to hide from me how much he was drinking. An effort that was fruitless, as Mrs. Brittle and I knew every hiding place in his study and would eventually clear the room of his empty bottles. How he could find the initiative to conceal them in the first place but not to remove them from the house, I never understood.

I pressed a hand wearily to my forehead and brushed the loose tendrils of hair that had escaped from my chignon back from my face. My anger and embarrassment spent, my fatigue from the long night and day of nursing Kate began to overwhelm me. Father kept pace with me, even though my steps had begun to drag, and I knew he must be anxious to return home to open his bottle of brandy. He might be a drunkard, but he was also a gentleman, and he would never have rushed ahead and left a lady, let alone his own daughter, to walk home alone.

From the furrow in his brow and the way he kept rubbing his temples beneath the brim of his hat, I knew he must have been craving his drink quite badly. I considered telling him I would look away if he wanted to take a swig of brandy straight from the bottle, but that would mean broaching this strange fiction that lay between us, and I refused to condone his actions even that little bit. He would simply have to suffer for the last quarter mile.

I thought perhaps he would question me about Kate's condition, or at least mention my imprudent trek through the marshes the previous evening. For I was certain if he had known where to find me, Mrs. Brittle had been the one to tell him, and she would not have failed to complain about the stupidity of my actions. But he said nothing. A vague twinge in the vicinity of my heart grew more and more pronounced with each silent step we took closer to home. That I actually wished he would scold me for my foolishness was a sad testimony to the state of our relationship. I wondered, as I had so many times of late, whether he simply didn't care or if he only couldn't be bothered, so consumed were his thoughts by other things. I wasn't sure which answer I preferred.

As we passed through the gate dividing our scraggy, overgrown front lawn from the end of the dirt track that served as a road, Father finally turned to me. "Will you take dinner in the dining room or retire directly to bed?"

I gazed back at him, trying to read the hopeful expression in his eyes. Did he want me to join him for dinner or, more likely, did he wish to avoid the strained ritual and instead barricade himself in his study for the remainder of the evening? I had planned to seek the solace of my bedchamber, hoping exhaustion would bring sleep and relief from my current uncomfortable emotions. But seeing Father's eagerness to escape me, yet another reminder of how he preferred the contents of a bottle to his daughter, I found myself responding the opposite.

"I believe I'll eat in the dining room this evening. Sleep can wait." I lifted my chin, worried he would choose this of all things to scold me for.

He merely nodded and turned to hurry up the walk. I watched him go, suddenly wishing I'd been kinder. Perhaps if I'd been nicer, he wouldn't have been quite so keen to leave me.

I lifted my face toward the deepening sky and closed my eyes, feeling the cool evening breeze play with the loose tendrils of my hair. I took a deep breath and released it, reminding myself it was useless to try to understand the quagmire of emotions associated with my father when I was in such a state. Exhaustion had a way of amplifying things better left unexamined. I already had too many worries dragging at me—Kate's illness, Robert and our past, my future, and now that Lantern Man I'd seen in the marshes the previous evening.

The Lantern Man. That's what I'd continued to call him in my mind, whether it was true or not, for I could think of nothing better. The luster of his pitch-black eyes fringed by thick lashes, the intensity of his gaze, appeared before my closed eyes and I blinked them open, startled by the clarity with which I could recall what little I had seen of him.

A crawling sensation began at the base of my spine, like the press of fingers inching up my back. I studied the windows of the house, wondering if Father or Mrs. Brittle were staring out at me, but the curtains and drapes remained undisturbed.

With growing unease, I slowly turned my head to scan the marsh grasses surrounding our house. Nothing seemed out of place. No dark eyes watched me from behind the waving curtain of reeds. At least, none that I could see.

I pushed away from the gate, deciding it was past time I sought the shelter of our cottage.

Chapter 4

WHEN I ENTERED THE KITCHEN, Mrs. Brittle looked up from chopping root vegetables to scan me once from head to toe before returning to her work. Her knife struck the table with a solid thunk, accenting her obvious agitation. "Nursed Miss Rockland through the night, did ye?"

"Yes," I replied, sidling closer. "Her fever broke this morning, but I thought it best to continue to dose her with your feverfew tea."

She nodded. "Ye look like ye're aboot to fall asleep on yer feet. Git yersel' off to bed."

My lips curled into a slight smile, used to her cantankerous nature. "Not yet," I answered, speaking to the top of her bent head and the faded white mobcap covering the steel-gray strands of her hair. "I told Father I would eat dinner with him in the dining room."

She glared up at me. "Noo, why'd ye do that?"

I sighed wearily and dropped my gaze to the scarred tabletop, hoping Mrs. Brittle wouldn't make me put it into words. I already regretted my silly impulse. Forcing Father to eat dinner with me would be no punishment for him, but it was beginning to be for me. Fatigue dragged at my limbs, and I sank onto the stool Mrs. Brittle often leaned against when her hip was paining her. I reached out to finger the soft green leaves of a sprig of parsley and snuck a glance at her. Her beady black eyes had narrowed in understanding.

"Aye. Stopped at the White Horse, did he?"

I nodded.

She harrumphed and lifted the hem of her apron to scrape the carrots and turnips she had diced into the little well she created with the fabric. She shuffled across the short space to the cook top and unceremoniously dumped the contents into the pot of boiling liquid with a cascade of splashes. I was grateful for the short reprieve from her knowing stare. Mrs. Brittle's shrewdness was often as unsettling as it was comforting, and as grateful as I was for her continued presence here at Penleaf—for she was often my only companion—I also tired of her disapproving ways.

I rested the side of my head in my hand and turned to gaze out the kitchen window at the deepening shadows cast by the cottage over the kitchen garden. Our lone tree, a stunted sycamore, always appeared so forlorn to me at this time of day. Its limbs, already withered and bent by the sometimes fierce winds that blew in from the North Sea ten short miles away, lost all definition and color in the dying light. Its flaky bark was drained of its silvery sheen, and the lush green leaves deepened to gray, resembling nothing so much as a once-lovely woman who has lost her beauty. I sighed, wondering if I was to become that woman—solitary, pitiful, my beauty and ultimately my life wasted away here by the marshes.

My options had always been few. My father's stipend from his family being only modest and his social connections limited, there was never to have been a London season for me, and so my suitors had been restricted to those of our acquaintance and proximity. I had never minded. My heart had been settled on Robert from as early as I could remember, and it had seemed Robert felt the same way. Until he went to

London that fateful November almost four years ago and met Olivia Deveraux.

The sour taste I always associated with Robert's late wife flooded my mouth. I swallowed hard, trying to wash away my memories of the woman, and my failings to befriend her. She had just been so very difficult to like, particularly as she never let me forget how Robert had chosen her over me. More than once I had been tempted to take her out into the marshes and abandon her to her own fate. Either she would find her way out or she wouldn't.

Or she would have been discovered by someone—or something—else.

I sat up taller, wrapping my arms around my middle. What would the Lantern Man have done if he'd found Olivia? Would he have let her go as easily? Or would we have found her floating face-down in the marshes like Joseph Bexfield?

"Is yer father all that be troublin' ya, lass?" Mrs. Brittle's eyes studied me beneath her scraggly eyebrows as she stripped the needle-like leaves from a sprig of rosemary with one swipe between her fingernails, releasing their evergreen scent into the air. I could tell my silent rumination had sparked her curiosity. "Did somethin' frighten ye oot there in the bogs?"

For a moment I considered telling her—about the marsh man, about how frightened I'd been, about how confused I was about who he was and why he'd let me go. But somehow I knew I would only be asking for more trouble. Mrs. Brittle was nothing if not superstitious, and I had no desire to hear her predictions for the dire consequences I now faced, whatever she thought they might be. There would be no doubt in her mind that he had been one of the men from the myth, and I needed to think logically about this, not indulge in a flight of fancy.

No, it seemed better to keep it to myself. After all, there was every possibility there would be no ill effects, and that

I would never see the Lantern Man, whoever he was, again.

Oddly, that thought did not comfort me.

"Just the fog," I replied, having no trouble sounding convincingly distressed. "I had no idea it could be so thick or disorienting."

Mrs. Brittle studied me for a moment and then nodded. "Aye. Mr. Brittle often spoke o' it, and he a retired seaman who'd seen his fair share o' fogbanks." She paused and then added with a searching look, "'Tis no' fer the faint o' heart."

I rose from my perch on the stool. "I'll set the table in the dining room," I told her, eager to escape her penetrating gaze before she dragged my secrets from me.

Mrs. Brittle didn't argue, as she sometimes did when I offered to perform the tasks that under normal circumstances would have been completed by a servant. As if Father and I could still afford to worry about such distinctions. However, she refused when I suggested for perhaps the thirtieth time that she dine with Father and me. She still clung to the long-held propriety that servants such as she ate their meals in the kitchen, even though I insisted that I had ceased thinking of her as anything but family years ago. She barely tolerated my dining with her in the kitchen when Father was too incapacitated to join me; but when he did dine with me, always in the dining room, she would not join us.

By the time I carried the soup tureen out to the dining room, Mrs. Brittle hobbling behind me with a fresh loaf of bread and butter, Father had had over an hour and a half to imbibe his French brandy. Though he wasn't completely sotted, he was well on his way to being tipsy. He reclined in his chair at the head of the table, cradling a glass of the warm caramel-colored liquid in his hand. Father had broken most of the tulip-shaped goblets traditionally used for holding brandy one-by-one over the past few years, and I had broken the last two in a fit of anger six months ago, but he seemed not to care what kind of cup he drank his preferred liquor from. I suspected he would use a dainty teacup if necessary, or simply swill it straight from the bottle.

Mrs. Brittle insisted on ladling the soup into our bowls and then retreated to the kitchen, leaving me to my father's dubious company. Knowing I was too tired to mind my tongue and effectively suppress my feelings, I had resolved to pass a quiet meal, but Father had other ideas. He refilled his glass from the already almost half-empty bottle on the table beside him, largely ignoring his stew of vegetables and a meager amount of mutton. Mrs. Brittle did an admirable job of stretching our often paltry resources with produce from the garden, but it was sometimes difficult not to recall how delicious her stews had been when we had beef and wine and spices for her to cook with.

"So, Rockland seemed perfectly civil," he drawled, his voice slurring only slightly.

I glanced up at him, wishing I could ignore him, but the levelness of his gaze told me he wasn't sufficiently foxed for me to try such a thing just yet. "Robert is always civil."

"Yes. But civil as an orange." He smiled at his own jest and I suppressed the urge to scowl.

Though that pun from Shakespeare's *Much Ado About Nothing* might have aptly described Robert's behavior toward Father, he had never acted bitter towards me. No, I would have to say I was the one with the tart tongue when it came to my and Robert's interactions.

I returned my attention to my soup, not liking the speculative gleam shining in Father's eyes. Hungry as I was, I was having trouble stomaching the meal, perhaps because of my worry over Kate and my fatigue. Or the uncomfortable emotions that had been dredged too close to the surface since last night. I silently prayed Father would leave me be, but I released a weary sigh, already knowing that was not to be the case.

"I expect he'll be paying me a call before long," he mused out loud, watching me for a reaction, which I gave him.

"Why, Father?" I asked in irritation.

"Don't play ignorant, Ella," he scolded. "It's not attractive."

I frowned.

He settled deeper into his chair. "You know Robert Rockland needs to take a new wife. And it makes perfect sense that he should look to you." He narrowed his eyes and took a sip of his brandy. "Should have married you years ago instead of Lord Deveraux's chit."

I stared at the handle of my silver spoon where it rested against the side of my soup dish. The old familiar ache squeezed my chest again, making it difficult to breathe. One would have thought I would have become accustomed to it by now.

"I considered suing him for breach of promise. But you said he never made you a formal offer." He looked to me and I shook my head. "Well, even so, the man had made his intentions clear to all of Thurlton. His behavior was shameful. And I let him know it."

"Yes, Father," I replied crossly. "You let *everyone* know it." I clenched my fists in remembered embarrassment of the scene he had caused in the Rocklands' front parlor in front of half the good society of Norfolk and Suffolk.

Father seemed to remember as well, for he shifted uncomfortably in his seat. "Yes, well, I'm of half a mind to tell you to refuse the cad. But…" His face fell. "I don't know that you'll receive another offer."

I looked up at him sideways, forced to physically bite my tongue to keep from speaking. Even so, I knew I had not done a sufficient job of keeping the anger and loathing I felt toward him from burning in my eyes. That he could state it so bluntly…that he could not even offer me an apology for his part in placing me firmly on the shelf—marked *unmar-riageable.*

His brow furrowed in some semblance of an emotion that resembled guilt. He lifted his glass and downed the rest of its contents. "Yes, well," he mumbled. His eyes darted toward my stew. "If you're finished eating…"

I waved him off, and he rose to beat a hasty retreat.

I glared at the dull wood of the table—solid oak that had once gleamed in the candlelight. If my mother had still been alive, she would have been horrified that we had allowed the furniture to go unpolished for so long. But then again, maybe she would have understood.

In that moment, I felt a sudden intense longing for her presence, as I hadn't allowed myself to feel in years. I couldn't help but think that she would have known what to do. And even if she hadn't, at least she would have been here to tell me everything would be all right. Even if she had to lie to me.

I pressed a hand to my forehead, reminding myself I could lie just as well. Hadn't I been doing so for years? A cynical smile curled my lips.

I glanced down at my still half-eaten meal and sighed. Sleep. I needed sleep. All of this would seem less troubling after a good night's rest.

Unfortunately, even the two trips I made back to the kitchen as I cleared the table, and the quarter of an hour I spent helping Mrs. Brittle wash and dry the dishes were not sufficient enough to untangle my nerves and bottle up the emotions that had been spilling out all day. So instead of making my way upstairs to my bedchamber, I carried a candle into the drawing room and set it down on the pianoforte. I lifted the lid and ran my fingers over the smooth ivory keys. Settling down on the bench, I stretched my fingers and began to play a Mozart sonata I knew from memory. The instrument hadn't been tuned in years—since my nineteenth birthday, an unex-

pected gift from my father. He'd forgotten my twentieth and
twenty-first.

I shook the distracting thought aside and closed my eyes,
trying to concentrate on the music, discordant as it was, but all
I could think about was my mother. I suddenly remembered
she had been the one to teach me this piece. My fingers stumbled to a halt, unwilling to finish.

I wrapped my arms around my middle. I was trembling,
whether from fatigue or pain I wasn't sure. All I knew was that
I had to escape this house, even if only for a moment. There
were too many ghosts here tonight. Too many memories bat-
tering at the barriers I'd firmly placed between myself and
the past. It had begun with my fear over Kate's illness, and my
exhaustion had only made my weakness worse.

I retreated to the hall and set my extinguished candle on
the bureau by the front door. The entry plunged into darkness, except for the firelight shining from beneath Father's
study door and another faint glow issuing from the direction
of the kitchen at the end of the passage. I pulled my cloak
down from its peg and carefully slipped out the front door,
not wishing to alert Father or Mrs. Brittle to my exit. Not
that there was much chance of either of them paying the least
bit of attention. Mrs. Brittle had sought her bed the same time
I should have gone to mine, and Father would be lounging
before the fire in his favorite chair, possibly already insensible.

I hesitated a moment on the front step, wondering if perhaps I was being foolish to leave the safety of the cottage,
especially after everything that had happened the previous
night. But the idea of retreating to my room to stare up at my
shadowy bed curtains while the bittersweet memories of my
youth played out before my eyes seemed torturous. So without another thought to any danger I might be placing myself
in, I plunged into the night, turning right to circle the house.
My skirts slapped against the overgrown grass as I stretched

out my stride. I passed the kitchen garden surrounded by its weathered white fence and the lonely sycamore and headed straight for the once well-trodden path that led out through the marsh grasses to our boat dock.

The water that lapped gently against the pier's wood eventually flowed out of our little inlet and into the channels that fed into the River Yare and the River Chet. Here on the Broads, the labyrinth of waterways was only truly understood by the wherry men, and perhaps the smugglers, who were often one and the same. The wherry men made their living by plying through the shallow waters with their boats to deliver goods from the larger ports on the coast. I could remember a time when entire packets of supplies had been delivered to Penleaf in much the same manner. Now we purchased our supplies from Thurlton, and consequently the dock had fallen into disrepair, its wood warped and worn and in a few places starting to splinter. It was a long dock, as those in the marsh were required to be in order to stretch far enough out through the boggy beds of reeds and grasses into the open waterways to be accessible by boat. The support posts were also built tall, rising several feet out of the water into the air, so that when the marshes flooded, as they inevitably did, no unsuspecting boats or barges crashed into the submerged dock.

My footfalls echoed off the wooden planks, sounding overloud to my ears in the silence of the surrounding fens. The wind was calm and I could hear little else but the soft cadence of insects and the occasional ripple of water as a bubble of marsh gas escaped to the surface or a passing fish stirred the water.

I pressed a hand to the rough wood of one of the support posts and leaned against it, staring out over the dark expanse of marshes. The sky was clear and peaceful, the stars bright and twinkling. The events of the past twenty-four hours might never have happened. Except I knew that they had. I could feel it in the tingling watchfulness along my spine, the tightness in my shoulders.

Wrapping my arm around the post to anchor me, I tried to force my thoughts away from wariness of my surroundings. I had taken the risk of venturing out here. The least I could do was enjoy it. Besides, the Lantern Men of myth did not walk on nights as clear as this, and the smugglers did not ply this stretch of the Broads. I had nothing to fear.

I lifted my face to the sky, automatically searching for The Hunter, Orion, like Kate and I had done since we were young girls. We would slip out to the balcony that ran along the north side of Greenlaws and lean out over the balustrade to look up at the stars and confide our secret wishes. My mother had told me once it was easier to share confidences under starlight, and I was inclined to believe her, for it had certainly proved true for Kate and me.

It had been on a night like this that I had told my best friend I was in love with her brother. That I hoped one day we would marry. And it had also been on a night like this that I had told her I was afraid my brother would never come back from the war. That I sometimes lay awake at night too consumed by worry to sleep.

I closed my eyes tightly, trying to blunt the sting. I couldn't see Orion anyway. It was too early in the year for the constellation to be seen. In another month or two he would be visible in the morning sky before dawn, but for now he was hidden from view. In any case, it seemed somehow traitorous just then to look for him without Kate. Perhaps she would feel well enough tomorrow evening for me to take her out to the balcony. We still wouldn't be able to see The Hunter, but there were other constellations to look for.

I would take my violin with me, as well. Kate enjoyed music. She told me she found it soothing. I doubted she would feel well enough to descend to the music room at Greenlaws, but I could certainly take my violin to her. And I could always sing. One of those outrageous folk tunes she was always humming, learned from an impertinent servant, no doubt. Or perhaps something calmer, something from the book of ballads Kate had given me last Christmas.

One of those haunting tunes weaved through my mind and before I knew it I was softly singing the words.

> *O fare you well, I must be gone*
> *And leave you for a while:*
> *But wherever I go, I will return,*
> *If I go ten thousand mile, my dear,*
> *If I go ten thousand mile.*

> *Ten thousand miles it is so far*
> *To leave me here alone,*
> *Whilst I may lie, lament and cry,*
> *And you will not hear my moan, my dear,*
> *And you will not hear my moan.*

My voice trailed away, but the stillness of the night was shattered. I was no longer alone.

I didn't know how I knew it, but I could sense it in every fiber of my being. Every inch of my skin seemed to come alive, prickling at the realization that someone was standing behind me.

I forced myself to inhale, and strained to see out of the corner of my eye without moving my head, but whomever it was stood too far behind me and the dock post was in my line of vision. I knew I would have to turn and look. It would be foolish to think that if I continued to ignore him he would simply disappear.

I flexed my fingers where they gripped the post, just to feel that my muscles were still under my control. Then taking another deep breath, I braced to turn my neck, and that's when I noticed the mist.

It was the creeping kind that often developed across the surface of the water, like steam rising from a cup of tea. However instead of swirling up toward the sky it spread outward, a soft billowing cloud of smoke that coated everything in its path. How had it spread so quickly? It could not have begun to develop more than five minutes before, and it still stood barely more than an inch or two above the water, but it had already crawled up into the surrounding marsh grasses.

I swallowed the nerves that seemed to climb up my throat and choke me, and forced myself to turn, knowing whom I would find behind me.

He stood on the dock at the edge of the grasses, his feet braced wide, still draped in a voluminous black cloak from head to toe. His lantern sat at his feet, its light shuttered. I wondered how it was that I hadn't heard his tread on the wooden boards, how I hadn't sensed their vibration. Were his steps so stealthy?

I sensed more than saw that he was looking at me; his eyes were too well hidden by the folds of his hood. But I could imagine them—their dark intensity, the way they narrowed upwards at the corners.

"Who are you?" I managed to gasp, though it emerged as barely a whisper.

He didn't answer at once, just continued to stare at me, and I began to wonder if he could speak. Then the folds of his cloak shifted just the tiniest bit in the starlight.

"Who do you think I am?"

The voice was humored and deep. It throbbed along my nerves like the swell of a well-played cello. My breath caught at the sensation and my body urged me closer, wanting to hear more of the sound. I dug the fingers of my left hand into the wood of the post beside me, forbidding myself from taking those steps.

"I...don't know."

Those words seemed to make him smile, for I could hear it in his voice. "Don't you?"

I tensed as he took several steps closer to me. He was near enough now that I could see the gleam of his eyes, but the rest of his face remained in shadow. He seemed to be studying me much in the same way I studied him, though with the confidence of knowing that *he* was in no danger from *me*. He was very tall and broad of shoulder. I imagined it would not take him much effort to subdue me should he wish to.

Had he been watching for me? Waiting for me to make such a stupid mistake as to return to the marshes at night?

I couldn't help but think about how I had been singing, and how everyone knew that nothing attracted the Lantern Men from the myth more. Why had I done that? Did I think to test my own resolve that he was human? Though, myth or not, singing in the marshes was a risk, for it would alert anyone nearby to my presence. And I had met the man before me in the marshes just the night before, for goodness' sake, and almost been ambushed by his cohorts. How could I have been so careless?

He seemed to sense my distress, for he tilted his head to the side in consideration, allowing me a glimpse of the right corner of his mouth and chin. There was a dusting of stubble across his jaw like any normal, red-blooded Englishman sported at this hour of night.

Noticing my interest, the corner of his lip curled upward in a smile—one that was decidedly arrogant. "You shouldn't be out in the marshes alone," he told me, that resonate voice even more captivating at this proximity. "Especially not at night."

"W-why not?" I stammered, trying to understand what was happening.

His dark eyes turned serious. "Because the next time, I

might not be the one to find you."

My heart leapt in alarm. "Oh."

He nodded once and swaggered another step closer to loom over me, blocking out the moonlight so that all I could see was the barest outline of his features. I could have easily reached out and touched him, but I was too afraid that if I released my grip on the pole I would lose my balance, and never find it again.

"And if I *am* the one to find you..." His words brushed against my skin as he leaned even closer.

My breath caught in my chest as I felt the warmth of his breath on my lips. I tried to move my head, to turn away, but I couldn't. My muscles simply wouldn't work. It was as if some unseen force held me in place, and I began to tremble. I closed my eyes as the Lantern Man continued, his voice deeper still.

"Well...I won't be held responsible for my actions."

The cold night air swirled around me then, raising goose-flesh on my skin. I blinked open my eyes in surprise, only to find he'd vanished. I turned toward the path that led up towards Penleaf. I thought I could see some of the marsh grasses at its verge swaying, as if in the wake of something passing, but I couldn't be certain it wasn't only the breeze, or my mind making it so.

I pressed a hand to my chest where my heart pounded, and I pivoted in a circle, surveying the marshes around me, but there was nothing. Nothing but the silence of the night, and the creeping mist. I pulled the edges of my worn cloak tighter around me and hurried back up the trail toward home, careful to move as silently and swiftly as possible. Even so, I saw nothing further to alarm me except the weathered boards of the cottage so badly in need of repair.

But at the corner of the house, I turned to look behind me, and I could have sworn I felt his eyes tracking me. From where, I couldn't say, but I knew he was there. As sure as I knew this was still my home, for however short of a time that remained true. What I didn't know was whether he was stalking me or seeing to my safety. It had been so long since anyone had bothered about the latter that I couldn't remember what that felt like. And if it was the former, well, I suddenly understood just how deeply in trouble I was.

Chapter 5

I WOKE EARLY THE NEXT MORNING to the shuffle of Father's footsteps in the corridor and the soft click of his bedroom door latch. I lay for a moment, staring up at the forest-green curtains over my bed, mulling over the strange mixture of emotions the sounds roused in me: gratitude that I would not be forced to wake him in his study and drag him up the stairs to his bedchamber so that the study could be cleaned and aired; irritation that once again he hadn't made it up to his bed before passing out; but mostly sadness that I should even have to think of such things.

I sighed as my gaze strayed to the pale sunlight spilling through the window where I had forgotten to pull the drapes the night before. The light was still milky and insubstantial, as if the sun had also not yet fully awakened. I considered closing my eyes and trying to go back to sleep, but then thoughts of Kate and her illness intruded, as well as memories of the night before, and I pushed myself up onto my elbows to reach for my dressing gown.

Pulling the warm cloth around me, I tiptoed across the cold floor to prod at the embers of the fire in my hearth. Not so very long ago, I could have relied on a charwoman to do such a thing, but she had quit along with the rest of the staff when her wages had gone unpaid. I recalled Fanny's cheery face, always grinning even when it was covered with soot and grime. She worked in the kitchens at Greenlaws now, but I never saw her, being perpetually belowstairs as she was.

Refusing to allow myself to dwell on such things, I completed my morning ablutions in the chill water left standing in the basin on my washstand, and dressed in an old but not unattractive gown of green sprig muslin. I stared into my tiny mirror and arranged my curls in their usual style before carefully pinning my mother's mourning brooch to my dress. It was the last of her jewelry left to me, the rest of it having been sold to settle our debts. I reached for my warmest shawl when something outside the window caught my eye. I moved closer to peer out past the gnarled branches of the sycamore and its sparse greenery to the trail leading out to the boat dock. My heart leapt in my chest at the sight of a man's silhouette striding out of the marsh grasses toward the cottage.

I leaned closer to the window, trying to get a better look at the visitor. A sigh of relief shuddered through me at the realization it was only Robert. Why I had thought it was the Lantern Man come to pay me a visit in daylight I'm not sure, but it suddenly seemed the height of foolishness. I could only attribute it to my nerves over the previous night's encounter, and the strange dreams that had plagued me during the night.

Robert passed the sycamore and followed the fence line toward the creaking gate that led into the kitchen garden, but something made him hesitate with his hand on the latch. His eyes lifted to my window. I knew he had already seen me, but still I had to force my feet from retreating into the shadow of the curtains. It was simply too familiar a scene—as if the last four years hadn't passed—especially when he grinned and touched the corner of his hat to me. I lifted my hand in acknowledgement, but no answering smile curled my lips, as it would have before.

How many times had I watched for him from this very window, waiting for him to call? I had been so happy then, so certain of what life had in store for me. I could feel the ghost of that girl standing beside me, her jubilant emotions, her all-consuming love for the man standing below her.

But that girl was gone now, never to return. And as if he sensed that, Robert's smile faded to something sadder.

As he lifted the latch on the gate, I turned away and reached for my bonnet and my violin, cushioned in its case. Descending the stairs, I began to wonder what Robert was doing here. I couldn't remember the last time he had come to Penleaf Cottage. Certainly it had been years. What could have induced him to seek me out now?

Kate.

Gripping the banister, I dashed the rest of the way down the steps and propelled myself around the newel post toward the back of the cottage. Robert already stood inside the kitchen doorway, speaking to Mrs. Brittle. They both looked up at me as I rushed into the room.

"Kate?" I gasped, braced for the worst.

Robert's eyes widened. "Oh. No, Ella. Kate was still resting comfortably when I left."

I closed my eyes and heaved a sigh of relief.

"I apologize," he said, approaching hesitantly. "I should have realized you would fear the worst when I appeared on your doorstep this early in the morning."

I opened my eyes to find him staring down at me in concern. I brushed his explanation aside and crossed to the kitchen table. "Did her breathing become constricted again last night?"

"Yes, but Nora took care of her. She said you had instructed her in what to do."

I nodded, glad the lady's maid had been there to care for Kate in my absence.

"Take another jar o' the ointment," Mrs. Brittle instructed us as she crossed over to the storeroom. "If the phlegm got in 'er lungs, Mistress Rockland may need it a few more nights."

"Thank you, Mrs. Brittle," Robert replied when she returned with the salve.

The old woman grunted and waved it off before turning toward the pot simmering on the cook top.

"Is that why you're here?" I asked him, curious what had brought him here if not concern for Kate.

"No. I knew you would visit Kate today, so…" he cleared his throat "…I thought I would offer my escort."

I furrowed my brow, uncertain how to respond. What, if anything, did this mean? Had Father been right? Was Robert planning to court me again? Or was he simply being more solicitous than normal, even for him? I was hesitant to believe this was anything more than a friendly gesture, but the fact that he had not made such an offer since our unspoken engagement had so ignominiously ended could not be ignored.

He shifted from one foot to the other, fiddling with the brim of his hat, reminding me I had yet to answer him. I certainly wasn't going to openly question his motives. Not here, not now. And it seemed churlish not to accept, especially as I was bound for Greenlaws anyway. If nothing else, Robert was still a friend. There need not be anything more to it than that.

"Thank you. That's very kind," I replied with a minimum of inflection, not wanting to offer him any encouragement if he intended for his actions to mean something more. Not after what had happened the last time.

I turned to pack my basket of sickroom supplies and cast a glance at Mrs. Brittle, who was watching us from across the room. From the sour look on her face I knew she was biting her tongue, but whether she was displeased with me or Robert I couldn't be sure.

I ignored her and turned to precede Robert through the

door he held open for me, avoiding his eyes as well. The early morning air was drowsy, making me suspect the afternoon would be warm. Even so, at this early hour I was grateful for my shawl, despite the numerous patches sewn near the hem.

As we picked our way down the tidy kitchen garden path I could hear the song of a bittern in the distance. The gate creaked, like everything else in the cottage, as we passed through it, and I was suddenly glad we were moving away from my home. This way I need not read the shock and pity in Robert's eyes at how dilapidated Penleaf Cottage had become. However, there was still our warped dock to be faced, though he graciously said nothing of its neglected state.

He helped me down into his rowboat and passed me my basket of supplies before bending to unwind the tether from one of the weathered posts. My eyes strayed out into the marshes, unconsciously searching for the Lantern Man. The thought that he still might be out there, watching me even now with his dark eyes, made a shiver run down my spine.

Robert glanced at me in concern as he dropped down into the boat. "Are you chilled?"

I offered him a weak smile. "It was just a passing breeze."

He eyed me closely as he settled onto his bench across from me, and I turned away from him, uncomfortable with his scrutiny. The boat lurched as he lifted one oar to push against the dock's piling, maneuvering us out into the waterway. Once we drifted past the tallest of the reeds and grasses, he dipped his oars into the water and expertly turned us north toward the River Yare and Greenlaws.

It had always amazed me how isolated one could feel gliding through the waterways of the broads and fens. Sitting so low to the water, the grasses and reeds seemed to stretch upward like trees, ensnaring you in their boggy world. Periodically, you would come across a stretch of marsh where an industrious landowner had cut back some of the reeds to reveal the shore, but for the most part you floated along through a sunken world of water and rippling stalks of vegetation, with only the occasional sighting of a dock to assure you there really was land beyond these swampy beds.

Just like on the paths, it was all too easy to become lost among the numerous tiny waterways stretching throughout the Broads like fractures in a broken piece of glass. When my brother and I were young, before Mother's and Erik's deaths and all that came after, Father used to tell us stories about the treasures sitting at the bottom of these channels and inlets, just waiting to be discovered. They'd either been thrown overboard to avoid discovery or sunken in tubs by smugglers in an attempt to hide their cargo from revenue men. If the casks then leaked and flooded, or the tubs drifted loose from their inconspicuous moorings made from a float of reeds, they sometimes became lost. Depending on the seal, the contents of many of these casks were undoubtedly ruined, but that had not stopped Erik from dragging me through the marshes with him to search for these missing treasures. Most of the time, I hadn't minded. Especially when Robert joined in the fun.

I risked a glance at him now. His brown hair was always cut neat and ruthlessly restrained by his valet, but that did not stop a wayward lock from falling across his brow due to all the effort of his rowing. As a girl, I would have been fascinated by that lone curl. As a young woman, I would have reached across the distance between us to brush it from his forehead. Now, I merely looked away, wrapping my fingers around the handle of the basket in my lap.

"You're very quiet this morning," he remarked as he turned the boat into a wider channel.

"I didn't sleep well," I replied truthfully, though that was not the reason for my silence.

I could feel his eyes on me, though I did not turn to meet them. The morning sun shone just over his shoulder, blinding me from any clear view of his expression but revealing every nuance of mine.

A stronger breeze blew across the water here, ruffling the shorter hairs framing my face, and carrying with it the salty scent of the North Sea. The fresh air was welcome, for if the day warmed as I suspected, they might be the last clean breaths I inhaled until after sunset. The stink of the marshes only increased with the heat of the sun, reeking of damp earth and rotten vegetation.

"Worried about Kate?"

I glanced at Robert in confusion, and then realized he was referring to my previous comment. "Yes. Partly." I could practically hear the questions forming in his mind in the silence that followed, but I wasn't about to discuss any of the other things that had kept me up last night, so I threw out a hand to gesture toward the height of the reeds. "They grow quite tall, don't they?" I pronounced lamely. "I haven't been out in a boat for some time, but I swear they've grown another foot since I last passed by here." It was inane, but it was the only topic I could think of on such short notice.

Robert cleared his throat. "Yes. They have. But it's high summer. They'll die back when the weather turns colder."

I smiled tightly at his polite response and turned aside to stare into the dense grasses.

"You know there's no need to feel awkward around me," Robert said.

I grimaced. So he'd noticed. Though in truth, it would have been difficult to miss.

"You do know that, don't you, Ella?" He leaned forward, his voice earnest. "I'm still the same boy you grew up with. The same man you've always known."

I looked down at the expensive leather of his shiny boots, curling my toes inside my mother's worn pair. "Except...you aren't." I lifted my gaze to meet his, watching as he opened his mouth to argue. "None of us are the same. How can we be? Too much has happened."

He lifted the oars from the water, allowing us to drift, and turned to stare out across the fens. It was my turn to watch and wait as he considered my words. I studied the pattern of rings created on the surface of the channel by the water dripping off the blades of the oars, and tightened my grip on the basket in my lap. There were so many things I was not prepared to discuss with Robert, but trapped with him out in the middle of the fens, as I now realized I was, I might not be able to avoid them. The air between us had become so heavy, it was almost as if his late wife, Olivia, physically sat in the tiny boat between us. I half expected to smell the cloying French perfume she'd persistently dowsed herself with.

I had disliked Olivia from the first, and our continued acquaintance had done nothing to change that. She had been vain, selfish, and manipulative, and as much as I had delighted in her extreme unhappiness at finding her new home with Robert so isolated from the high society she loved, I had also wished for Kate's and even Robert's sake that she wasn't so difficult. I had never been able to warm to Olivia, no matter how I tried—a failing I feared I would always regret, particularly since she and the child she carried had died in such a horrible way.

But that was almost two years ago now, and by necessity most of us had carried on with our lives. Robert, on the other hand, had grieved long and hard, though whether that was because he had truly loved her or because his conscience insisted upon it, I didn't know. I was not privy to his private thoughts. I hadn't been since even before his marriage, though I hadn't realized it at the time. Whatever had been between us had begun to break when we received word of my brother's death on a battlefield in Portugal, but in my own grief I had not seen it. Not until three months later when he'd returned from London with Olivia on his arm as his new bride.

"Do you remember that last trip Erik and I made to London?" Robert finally asked.

I began to nod, but then realized he wasn't looking at me. "Yes."

His eyes seemed to search for something on the horizon, perhaps something in his memory. "Your mother had died only a few months before."

"I remember," I replied, unsurprised my voice had grown hoarse. "That's when Erik bought his commission in the army."

Erik had looked so proud when he came home to tell us, as if a weight had been lifted from his shoulders, but Father had been furious. Mother's death had truly shaken him, and he'd begun to drink more often in the evenings. He'd railed against Erik's decision and ordered him to sell out, but my brother had remained steadfast in his conviction. I sometimes wondered whether Erik had known what was coming, whether he was escaping the only way he knew how.

Thinking back on it now, I tried not to feel resentful. After all, I knew he'd had every expectation that Robert would marry me. He had no reason to believe he was abandoning me to the fate he was so eager to avoid. But the truth was that Father had never improved, and when Erik had been killed a few months later, he'd sunken even deeper into despair and the temporary release of the bottle.

"Did I ever tell you I almost bought a commission as well?" Robert looked up to see my brow furrow in disbelief.

"No. Although," I added, considering the matter, "I suppose it's not surprising you would keep such a thing from the girl who believed you were going to marry her as soon as her period of mourning was up." He blanched, but I refused to feel bad for stating the matter so bluntly. "But who would have managed the estate, and looked after your sister?" I rushed on to ask, not wishing to dwell on the impact his commission would have had on me.

He stared down at his hands where they flexed on the handles of the oars. "That's what Erik said. He told me my place was here. That I had no business purchasing a commission in His Majesty's army."

"He was right."

"Maybe," he admitted. "But you know, sometimes I still wish I had."

I frowned at the top of his head, wondering what on earth he meant by that.

The boat drifted into a bank of reeds behind Robert, forcing him to act swiftly lest we get tangled at the boggy edge of the waterway. He expertly steered us away from the verge and into one of the tighter channels which would take us west toward Greenlaws—a shortcut known only to those of us who traveled this way often, and one to be avoided during a dry season.

I did not question the luck of my temporary reprieve from further discussion of our painful past, and did not dare ask him about his strange confession, despite my burning curiosity. I knew better than to think Robert would divulge more without expecting me to do the same. Instead I helped guide him through the reed-choked passage and out into the broader waterway where the Greenlaws docks perched.

I waited patiently as Robert tossed the boat's rope to one of his wherry men and climbed out. I even accepted his assistance in disembarking. But once my feet were planted firmly on the pier with my basket of sickroom supplies and violin in my hands, I thanked him and made my excuses, only having to partially feign my eagerness to see Kate. Robert did not delay me, but I could tell he was also not fooled. His troubled gaze told me he knew I was fleeing.

Chapter 6

I FOUND KATE MUCH IMPROVED. THE rattle of phlegm in her chest was less pronounced, her appetite had returned, and her hacking cough, while still bone-rattling, at least proved some of her strength had returned. Though by no means was she well enough to rise from her bed. However, by afternoon the color in her cheeks and the renewed vitality of her voice had convinced me it would be safe enough to allow her to lounge on the balcony; in fact, the fresh air might do her some good.

The balcony spanned the entire length of the house at the rear, connecting a number of the bedrooms. It looked out over the fens and Greenlaws docks, and because of its shaded covering and heightened vantage point, often remained the coolest part of the house even on the warmest of days. Breezes that failed to penetrate the thick tangle of grasses down in the marsh, or even at the top of the hill on which the manor perched, blew refreshingly across the gallery above. So much so that I insisted Kate drape a blanket across her lap.

I left her on her fainting couch and stepped closer to the railing, closed my eyes and breathed deeply of the cooler air. Kate's bedchamber had grown stuffy and close in the after-noon heat, and the effort it had taken for Nora and me to move her out to the balcony had made the sweat gathering at the back of my neck run down my spine. I pulled the bodice of my green sprig gown away from my chest and fanned myself. I sighed as the air rushed down my chemise to dry my skin.

The sails of Reedham Windmill turned slowly in the distance, catching what wind there was coming in from the North Sea. It was the tallest structure for miles around, breaking up the monotonous expanse of water and grasses that made up the marshes. The faded white of its cap and sails and the weathered red brick were also the only spots of bright color visible in the sea of brown and green and faded yellow.

Hearing a man's deep voice, I opened my eyes to see Robert striding across the lawn below toward the docks. He was issuing instructions to two servants standing at the edge of the waterway. In the distance, I could see two wherry boats approaching, loaded down with cargo.

Whatever was being delivered, Robert seemed particularly animated about it, waving his hands in broad gestures. The two servants shouted to the men on the boats while Robert looked on. His hands planted on his hips, he glanced from side to side, and something in the tightness of his posture communicated to me his agitation. I frowned, trying to understand why he seemed so vexed.

"Robert is always like that when a shipment of supplies is delivered," Kate murmured behind me. I turned to find her watching me with taut brackets between her eyes. "You would think they were transporting a load of porcelain for all he fusses."

I crossed to perch on the edge of the seat next to her couch. "Does he not trust his men?"

Kate lifted a shoulder negligently, as if the matter didn't interest her. She started to cough, and I waited while her chest worked to clear itself of the phlegm constricting it. When she sat back, breathing heavily, I handed her a glass of water and watched as she swallowed large mouthfuls.

I returned the glass to the small table between us, shifting the jar of precious ointment further from the edge. When I looked up, it was to find Kate watching me through half-closed lids.

"Nora said Robert went to collect you in the skiff this morning."

I turned to stare out across the flat expanse of the fens. I could hear the speculation in her voice, even as she tried to restrain it. I couldn't fault her for her curiosity—Robert was her brother and I was her closest friend—but that did not mean I wanted to discuss it.

"Yes. It was very kind of him," I replied carefully.

"I suppose."

I glanced up at the annoyance in her tone. Her lips pressed tight together as she waited for my response. When I gave none, she huffed.

"Oh, come now. We both know kindness had nothing to do with it."

I turned away and pressed my damp palms against my knees. "I have no idea what you mean."

The lie rang hollow in the silence that fell between us, but I wasn't about to correct it or qualify it. This was Kate, and I knew I should have been able to talk to her about it, but I simply couldn't. There were too many painful memories, on both sides, and I couldn't dredge those up again. I often suspected Kate had been hurt almost as deeply as I had been by her brother's treatment of me and his hasty choice of a different bride. I knew it had caused a rift between them that had only recently healed, and I had no intention of opening it up again.

But Kate had never been one to leave things unsaid. She was stubborn and argumentative, even when it was clear she was in the wrong. It was something she and my brother had had in common. So I braced myself for her reply, but when it came, it was far more surprising.

She inhaled wearily, her chest rattling. "I know you do. But I suppose it's pointless to talk about at this point."

I turned back to find her eyes closed, her head resting against the couch arm.

I shifted toward her, the chair creaking beneath me, and she lifted her eyelids to peer up at me.

"No fussing. I'm just tired." Her eyelids drifted shut again. "I can just as easily rest out here as I can in my room."

I supposed that was true, and the air was so much cooler on the balcony. I fanned myself with the front of my bodice again and scanned Kate's face for any sign of distress.

"Besides," she added, her lips curling at the corners, "I can't hear the maids gossiping from my bed."

We both fell silent, and I noticed for the first time the excited chatter of several women. They must have been gathered in the shade of the balcony below us. At first I couldn't make out much of what they were saying, but then I realized from their giggles and sounds of approval that they were admiring the men who unloaded the barges and wherry boats.

I glanced back at Kate, who was now smiling broadly. Her eyes twinkled, and I was glad to see it was with amusement rather than the fever that had brightened them only a day and a half earlier.

"I take it they've done this before?"

"Oh, yes. Every time a shipment arrives." She stretched her toes out beneath the blanket. "They're not restrained by the rules of decorum like we are."

I arched an eyebrow at her mischievous smirk.

"Go ahead. Take a look at what they're cooing over."

I frowned.

"And don't give me that look. You know you're curious."

I wanted to argue, but seeing Kate's enjoyment of my embarrassment I decided that would only make it worse. Fighting a blush, I rose to my feet to watch as the men began to unload the boats.

There wasn't anything to truly be discomfited about. Robert would never have allowed it. The wherry men were all dressed, though what constituted being fully-clothed as a wherry man was considerably more revealing than the many layers that any gentleman would wear in either Kate's or my presence. But I had seen plenty of men in the village of Thurlton dressed in similar attire—their coats and neckcloths discarded, their sleeves rolled up to their elbows. However, none of the local men had quite so muscular forearms, nor did their bodies fill out their clothing in quite the same way.

Something in my abdomen tightened at the sight, and I thought I understood why the maids below us were chattering so excitedly. Two of the wherry men seemed to interest them in particular, though there seemed to be some debate over who was more appealing. The first had upper arms that strained the fabric of his shirt and hair streaked guinea-gold from the sun, while the second stood several inches taller than the men around him and sported a head full of disheveled dark hair.

Kate chuckled. "Who are you studying so raptly? Achilles or Hector?"

Knowing she was watching me, I resisted the urge to squirm. I wasn't sure why, but I resented her amusement. Perhaps because her comfort with this situation only reminded me of how isolated my own existence was. The only men I encountered on a regular basis were my father, Robert, the butler here at Greenlaws, and fifty-one-year-old Vicar Tilby from the Church of All Saints in Thurlton. There were no gentlemen callers, no male servants at our cottage, no wherry men delivering supplies, and no young maids to ogle them had there been.

"I doubt that's how the maids refer to them," I replied, skeptical that their limited education included the classics.

"No. But if you're this hesitant to tell me who is the more attractive, then I think it best to keep their nicknames for them to myself."

I scowled at Kate over my shoulder. "I'm not hesitant," I grumbled, turning back toward the marsh. One of the wherry men pointed at something in the distance. "Besides, who says I find either of them…"

I stiffened as I caught sight of what had so interested him. Reedham Windmill had stopped turning, its sails paused diagonally in the shape of St. Andrew's cross. It was well-known among the people living amongst the fens that a windmill temporarily stopped in such a position meant that revenue men were abroad, searching for smuggled goods. Once the signal had passed to the next windmill down the line, the sails would be allowed to turn again. A clear signal was communicated by stopping the sails in the square shape of St. George's cross.

It was merely a fact of life that smuggling occurred in this part of the country. If a family wasn't directly involved, then they purchased or were bribed with the contraband from the smugglers' runs to France and the Netherlands—tobacco, snuff, tea, sugar, chocolate, bolts of fine cloth like silk and India cotton, wine, gin, or my father's beverage of choice, brandy. It was why the illegal trade still flourished. Everyone had reason to keep quiet. Including me.

Panic shot through me. I'd been in such a hurry this morning I hadn't cleared the empty bottles from Father's study. Perhaps Mrs. Brittle had searched the room and sunk the incriminating flasks in the marsh, but our lone servant had enough to do without worrying about saving her employer from a hefty fine.

"I have to go," I exclaimed, rushing inside Kate's room to gather my things.

"What?" she called after me in surprise. "Ella, I was only teasing."

"It's not that," I replied, tucking the fichu back into the collar of my dress. I could already feel the sweat gathering under my bodice again. "The revenue men are about."

Kate needed no further explanation, which bothered me more than I had time to contemplate. It was a neat fiction between me and Robert and Kate that everything was well with my father. I knew they suspected the truth, but we had an unspoken agreement never to talk of it directly.

The heat of the day became heavier the farther I descended, through the house and down the hill to the marsh path. I felt a moment's apprehension about entering the fens on my own, especially after the warning the Lantern Man had given me last night, but I had no choice. The path through the Broads was by far the quickest route to my house.

When I emerged from the marsh at Penleaf Cottage, flushed and damp with sweat, I was pleased not to have been harassed by man nor myth. But my relief was short-lived. A trio of horses stood on the road outside our front gate, bending over to chomp at the overgrown grass growing between the slats of our fence. I lifted my skirts and raced toward the house.

The kitchen door stood open, as Mrs. Brittle often left it on hot days while she cooked. The room was empty, though there was a pot simmering on the stove, and I hurried into the hall, skidding to a halt at the sight of Mrs. Brittle standing next to the open door to Father's study. Her face was red from more than the heat and her hands were clenched into fists as she glared up at the man standing before her holding an empty bottle.

My stomach dropped.

It was Sergeant Watkins, a riding officer with the Board of

Customs. This wasn't my first encounter with the portly revenue man. He had "randomly" searched our cottage on several occasions looking for evidence of smuggled goods. I wasn't certain why our home was chosen so often for his raids. Perhaps it was the location, deep within the Broads next to the waterways through which the contraband was trafficked, or perhaps it was Father's status as a gentleman. Maybe someone had informed him about my father's drinking preferences. Whatever the reason, I was far more familiar with Sergeant Watkins' perpetually stubbly face than I would have liked.

And now it appeared he'd finally found what he was looking for.

I must have made some sort of noise, for they turned to look at me. Mrs. Brittle's angry gaze softened in apology while Sergeant Watkins's only sharpened.

His mouth curled in an unctuous smirk. "Miss Winterton. Good of ye to join us." He lifted the bottle with a single drop of Father's precious French brandy still circling the bottom. "Care to explain this?"

"What is it?" I asked, deciding to brazen it out.

I tried not to squirm as he surveyed me from head to toe. "Ye know very well. Where is yer father?"

I glanced at Mrs. Brittle out of the corner of my eye, wishing I knew what she'd already told him. "He's not feeling well," I finally replied, falling back on our standard excuse.

"Is he, now?" The malicious light in his eyes told me he was not fooled, and that he derived far too much enjoyment from his job. "Well, I'm afraid we'll still need to speak to 'im."

I stared over his shoulder for the first time at the two men standing behind him. The younger one sported a head full of ink-black hair and looked distinctly uncomfortable, while the other seemed to be enjoying himself as much as Sergeant Watkins.

"Is that really necessary?" I stalled. Father was likely nursing a thick head, which often made him belligerent. His presence could only make matters worse. "Surely I can clear up this... misunderstanding."

Sergeant Watkins' eyebrows lifted. "Oh?"

"That bottle was a gift from a friend. I'm sure you wouldn't want to punish my father for someone else's poor taste." I tried to smile, but I'm sure it looked more like a grimace.

"I see. And who is this...friend?"

"Oh, I don't wish to get him into trouble."

"That's a shame." He grinned, flashing crooked yellow teeth. "Then I'm afraid yer father'll have to pay his friend's fine in addition to his own."

I gasped. "You can't do that!"

"But I can," he assured me, naming the crippling amount of money we now owed the Crown.

"We don't have that kind of money," I protested.

"I'll collect it later," he replied. His gaze cut me like a knife. "I know ye're not goin' anywhere."

"No. I mean, we *don't* have the money. At all." *Just look at our cottage.* Did he honestly think it would be in such a state of disrepair if we had the money to keep it up?

"Then I suggest ye find it. Unless..." He sidled closer, and the look he gave me made my skin crawl. "Ye wish to make other arrangements."

I swallowed the bile at the back of my throat and glanced at his associates. Neither man made a move to interfere with their superior's inappropriate behavior.

"I'll find the money," I replied stonily.

The oily smirk never left Sergeant Watkins' face. "See that ye do."

Chapter 7

MRS. BRITTLE AND I STOOD silently by the front door, watching as the three men mounted their horses and rode away. When they disappeared behind the tall marsh grasses, she turned to me, her words sharp with anger that I knew was not directed at me. "What are ye goin' to do? Ye've already sold everythin' o' any value."

I tightened my arms around my middle and stared stiffly into the distance, where the dirt kicked up by the riding officers' horses had finally settled. "Not everything."

Her voice softened in understanding. "But ye love that pianoforte."

I didn't deny it. It was obvious the instrument meant something to me, otherwise I would have sold it long ago. Now I had no choice.

"There mun' be somethin' else. A paintin'? Somethin' o' yer father's?"

I shook my head. All of the artwork and furnishings of any value had already been sold. The house had been picked clean, even of Father's gold cufflinks.

"Ye could ask Master Rockland," she suggested, carefully avoiding my eyes, and for good reason.

"No," I replied. I would not bring Robert into this. Things

were already strained and awkward between us, our past always overshadowing our interactions. I would not be indebted to him, too. Not if I could help it. Not until I knew.

Robert had begun to show signs that he wished to return to the way things had been before Olivia. The problem was I didn't know if I could. If I even wanted to. Though Father's financial troubles might soon make it impossible for me not to at least seriously consider it. I was practical enough to understand that marriage to Robert, whatever our true feelings, would be better than most of the other options I faced once Father drank us out of our home or killed himself with brandy.

Suddenly feeling bone-tired, I pushed the door closed. "I'll write to our solicitor tomorrow." I trudged toward the stairs, then paused with my hand on the banister. "Should Father ask, tell him I'm not feeling well enough to join him for dinner."

I was grateful when Mrs. Brittle didn't question me or offer me one of her tinctures, even though that meant she knew I was lying—that I would rather go to bed with an empty stomach than face my own father.

I blinked open my eyes into the murky light of dusk that filtered into my room through the still-open curtains. It took me a moment to remember why I was lying in my bed at this hour of the day, and then it all came back to me, permeating my mind like the water rising over the marsh paths in the spring. I closed my eyes, wishing myself back into oblivion, but I could already feel the tension returning to my muscles. Once a list of things to do began to run through my mind, I realized sleep was hopeless.

I dragged myself out of bed and across the room to splash

water on my face and straighten my hair. I stood for a moment in the hall outside my door. The cottage was quiet except for its normal creaks and groans. Mrs. Brittle, I knew, would be in her room off the kitchen, and I suspected father was either out or in his study, for I didn't hear the sound of his snores coming from his bedchamber. Whether he had gone in search of or found another bottle of brandy stashed somewhere in the house, I didn't know. And for once, I didn't care. Let him drink himself into a stupor. Just so long as I didn't have to see him.

I crept down the stairs in the gray light of evening and into the drawing room with its mismatched chairs and bare tables. I didn't light a candle, the better to ignore the bright squares of wallpaper untarnished by soot, where our paintings used to hang. I didn't really need the light anyway, not for what I wanted to do.

I sat down on the stool and opened the lid to the piano-forte, staring down at the pale blur of keys. I rested my fingers against the cool, smooth ivory and closed my eyes. It didn't require much effort to imagine my mother seated in a chair beside me, offering encouragement and instruction as I stumbled through a new piece of music. Or to recall how she tilted her head back whenever she reached a particularly powerful passage, as if allowing her fingers to carry her away. Or to see my father leaning over her, adoration shining in his eyes as he waited for her nod to indicate he should turn the page of music.

I opened my eyes, hoping to banish that particularly painful memory. At least I could remember Mother as she had been—at her best. Father, on the other hand, had provided me with years of unwanted recollections of him slowly killing himself with drink.

I flushed with anger. Why could he not stop? If not for himself, then at least for me. I knew how much he loved

Mother. I knew how much it devastated him when she died, and then to lose Erik so soon after. But what about me? Was I of so little account? After all, I had lost them, too.

Not for the first time, or the last, I was sure, I pressed my hand to my chest over my aching heart and wished Mother was there. Everything would be so different if she was still alive.

But she was not. And so I must do what I must.

I inhaled through the tightness in my chest as I stared down at the shadowy outline of the pianoforte. Sentiment was the only reason we still owned it. It would have been far more practical to sell it long ago, before I began picking through the furnishings and less expensive artwork. It would fetch far more money than an armoire or my string of pearls. But the pianoforte had been Mother's, and I always felt closer to her when I was playing a Bach concerto or a Haydn sonata, so I had delayed it as long as possible.

I'd hoped this day would never come. Though now that it had, I could tell I'd been bracing for it for months, and not just for emotional reasons. Once the money from the sale of the pianoforte was spent, we would truly be near destitution. All of the furniture and clothing we had left were worth very little. Even my old, battered violin would not fetch more than tuppence. The only thing of value I still owned was my mother's brooch, and I would never part with that. Garnets and seed pearls surrounded the center of the gold brooch, which contained woven locks of my maternal grandmother's auburn hair carefully set behind glass. Hair the same shade as my mother's, and mine.

I reached up to feel its familiar weight, but my fingers merely brushed against cloth. I looked down, patting my hands over my bodice to see if it had shifted, but there was nothing there.

Panic stiffened my spine. Maybe it had fallen off while I slept? I dashed up the stairs to my room, feeling nauseated with the need to find the precious brooch. I frantically searched the sheets and blankets then dropped to my knees to run my hands over the rug and bare floors around and under my bed. Nothing.

I tried desperately to recall the last time I had touched it. I remembered fingering it as I read to Kate just before luncheon, and the heft of it as it bounced off my collarbone as I fanned myself with my dress on the terrace at Greenlaws. That was the last distinct memory I had of seeing or feeling it.

A sick feeling of dread took hold of me, and I moved toward my window. The fens spread before me, swallowing the light from the hazy summer moon. I wanted to deny the possibility, to argue that the brooch could just as easily have fallen off after I'd returned to the cottage, but I knew with an unsettling certainty where it was.

I'd chosen to take the marsh paths because they were the quickest route between Greenlaws and home. I'd reasoned that they would be safe because it was daylight, and I'd even breathed a sigh of relief when I'd emerged unscathed, without any sign of trouble from the Lantern Man. But I'd been wrong.

I had never thought of myself as superstitious, but under these circumstances it was difficult not to believe some kind of magic or trickery was at work, for I was going to have to venture back into the fens. There was no doubt about it. I couldn't leave my mother's brooch lying somewhere among the grass and reeds until dawn. It could sink into the bog at high tide or be carried away by some small creature. There was every chance it already had, but I couldn't think about that. I refused to.

Just as I refused to contemplate just what sort of mischief awaited me at the hands of the Lantern Man should he find me in the marsh after dark. Again. I'd had every intention of heeding his warning to stay away, but my mother's mourning brooch was more important. I'd already lost too much. I wouldn't lose that, too.

I crept through the kitchen, grateful for once for the worn soles of my boots that made little sound. Soft snores carried through the door to Mrs. Brittle's room, letting me know her slumber was uninterrupted. I grabbed the tinderbox and lantern from the shelf by the back door, and winced when the metal handle squeaked. For a breathless moment I thought I had woken Mrs. Brittle and would have to explain myself, but then the whistle of her snore began again.

I closed the door softly behind me and made my way through the garden and out the gate. A welcome breeze brushed across my skin, almost shockingly cool after the heat of the day still trapped in the house. The moon hung low in the eastern sky, its light veiled by thin, gossamer clouds, but I could see the mist condensing from the moist summer air already beginning to spread its tendrils through the reeds.

I knelt at the edge of the fen to light the lantern, trying to ignore the voices clamoring inside my head telling me to turn back. It wasn't easy, with the hairs on the back of my neck standing on end. I felt vulnerable and exposed, nervous that someone might sneak up behind me while I struggled to light the wick with shaking hands.

When the fire finally caught, I closed the glass panel with a snap and stood. Holding the lantern high, I swiveled left and right, searching the lawn around me and the edge of the marsh. I couldn't see any eyes peering out at me through the tall grasses, but that did not mean they weren't there. I inhaled sharply, gathering my courage, and plunged into the fen.

I moved as quickly as the task allowed, sweeping the lantern from side to side to search the path and the soggy edges. I wanted to push aside the marsh grass that lined the trail in some places, but I knew that was a waste of time. If the brooch had fallen into such a patch I would never find it.

I was ever conscious of the time passing and the number of steps I was taking deeper into the fen. I prayed I'd dropped the brooch closer to home than to Greenlaws, but there was no way of knowing. I could be at this for hours. The thought rattled my already shaky nerves.

At each turn in the path I had to talk myself into moving forward. I feared that someone stood around the bend, lying in wait for me, and the further I journeyed into the marsh, the worse that feeling became.

When I reached the bend in the path just before it paralleled the River Yare, the spot where I had first seen the lights from the Lantern Men, I stopped dead. My feet seemed unwilling to move forward.

I shivered, wishing I'd brought my cloak. I pressed a hand to my heart, trying to slow my breathing. It escaped in short staccato puffs, sharp bursts of sound in the stillness around me. Even the ever-present wind that blew off the North Sea through the Broads, rustling the marsh grass, seemed to have ceased.

That's when the prickling sensation began—up my back, over my shoulders and neck, and into my tightly bound hair. I stiffened and tightened my grip on the lantern.

He was here.

For a moment, neither of us moved, and I became aware of almost a sense of resignation, of relief, stealing over me. What I'd feared had happened, and I realized—if I was honest with myself—that I'd been expecting it.

I was the one who finally moved, pivoting so that I could face him. The Lantern Man stood just a few feet away amidst the thickening fog. As always, his face was hidden in shadow. Would he ever let me see what he looked like? Perhaps I should be grateful he hadn't. Perhaps it was only his disguise that kept me safe and allowed him to let me go.

He stood staring at me, and the silence stretched so long

that I began to question whether this was the same man. The thought made my heart leap in alarm. After all, I knew that first night there had been more than one man with a lantern, and from this distance I could see nothing to reassure me he was the fellow I'd already confronted twice.

However, the longer we stood regarding each other, the more certain I became that it was him. I'm not sure how. I just knew it, deep in my bones.

"I warned you to stay out of the marshes," he said, his deep, resonate voice washing over me.

I swallowed against the stickiness coating my mouth. "Well, I…I would have," I stammered as he took several steps closer, the folds of his dark cloak swirling around his legs. "If…if it weren't so important."

He stopped just outside the circle of light cast by my lantern, and shifted to the left so that the moon was positioned over his shoulder, casting his features in deepest shadow. I considered raising the lamp so that I could see him better, but I knew he would stop me. Whoever he was, he was strong and tall. That was obvious in the breadth of his shoulders and the sense of restrained energy conveyed in his stance.

I could feel his eyes travel over the skin of my neckline, across the bodice of my gown and down my arm to the lantern. Though he never physically touched me, the weight of his stare was as tangible as if his fingers had followed that trail. It made my stomach flutter.

"Looking for something?"

My head reared back, and I could just barely see his firm lips as they curled upward.

"Perhaps a brooch?" He pronounced the word strangely, but I understood him.

"You found it?" I gasped, taking a step closer to him in eager relief.

He didn't move to stop me, even though the light of my

lantern now revealed the cleft in his stubbly chin.

His arm lifted and he slowly opened his hand. The garnets of my mother's mourning brooch sparkled up at me.

I reached for it, but he pulled his hand back. I looked up at him in alarm.

"Did you honestly think I would just return it to you?" His voice rippled with amusement.

"Well, I…" I stumbled over my words, recalling just who I was facing. I wished I could see the expression in his eyes, but they were hidden in the deep shadows of his hood. He'd cautioned me to stay out of the marsh, that if I didn't there would be consequences. "What do you want?"

He took another step nearer, allowing the light of the lantern to clearly reveal his mouth, and simultaneously wrapped his fingers around my wrist to prevent me from lifting it higher. I startled at his warm touch.

"How about a trade?"

"A trade? For what?"

I'm not sure what I expected him to say, but it certainly wasn't the words I heard next.

"The brooch for a lock of your hair."

It took me a moment to grasp the implication of his words, but when I did all the heat that my body seemed to have absorbed just by standing in such close proximity to him drained away, leaving me cold. "My hair?"

"Yes."

The myth of the Lantern Men was not the only bit of folklore those of us living among the fens were told as children. Mrs. Brittle had warned me of the dangers of a lock of hair—a bit of nonsense I had dismissed. Until now.

Legend said that if you freely gave someone just a few strands of your hair, it gave them power over you. Because I'd never truly believed it, I'd never bothered to ask Mrs. Brittle just how far-reaching that power was; but from the manner in which she'd spoken of it, I'd deduced it wasn't a small matter. However, I had read *Sense and Sensibility*. It was, in fact, my favorite book. I couldn't help but think of Marianne. Of the lock of hair she'd given Willoughby. And how the power of her love for him, and her despair at his marrying another, had led to the foolish actions that almost caused her death.

Was this how it began, then? Was this the reason the Lantern Man had not already harmed me? Had he been biding his time, waiting for a moment just like this? A moment wherein he could enthrall me?

My common sense reasserted itself, telling me it was ridiculous—that possession of a lock of hair granted no magical qualities—but I was shaken. After all, Lantern Men weren't supposed to be real either, and yet here stood a man masquerading quite convincingly as one, his rough hand gripping the tender skin of my wrist. I had to fight to keep my imaginings from overcoming my reason.

"But why?" I finally managed to ask.

I could not truly see his eyes, but I swore a glint entered them. "I think you know why."

My chest tightened. "Surely there's something else—"

"No." His voice was firm, brooking no argument.

My mouth drifted closed as I considered the choice before me. I'd already come so far and risked so much to find my mother's brooch. Could I really return home without it? The idea of doing so left a hollow feeling in my chest. I knew it was just a piece of jewelry, a lump of gems and metal and hair, but it was also my last link with my mother, especially now that I'd come to the conclusion that the pianoforte must be sold. It was a part of me I wasn't prepared to lose, I realized, even if there was a chance that agreeing to the Lantern Man's terms could place me in even more peril.

I nodded slowly and reached up to unpin a tendril of my hair.

He stopped me. "Allow me."

Too overcome to protest, I began to turn around, but he halted me again, pressing the brooch into my hand. My fingers tightened around the gold and stone warmed by his palm, welcoming the bite of the metal into my flesh. He shifted to stand behind me and I heard the snick of what must have been a knife opening.

Belatedly, I realized that perhaps I should have been more alarmed by the idea of this man hovering over me with a knife, but I was so dazed by what was happening that I could only stand there stiffly. I felt a tug at my scalp as he pulled a strand of my hair loose from its pin. The back of my neck prickled as I imagined him folding the hair around his blade and slicing upward. The long tendril of my hair landed between my shoulder blades, and I realized he must have only taken a small snippet from the end.

I glanced over my shoulder to find him tucking the lock of my hair inside his cloak. While he was distracted, I twisted, hoping to glimpse all of his face, but he pivoted with me. His hands fell heavy on my shoulders, holding me immobile.

I sucked in a rasping breath, worried I'd angered him. The marshes were silent—the hush of the already still night augmented by the dampening effect of the fog that had continued to gather around us. I had the disturbing thought that if I screamed the sound would be swallowed up by the dense air almost before it left my mouth.

I felt the brush of the fabric of the Lantern Man's cloak hood against the back of my head, and then the heat of his breath feathered over my cheek. My heart fluttered in my chest as I braced for his words.

"Now, you will listen to me."

Before I could react, the pressure on my shoulders suddenly vanished and a chill replaced the warm gust of his breath against my skin. By the time I had the presence of mind to turn around he was gone. Only a swirl of mist marked his passing.

I opened my hand and stared down at the dull gleam of mother's brooch, wondering if this encounter had all been an illusion. Perhaps the mist had momentarily mesmerized me, bringing my own fears to life.

But then I felt a tickle against the back of my neck. I reached back to touch the single strand of hair trailing down my back. The tip was blunt, the ends crudely cropped.

Chapter 8

IWOKE LATER THAN USUAL THE next morning. Through my open window I could see that the sun had already risen high in the sky, burning away the lingering fog that swathed the fens. I dressed slowly, twisting my hair up into a tight knot, and affixed my mother's mourning brooch firmly to my bodice. But rather than hastening downstairs, I sat staring at myself in the reflection of my mirror.

I could not pretend I wasn't shaken by what had transpired in the marsh the night before, just as I could no longer pretend that everything in our household would resolve itself without my interference. Father was drinking more than ever, barely able to function without it as far as I could tell. Eventually he was going to cause us to lose this cottage or drink himself into an oblivion so deep he never woke. I was one more crippling fine, one more harsh winter, or perhaps just one more bottle of brandy away from destitution.

I knew that Robert and Kate would not let me starve, but I could not stay with them indefinitely. Not unless I married Robert. The idea held less appeal than I expected, given that I'd been heartsick over him what seemed like such a short time ago. If nothing else, I certainly didn't want his hand to be forced. I didn't want to spend my entire life wondering if he'd wed me only out of pity and obligation.

I was beginning to accept that I needed to leave the marshes, at least for a time. There was nothing left for me here but remembered heartache and painful memories. Perhaps if I put a little distance between myself and the fens, I could gain some perspective.

I pressed a hand to my quavering stomach.

And escape the Lantern Man, whoever he was, and this strange hold he seemed to have on me. Whatever forces were at work—supernatural or, more likely, not—I couldn't continue to deny the danger he posed. A bit of distance could only be good. Unless he followed…

I shook my head, unwilling to think of it.

So, it was decided. Sooner or later, depending on Father, I would leave. Which meant I needed other options.

I ran my fingers over the garnets in my mother's brooch, watching them flash in the reflection of the mirror.

We hadn't always been poor. Once upon a time, my mother had been Lady Eve, beloved eldest daughter of the Earl of Pembroke. But her family had not approved of my father, an unfashionable second son of the third son of a viscount, a man with very few prospects. Why my mother's family allowed the marriage and gave them her not-insignificant dowry—with which they'd bought this cottage—I didn't know, but they had cut off all contact with her after.

Consequently, I knew almost nothing about my mother's side of the family, and that which I had gleaned from comments I'd overheard my parents make was not very complimentary. Despite my and Father's strained circumstances, I had never tried to contact them, but perhaps it was time. Maybe if I wrote to the earl he would feel at least some filial responsibility to his granddaughter and find me a place in someone's household. I could work as a governess or a companion if I had to.

In any case, there was no risk in writing, except my hurt feelings and wounded pride—sentiments that were less important when faced with the prospect of homelessness and starvation. I would ask Mr. Fulton, my father's solicitor, to look into the matter while he was making inquiries about selling the pianoforte. Surely he could locate the earl for me, and perhaps advise me on the best way to approach him.

I pulled out a sheet of foolscap and dashed off the message before folding it into a tight square. Then I grabbed my poke bonnet from the top of my dresser and padded down the stairs. I hesitated at the door to my father's study, knowing he was likely inside asleep in his chair. But the letter had to be sent today, so I rapped before entering.

Father's head rested on the back of his chair, his neck exposed and his mouth gaping open like a fish. Soft snores rattled up from his throat. His frockcoat and cravat were discarded, tossed over the arm of an old horsehair settee. An empty bottle of brandy set at his feet.

I felt an uncomfortable stab of fury. He should be the one sending this note, not me. But it was clear that if things were left to him I would find myself standing on the side of the road, all of my remaining possessions packed into a valise as I watched him be carted off to debtors' prison, or worse.

I pulled open the top right drawer of his desk and took out the sealing wax. Rather than light a candle, I kneeled over the hearth, stirring up the embers enough so that I could heat the red wax. Once a sufficient amount had dripped over the letter, I approached my father. Lifting his limp hand, I pressed the signet ring still attached to his pinky finger to the wax.

He snorted and blinked open his bloodshot eyes as I released his hand. I returned the sealing wax to the drawer and tucked the missive into my pocket before he could see it.

"Ella?" my father slurred, swiping a hand across his mouth. "Is something wrong?"

"No," I replied. "Just looking for my book." I lifted a random leather volume from the corner of the desk.

He stared at me, as if trying to comprehend what I said.

I pressed the book between my hands, irritated and anxious to make my escape, but the sight of him bleary-eyed and disoriented with his hair standing on end twisted something inside me. "Wouldn't you be more comfortable upstairs?" I asked more gently than I felt.

"Probably," he replied. He pushed himself upright and leaned forward with his elbows braced on his knees.

Again I wanted to leave, but my feet remained rooted to the spot. This was my father, after all. Regardless of what he'd done, that hadn't changed. It never would. I sighed, as frustrated with myself and my tender emotions as I was with him.

I rounded the desk and bent to grip his arm. "Come."

He allowed me to help him up and guide him through the door and up the stairs. I left him at his bedroom door, deciding he could make it to the bed himself, even if he fell into it still clothed. I hurried down the stairs and out the front of the cottage, wanting to distance myself from the confusing array of feelings that churned inside me.

It took all of my self-control not to confront Mr. Ingles, the proprietor of the White Horse and our local postmaster, as I strode into the inn. I knew Father had gotten his latest bottle of brandy from the White Horse, just as he'd gotten all his other bottles, collecting his bribes for his silence about the local smugglers. But as much as I wanted to give Ingles a piece of my mind, the mortification I would feel at revealing the stark truth of my position kept me in check.

I wasn't dimwitted. I knew the villagers must have deduced our strained situation. They might not discuss it openly, at least not in front of me, but it was obvious from our unpaid bills at the shops and the ease with which Father could be bribed that we were living in reduced circumstances. Regardless, I could never speak up and remove all doubt, could never reveal my shame in such a public way, especially not to someone like Ingles.

As a gentleman's daughter, perhaps I should have been able to go to them and demand that they stop bribing my father, that they stop smuggling. Perhaps I should have been able to apply to them for help. But it was precisely that same difference in our social classes that prevented me from doing so. It would have been absolutely beyond the pale, and the very thought of doing so made me cringe in humiliation.

So instead I glared at Ingles, managing to bite out as polite a request as I could manage for him to post my letter, and turned on my heel before my anger got the better of me. It was difficult. Especially with Albie Turner and Ralph Conner sitting at the bar watching me, two men who supported their families by working far too little *not* to be smugglers.

The conflicting emotions of both defiance and despair crashed inside me. I wanted to threaten these men that I would inform on them to the Board of Customs, to make them feel for just a moment the fear and frustration I choked back daily, but we both knew I would never do it. As much as I hated the fact that some of their smuggled goods came from France—the country whose soldiers had been responsible for my brother's death—I knew that stopping their enterprise would do far more harm than good.

In any case, the small amount of contraband that was transported back and forth through Thurlton did little, if anything, to support Napoleon or his troops, but mainly benefited the small villages along the coasts of France and the Netherlands where they docked—villages as poor as Thurlton. Which was why I'd pretended it wasn't happening for so long. I'd overlooked it because without the added income from smuggled goods, I wasn't sure how many women would be forced to mend their tattered and faded dresses yet again, or how many children might go to bed hungry. I wasn't sure I could live with myself if I caused such suffering, even if by tattling I would legally be in the right.

Besides, even if I shut down the smuggling operation in Thurlton, the contraband would still find its way to London by another route. It would all be for naught. My petty vengeance might force my father to stop drinking, but for how long? He could always travel to the next village to obtain his beloved brandy. And my retaliation might only beget more, when the shopkeepers who had kindly refrained from demanding my father pay his debts suddenly reported them to the authorities.

Several days later, I arrived home in the late afternoon to find Father waiting for me. Instantly I was on guard, for he so rarely had anything to speak with me about. I could tell from the slur in his raised voice calling me into his study that he was not sober, though the fact that he could string his words together without confusion suggested he was not completely foxed either.

I took my time hanging my bonnet on the hook before crossing the hall. At the door, I paused to smooth my hands over my skirt and took a calming breath. "Yes, Father?" I asked, pushing the door wide.

He waved a piece of paper at me. I could tell from the creases it was a letter.

"What is this?" he demanded.

My stomach dropped. I'd arrived home early every day from my visit with Kate at Greenlaws, hoping to intercept Mr. Fulton's reply before Father quit his chamber, but today I'd been held up by Mrs. Tate outside the church in Thurlton. She wanted me to ask Mrs. Brittle to bake one of her strawberry trifles for the church's anniversary dinner in two weeks' time. The encounter had been awkward, considering we didn't have the money to purchase the lemons or sugar needed for the recipe. Awkward enough to make me reconsider my decision to avoid the marsh path, even during the day. But the thought of the Lantern Man and his shadowed eyes unsettled me more.

Father lurched to his feet, still flapping the letter in the air. "When did you write to Fulton?"

"After our visit from Sergeant Watkins," I replied cautiously, not wanting to rile him further.

He lifted a hand to rub the bridge of his nose, a tactic I knew well. He was stalling for time, trying to recall. I'd informed him of the revenue men's unexpected visit and the exorbitant fine they'd levied on us the evening after I'd mailed my letter to Mr. Fulton. Father had been drinking again, but he had not yet been insensible to his surroundings. But Father's memory was not what it had once been, even sober.

That, or he simply chose not to listen.

I felt a sharp sting in my chest, a faint echo of the pain I'd once felt at the prospect that he didn't care enough to attend his daughter.

"He found your empty brandy bottle," I reminded him. "He says we must pay—"

"Yes, yes," he replied impatiently, as if he'd remembered all along. "And so you wrote to Fulton and asked him to find someone to purchase our pianoforte?" His voice was incredulous and angry.

I fisted my hands at my sides, wanting to lash out at him, but I knew from experience that doing so would only infuriate him further. Father had never hit me, but there were other ways to wound.

"I don't see that we have a choice."

He paced in front of the empty hearth, giving no sign he'd

heard me. "So it's come to this, has it?" He scoffed. "I can't believe you would sell your mother's pianoforte." His eyes were hard and accusing.

His words were like knives being thrust into my gut. "Do you think this is easy for me?" I implored in a voice raw with pain. "I had no choice. We have nothing else to sell."

"What about that landscape in the dining room?"

"Gone."

"Then the Hepplewhite settee in the drawing room—"

"Gone."

He faltered. "The Dresden shepherdesses...?"

Did he pay attention to nothing?

I struggled to keep the bitterness from my voice. "They're gone, too."

He looked around him, as if seeing for the first time how sparse our surroundings had become. It was a testament to his preoccupation with drowning himself with drink that he'd not noticed before.

"There's still no need to sell the pianoforte," he insisted in a calmer voice. "We'll simply have to make do."

I lifted my hands in frustrated entreaty. "But how else will we pay the fine? We don't have nearly enough ready money to cover it."

"We won't." He turned away and I heard the clink of glass against glass as he poured himself another drink. "We won't pay it."

"Father, you do understand that's not an option? If we don't pay the fine, they'll have you carted off to debtors' prison."

"They'll do no such thing."

I was stunned he could be so unconcerned about something so serious. "But Father—"

"I'm the grandson of a viscount." The leather of his chair creaked as he settled into it. "Sergeant Watkins can't do anything to me."

He might be the grandson of a viscount, but no one in his family was going to vouch for him, or pay his debts, or protest when he was thrown into the Marshalsea Prison. Or offer me a place in their household. Unlike my mother's family, I had met my paternal grandfather and uncle, and I knew better than to expect anything from them, and neither would I want it. Even though I was barely five years old at the time, I recalled how much they had frightened me. I was braver at age twenty-one, but that did not mean I would be comfortable in their presence.

I watched as my father tipped back his glass and drank. His throat worked as he swallowed greedily, eager to forget.

"Might I see the letter?" I finally asked, recognizing it would do no good to press the matter now.

Father flipped his hand toward the desk and I moved to retrieve it from where he had set it down to pour his drink. Then I slipped from the room before he could protest.

I retreated to my chamber, sitting on the edge of my bed to read it. Mr. Fulton wrote that he had found a buyer for the pianoforte, and if it pleased me he would come the day after next with a pair of hired men and a cart to retrieve it. Fortunately, he had not mentioned my request that he advise me on how to contact my mother's father, referring to it only as "that other matter." Perhaps he had sensed my desire for secrecy. In any case, his discretion turned out to be prudent.

I was surprised he'd found someone to purchase the pianoforte so quickly, but I wasn't about to question our luck. Instead I dashed off a reply and slipped out of the cottage and down to the village to post it before Father could stop me.

Chapter 9

IDAWDLED ON MY WAY HOME, not eager to return to the strained silence of Penleaf Cottage. The sweet scent of roses beckoned me toward the lychgate leading into the churchyard. I followed the path toward the narrow, battered stone façade of Church of All Saints. Its stolid Norman simplicity and thatched roof somehow seemed more fitting to the bleak landscape surrounding it than the profusion of bushes and flowers the women of Thurlton so lovingly maintained along its pathways and around its perimeter. Like a worn and wind-beaten old man, no amount of ornamentation could hide the pockmarks and patches time had wrought on the building's craggy surface, not even the porch and arched doorway added in the late fifteenth century, complete with angel-carved spandrels.

I veered to the right of the building, passing beneath the cool shade of a pair of yew trees. Near the stone wall marking the churchyard's eastern border sat my mother's and my brother's graves. I stood before them as perhaps I'd done hundreds of times since their passing. I often dallied over their gravestones on Sundays following church service, avoiding awkward small talk with the other parishioners, who could not have failed to note my father's perpetual absence. Mrs. Brittle and I usually arrived just before the bells chimed to begin worship, and having kept her from chattering before the service, I tried to wait patiently while she did so after. I could have walked home without her, but it somehow seemed lonelier to travel that mile alone after church, especially when I knew others were gathering together to share Sunday dinner.

I puttered around their graves, as I did now, pulling wayward strands of grass or arranging at a more pleasing angle the petals of the flowers I planted there from time to time. When the churchyard buzzed with conversation after Sunday morning worship I felt uncomfortable, ever conscious of the eyes that might be watching me. But in the softening light of early evening, with the hum of insects and the rustle of the wind through the trees all there was to break the silence, I could sense the peace that so often eluded me.

I tossed aside the piece of grass I'd plucked from in front of my brother's gravestone and sat back on my heels. I wondered as I had so many times before whether my mother and Erik were together in Heaven. Whether they looked down on me and saw my troubles, or whether they had ceased to care, forgetting me much as Father had.

I'd heard about how the Papists sometimes prayed to the Virgin Mary to intercede on their behalf. I knew it was sinful, or so Vicar Tilby said, but I couldn't help but wonder if it was so wrong to hope for such a thing. I wondered if I prayed to Mother or Erik whether they would intercede on my behalf. But perhaps they weren't even listening.

Pressing my hands to my thighs, I prepared to rise to my feet when I felt the hairs on the back of my neck stand on end. Someone was behind me. I wasn't sure how I knew. I hadn't heard them move or inhaled their scent on the breeze. But somehow I sensed their presence, as sure as the grass beneath my knees.

Instantly, I couldn't help but think of the Lantern Man. He

had dogged my thoughts and my steps for days as I pondered when and where he would appear next. My scalp near the base of the shortened tendril of hair from where he had clipped the end seemed to tingle in remembrance of his actions just a few short days ago.

But on this long summer day it was still hours from dusk, and we were several hundred yards from the edge of the marsh. The Lantern Men had never ventured this far afield before, nor in broad daylight. And although I didn't doubt he would be so bold, it seemed like an unnecessary risk. Especially when I already lived deep in the marshes with only an old woman and an inebriated father unable to prevent him from doing whatever he wished.

My mind shied away from the possibility, unwilling to contemplate how precarious my situation truly was. Instead, I pushed myself to my feet, determined to face whatever was behind me before my imaginings became worse than reality.

It was only Robert who stood several feet away next to a weathered, leaning gravestone, watching me with a curiously unguarded expression. There was regret and uncertainty stamped across his features, and also something akin to tenderness. It was different from the warmth I had once seen reflected in his eyes when he looked at me, but no less potent, considering how unprepared I was for it. My stomach dipped, and I wasn't sure I didn't wish it had been the Lantern Man behind me instead.

I brushed the grass from my knees, stalling for time, hoping Robert would once again veil his thoughts from me. He dropped his gaze as he wove between the gravestones separating us, and when he lifted it again much of what I had seen stamped there was gone.

I inhaled shakily. "How long were you standing there?" I asked, still wondering why I hadn't heard his approach.

"A few minutes," he admitted. The corners of his mouth

curled upward in chagrin. "I didn't want to disturb you."

I nodded.

An awkward lull fell between us as we turned to look at Erik's grave. We had both said everything that needed to be said to each other about my brother and his best friend long ago, and yet standing there discussing something else seemed inappropriate somehow. As if we were disrespectful of his memory. Or perhaps it was the knowledge that upon Erik's death what we had once been to each other was no longer true.

Robert cleared his throat. "Walk with me?" he asked, offering me his arm.

I linked my arm through his, grateful for the excuse to escape our uncomfortable situation.

Rather than turning me toward the lychgate and the street, he led me deeper into the churchyard. We wound our way between gravestones, the grass soft beneath our feet as we passed through the shadow cast by the church. The air was heavy with the scent of roses, delphinium, and cornflowers, a sharp contrast to the boggy musk that perfumed the breezes in summer at Penleaf Cottage.

I couldn't help but wonder at Robert's presence here. Or was our encounter merely a coincidence? I was trying to decide how to ask him when he answered for me.

"Vicar Tilby wanted to discuss the church's anniversary celebration. Greenlaws is donating a roasted hog for the dinner," he explained, tilting his head down to me as he'd done since he'd turned fourteen and grown a head taller than me.

I felt a tingle of something—a memory in my muscles. The feel of his arm linked with mine, the sight of his head angled toward me, almost but not quite brushing my temple. The sensation was at once familiar and foreign; it had been so long since we'd simply strolled this way, side by side, with no destination in mind.

He shook his head. "I hadn't expected the vicar to be so anxious about this dinner. But then again, it's not every day that one celebrates a building's 600-year anniversary."

I, too, had been surprised by how much our normally easy-going vicar seemed to be fretting over this celebration, until I'd overheard Mrs. Harper gossiping outside the White Horse.

"Archdeacon Soames is rumored to be attending."

Robert's eyes met mine in understanding.

"And the bishop as well," I added. "Though that seems less likely."

"Well, that would explain the nerves. Having one's superior watching over your shoulder cannot be enjoyable." His lips twisted. "Especially when that man is Archdeacon Soames."

As affable as Vicar Tilby was, Archdeacon Soames was not. He scoured everyone and everything with a critical eye, determined to find fault, even in babies. He rarely made visits from neighboring Raveningham, but I supposed it was too much to hope he would miss out on the pomp and ceremony of a 600-year anniversary.

"I suppose the children's games will be more subdued, then?" Robert asked.

"I imagine so. And the barrel race cancelled."

He laughed suddenly. "Do you remember the year Erik decided to climb inside Carter's barrel on Bonfire Night?"

I smiled. "After he'd snuck a glass or two of Mrs. Ingles' special punch?"

"And Carter's face when he crawled out of it at the end of the street."

I started to giggle. "Poor Erik was so sick he couldn't even hide what he'd done from Father."

"As far as I know, no one's tried riding in a barrel since."

Our laughter filled the churchyard, and as it faded I couldn't help but speculate. "I imagine Ingles won't be serving his special punch at the anniversary celebration either."

Robert sighed contentedly, regaining control of himself. "No. Too many questions."

Vicar Tilby might have been happy to be bribed with a cask of brandy or claret or beer, or perhaps some tobacco, but it was doubtful Archdeacon Soames would be so understanding of his parishioners' clandestine activities.

I glanced at Robert, wondering not for the first time how the local smugglers induced him to keep quiet. Did he receive payment in French brandy as well, or was it bolts of silk and lace, or maybe chocolate and coffee? Perhaps all of it. Kate did own exceptionally lovely clothes, made with the finest fabrics. Even her day dresses were made from India cotton and calico. And Greenlaws was never short on coffee, or tea, or chocolate, but perhaps that only seemed remarkable because of our own deprivation at Penleaf Cottage.

We paused near the border of the church's property next to the crude stone wall that separated it from an open field beyond. In the distance a marsh hawk wheeled over the waving tufts of tall grass that marked the beginning of the fen. Robert's eyes followed its flight, and I realized his thoughts had not followed mine when he spoke again.

"I sometimes forget how mischievous Erik could be. I seem to always remember him as he was at the end, suddenly shouldering such great responsibility marching off to war."

I nodded, understanding what he meant. Even now I could see him quite clearly as he'd looked that last morning before he left to join his regiment, the pride and determination shining in his eyes. Growing up, Erik had been the one who had most often led the four of us into trouble, but he'd also been the first one to embrace adulthood and all it entailed.

"Did you know it was Erik who introduced me to Olivia?"

I turned to him in surprise. "No."

He nodded, still staring off into the distance. "On that trip we took to London. The very same one when he bought his commission. He collided with her coming out of the Temple of the Muses Book Shop."

Where he'd probably gone to purchase something for me.

Robert's expression tightened. "He felt a right dullard, but later Olivia admitted she'd purposely stepped into his path. She found him to be quite dashing in his new regimentals."

My head spun at the implication of his words. "So they…" I broke off, uncertain how to phrase what I needed to know.

But he knew what I meant. "I thought so. At least at the time. And later, after his death, when I returned to London." He inhaled as if he'd been carrying something heavy. "But then I began to suspect not."

I stared out at the field of dirt and stalks of straw-yellow grass without really seeing it. "So that's why you went to London?"

Once again he didn't pretend to misunderstand. "Yes. I thought…" He shook his head in agitation. "Oh, I don't know now. I guess I *did* worry Olivia hadn't received the news. Or that she would be grieving, with no one to share her loss. But it wasn't entirely as altruistic as that." He shifted from one foot to the other. "The truth is, I found her fascinating. Exciting. I'd never met anyone like her before. And I'm not sure I didn't go there with the intention of courting her, if she would have me in Erik's place."

I didn't know what to say. His words certainly explained the distance I'd felt growing between us after Erik's death, but they didn't blunt the pain of knowing he'd been lost to me long before I'd even realized it. Self-consciously I removed my arm from his, and half turned away.

"When Erik was alive, I never even thought of pursuing her," he hastened to say, and I knew he was trying to soften the blow. "I had you, and I was quite happy, quite…content. But when Erik died…things changed."

That break in his words was weighted with so many things,

chief of which was my father. And *that* I couldn't blame him for. As for the rest…

I finally turned to face him, unswayed by the concern reflected in his eyes. "Why are you telling me all this now? What good does it do?"

He swallowed and dropped his gaze, as if gathering his thoughts. "Because…I thought you should finally know the truth. Because I was wrong, *so* wrong about Olivia, about everything."

He moved a step closer to me, but seeing my arms wrapped tightly around my torso, he wisely decided not to touch me.

"I know I hurt you, Ella. I could say that I wish I had never been foolish enough to fall prey to her charms, but that would also mean I wish my child had never been—"

"I don't want that."

He must have heard the distress in my voice, for he broke off from saying whatever he'd been about to say.

I shook my head fiercely. "I would never want that."

There might be some doubt whether Robert had truly mourned his wife, but I knew for certain he had grieved the loss of his unborn child. Even now I could see the pain in his eyes when he spoke of him.

His chin lifted up and down above his crisp white cravat as he swallowed. "What I'm trying to say is that I'm sorry, Ella. I realize I never made a proper apology, and I thought it was long past time I did."

I studied his face: the lines radiating from the corners of his eyes wrought by both joy and sorrow; the deep furrows of uncertainty in his brow; the genuine contrition darkening his topaz eyes. And I felt something loosen inside me I hadn't known I'd been holding tight until that very moment.

I had not realized how much I'd needed Robert to express his regret. I'd lived so many years believing it would never happen that I supposed I'd stopped hoping for it. And now that he had, I hardly knew what to say. It was balm for my bruised pride to hear him apologize, but it did not change what had happened. The hurt did not miraculously vanish, nor did the discomfort his presence caused me. If anything, the emotion I experienced was relief—that he'd finally acknowledged the pain he'd caused, that he cared enough to make amends. But I supposed that was as good a place to start as any.

When I said nothing, his eyes dropped to the toe of his boot where he nudged at a stray twig fallen from one of the trees overhead. "I've been thinking about what you said the other day in the fen, and you're right. None of us are who we were four years ago. And I'm afraid I've been, perhaps foolishly, behaving under the misapprehension that we could be." He lifted his eyes to stare at me through their lashes. "So if we can't go back, then let's go forward."

This time I didn't tense when he reached out to take my hand, but I was far from comfortable with his touch or close proximity. My heartbeat accelerated, afraid of what he might say next.

"I know things are strained between us. I hate the wariness I see in your eyes when you look at me, justified though it may be. But I would like it to be different." His fingers squeezed my palm in emphasis. "I would like for us to at least be friends again. Do you think that's possible?"

I searched his face, trying to interpret what he meant. Was friendship truly all he wanted from me, or was this a stepping stone to something else? All I could see was sincerity shining in his eyes, but that didn't mean there wasn't more to it than his words would lead me to believe.

Regardless, I did want to be friends—at least better friends than we had been these past four years. For Kate's sake, if nothing else. Though she said little about it, I knew our awkward relationship troubled her. Neither of us had ever asked her to choose sides, but that didn't mean she hadn't felt pressured to do so.

In any case, whether Robert intended more meaning behind his words or not didn't matter. Later, if he pushed for more before I'd decided if I wanted it, I could simply feign ignorance.

"I would like that," I replied, offering him a small smile.

His face brightened. "Good."

Chapter 10

TWO DAYS LATER, AS PROMISED, Mr. Fulton arrived with two workmen and a cart to retrieve the pianoforte. They clattered to a stop outside of Penleaf Cottage just after midday, while Father was still asleep in his bedchamber. The rainclouds that had been threatening all morning had blown over and the sun shone down, burning through the wisps that remained.

Mrs. Brittle and I had dusted and polished the wood of the pianoforte, making it gleam as it hadn't in years. Perhaps the effort was silly given the fact that the new owner had been willing to purchase it unseen, but I didn't want them to feel cheated. Besides, it was a good instrument, one that deserved to be cherished. I was only sad I hadn't cleaned it so well sooner.

I was grateful when Mr. Fulton didn't question Father's absence, but by now he must have grown accustomed to this strange fiction we pretended. That Father was aware of our selling off the home's assets to pay our debts. That most days he wasn't incapacitated by drink.

Mr. Fulton followed me into the drawing room, issuing directions to the men. I tried not to feel embarrassed by the bareness of the walls and the absence of much of the furniture, but if the workmen thought it odd they didn't let it show.

As Mr. Fulton and I stood side by side watching the workmen drape heavy blankets over the pianoforte, it must have been obvious how unhappy I was, for he leaned over to promise me it would be well cared for. I nodded and forced a smile to my face for his benefit. After all, the silver-haired solicitor had been nothing but kind and efficient. He didn't need to contend with a blubbering female as well.

I took a deep breath and made myself focus on something other than the sight of my mother's pianoforte being wheeled toward the door. "I trust there will be enough funds to cover some of our debts?" Including what we owed him.

"Yes," he said, handing me a folded piece of paper. "I've listed all of the bills and the amounts that will be paid. And as discussed, I'll also handle the payment of the fine."

"Thank you," I replied, grateful I wouldn't have to face Sergeant Watkins, and that I could be certain the full amount would be paid to the Board of Customs and not partially into the odious riding officer's pocket, angry as that would surely make him.

Mr. Fulton rocked back on his heels with his hands clasped behind his back. "To be honest, I think the fine is excessive. I may be able to negotiate to have the amount reduced."

"That would be wonderful."

"I can't make any promises. But I'm well acquainted with the Collector of Customs at Yarmouth. He's a reasonable man." A little frown formed between his eyes. "Most of the time."

I squeezed the paper he'd given me between my fingers, feeling several round lumps inside. "What's this?"

He pulled his watch from the pocket of his dark coat to check the time. "Just a bit of extra ready, to use as you see fit."

I cradled the paper tightly, the sharp corners biting into my palm. That Mr. Fulton should set aside even a small amount of the money to give me instead of directing it all towards our debts was incredibly thoughtful, and it affected me more than I would have expected. I blinked against the sudden wash of emotion, grateful that the solicitor had courteously averted his eyes.

We watched as the men carefully maneuvered the piano-forte through the drawing room door. Their rough voices echoed in the front hall. I glanced nervously at the stairs as we followed them through the doorway. Normally I wouldn't have worried about the noise waking my father, but after his adverse reaction to Mr. Fulton's letter, I was justifiably tense.

Mrs. Brittle stood to the right by the entrance to the kitchen, wiping her hands on a towel, which reminded me of my manners.

"Would you care for tea?" I asked Mr. Fulton, hoping he couldn't tell how anxious I was for him to say no.

"No, thank you," he replied, running his fingers over the brim of his hat. "My daughter and her family are joining us for dinner tonight, and I promised Mrs. Fulton I wouldn't be late."

I smiled, imagining the cozy scene. At one time, I had hoped for something similar. Now I could barely anticipate sitting down to dinner with Father at all, never mind his remaining sober enough for me to actually enjoy it.

I turned aside to watch the workmen lift and maneuver the pianoforte over the threshold. The instrument made a loud thunk on the floorboards of the front porch as the man on the outside set it down a bit too hard. His head disappeared as he bent to examine the base, but he must have decided it was undamaged for they began to move it again. They slid it forward so that the man pushing from our end could lift his side of the pianoforte.

Mr. Fulton cleared his throat. "Now, about the other…"

I glanced back at him expectantly, when something caught

my eye. I pivoted toward the stairs in alarm.

"What is the meaning of this?" Father demanded, leaning heavily on the banister as he descended. He still wore his clothes from the night before, though now they were wrinkled from sleeping in them. He had discarded his coat, and his cravat hung limply around his neck. Dark stubble speckled his jaw, and his graying hair stood on end.

"Father," I gasped, moving to intercept him.

He halted at the base of the stairs, clinging to the newel post, and stared past me toward the door.

"Father, I…"

He glared at me. "I *told* you to forget this nonsense. Bring that back inside," he shouted at the workmen and then winced, cradling his head in his other hand.

I glanced at the workmen who had paused to look back at us through the door.

"Father, *please*," I whispered. "You know this must be done."

"I know no such thing!"

I lifted my hands to try to soothe him, but he'd already dismissed me.

"Fulton, I'm sorry. There's been a mistake." He pushed past me. "You there," he called out again, though less loudly than before. "Bring that instrument back in here."

The men glanced at each other in confusion and then looked to Mr. Fulton.

I wrapped my arms around my middle, feeling a hollow space open up inside my chest. My cheeks burned with shame.

The solicitor raised his hand to tell the men to wait. "Mr. Winterton, what seems to be the problem?"

"I do not wish to sell that pianoforte. I never authorized it."

"I see. Well, then I assume you have other means to pay this fine from the Board of Customs?" He eyed my father expectantly.

But Father brushed it aside. "It's not necessary. They cannot honestly expect me to pay."

Mr. Fulton tapped his fingers against the brim of his hat. "Oh, dear. Mr. Winterton, I'm afraid they do. As your solicitor, I've already received written notice of it in my office. And if it is not paid within a fortnight, they threaten to take action."

I watched my father's profile, praying that now he would listen to reason.

His brow furrowed in outrage. "But it's preposterous. A gentleman can't drink whatever he chooses in his own home?"

"Not if it comes from France," Mr. Fulton replied carefully. "And the government questions how you obtained it, considering most trade with that country has been outlawed for the duration of the war."

"You can't tell me that noblemen down in London, sitting in their cozy studies or conversing in their clubs, aren't drinking the same swill," he argued, stabbing his finger in the air in that direction.

"You're right. But I'm afraid the government is less concerned with those who are at the bottom of the chain than with those whom they are suspicious of being at the top, smuggling the items into the country." He paused a moment to let Father contemplate that before adding, "And perhaps more important, those gentlemen in London have connections. You, sir, do not."

Father fisted his hands at his sides and inhaled as if to argue, but then abruptly he turned away. All of the energy that had bristled through him seemed to drain away. He reached out to brace a hand against the wall.

I moved forward, worried he might be unwell, but then I stopped just before touching him. The sting of his rejection such a short while ago hadn't faded, and I didn't know if I was willing to risk it again.

"Do what you must," Father muttered, raking his free hand through his already unruly hair. "Just...leave me be." He pushed away from the wall and disappeared into his study.

I stared at the door as he closed it behind him, shutting us out. Shutting me out. Again.

My chest tightened painfully, making it difficult for me to breathe. I could feel Mrs. Brittle watching me, but Mr. Fulton had the good grace to look away. He moved to direct the workmen to finish loading the pianoforte, giving me a moment to compose myself.

I swallowed hard and forced a deep breath into my lungs. When I was certain I wouldn't embarrass myself further by weeping, I turned toward where the solicitor stood a discrete distance away. His expression was scrupulously blank.

"About the other," he murmured, pulling another folded sheet of foolscap from the inside pocket of his dark coat. "Your grandfather's direction."

I reached out to take the paper from him, more nervous than I'd anticipated to hold the information in my hand.

"I also took the liberty of including the address of your great-aunt. Lady Bramford lives not far from here, in Suffolk."

"Thank you," I replied, not having even known I had a great-aunt.

"Should Lord Pembroke prove stubborn, Lady Bramford might be more amenable."

I nodded my understanding. There was no telling how my grandfather would react to a letter from a granddaughter he'd never met. If it came to it, someone of the same blood but with a bit more emotional distance might respond more reasonably.

I couldn't watch Mr. Fulton and the workmen drive away with my mother's pianoforte. It was simply too difficult. So once the solicitor had exited through the front door, I departed through the back. Mrs. Brittle didn't offer any useless placations or try to stop me.

But from the garden I could still hear the jangle of the harnesses and the men's rumbling voices. So I allowed my feet to carry me through the gate and across our overgrown lawn, and before I knew it I was walking into the fens. Without conscious thought, I let my steps lead me where they would along the marsh paths. Had I been someone less familiar with the Broads, my careless wandering would have been dangerous, but I knew these waterways. I'd explored them in every season since I was too young to remember. In daylight and fine weather, there was nothing to harm me.

Or so I used to think.

Somehow in my agitation, in my eagerness to block out all thought, I had forgotten about the Lantern Man and the lock of my hair he now possessed that might or might not give him power over me. I was deep in the marshes before reason asserted itself and I realized how reckless I was being. My footsteps slowed as I tried to figure out exactly where I was. With my heart suddenly beating loud in my ears it took me longer than I was comfortable with to recognize my surroundings.

I was on a little-used side trail that flooded during the winter, roughly halfway between Greenlaws and Penleaf Cottage. Few people risked this part of the fens, even though it was entirely safe during high summer. It was that very fact that alarmed me now. The absolute solitude.

I glanced around me frantically, and then stopped. I made myself stand still and close my eyes, trying to sense if anyone was near. Each time I had encountered the Lantern Man, he had been able to sneak up on me. One moment he wasn't there, and the next he was. My eyes and ears seemed unable to detect his approach, but perhaps something else inside me would.

I inhaled shakily and then released it, waiting for that moment when I would feel his presence. The reeds and marsh grasses whispered around me, pitched in hushed speculation.

A breeze rippled across my skin, raising bumps along my arms as the sun passed behind a cloud, dropping a shadow like a veil over my eyes.

I stood suspended, my entire body tingling as I waited for something to happen. But then the cloud passed and the breeze died, stifling the murmurs of the marsh. The sun shone hot on my skin again. I blinked against its glare and turned to survey the marshes around me. There was nothing there.

Or there wasn't now.

Had the Lantern Man been watching me? I hadn't directly perceived his presence, but something had stolen my breath and directed the wind and the sun.

I pressed a hand to my heart where it still raced in my chest and frowned. I was being ridiculous. The Lantern Man, whoever he was, could not control the elements. This entire supposed encounter had been contrived in my imagination out of fear.

A cluster of marsh grass rustled loudly to my left, and I jumped and turned to stare at it. There was nothing there, except perhaps a small animal. Regardless, I decided it was time to leave. I wasn't ready to return home, so I directed my steps toward Greenlaws.

Maybe it was past time I told someone about my encounters with the Lantern Man. Kate was the obvious choice for a confidant. I wasn't sure why I had been so hesitant to tell her before. At the beginning, her illness had kept me from sharing, but once she had recovered there had really been no reason for me to remain silent. However, with each passing day and each subsequent encounter with the cloaked figure, it became harder to talk about.

Perhaps it was the absurdity of the entire situation. It was difficult enough for me to believe these meetings had really happened, let alone Kate who hadn't seen him or felt his breath against her skin. I could only imagine her reaction to

such a story, and her suspicions as to why I had waited so long
to share it.

Or, more disturbing, maybe I hadn't said anything for a far
more personal reason. As frightening as some of my encounters with the Lantern Man had been, I couldn't deny they'd
also been thrilling. Nothing so exhilarating had ever happened to me. I'd lived my entire life insulated by the marshes.
The few glimmers of excitement I had ever felt had been at
the balls and parties hosted by Kate's mother, and then later
Olivia. And the latter events had been tempered by wariness
and nerves after what had happened between me and Robert. My encounters with the Lantern Man were completely
different and solely mine, as almost nothing seemed to be
anymore.

I passed out of the marshes and began to climb the steep
slope of lawn leading up toward Greenlaws. I was halfway to
the summit when Robert appeared around the corner of the
manor. I lifted my hand in greeting, thinking he would wait
for me at the top, but instead he surprised me by striding
quickly down toward me.

"You could have waited for me," I called, feeling the burn
in my legs from the climb.

"Didn't you see Kate?" he replied, a hint of urgency in his
voice. "She went looking for you."

"Through the marshes?"

Robert glanced back at the house before nodding. "About
a quarter of an hour ago."

"Well, I didn't take the usual path, so perhaps we just missed
each other."

"That's probably it."

We stood awkwardly side by side. Normally I would have
expected him to invite me up to the house for some refresh-
ment on such a warm day, but he seemed impatient somehow,
and his gaze kept straying back toward the house. I couldn't

decide whether he was anxious for his sister or simply eager for me leave.

"Perhaps I should go look for her," I finally said.

"Yes," he gasped in relief. "That's a good idea."

I frowned at his odd behavior and turned to go.

"Kate seemed distracted."

I glanced over my shoulder at him.

His brow furrowed. "I just want to be certain she's well," he offered in explanation.

"I'll find her," I assured him.

I wasn't concerned. Kate's illness had passed days ago, with no sign of returning. If she was seeking me out, then that meant it was regarding a matter she didn't want to share with her brother. That, or she simply wanted to escape the confines of Greenlaws and the watchful eyes of the servants. As carefree as Kate's life was, and as indulgent as Robert was with her, my friend still chafed from time to time at the restrictions placed on her.

I'd never understood why Kate had not spent a season or two in London like most women of her station. Olivia would have been more than happy to sponsor her and escape the dullness of life among the Broads. Whenever I tried to ask Kate about it, she refused to answer. Sometimes I worried she'd not gone because of me, but I knew there had to be more to it. Kate was loyal, but not so much so that she was impractical.

I fully expected to cross paths with Kate on my return to Penleaf Cottage, so when I reached our garden without seeing her I felt a tiny flutter of worry. Thinking she might be sitting in the kitchen chatting with Mrs. Brittle, I hurried past the herb beds and through the scuffed door. I inhaled the scent of fresh bread baking in the oven, but there was no sign of Kate.

"Did Kate pay us a visit?" I asked, hoping she hadn't encountered Father in his current state.

Mrs. Brittle looked up from chopping vegetables. "I havena' seen Mistress Rockland today."

I bit my lip, wondering how that could be. If Robert said she had come looking for me, she should have arrived long ago. "Could she have spoken to Father instead?"

Mrs. Brittle's mouth tightened in disapproval. "'Tis no' likely, since he's no' left his study." She glanced up at me. "Why do ye think she's been here?"

"Robert told me she was on her way here. That we'd probably just missed each other."

"Through the fens?"

"Yes."

Her knife thunked against the wood of the table. "Well, I wouldna worry. It's still daylight, isna it? And she's as familiar wi' those paths as you are. Mayhap she just needed some time to hersel'." Her gaze lifted to stare at me through her lashes, and I knew she was thinking of me. "Unless ye're worried she's fallen ill again?"

"No." In general, Kate had a hearty disposition, which was why her recent sickness had been so distressing. But she was fully recovered now, I was sure of it.

Still, there were other things in the marsh that could have waylaid her. She could have twisted her ankle. Or encountered an unwelcome stranger. However, as Mrs. Brittle pointed out, it was daylight, and the Lantern Men of myth, as a general rule, did not walk the marsh while the sun was still high in the sky. And whether by necessity or because he'd chosen to heed the legend, I had yet to meet my Lantern Man during the day either. Though, unsurprisingly, such a thought did not make me feel better.

"Is there somethin' else she should be concerned wi'?"

I looked up to find Mrs. Brittle studying me with her sharp eyes. She had never missed much, and I began to wonder if she knew far more than she was saying.

"It's just that Robert was acting so strangely," I replied, wanting to misdirect her.

She stared at me a moment longer and then returned to her chopping. "Mayhap today was no' the day to visit Greenlaws unannounced."

I frowned at the top of her gray head, uncertain what she meant. But before I could ask, we heard a crash. I dashed down the hall to Father's study and flung open the door. He sat among the broken pieces of an old wooden table, trying to push himself to his feet. Amazingly, or perhaps not so, the bottle of brandy in his hand was unharmed.

"Father, are you all right?" I hurried across the room to help him.

"Go away," he slurred drunkenly.

I couldn't help wondering where he'd hidden this latest bottle. Mrs. Brittle and I had cleared the house just this morning. I bent to grab his elbow, but he pushed me away.

"Go away," he repeated, louder this time.

"But Father—"

"I said go away!"

The ferocity of his voice made me shrink back. He glared up at me with bloodshot eyes, and my heart, which I was forever believing could not be hurt any further, shriveled inside my chest. Mrs. Brittle stood in the doorway as I whirled around to flee, her eyes swimming with compassion. In that moment it was simply more than I could bear.

I ran.

Chapter 11

I RAN THROUGH THE KITCHEN AND out the creaking garden gate, down the hill to the trail that led to our dock. The weathered wood thudded and rattled beneath my feet. I skidded to a halt just at the edge, wrapping my arm around one of the posts lest I plunge into the channel.

The water below rippled and swirled, murky and dark with vegetation. I felt an almost desperate need to dive into it, to disappear among the submerged reeds and grasses and lost caskets of treasure, and resurface somewhere else, somewhere far away. I hugged the pillar to stop myself. Far too many people had become tangled in the vines growing just below the surface of the water and been dragged down to a watery death. I knew better than to trust the placid, harmless appearance of the Broads. They were as treacherous as any current or tide.

Tears stung my eyes. I swiped at them with the back of my hand, chastising myself for letting them fall. Father's outburst was nothing new. I should be immune to the pain by now. I should refuse to let it hurt me. But it did all the same.

I sank down to my knees and sat, dangling my feet over the edge of the dock. A wooden splinter bit into the palm of my skin, but I barely felt it next to the dull throb in my chest. I knew I should pick it out, but I couldn't be bothered to. I was just so tired. So very tired.

I stared off into the distance, watching the wheeling flight of two corbels. Their movements were like a dance, but I couldn't tell whether it was playful or aggressive the way they swooped and dived. The light slowly began to fade from the sky, turning orange then pink and then purple, and still I didn't move. I couldn't seem to dredge up the energy or the will. I was conscious of the danger I was courting, but I simply didn't care. Or maybe I did and I just wanted to feel something other than this numbing pain, this despair.

Whatever the reason, I sat and waited for darkness to gather and the mist to appear. My only movements were to alleviate the pins-and-needles sensations in my limbs as they fell asleep.

I'd just begun to give up on him, becoming unaccountably angry that he, too, had abandoned me, when I sensed his presence behind me. I don't know if it was a small vibration of the boards beneath me from his footsteps, or solely this connection that seemed to exist between us that alerted me, but I was certain he stood just a few feet away. He didn't speak, only looked at my back. I could feel the intensity of his gaze crawling along my skin, raising the fine hairs on the back of my neck. It was at once frightening and exhilarating, and thoroughly exasperating that he should affect me so.

"Go away," I snapped. When he made no effort to move or reply, I scowled. "Clearly your possession of a lock of my hair gives you no power over me, for here I am…" I gestured broadly with my arms "…alone in the marshes at night." I knew I was being belligerent, deliberately egging him on.

"How do you know I didn't make it so?"

The low timbre of his voice trembled through me. "If you…" My words broke off as the meaning of his words penetrated my consciousness. I felt a moment's hesitation, but then I shook it aside. "That's ridiculous," I declared, though with less heat than my previous comments. "You've been try-ing to keep me out of the marshes. Why would you suddenly change your mind?"

"Perhaps I missed you."

My breathing hitched as I realized he had moved closer and I hadn't even known it.

"Perhaps I want you near as much as I want you to stay away," he continued in his smooth, steady voice. His words seemed to weave about me. "Or perhaps I've decided there's a better way to deal with you."

I felt the hem of his cloak brush against my back and I sud-denly realized how incredibly stupid I was. Here I sat trapped at the edge of our dock with nowhere to run. The Lantern Man could choke me, drown me, do whatever he pleased, and I would be almost helpless to stop it. What's more, no one would hear my screams. Father was almost certainly insensible and Mrs. Brittle's hearing had diminished to the point that she sometimes couldn't hear a knock at the door. And if she did hear me, what could she do?

However, he didn't move any farther, simply stood towering over me, as if he'd expected me to cower in fear. Exactly as I was doing. At that realization, my dampened temper flared back to life.

"What utter twaddle," I snapped, forcing him to back up a step as I rose clumsily to my feet. "I'm not some moonstruck girl. Don't play your games with me."

He moved so quickly, I wasn't prepared. Reaching out to take hold of my arm as I backed away, he angled my body so that my shoulders came up against the post behind me. "Who says I'm playing games?"

The sky overhead was strewn with clouds, obscuring what little light from the moon there was. So even standing as close to me as he was, I could only sense rather than see his dark eyes boring into mine. Still, my heart beat wildly in my chest at his proximity.

In the past he had been almost careful *not* to touch me, but now he crowded against me, his strong hands gripping my upper arms. My hands pressed into the coarse fabric of his cloak, feeling the heat of him.

"You must be," I challenged. "If not to toy with me, what else could you want?"

His already deep voice seemed to drop another octave. "That's a dangerous question."

Unbidden, my eyes dropped to the shadowed place where his words feathered against my skin when he spoke. I inhaled a ragged breath. "Is it?"

"Very."

There was an odd note in his voice I couldn't identify. Was it amusement, or something else? Something I hadn't heard in a long time.

I couldn't seem to form a reply. My whole body tingled with awareness and I felt my eyes begin to close as I swayed toward him.

But then he chuckled—a throaty sound of self-satisfaction. My eyes snapped open as he backed away, removing his solid warmth. Heat suffused my face as he tipped his head toward land, clearly signaling he was finished with me.

I stumbled forward a few steps, bemused and disconcerted, until he offered a few parting words.

"Stay out of the marshes."

His voice was tight, though still laced with dark humor. It felt like an arrow shot into my spine.

I gathered my composure, striding down the dock with my head held high. I refused to look back though I wanted to. I refused to give him that satisfaction. Clearly, I'd behaved exactly as I said I wouldn't, though he'd seemed to give every indication that's what he wanted.

I pushed through the reeds and grasses up the path to our

cottage as my indignation drained away to leave only confusion and disillusionment. I'd gone out into the marshes
seeking something, and now, not having found it, I felt ludi-
crously disappointed. What did I expect from a cloaked figure
who only approached me at night to frighten and unsettle
me? I would be better off trusting Robert despite our painful
past than a man whose face I'd never seen.

Mrs. Brittle had left a plate of bread and cheese covered
with a towel on the table in the kitchen, and I was surprised
to find I was actually hungry enough to eat even though my
stomach felt twisted in knots. There was also a note addressed
to me in Kate's handwriting. In it, she explained that she had
gone for a walk that afternoon, but not in the direction of
Penleaf Cottage, and she didn't know why her brother had
told me so. I was somewhat shocked to realize that in my own
distress I'd completely forgotten about her.

Kate's note made me consider Robert's conduct earlier that
afternoon as even odder. Had he truly been mistaken about
Kate's whereabouts or was there something else behind his
evasive behavior? Or perhaps Kate had been the one to lie.
It wasn't the first time she'd used me as an excuse. In the
past, I hadn't minded, especially when she wanted to escape
Olivia. But now I wasn't as comfortable with it, particularly
knowing there were figures like the Lantern Men prowling
the marshes.

Attempting to push the bothersome suspicions from my
mind, I climbed the stairs and readied myself for bed. As
exhausted as I was in mind and body, I should easily have
tumbled into sleep, but my brain did not wish to cooperate. I
stared into the shadows, trying not to think about the Lantern
Man, about how much I'd wanted him to kiss me.

I'm not sure how long I had lain there like that, praying
for the oblivion of sleep, when I heard the creak of my door
opening.

"Ella."

I turned toward the sound of my father's voice, but I didn't speak. I was torn between wanting to hear what he would say and wishing he would leave me be. So I held my breath, pretending to be asleep a moment longer.

But I should have known better. This was a song we'd danced to many times before.

"Ella," he whispered louder, opening the door wider and stepping inside. "Ella, are you awake?"

Father was never going to let me sleep through what he needed to say. In his inebriated state I didn't think it even occurred to him that his actions ensured that I was awake rather than the other way around.

I sighed. "Yes, Father."

He crossed the room unsteadily and sat on the edge of my bed next to my hip. "Ella, I…" His words faltered, and I could hear him swallow. He inhaled, trying again to get the words out, but he stopped and pressed a hand to his eyes.

I choked on an answering knot in my throat.

He grunted angrily and then inhaled a deeper breath. "I…I…I'm sorry," he blubbered, dissolving into tears.

I sat listening to his broken weeping, wanting to reach out to him, wanting him to go away. He was my father after all. I wanted to comfort him, to tell him all was well. But it wasn't. It never was. I'd received too many of these tearful, rambling apologies in the middle of the night to ever fully believe it would all be well again.

Father would eventually choke out something that resembled a confession—one that at first made me feel guilty at seeing the depth of his emotion, and then, as it became less and less coherent, annoyed—just before falling asleep. I would shake him awake and help him to his room where he would collapse on his bed, completely insensible to the confusion and heartache he'd caused me.

Inevitably, the morning after he would offer me another apology, this one short and sheepish, along with a promise that he would stop drinking. A promise he would keep for a day or two—although he had once kept it for an entire week—before returning to the bottle.

I knew what was coming, like following a script written specifically for us. And yet every time I hoped *this* time would be different. *This* time he would really mean what he said. *This* time he would give up his brandy. So when he failed and I stumbled upon him defiantly swigging from a flask or passed out in his chair, an empty bottle at his feet, it was doubly painful.

It was for that hope that he so tearfully gave me and then carelessly snatched away that I came closest to hating my father.

And so this time played out like all the rest, overwrought and nearly incoherent, until I was sick at heart as well as to my stomach. After depositing my father in his room, I lay back down and rubbed my abdomen, wondering why I always seemed to suffer more from Father's attacks of conscience than he did.

Chapter 12

I WATCHED AS MY FATHER STUMBLED through several days without a drop of brandy, and I couldn't stop the buoyant feeling that continued to fill my chest with every day that passed. Maybe this time truly was different. Maybe this time Father would change.

So I stashed the letter Mr. Fulton had given me with my grandfather's and great-aunt's addresses inside my desk. I knew I would likely regret not writing them immediately, but I could not resist that fickle hope. If this was the time Father finally stopped, then I would repent having exposed our situation to my mother's relatives.

I remained at Penleaf Cottage much of the time, thinking that perhaps if I was nearby Father would be less likely to return to drinking. This may have been faulty logic on my part—my presence had never made a difference before—but I convinced myself of it regardless.

Besides, without a staff of servants to clean and maintain the property there were always chores to be done. Mrs. Brittle and I dusted, scrubbed the floors and windows, stripped the beds to clean the sheets, and pulled weeds in the garden. And all the while we searched the house from top to bottom for any bottles of brandy, empty or otherwise, which Father had stashed about the premises. I took great pleasure in sinking the last of them into the marshes, hopefully never to be seen again.

I also made a trip into Thurlton to purchase the sugar and lemon Mrs. Brittle would need to bake her strawberry trifle for the church dinner with some of the money Mr. Fulton had given me. She protested when I presented them to her, arguing that she could have made something else, but I could tell she was pleased. Mrs. Brittle was vain about few things, but her baking was rightly one of them.

In exchange, Mrs. Brittle handed me a note that had been delivered while I was gone. It was an invitation from Kate in her always exquisite handwriting to dine at Greenlaws that evening.

> *Please, Ella, you must come.*
> *Monsieur Reynard is visiting again, and I vow I cannot sit through another insuffer-able dinner with only that odious man and my brother for company. If word of his obnoxious presence sours your appetite, as it does mine, then at least come to save me from myself.*
> *Impaling myself on the silver never appeared so tempting.*

I smiled at Kate's melodramatic commentary. I was not particularly fond of Monsieur Reynard either, especially given the fact that he was Olivia's cousin, but Kate's dislike ran far deeper. I'd never asked why, figuring that if I'd been forced to spend as much time in his company as she had, then I would probably loathe him too. I was eager to see Kate, for I'd been absent from Greenlaws for almost a week and we rarely spent more than three days apart, but still I was tempted to decline, anxious about leaving Father.

Mrs. Brittle must have guessed at the content of the letter and correctly deduced my hesitation. "Go," she told me. "Ye canna' hang aboot here all the time." She picked up the sack of sugar to carry it to the pantry. "I'll look after yer da." When still I dithered, she shooed me with her hand. "Go!"

I thanked her and hurried to wash off the sweat and grime of the day. My lavender sprig dress was by far the nicest and cleanest gown I owned, even with the patches where the color was beginning to fade. It was far from an evening dress, but the only one of those I owned no longer fit, and Mother's had long since been sold. Fortunately, Robert and Kate had never been ones to dine in strictly evening attire, so they would not care what gown I wore. Monsieur Reynard would likely make a derisive comment, but his opinion mattered little to me anyway. I twisted my hair up onto my head and pinned my mother's brooch securely to my bodice before setting out.

The residents of Greenlaws House had always observed country hours, partaking of their meals far earlier than those in town. When Olivia first arrived at Greenlaws she had complained about this endlessly, finding it abominably unfashionable. It had been one of the only things I knew of that Robert had fought her on. He insisted that he rose from bed far too early to hold breakfast until midday and retired too early to eat dinner after sunset. So we supped while the sun was still high in the sky in the summer.

Monsieur Reynard was just as contemptuous of the practice, and was in fact bemoaning the Rocklands' bourgeois tendencies when I entered the drawing room. Kate's blatant annoyance and Robert's long-suffering expression would have been humorous if I had not been confused as to why they continued to endure the man's presence.

"Ella," Kate exclaimed, making no effort to hide her relief to see me. She bounded across the room to me in a lovely amber and ivory lace confection that put my own gown to shame. "I'm so glad you could join us." She embraced me briefly and then pulled back, wrinkling her nose in distaste. "You remember *Mister* Reynard." Her words were all sweetness, but for the mocking title.

Reynard scowled but did not bother to correct her, knowing it was no use, nor did his proper title matter in such company. Mister Reynard was in fact Monsieur Reynard, or more accurate still, the Comte de Reynard, though he and his family had lost much of their consequence when they fled France during the Revolution when he was just a boy. In an attempt to make polite conversation, I had once tried to ask him about his family's history and the story of their flight to England, thinking he would be happy to boast of his importance, but he had rebuffed me. I didn't know whether this was because it would be too painful to discuss or if he felt the tale would be wasted on me. I had always strongly suspected it was the latter.

His eyes flicked up and down me contemptuously. "Miss Winterton, lovely to see you," he said in such a way that I knew he meant the exact opposite.

I smiled tightly and replied in the same voice, "Likewise."

Robert greeted me far more warmly, even going so far as to take my hand. "I apologize about the other day," he leaned in to say. "I could have sworn Kate had told me she was going to visit you, but apparently I wasn't attending properly."

"There was no harm done," I assured him with a dismissive huff of laughter. Though I had no reason to be, I felt uncomfortable with Robert's familiarity in front of the others. Particularly when Reynard narrowed his dark eyes in speculation. The Frenchman was too strong a reminder of Olivia.

"I hope Robert isn't blaming me for his mistake," Kate leapt in to say. "It's not my fault he doesn't listen to his younger sister."

He glowered at her. "I claimed responsibility. Though you could have made certain I heard you."

"You nodded in understanding," she protested.

"That doesn't mean I was actually listening."

"What's this about?" Reynard interjected before the siblings could resort to fisticuffs.

"I came looking for Kate a few days ago and Robert told me she had gone to Penleaf Cottage to visit me," I explained.

"But I hadn't," Kate pointed out unnecessarily, still glaring at her brother.

Reynard swirled the drink in his glass. "Which day was this?"

Robert turned away suddenly, crossing the room to the sideboard to refill his drink. "Monday, I believe."

"Ah," Reynard replied in his nasally voice, as if that meant something.

I glanced between the two men, confused by their exchange.

Reynard lounged back in his dark evening kit, with one elbow propped on the back of the russet settee, and offered me a secretive smile.

Kate rolled her eyes at this display. "Let's adjourn to the dining room, shall we?" she suggested and then linked her arm through mine, snubbing Reynard, who should have escorted her. Not that the man truly cared. He seemed amused by Kate's aversion.

I had dined at Greenlaws more times than I could count, and every time I was struck by how elegant but restrained the dining room was. Somehow Kate's mother had managed to create the perfect balance of beauty and comfort. It was the one room in the house that Olivia had been content to leave as it was.

The walls were papered in Chinese silk with azure-blue birds perched on golden branches. The curtains flanking the wide picture window were almost a perfect match to the birds, and seamlessly guided the eye toward the expansive view. The table and furnishings were ornately carved in warm oak, and the chairs upholstered in gold. Their stiff appearance was deceiving, though, because once you sat in them you realized how well cushioned they were. At least, they were far more padded than the hard seats remaining in the dining room at Penleaf Cottage.

"So, Ella, how have you been spending your days since we saw you last?" Robert asked as a bowl of Lorraine soup was placed before each of us.

"Helping with the inventory and overseeing the cleaning of some of the rooms we don't often use. Just household management. Nothing very interesting," I fibbed, taking a sip of my soup. Robert and Kate knew that Mrs. Brittle was our only servant, and it must have been obvious she was more family at this point than a member of our staff, but Reynard did not need to know that.

Kate groaned. "I dread inventory. Every time, I wonder why I can't allow Mrs. Griggs to handle the matter entirely."

I offered her a grateful smile, for I knew she did just that, barely taking the time to listen to her housekeeper's final report. She could have cared less whether there was a set of sheets missing or if one of the rugs needed to be replaced.

"The riveting life of domestic bliss," Reynard mocked. "But tell me about this illustrious anniversary dinner the church in Thurlton is having tomorrow. I hear your humble village may be graced with the presence of an archdeacon, and perhaps even a bishop." He arched his eyebrows over his wineglass in feigned astonishment as he took a sip.

Robert frowned.

"I haven't the least idea who shall actually attend. But I imagine it would be deadly dull for someone as riveting as yourself," I snapped sarcastically.

"Nonetheless, I look forward to it."

I looked up at him in perplexed annoyance. Why did he wish to attend the Church of All Saints anniversary dinner? To amuse himself with our provincial quaintness?

"I hope you can give me a tour of this 600-year-old building, Rockland. The sanctuary, the vestry, the bell tower, the cellar. Olivia always talked about how charming it was."

Robert looked like he'd bitten into a bitter piece of onion. "I'm sure that could be arranged."

I stared across the table at Kate, wondering if she was just as bewildered as I was. She appeared to be doing her best to ignore them, scowling into her bowl. I was curious what bothered her most—Reynard himself or his calculated mention of Olivia. Robert's late wife certainly hadn't found the church, or anything here in the fens for that matter, charming. I knew that for sure. So why was he bringing her up now?

I listened absently as Robert and Reynard discussed their mutual acquaintances and the events happening in London—people and places I knew nothing about. Kate was able to add small comments, for she'd at least been to the city on short trips, but even she was mostly silent. I did notice that Robert tried to steer the conversation away from talking about the war or matters abroad. I guessed this was out of courtesy to me because of Erik, but as much as I appreciated it, shielding me in such a way was futile. I might not visit London, but I sometimes read the London newspapers Robert had delivered to Greenlaws. I wasn't oblivious to what was going on elsewhere.

When the meal was over, Robert and Reynard elected to forgo their usual glasses of port and join me and Kate in the drawing room for tea. I can't say that we were altogether pleased by this. I suspected my friend was as eager as I was to chat privately, and to escape the obnoxious Frenchman.

However, Reynard had other ideas. "Rockland, why don't we adjourn to the music room instead?" he suggested as we rose from our chairs. "Then we can hear how well this new pianoforte of yours sounds. A rather tattered old thing. Not sure why you bought it." He turned toward me with a far too innocent expression. "Miss Winterton, do you play? If I remember correctly, Olivia told me you were quite tolerable. Of course, my cousin Sophie is an exquisite pianist, so I'm afraid I'm ruined for even acceptable performances. But beggars should be no choosers."

I scarcely heard the last of his words or registered his insult, for my ears were still buzzing from what he'd said about the pianoforte. A tingling sensation ran up my limbs as I turned to Robert and Kate. The panic stamped across their features told me all I needed to know.

I moved toward the door, ignoring Robert when he called for me to wait. I lengthened my stride as I turned down the corridor toward the music room, not wanting the quick patter of Kate's pursuit to catch up with me until I'd seen for myself.

"Ella, *please*. Wait!" she cried.

I threw open the door and there sat my mother's pianoforte, tucked between their Broadwood grand and a harp. My face flushed hot and tears stung my eyes as I stared at the evidence of how very far my family had fallen. At the proof of my dearest friends' knowledge of this—and their deception.

"Ella," Kate gasped as she reached me. She touched my shoulder, but I brushed her aside. "Ella, please. We were going to tell you, but we didn't know how." Her eyes were stricken with guilt. "We never meant to hurt you," she added in a hushed voice as Reynard and Robert entered the room.

Robert was glaring at Reynard, his color high, while the

Frenchman could only offer me a self-satisfied smirk. I could do nothing to hide my upset, to arm myself against his pleasure at my discomfort. But at least he was honest. At least I knew where I stood with him.

I dropped my gaze, unable to meet Robert's and Kate's eyes. Now Robert's behavior that day made sense. I had likely arrived at Greenlaws through the marshes just as the pianoforte was being delivered via the road. My lips twisted bitterly. "You must have been horrified by the sight of me climbing the hill that day."

Robert glanced at his sister before having the grace to admit, "It was somewhat of a shock."

"And I suppose Kate told you what lie to feed me."

"Ella," she pleaded, reaching for me again.

I side-stepped her touch, and pushed passed Reynard through the door, unable to stand there a moment longer. Shame burned inside me, hot and all-consuming.

"Ella," she called again. But Robert said something to stop her before I escaped out of earshot. I wasn't certain whether I was grateful for his interference or angry that he didn't care enough to let her come after me or pursue me himself.

I dashed down the front steps, and then hesitated, uncertain where to go. I didn't want to return home through Thurlton, not when there might be people about to witness my distress, but I also didn't want to venture out into the marshes. Not after what had happened the last time I'd been there. The Lantern Man's rejection and amusement were still too fresh in my memory. So I turned my feet toward the road that led west to Chedgrave.

My mind turned round and round as my feet churned up the dust, carrying me farther and farther away from the embarrassment and the pain. It seemed lately I was always fleeing, for good reason, and this time I was contemplating continuing to do so until both Penleaf Cottage and Greenlaws were just a distant memory.

The sun began to sink lower in front of me, casting long shafts of light over the softly undulating grasses of the marsh to my right and the bright green fields to my left. I knew it was time to turn back, or else I might be caught out on the carriageways after dark. Not far off I could see the white sails of a windmill turning. From the direction I'd been walking I deduced it was Hardley Mill, but in my distraction I wanted to be sure. There were at least two people moving about outside the mill, so I decided it would be best to ask them before turning around.

As I neared the mill, I could see that there appeared to be a trio of men. They would unload a barrel or crate from a boat and then disappear inside the mill. At first it seemed as if they were simply stocking supplies, but then I began to wonder at the quantity. These windmills were used to drain the marshland, not to grind wheat or grain. What could they possibly need to store so much of?

A sinking feeling entered my stomach, and my footsteps faltered. Perhaps I shouldn't draw their attention. But by then it was too late. One of the men stopped as he exited the mill, finally taking notice of me, and a second man joined him. They looked familiar, though I couldn't recall why, but that didn't mean they were harmless. I was considering turning back without speaking to them, even though such an action might appear suspicious, when the first man began to move toward me with long, quick strides. I stiffened, knowing my shorter legs could never outpace him.

It was then that I heard the sound of a horse approaching at a fast pace. I swiveled about to see Kate's chestnut gelding galloping toward me. Kate sat astride, her skirts pushed up around her legs, displaying her ankles, and her caramel-brown hair falling from its pins. She waited a bit too late for my comfort to rein in her horse.

"When did you start walking so fast?" she accused as her horse danced to the side. "I couldn't keep up with you. I had to turn back for Samson."

I almost apologized, but then I recalled why I'd been fleeing from her in the first place.

"Where did you intend to go?" she demanded. "Were you going to walk all the way to Norwich?" She glanced past me, her hazel eyes still narrowed in challenge, and I turned to face the man approaching us.

I remembered now where I'd seen him. He was Achilles—though I supposed that wasn't his real name—the wherry man with the guinea-gold-streaked hair that the maids had been giggling and cooing over at Greenlaws, and he didn't look the least bit happy to see us. Though I noted his displeasure was tempered by the sight of Kate on horseback. I had to admit, she did look rather magnificent, like a warrior maiden. Boudicca and her tribe of Iceni had ruled this part of East Anglia, so perhaps the comparison wasn't inapt, minus the flaming red hair and spear at any rate.

"Well, if it isn't Her Highness," the man drawled, not bothering to hide his admiration of Kate's ankles. "How can I help ye?"

She arched a single eyebrow imperiously. "You can't."

"Actually…" I spoke up before Kate angered the man. After all, she was the one on horseback, several feet above him. I was not. "Is that Hardley Mill?"

He flicked a glance at me before turning back to Kate. "Aye. Why? Did ye have business here?" he asked dubiously.

She scoffed, as if the idea was ludicrous.

"We'll just be going then," I said. There was something about this man that made me nervous, and one of his cohorts was now making his way toward us as well. He stopped a short distance away, but close enough that I could tell it was the dark-haired wherry man—the one Kate had dubbed Hector.

"What's the hurry?" Achilles moved a step closer to Kate, a ribald grin stretching his mouth.

But Kate was far from intimidated. Rather than backing away, she danced Samson closer, swinging his mouth full of large teeth toward the impudent man.

"Is all well?" the second man called out. I couldn't tell whether he was asking for our benefit or his cohort's, but he didn't move closer.

"Let's go, Kate."

She continued to stare down at Achilles with a sparkle of challenge in her eyes, but this only seemed to please him more if the broadness of his grin was any indication. It was suddenly quite clear to me that this wasn't Kate's first encounter with the man. Though what or when that previous encounter had been, I couldn't have guessed.

She removed her foot from one of the stirrups so that I could use it and reached down to help pull me up behind her. With one last toss of her head, she urged Samson forward with her riding crop. I wrapped my arms around her waist, but couldn't help one last glance behind me. Achilles' and Hector's heads were bent together, watching us as we disappeared down the road.

We rode for several minutes in silence, putting some distance between us and the mill, before Kate slowed her horse to a walk.

"Those were two of the wherry men who deliver supplies to Greenlaws," I remarked. "I wonder what they were doing at the windmill."

"Probably delivering supplies. They don't work exclusively for Robert," she replied blithely.

"No, but…it did seem odd." I couldn't tell if Kate truly didn't find their actions strange or if she was merely fobbing me off. Regardless, I was grateful she'd ridden up on her horse when she had. There was no guarantee they would have acted like gentlemen. In fact, there was every chance they wouldn't have. But having witnessed her too-familiar interaction with Achilles, I couldn't quite dismiss the matter.

However, she wasn't interested in discussing him. "You know my brother meant no harm, don't you, Ella? When he heard you were being forced to sell your mother's pianoforte because of that revenue man, he decided he couldn't let it go to a stranger. It wasn't right."

"Did you know?"

"Not at first. And I truly wasn't home when you arrived at Greenlaws that day," she hastened to add. "But I found the pianoforte that night. And heard his *stupid* excuse for sending you away."

"Where were you?" I couldn't help asking.

"Walking."

I could tell she was being deliberately vague. "In the marshes?"

"Mmmm."

I frowned, wishing I could see her face. Did her evasion have something to do with the golden-haired wherry man? It was on the tip of my tongue to ask her, but then it occurred to me that I hadn't exactly been forthcoming about my interactions with the Lantern Man. Was it fair for me to pry when I still hadn't decided if I wanted to share my secrets?

"Would you rather Robert had let your pianoforte be sold to someone else?" Kate pointed out. She guided the horse to the right, down the road leading to Thurlton.

"I would rather he hadn't known about it at all." I frowned at the passing landscape. "How did he?"

She shrugged. "Maybe your solicitor wrote him."

A possibility, but I didn't think Mr. Fulton would have done such a thing. He was kind, but not meddlesome. And no matter how well-intentioned this sale had been, it was still meddlesome.

Kate turned to look over her shoulder at me as best she could on horseback. "Don't be cross with him, Ella. He was only trying to help."

I sighed and lifted my eyes to gaze out across the field speckled with marsh marigolds at the stark tower of the Church of All Saints. "I know."

A companionable silence fell and I thought for a moment that she would let the matter go. After all, I had reluctantly agreed not to begrudge Robert his act of kindness. Once he found out about the sale, he had been placed in an awkward situation. But Kate knew there was far more at stake than the loss of my mother's beloved instrument. Our days of pretending all was well at Penleaf Cottage were over.

"How awful is it?" she murmured.

This time I was glad I couldn't see her face.

"Awful," I admitted through a tight throat. "But maybe getting better."

She didn't ask me to elaborate, and I loved her for that. Just then, I didn't want to admit aloud how I was clinging to the hope that my father had finally stopped drinking. It was still too fresh, too fragile. If I was proved wrong yet again, I didn't want to have to face someone else with my foolishness.

She reached down to squeeze my hand where it wrapped around her waist, and I turned my hand over to squeeze back.

Chapter 13

IN THE END, THE CONGREGATION of the Church of
All Saints was not graced by the presence of the Bishop of
Norwich for the anniversary celebration; however Archdeacon Soames did, unhappily, attend. I couldn't help but feel
sorry for Vicar Tilby, whose normal quiet exuberance was
squashed by the presence of his superior. The rededication
service, which the vicar had intended to be joyous and uplift-
ing, was nearly brought to a halt when the archdeacon stood
up and began to drone on about service, humility, and tem-
perance.

If he expected the congregation to be grateful for this somber reminder of their Christian duty, he was sadly mistaken.
When the women of the church began to frown and grumble,
worrying the food they'd spent days preparing would spoil
because the man before them—who spent very little time in
service to their tiny corner of the parish—didn't understand
when it was time to "shut his gob," he should have realized
he'd lost us all.

I admit I heard very little of the archdeacon's impromptu
sermon, distracted as I was by the company of my father
seated beside me. More than one person had glanced at him
in surprise, though no one had been ungracious enough to

comment. I tried and failed to remember the last time Father had attended church with me. I knew it was before Erik's death, when he had declared he washed his hands of God since God had washed His hands of him. His coming to the rededication service was a big step forward, one that Vicar Tilby seemed to appreciate when he shook Father's hand as we filed out of the building.

Archdeacon Soames, on the other hand, did not.

"Mr. Winterton, have you decided to return to His flock, or are you just here for the food?" he intoned as he shook Father's hand. Apparently, the archdeacon was kept apprised of such important things as attendance even if he rarely deigned to visit us.

Father's shoulders stiffened.

"Mr. Winterton has been ill," Vicar Tilby interjected with a gentle smile.

Archdeacon Soames narrowed his eyes behind his spectacles as if he didn't believe it.

"Archdeacon, I enjoyed your sermon," I rushed to say, hoping to distract him.

"That wasn't a sermon, child. Vicar Tilby delivered that." He flicked a critical glance at the other man. "Mine was merely a short devotional."

Mrs. Brittle harrumphed loudly at that before hurrying off to assist in laying out the meal on the long tables that had been set up in the shade of a pair of yew trees.

I followed Father toward another shaded area and stood next to him as he ran his hands distractedly around the brim of his hat rather than putting it on his head. His gaze kept straying toward the area of the churchyard where Mother and Erik's graves lay. I wondered whether he'd been back to visit them since my brother's body had been laid to rest. I was about to ask if he'd like to go see them when Robert, Kate, and Reynard approached.

"Well, that was a stimulating service," Reynard drawled.
Father stared at him blankly and I scowled.

"What?" the Frenchman goaded. "You enjoyed it?"

I ignored him. "You made it home safely, I see," I told Kate.
Her eyes twinkled. "Did you think I wouldn't?"

Robert shook hands stiffly with Father and introduced
Reynard before turning to me. "Miss Winterton," he greeted
me with a nod of his head. There was a question in his eyes,
but I knew him well enough to know he wouldn't ask it. At
least, not in our present company. Given the way dinner had
ended the night before, I couldn't blame him for his uncertainty.

I cleared my throat. "I see the hog Greenlaws contributed."

The delicious scent of roasted meat filled the air, making
everyone's mouth water.

Robert's brow seemed to smooth in relief. "Yes. Though
perhaps I should have asked that it be delivered a bit later. I
thought some of the men were going to come to blows when
the smell started drifting into the church halfway through the
service."

"I thought Archdeacon Soames would take that as his cue
to stop talking," Kate added with a mischievous smile.

"Excuse me a moment," Father suddenly said, before slipping away.

As I watched him cross the churchyard and disappear behind
a cluster of people, I tried not to feel concerned about him.

"Speaking of the archdeacon," Reynard said, closing the gap
left by my father, "for a moment there I thought your housekeeper was going to swat him with her bonnet." A lock of his
brown hair draped over his forehead as he leaned toward me.
"Now that's something I would have liked to see."

I arched my eyebrows. "I'm sure you would."

Vicar Tilby called us all closer to give thanks for the meal.
Then the Rocklands, Reynard, and I made our way to the

front of the line with the vicar and the archdeacon, knowing none of the others would venture forward until we had filled our plates—yet another reminder of the class divide. By birth, I was ranked with the Rocklands, and yet I was as poor as, if not poorer than, everyone else here.

I glanced around, wondering where Father was and whether I should go search for him, but I didn't want to confuse matters. If I stepped out of line now, would the others serve themselves food or wait for me to return? Besides, he'd probably only gone to take care of his needs. I would feel foolish if that was the case, and embarrass him with my worrying.

Kate invited me to share their blanket. One of their servants had spread it in the shade of a large yew tree along the northern border, not far from where Robert and I had talked just a short week ago. I tried to enjoy the others' conversation and join in as best I could, but I found it difficult to concentrate when I still hadn't seen my father return. I kept an eye on the food tables, but he never passed through the line.

I began to set my plate aside, wondering if I should go look for him, when Robert leaned in to murmur, "Would you like me to discover if he's unwell? Maybe his breakfast did not sit well with him."

I nodded in gratitude, knowing he didn't have to phrase it so diplomatically. Though we might dance around it, I knew he was aware of my real concerns. "Yes, please."

He disappeared around the building and I tried to eat more of the delicious food the women had worked so hard to prepare, but it all settled in a heavy lump in my stomach.

The children's games began at the far end of the lawn and Kate went to have a closer look. She urged me to join her, but I wanted to stay where I was. It afforded a better view of the front of the church. She shrugged and trotted off, leaving me with Reynard, who remained blessedly silent. Every so often I could feel him watching me, but I ignored him, not wanting to encourage conversation, which was sure to be filled with his snide remarks.

The longer Robert was away the more nervous I became. There was no reason it should be taking this long to find my father. Unless he went home. But would he have left without telling me? When he had been drinking, I would have said unequivocally yes. However, when his mind was clear he never behaved so discourteously. So where was he?

Kate weaved her way back through the throng to our blanket and abruptly launched into a long, rambling account of the hoop race. At first I thought nothing of it, despite the excessive amount of excitement she displayed over a rather dull event, but I quickly realized her behavior was far too peculiar, even for Kate. I glanced about me, wondering what it was her big gestures were supposed to distract me from.

There, at the edge of the crowd, people were pointing and gawking at something at the front of the church, something currently hidden from my sight by the building. I rose to my feet and started walking towards it, ignoring Kate's protests. My heartbeat accelerated along with my steps, until it was pounding loudly in my ears. A fitting accompaniment to the yelling I heard as I drew closer.

I knew that voice raised in anger. I knew its sharpness, its frustration. And the slur I heard in his words was like a knife thrust to my midsection.

I lifted my skirts, dashing around the corner of the building. Father stood on the front walk, shouting belligerently at Robert and Vicar Tilby, who appeared to be trying to coax him out of the churchyard. He twisted and turned, staggering about as he rebuffed their assistance. The liquid in the bottle in his hand sloshed against the sides, though having been drained of nearly three-quarters of its contents, it never spilled.

The fragile, foolish blossom of hope I'd been nursing withered and died, smashed under my father's heel.

I pushed forward through a group of men, only to be brought up short by Mrs. Brittle. She wrapped an arm about my waist, urging me backward.

"Come away, my dear. Let the men deal with it."

For a second, I considered listening to her. I was perilously close to tears. But everyone was staring at my father: the villagers, Archdeacon Soames with his pinched face, Kate and Reynard who had followed me, along with a dozen others. Even Achilles and Hector were there, standing near the lychgate. They were all gaping and whispering, just as they'd done at Erik's funeral when too much drink had made Father maudlin and unable to hold back his grief, and at Robert's and Olivia's wedding reception when he'd hurled insults and accusations at Robert. I couldn't leave him to face that alone, no matter if it was of his own making.

I shook my head at Mrs. Brittle and she nodded resignedly. Her eyes held all the compassion I thought I could bear. Then I waded into the fray.

My skin prickled like it was being stung by hundreds of tiny midges as some of the attention shifted to me. I wanted to scream at them all, to demand to know who had given Father the bottle of what was sure to be brandy. I wanted to throw the entire smuggling operation in their faces, to bring into the open the thing that everyone knew about but never spoke of. To reveal it all to Archdeacon Soames and any other important guests who might be present. After all, if my secrets were to be laid bare, why shouldn't everyone else's?

But I bit back the words, even though they scalded my tongue. Adding my hysterics to Father's would not help the situation. I knew from experience that if I was to persuade Father to do anything when he was this inebriated, I had to remain calm.

"Father," I called, and when that didn't gain his attention, louder still to be heard over his recriminations. "Father!" I pressed a hand to Vicar Tilby's shoulder, telling him to let me past. "Father."

He swerved toward me and I took hold of his free hand. "Father." I tugged harder as he tried to pull away, prepared to duck if he swung around with his bottle. "Father, look at me," I pleaded.

"Ella?" He blinked, as if to bring me into focus. "Ella."

"Yes, Father," I replied calmly. "Come—"

"Tell 'em," he ordered. "Tell 'em." He shook his head. "They just don't understand. None of 'em," he barked in Robert's direction. "Tell 'em."

"I will, Father. But...but I'm not feeling well." My voice shook from the strain, making it all too easy for me to feign illness. "Could we please go home?" The last emerged as almost a whisper, and I thought I might have to repeat myself.

Father lifted his other hand, the one that still held the bottle, so quickly that I jumped, thinking he meant to strike me with it. Robert clearly thought the same thing, for out of the corner of my eye I saw him lurch forward a step. But Father only touched my cheek clumsily. "Oh, yes. Of course. Mayhap it's the heat," he slurred and reached up to tug at his cravat, rumpling it. "It's swelterin'."

I smiled tightly in agreement, though inside I felt as cold as winter.

Father turned to walk me toward the lychgate, his head held high as if he was doing a noble deed even as his footsteps veered to the right. I didn't know if he was truly too far gone to comprehend why everyone was watching us, or if this display was meant to salvage his dignity. Whatever the case, he couldn't seem to resist tossing one last comment at Robert as we passed, loud enough that half the people in the front of the churchyard could hear.

"She may be soon, Rockland, but she's not yours yet." He

paused and leaned toward Robert unsteadily. "And you don't deserve her."

I frowned as a blush burned its way up into my cheeks, surprised I was capable of feeling any more embarrassment than I already did.

As we turned to move away, Robert murmured, "I know."

I was surprised by the fervency of those words, but I refused to look back, lest I discover I'd heard wrong and he was mocking me.

I lifted my eyes as we neared the lychgate, and my gaze collided with the dark-haired wherry man's—the one I now thought of as Hector. His expression was carefully neutral, his posture relaxed and uncaring, and I was grateful to him for that. I wasn't certain I could have withstood anything else, be it disapproval or sympathy. But there was a glint of something in his eyes, something I couldn't name, though I tried.

Father staggered, pulling my attention back to him. I gripped his arm tighter where it looped through mine and escorted him out into the street.

Chapter 14

A S WE WALKED HOME, FATHER blathered on in his usual meandering, nonsensical way when he was ine-briated. His chief complaint seemed to be Robert and the other men's ill treatment of him. He kept reiterating how he'd done nothing wrong. What did it matter to them if he'd had a bit to drink? I mostly remained silent, only replying in the affirmative from time to time when he demanded to know if I was listening.

But when our cottage came into view and he launched into his fourth vehement retelling of the same events, my patience grew thin. Though I knew better, I sighed and suggested that Robert and Vicar Tilby were just trying to help. It was the wrong thing to say.

"They weren't helpin'," he argued in his garbled voice. "They were only worried about themselves and their pre-cious anniversary service."

"Well, that *is* why everyone was there." I didn't know why I was arguing with him. He couldn't be reasoned with in this state.

"I know that," he snapped. "I'm not stupid. I know what's happenin'."

I nodded, keeping my gaze fixed on our cottage. I could feel him glaring down at me.

"So I had some brandy. I know I said I wouldn', but I can control myself. There's no reason I shouldn' be able to 'ave some if I want it. I can stop anytime I want. This is my house. I'll do as I please." He kept growing angrier and angrier with each sentence, trampling on my already aching heart.

I pushed open our front gate. "Where did you get it?" I asked, pitching my voice as neutral as possible. I had to know.

"That's none of your concern," Father growled.

Oh, but it was.

He huffed. "You're jus' like them. Meddling in somethin' that's none of your concern. I thought my own daughter would know better." He brushed me aside and threw open the front door.

I stood on the porch, listening to his footsteps stomp down the hall and then the slam of his study door.

Mrs. Brittle found me still standing there when she returned home. She didn't ask me what happened, just coaxed me inside and led me down the hall toward the kitchen. She harrumphed and shook her head as we passed the closed door to Father's study.

The kitchen was the only room in the house that ever saw a regular cleaning, and it was immaculate as always, even after a busy evening and morning of baking and cooking. I ran my hands over the scarred wooden table while Mrs. Brittle made us tea. When the liquid had cooled enough for me to take a few sips and she had settled herself in the chair across from me, she finally spoke.

"Ye mun' have kenned this would happen," she said gently.

I stared at the cup between my hands. "Yes."

"Though I s'pose none o' us thought he'd tipple at the kirk's anniversary dinner."

"Who gave him the bottle? Do you know?" I looked up to see her craggy face creased in a frown. "Was it Ingles?"

She tilted her head. "I dinna ken, lass. Does it matter?"

"Yes."

They'd given Father the very thing he needed least in the world at a time when he was most vulnerable. Had they seen how uncomfortable he had been in church? Had they witnessed our exchange with Archdeacon Soames? Had they guessed how badly Father must have been wishing for a drink? Whether or not it had been intentional, I couldn't help but feel it was.

Mrs. Brittle seemed to understand that. "Maybe it does. But there's no' much ye can do aboot it. Unless ye plan to tattle on all o' 'em."

I'd already considered that and realized I couldn't. Too many innocent people would be hurt in the process. I wrapped my hands tightly around the cup, trying to absorb the warmth. I hated this feeling of helplessness. It weighed down my limbs even as my insides urged me to take action. Only I didn't know what to do. My mind scrambled for purchase, frantic to clasp onto anything rather than face this pit of despair.

"Have ye written to yer relatives?"

I looked up at Mrs. Brittle, surprised she'd known I had been considering just that. That is, before I latched onto the forlorn hope of Father's latest promise.

"Do you know anything about them?"

"Nay. Though yer mam told me once how much ye looked like yer granny."

I was surprised by this. My mother had never told me much about her parents. I knew I had the same hair color—a lock of her hair was clasped inside my mother's mourning brooch— but that was all.

"Write to 'em, lass," Mrs. Brittle urged. "Ye willna ken how they'll respond unless ye write."

I nodded, knowing she was correct even though my stomach was tied in knots at the prospect. "But Father…"

"If ye ever owed him your silence, ye dinna anymore," Mrs. Brittle stated firmly, though not unkindly.

In principle, she was right. But that didn't make it any easier. Mentioning my father's drinking felt like a betrayal of some kind. Although after today I supposed there was no use continuing the pretense.

Mrs. Brittle reached across the table to take my hand in a rare show of affection. "I'm old, lass. I dinna have many more years. And the way yer Father is, he doesna have many years left either."

I knew all of this, but hearing her declare the bald truth troubled me.

"Ye need to plan noo, lass. Afore it's too late." Her voice turned wry. "And afore ye have no choice but to accept whatever Master Rockland offers ye."

I looked up in surprise.

Her black eyes were hard.

"You don't like him?"

"'Tis no' for me to say," she replied, lifting her chin, and then proceeded to do just that. "But I didna like the way he treated ye when he ran off and married that lightskirt from London. I dinna care how much he lived to rue it. That didna make any difference for you."

I was surprised to hear her describe Olivia as a lightskirt. I didn't know whether she understood exactly what the term meant. There had been some vague suspicions that Olivia had been unfaithful to Robert, but none that anyone had discussed openly with me. Not that they would have, since I was a gentlewoman and Robert's former intended. However, all gossip on that subject had ceased after the carriage accident that killed her and the child she carried. Did Mrs. Brittle know more than she was saying, or was she just repeating an oft-heard phrase?

"Me point is, ye need options, lass. I dinna want ye acceptin' an offer from Master Rockland because ye dinna have a choice."

She was right, of course. I had contemplated the very same thing. The last thing I wanted was for Robert to marry me out of a sense of obligation.

I didn't know who would inherit the cottage upon Father's death, but I was well aware it wouldn't be me. In truth, since Erik's passing, I wasn't even certain Father had changed his will. But regardless, as a rule, young, unwed daughters didn't inherit property, and I couldn't very well go on living here with some distant male relative I'd likely never met. Even if I could, my mother's dowry was long since spent and the small income Father still received from his family would stop upon his death. Our property had never generated income—which now seemed a foolish oversight on my parents' part, given the fact that neither of their families approved of the match. So the stark reality was I would have no money to support myself. If my mother's family did not help me, I would be forced to search for work as a governess or lady's companion—or wed Robert. That is, if he even asked.

"I'll write my grandfather and great-aunt," I told Mrs. Brittle.

She patted my hand in approval. "Noo, do ye wish me to make ye a wee bit o' supper?"

I declined, not certain I could stomach it. "I doubt Father will either." He also hadn't eaten anything at the church dinner—the better to fill his gut with brandy.

I retreated to my room upstairs to lie down, but sleep eluded me. Stupid as it seemed, I found myself worrying about Father. He had begun to imbibe rather early and quickly, and he was closed away in his study alone. If something happened to him, would we even know before it was too late? He could stumble and hit his head, or fall on something sharp, or simply sleep too deep and never awake.

I strained to hear any sound from below, just to reassure myself he was well, but the cottage was quiet. Mrs. Brittle had gone to bed early, and Father was apparently still. But was that because he was in trouble or because he'd merely drank himself into a stupor?

I flopped over on my other side, agitated with myself for worrying so. Father didn't deserve my concern. I should just be able to forget him and close my eyes.

But I'd realized long ago that love and family were complicated. One couldn't simply stop caring because the person didn't merit it.

I sighed and gave up. Rolling over, I pushed myself up from the bed and made my way downstairs on silent feet. At the door to Father's study, I pressed my ear against the wood, listening for any sign of movement. When I didn't hear anything, I slowly turned the knob and opened the door.

Everything in the room was cast in muted hues from the hazy light of dusk filtering through the curtains. Father sat slumped over in his chair, his head resting against his chest as it rose up and down evenly with his breaths.

I watched him for a moment, wishing I understood. The one time I'd drunk too much wine at a dinner at Greenlaws, I'd felt wretched afterward. Erik had laughed at me and told me brandy or whiskey would be much worse. To live day after day like that seemed more akin to torture than escape, but then I hadn't ever drunk enough to reach true forgetfulness.

I considered trying to wake him, knowing he would end up with a terrible pain in his neck if he slept that way all night, but then decided against it. The last thing I wanted was another confrontation. If I woke him from a sound slumber now, I was sure to get one. So I left him where he was.

I wandered through the cottage, not yet ready to return to tossing and turning in my bed. In the waning light I could squint my eyes and almost pretend the furnishings and artwork we'd sold to pay our bills were still there. Their images were still fresh enough in my memory to form shadowy apparitions out of the fuzzy light. The landscape of Dedham Vale still hung above the table in the front hall. The Hepplewhite chairs still sat in the dining room. And in the drawing room the pianoforte still stood in the corner, waiting to be played.

That is, until I crossed to where it had once stood and felt the slight indentation in the floor it had left behind. I brushed the toe of my slipper over the worn floorboards, wondering when the last time was that someone had stood in that spot. Perhaps it had been my mother, happily directing the servants where to position her instrument, just beside the window so that she would have the optimum amount of light to read her music by. I could almost see her pressing her hands together to contain her excitement.

I turned away abruptly. I was doing it again. Mrs. Brittle had warned me of the dangers of conjuring up ghosts. Our memories were powerful things. They had the ability to both comfort and cause great pain.

I lifted aside the soft mint-green drapes and stared out at the fens. Fog had begun to gather as the temperature dropped, climbing up from the waterways through the reeds. It cast a bleary, unearthly quality over the landscape, one that caused tingles to run up my spine, warning me to stay safe inside.

That thought alone should have deterred me, but suddenly I felt confined by the cottage—its shabby rooms and musty air and heavy silence. It pressed in around me like a weight pushing down on my chest. My limbs actually physically ached with the need to move.

In my current frame of mind, it was impossible not to wonder, even if briefly, whether these sensations were being caused by the Lantern Man and the power he might have held over me. Either way, I suddenly didn't care. I wanted out. I wanted to be free of this house and its bittersweet memories.

Of Father and his blind destruction. Of my foolish, stupid hopes. I decided I much preferred the company of the Lantern Man, whoever he might be, than my own despondent thoughts.

I stole through the house to the back door and snatched up the lantern. The air outside was cool and damp against my bare arms, a welcome relief from the oppressive atmosphere inside. I inhaled deeply, filling my lungs, and deliberately slowed my steps as I crossed the lawn, taking time to savor the tranquility surrounding me. It was like standing in a void between two maelstroms—one within and one without. With each step I took toward the marsh, I could feel the prickling of anticipation.

I stopped at the edge of the fen, reminding myself I didn't have to go in. I could stay here on the lawn, cocooned in this in-between space. There was little chance the Lantern Man would leave the marsh, and almost none that Father would come outside. I could make this place all my own.

But that was the trouble, wasn't it? I was too often on my own, separated from others in all the ways that really mattered, and I was tired of it. Tired of not belonging anywhere with anyone, merely a visitor in other people's lives. It would be nice to choose something for myself for once. To seek out something rather than running away, even if that something was the Lantern Man. To take the risk, reckless though it might be, instead of cushioning myself, waiting for the next blow.

I breathed deep of the musty scent of the Broads, and strode into the fen. As my foot touched the pliant earth of the marsh path a soft breeze gusted through the tendrils of my hair that had escaped from their pins. They tickled against my ears and neck like fingertips brushing gently over my skin.

I walked with a slow and careful tread, knowing there was no need to rush, or even to search. The Lantern Man would find me. All I needed to do was not stray from the path or become lost in the fog, so that eventually I could find my way back.

I strolled for what must have been five or ten minutes, long enough for me to begin to question the wisdom of my actions. Not only had I willfully entered the fens on a misty night, knowing how perilous they could be, but I was also seeking out the Lantern Man, a man who had proved he was clearly up to nothing good.

I was on the verge of turning back when he appeared, materializing in the corner of my eye to the right. Once again, he seemed to step out of the heart of the bog, with the mist swirling around him and his dark cloak.

I swiveled to face him, startled by his proximity. Before I could lift my lamp, he reached out and with a flick of his wrist the flame flickered out. My breath caught in my throat as we were plunged into darkness.

Chapter 15

BLINKED, TRYING TO ADJUST MY vision. The Lantern
Man stood over me, close enough to feel the heat radiating
from him. It appeared this time he'd left his lantern behind.

"Why are you here?" he demanded with none of his normal charming pretense.

I fumbled to form a reply. "I...I suppose I wanted to see
you," I said, opting for honesty, imprudent though that might
be. I wasn't sure I could prevaricate.

It was obviously not the response he expected, for his head
jerked backward. He stared down at me, and as my vision
improved I could begin to make out the cat-like shape of his
eyes, the cleft in his chin. "Bloody woman," he murmured in
exasperation, though there was an oddly tender note to his
voice. "I've been trying to keep you *out* of the marshes, not
lure you in."

It was a surprisingly candid remark.

"Why?"

He sighed. "Are you normally this nosy?"

"Never."

The corners of his lips curled upward. "And I suppose
you're not normally this forthright either."

I thought of all the ways I danced around ever revealing the truth of what I was thinking. How I carefully chose my words lest I upset my father, or Robert, or sometimes even Kate.

"No."

He must have heard something in my voice, for his head tilted to the side as he searched my face. I wished he wasn't wearing a hood. Then at least I could see him as well as he saw me.

"You visit Greenlaws a great deal."

I nodded, wondering just how much of his time he spent observing me. Or did he have help?

"The Rocklands are friends. There's not much society in this part of the Broads."

I wasn't sure why I added the last, but he seemed to understand.

"Is that all?"

At first I wasn't sure what he meant, but as he stared down at me in anticipation I grasped his implication. "Yes. That is... there used to be more. But not for some time. It's just..." I exhaled, halting my stammered response. Why was I telling him any of this? "Kate and I are friends. That's why I visit so often," I stated more succinctly.

His dark eyes saw too much. "And yet Mr. Rockland seems quite protective of you."

I turned away, uncomfortable with the question.

"Although clearly not protective enough."

I glanced sideways at him as his jaw tightened.

"You really shouldn't be out here in the marshes. Especially at night. What do I need to do to make you understand the danger? Or are you always so reckless?"

I stiffened. "Why are you so intent on keeping me out?"

He loomed over me. "Because, you daft girl, I'm not the only one who roams these marshes. And the others would not be so considerate."

"You mean the other Lantern Men?"

He sank back on his heels. "Yes, if that's what you want to call us. I imagine you rarely encounter dangerous men, but I assure you, they are all around you."

"I'm well aware of the damages men can inflict on others," I shot back. I was all too familiar with the pain and suffering and cruelty people could cause. All I had to do was look at my own father. I pressed a hand to my stomach and added, more calmly, "Well aware."

"Then why risk it by repeatedly venturing into the marsh?"

I considered the matter. "What was at stake—my friend's health on our first meeting, and my mother's brooch on our second—was priceless to me. I don't think of standing on my own dock as actually being out in the marshes," I challenged. "So by my estimate, this is the only time I've taken an unnecessary risk. Though I suppose *you'll* have to decide whether it was for no good reason."

He fell silent, and I began to wonder if I was a fool. Was I so desperate for companionship, for sympathy, that I would place myself at an unknown and potentially dangerous man's mercy?

But then, there had been that first night when I was returning to Greenlaws with medicine for Kate. At the time, I'd thought I'd escaped from him. But now, having been near him several times and seen his height and the breadth of his shoulders, I was certain he could have easily caught me if he'd wanted to.

"Who are you?" I asked, trying to comprehend.

"Who do you think I am?" he replied, repeating the same response he'd given me on the dock, intentionally, I was sure.

"That's not an answer."

"It's the only one I have to give."

I scowled in frustration. "Can you tell me why you let me go?"

His head tilted in question.

"That first night, near the river, when your friends were closing in. Why did you let me escape?"

He crowded in closer, but I stood my ground.

"Did I?" he asked silkily.

I felt the potency of his nearness, but I refused to be distracted. "Yes."

His eyes traveled over my face, making my skin flush from their intensity. This was the clearest I had ever seen them, and I was captivated—memorizing every detail I could make out in the dim light. The slant at their corners, the depth at which they sat in his face, the heaviness of his brow. I almost didn't hear him when he finally answered.

"I had my reasons."

My brow furrowed. "Must you be so vague?"

"Yes."

"Then tell me one thing."

"I'll try."

"Are you always watching me? How do you know where I am?"

He smiled. "That's two things."

I glowered.

"No, I'm not always watching. Which is *why* I keep warning you," he muttered in frustration. "I might not always be the one who finds you."

"So…you *are* protecting me? You did let me escape?" I asked doubtfully.

His mouth pressed together into a tight line of displeasure.

"Perhaps you should give me back my lock of hair, then," I goaded. "Clearly it's not working for you."

But rather than respond in anger, his voice was thoughtful. "No. I think I'll keep it."

I felt a strange tingling sensation all over me, but whether that was because of the way the Lantern Man was standing so close to me or my own frustration, I didn't know. I didn't understand him. I couldn't. He was being deliberately mysterious and evasive. But while part of me was urging me to run from him, that his proximity only meant danger, another part of me was urging me to move closer.

His presence here, wandering the marshes at night, masquerading as a figure of myth, could only mean he was involved in something nefarious. And yet, still, I didn't hurry away from him. My body seemed determined to listen to the half that trusted him, that wanted to move nearer to the welcome heat his body produced. If he had been fae, I would believe these impulses were his doing.

I shivered in my cap-sleeved gown.

His hand rose to the clasp of his cloak under his chin and then stilled. "You shouldn't be here."

I nodded, knowing he was right, and suddenly felt too disconcerted to argue. But I couldn't take my eyes from his.

He inched a step closer. I could feel the length of his cloak pressing against my skirts. "Can you find your way back?"

I nodded again, tilting my head back farther to see into the darkness of his hood.

His eyes glittered as he leaned down toward me. My breath caught as he hesitated, as if he was waiting for something. For me to move closer? To push him away? When I did nothing, he closed the distance himself.

His mouth was warm and assured, and made my insides flutter like the leaves of our sycamore tree in the evening breeze. I had been kissed before. Robert and I had exchanged fumbling kisses and more than a few inappropriate embraces in the years before he married Olivia. But none of his caresses had made me feel anything close to this.

The Lantern Man pulled back and opened his mouth as if to tell me something, but then he stiffened. I could tell his gaze was fastened over my shoulder, and I turned to see what he was looking at. In the near distance there was a hazy orb of light hovering over the marshes. It flitted and danced in the midst of the fog.

One of his associates? Or something else?

Either possibility made the blood that had been flowing hotly through my veins suddenly run cold. Especially when the Lantern Man whirled me back around to face him and pressed something into my hand. "Go quickly," he whispered. "But wait as long as possible before you use that." Then he turned my shoulders toward the path leading to Penleaf Cottage. "Now go."

I stumbled forward as fast as I dared, glancing over my shoulder only once, just long enough to see him move off in the direction of the light. His body seemed to dissipate and scatter in the mist.

I rounded a turn and then another and another before I risked another look. There was nothing but fog surrounding me, and yet I still felt a tingling sensation along my neck as if I was being watched by someone I couldn't see. I opened my palm to see what the Lantern Man had given me. It was a tinderbox.

I stared at it a moment in surprise before fumbling it open. I knelt to light my lantern, feeling the seconds tick away like water through my fingers. My hands shook, making it harder than it should have been to light the wick. When it finally caught, I pushed to my feet and hurried toward home as swiftly as the mist allowed. I had no idea if anything was still following me, but my instinct drove me onward as if there were dogs snapping at my heels.

When I pushed through the reeds onto our lawn, I nearly tripped over my feet at the change in incline. I righted myself and finally dared to glance behind me again. Nothing stared back at me as I half expected. There was only the white wall of fog deflecting my lantern light about me and the heaving sounds of my own breath.

Nevertheless, the relative security of the cottage suddenly seemed very appealing. When I passed through the garden gate it creaked comfortingly, like it always did, and the green scent of herbs permeated the air even through the damp of the fog. I stopped just outside the kitchen door and stared up at the weathered wooden exterior of the cottage. In the mist it appeared as if it stretched upward forever, the roof disappearing in the veil of white. I inhaled deeply once, steadying my quivering nerves, and then reached for the door handle.

I doused the lamp before entering, and propped it carefully on the shelf inside. The latch on the door was old, and often rattled, but I fastened it as quietly as I could and then turned to creep through the house. Which was when Mrs. Brittle shifted in her seat at the table, making her chair creak.

I lurched to a stop. Guilt washed over me. Even in the dim light I could sense her disapproval.

"Ye ken ye're courtin' trouble?"

Mrs. Brittle never raised her voice. Whether scolding me for stealing a biscuit or tracking mud onto the floors, her words had always been measured and even, and tight with condemnation. It was a sound I'd learned to loathe, and it sparked my temper.

I was no longer a child. She had no right to question my actions.

"I'm well aware," I replied in a clipped voice.

"Are ye?" she challenged. "Because I'm no' so sure."

I wasn't certain what she thought I'd been doing, or if she suspected something even close to the truth, but I was not about to apologize or explain myself. So instead I ignored her, taking another step toward the hall.

"I've half a mind to tell yer father."

I rounded on her. "Do that. I'm sure he'll rouse himself from his stupor for half a minute to care," I snapped sarcastically.

She slowly pushed to her feet. "Dinna talk so disrespectfully aboot yer father, lass. It doesna become ye."

The comment stung. I crossed my arms and turned away.

"Yer father just might care aboot this."

"Well, he can't have it both ways," I said, speaking to the wall. "He can't ignore me, and the house, and everything that matters for almost four years and then suddenly decide he deserves an opinion. But it's of no concern anyway," I added before she could refute my statement. I glowered at her through the gloom. "He *doesn't* care. He's made that abundantly clear."

I left the room before she could censure me for my angry words or, worse, before she tried to comfort me.

A pounding sound woke me the next morning. I blinked up at the ceiling, trying to clear my head of sleep. Below, the front door opened with a groan and then the heavy tread of footsteps crossed the floor, followed by the sharp sound of raised voices—first Mrs. Brittle's and then a rough, masculine jeer.

I bolted upright. I knew that voice.

Panic flooded me as I leapt out of bed and pulled on my rumpled dress from the day before. Leaving my hair in braids, I dashed down the steps. My heart plummeted as I saw Father's study door standing open. The young, dark-haired revenue man stood in the hallway just outside of it and he flushed when he saw me. I ignored him, knowing the real cause for concern was inside.

Sergeant Watkins stood over Father where he still sat slumped in his chair, triumphantly brandishing the empty bottle of brandy. I cursed myself for not having the foresight to throw out the bottle when I'd checked on Father before venturing into the fens the night before. If only I'd sunk it in the marsh there would have been nothing for the odious man to find.

Mrs. Brittle was doubled over on the settee, her hand pressed to her chest as she wheezed. I hurried over to take her hand, not liking the mottled color of her cheeks.

"Ah, Miss Winterton," Sergeant Watkins boomed. "How good of ye to join us."

I glared up at him. "What did you do to her?"

His eyes narrowed. "She was attemptin' to impede the lawful search of His Majesty's agents."

"So you injured her? An old woman?" I demanded in outrage.

"We…moved her aside."

"He shoved me into the wall," Mrs. Brittle panted. Her eyes burned with hatred. "The cur."

Sergeant Watkins's face reddened. "I'll have ye thrown in jail, ye old hag."

"What are you doing here?" I interrupted, before Mrs. Brittle could egg him on further. "We paid the fine."

His attention swung to me. "Aye. I heard. But apparently ye didn't learn yer lesson."

Father pushed himself upright with some effort, seeming to finally grasp the import of our conversation. "What are you doing in my house? You have no right to be here."

"Oh, but I do."

I hated the way he stared down at my father, as if intent on squashing an insect.

"'Specially after that scene ye caused in front of all the good people of Thurlton yesterday."

Father's waxy face turned even paler and I feared he might cast up his accounts all over Sergeant Watkins's shoes. As satisfying as that might have been, there was no telling how the riding officer would react.

I began to wonder who had informed on my father, but

then realized there were really only two possibilities, and Reynard would never have made the effort.

"I suppose Archdeacon Soames was concerned for his flock," I sneered.

Sergeant Watkins grinned. "He confessed to being worried about Mr. Winterton's corruptin' influence."

It was on the tip of my tongue to tell him there wasn't anyone in the village left to corrupt, including our vicar, but I bit it back. Watkins already knew what was going on in Thurlton, and he didn't care so long as he received his bribes. Perhaps I should have told Mr. Fulton to pay our fine to Watkins. He could've taken his cut and then maybe he would have left us alone.

Or maybe not, given the censorious archdeacon's complaint.

Watkins tsked. "Under the circumstances, I'm afraid I have no choice but to fine ye again." The spiteful twinkle in his eye told me he wasn't the least bit sorry. And when he named a sum even more outrageous than the last time, I nearly staggered.

"But we can't possibly pay that," I gasped.

"Well, now, ye said that afore and yet ye found the money somehow."

The look he gave me made my face burn with indignation at his insinuation.

"I'm sure ye'll find it again."

Father failed to notice, but Mrs. Brittle did not. Her hand squeezed mine. "How dare you!"

"I won't pay it," Father protested, finally struggling to his feet. "You're a grasping blackmailer, and I won't give you a farthing."

"Then ye give me no choice but to arrest ye," Watkins replied as if he'd been waiting to do just that. He reached out to grab his arm, but Father shook him off.

"Take your hands off me! I'm not going anywhere."

"Resistin', eh? Well, if ye don't come with me quiet-like now, I'll just have to return with a warrant and more men."

"No!" I moved to place a staying hand on Father before he said anything more. "We'll pay the fine."

"No, we—"

"*We'll pay the fine*," I shouted, making Father wince and cradle his head.

Watkins glanced from me to him, as if willing Father to fight this outcome. I glared back, letting him know I wasn't about to let him do that.

Watkins grunted and leaned in threateningly. "I'll be back," he murmured, letting his gaze drift down my body insultingly.

This time Father did see it. He stiffened and I had to tighten my grip on his arm.

We stood rigidly side by side, listening to Watkins's and the younger revenue man's footsteps as they retreated down the hall and out the door. I released Father's arm and sank back down on the settee next to Mrs. Brittle, pressing a hand to my brow.

What were we going to do? There was nothing else of significant value left to sell. My mother's brooch wouldn't even fetch a quarter of the amount. There was the cottage, but then where would we live?

Mrs. Brittle's hand covered my other hand where it rested against the cushions of the settee.

I inhaled to steady myself and turned to her. "Are you well? Shall I fetch the surgeon?"

"Nay, lass. Just winded. I'll do."

I searched her face to be sure she was telling me the truth. She did already look recovered.

Father stood looking down at us, as if he wasn't sure whether we were real or he was dreaming. I waited for him to say something, anything, but he remained silent. His gaze drifted to the wall behind his desk and I frowned, making a mental note to search it later for any hiding places Mrs. Brittle and I had missed earlier in the week.

"I'll write to Mr. Fulton," I said.

He nodded, leaving the matter, like everything else, in my hands.

I sat a moment longer, hoping he would protest, or scold me, or throw something across the room. Anything but this blank stare. But he seemed to have forgotten my presence altogether.

I pushed up from my seat and hurried out of the study, down the hall, and out the kitchen door. If only I could escape this suffocating weight pressing down on my chest as easily as I could escape the cottage. I pressed my hands to my hips and breathed deeply of the morning air, trying to calm myself. But the longer I stood there, the more furious I became.

I cursed Mr. Ingles, and Vicar Tilby, and all the villagers of Thurlton. Who had given Father that bottle of brandy at the church? What had they been *thinking*? Did they *want* to draw attention to their illegal activities? They had to know Father would drink it immediately. I clenched my fists and considered marching down to the White Horse Inn just to give them all a piece of my mind.

But almost as swiftly as it came, my anger faded and I slumped down on the threshold, burying my hands in my hair. What did it matter? The damage was done. Watkins had caught Father again and issued an even heftier fine. If we didn't find a way to pay it, Father would be locked up in the Marshalsea Prison until I could find a way to raise the funds.

If only I'd had some warning, some way of knowing that Watkins would come again so soon. I should have realized Archdeacon Soames would guess that Father's drink was smuggled contraband. I should have known he would report it to the Board of Customs. Maybe if I hadn't gotten so upset at Father for doing exactly what I'd known he would do, then this morning's debacle would never have happened.

I lifted my gaze heavenward, biting back tears. For the first time, I was completely and utterly out of ideas, and I didn't know where to turn. If there were ever a time for Mother and Erik to intercede on my behalf, this was it.

Chapter 16

I RAPPED ON THE FRONT DOOR of Greenlaws and stepped back, turning to stare out over the fens. The late afternoon breeze was soft and blessedly cool, tickling the stray hairs around my face and neck. It was the sort of day that invited activity, and I had taken up the challenge, walking for hours through the countryside. I'd avoided the marshes, not ready yet to contemplate my encounter there the night before. Instead, I thought of Father and the fine, and I'd come to a decision easier than I'd anticipated.

Though, now that I was standing here, bouncing on the balls of my feet as I waited for the Rocklands' butler to answer the door, that decision suddenly seemed less straightforward.

I clasped my hands together and glanced back at the door. It was taking much longer than usual for someone to respond. Should I knock again?

As I'd approached, I'd noticed that Greenlaws seemed almost as if it were slumbering, quiet and still. None of its usual bustle and commotion could be seen or heard. Had the servants been given the day off?

I shifted my steps toward the corner of the house, preparing to peer around the side of the manor, when the door finally clicked open.

"My apologies, Miss Winterton," the butler told me with a small bow. "If you're looking for Miss Rockland, you should find her in the garden."

"Oh, thank you."

He nodded and began to close the door.

"But actually I'm looking for Mr. Rockland." I cleared my throat. "Is he in?"

If the butler was surprised by my request, he didn't show it by even the flicker of an eyelash. "Let me see if he's available."

He stepped aside, so I could enter the front hall. My eyes trailed up over the dark wood around me as if I'd not been in the room a hundred times before.

The butler gestured to the door on the right. "Would you like to wait in the drawing room?"

"Oh, yes. Of course."

I paced across the room, chastising myself for my silly nerves. This was Robert, for goodness' sake. Not some stranger. But my stomach didn't seem to receive the message. It fluttered and churned like a flock of birds taking flight.

I crossed to the bow window, staring out through the rose-colored damask drapes at the shifting light and shadow on the fens below as clouds chased the sun across the sky. It was there that Robert found me, fingering the fine fabric and reconsidering my decision to come here.

"Ella," he murmured softly. His brow crinkled in concern. "Is everything all right?"

"Yes," I replied automatically, and then shook my head as he took hold of my hand. "Well, no. But…" There was no use pretending anymore. He had seen Father at the church anniversary dinner, and given what I was about to say, it was silly to pretend all was well. But still the words I'd rehearsed stuck in my throat.

Robert's eyes swam with sympathy, but rather than comfort me, his compassion stung like nettles. I glanced away, unable to continue to meet his gaze.

"Oh, Ella, you do realize none of this is your fault," he hastened to tell me, misinterpreting my discomfort. "No one could think that of you. And the fact that you've been contending with this all alone... Well, we suspected, but we didn't know it was as bad as this."

My cheeks heated at the implication that he and Kate had conferred about it, but of course they would have. It was ridiculous to think otherwise.

"I only feel guilty I didn't step in sooner," he went on. "But I knew it was something you didn't wish to discuss, and I suppose I felt I had no right to intrude on your privacy."

I pulled my hand away and paced toward the empty hearth.

"Was I wrong? Should I have pried sooner?"

I shook my head. "No. You were right. I...didn't want anyone to know." And then realizing how absurd that sounded, I added, "Not for certain, anyway."

I stared down at the pristine fireplace, swept clear of all remnants of its last fire. I couldn't remember the last time the hearth in the drawing room at Penleaf Cottage had been cleaned. It had been so long since we'd lit a fire in that room, saving the costly luxury for the kitchen, bedchambers, and Father's study.

"When did it start?" Robert asked, following me across the room. "With your mother's death?"

"Yes. Though it grew worse when Erik left and...and then never returned." I swallowed. "After that, I think he stopped caring."

I hated how pitiful I sounded, but it was the truth. And it hurt far more to admit out loud than I would ever have expected, given how much it burned just to think it.

"When were you forced to begin selling the contents of your cottage?" His voice was gentle, as if he sensed how fragile I felt.

I wrapped my arms about my waist. I knew, of course, but I didn't want to admit I'd been bartering off our property for years, praying each piece would be the last. So I turned the question back on him instead. "How long have you known?"

When he didn't answer, I glanced over my shoulder to see him shift awkwardly from one foot to the other. "Long enough I should have said something."

That realization stung, but only because I'd thought I'd done better at hiding our reduced circumstances. I knew I hadn't worn a new dress in over two years, but I'd hoped that either he hadn't noticed or that he would assume we simply didn't have money to buy new things, not that we didn't have enough to even keep the things we already owned.

Then a thought struck me. "Have you bought anything other than the pianoforte?"

Robert looked to the side and my stomach twisted. "A painting and a pair of pearl earrings," he admitted ruefully.

I pressed my lips together. So he'd known for at least six months. I'd sold my pearl earrings—a gift from my mother on my sixteenth birthday, a year before she fell ill—just before Christmas.

"I wanted to help. You can have them back—"

I held up my hand to stop his words and turned aside.

"Ella, I didn't buy them for myself," he said, advancing toward me. "You must know that. Don't be stubborn. You must take them back."

"Why? So I can sell them to you again?" I snapped.

His brow furrowed in hurt.

I closed my eyes and exhaled forcefully. "I apologize. That wasn't fair. I know you were only trying to help." My voice wobbled and I pressed a shaking hand to my throat. "I should be thanking you, not berating you."

"I understand. It must be a shock."

I nodded. "To say the least."

I wondered if Mr. Fulton had been aware who was purchasing each of the items. But of course he was. He'd delivered the pianoforte to Robert a week ago. Had he written Robert directly about the instrument? That would explain the speed of the sale, sight unseen. I knew I shouldn't have felt betrayed by the solicitor, but I did. He should have told me Robert was purchasing some of our possessions. Even if he hadn't been aware of my and Robert's past, he had to appreciate how uncomfortable it would be for me to stumble upon our former property at a neighbor's home.

Maybe Robert had convinced Mr. Fulton to let him tell me, for surely he realized with how often I visited Greenlaws he couldn't hide the musical instrument from me forever. A painting and a pair of earrings were far easier to conceal than a pianoforte.

"What I don't understand," Robert mused, breaking into my thoughts, "is why you didn't come to me from the beginning when you knew you needed money." His expression betrayed how wounded he must have felt. "I would have given it to you."

I felt my cheeks begin to heat again. "Even while Olivia was still alive?"

I watched as his countenance changed with the realization of how long this had been going on.

I shook my head. "I couldn't do that. We were barely speaking then. And how would it have looked if anyone found out you were loaning me money? Even if it had been directed through my father, I know the insinuations people would have made. And they would have made the same insinuations after her death."

Robert frowned, but he didn't look surprised, and I realized he'd heard this before.

"That's why Mr. Fulton recommended you buy the painting and the jewelry and the pianoforte," I guessed. "You tried to give him money on my behalf, but he wouldn't accept it."

"He said that if you and your father suddenly started receiving money from an anonymous benefactor it could damage your reputation. That you would know it was me anyway."

He was right. There was no one else. No one who would attempt to do it anonymously, in any case.

"Well, I still wish you'd come to me," Robert said. "We could have figured something out."

I dropped my gaze to my feet, trying to gather my courage and stifle my pride to ask him what I'd come here for. He'd offered me the perfect opening. I only needed to open my mouth and take it.

But before I could speak, he crossed back to the window, clasping his hands behind his back. "In a way, this is my fault."

I trailed after him, confused by his comment. "I don't see how—"

"I promised Erik I would look after you, you know?" His voice sharpened with recrimination and regret. "Before he left for the continent, I promised him I would care for you and keep you safe. But I didn't do any of that, did I?"

His gaze swung to mine before I was prepared for it, and I was certain he could see the pain his betrayal still caused me.

"Maybe I don't bear responsibility for your father, but I certainly do for you. I should have wed you four years ago as I'd intended to and protected you from everything that came after."

His confession stunned me, but far from comforting me, it turned my insides to stone.

His fingers touched my cheek gently before falling back to his side. "I can't undo the things I've done wrong. But perhaps I can fix them." His topaz eyes gleamed with hope. "If you'll let me."

I stared up at him, realizing exactly what he was offering me. With one word, all of my worries could be at an end. It was more than I'd ever thought to achieve when I came here intending to ask him for money. With one word, my girlish dreams could come true. I could marry Robert and my future would be secured. No more sleepless nights wondering when our cottage would be taken, or if Father would wake up the next day, or what I was going to do after he was gone.

Despite everything that had happened in the past, Robert was a good man. He was kind and steady. We would raise a family. Kate would become my sister-in-law. I would continue to call the place I knew and loved home. Robert and I would undoubtedly be content together. And yet his proposal made me feel nothing but sadness.

I should say yes. It was the wisest, the most logical, thing to do.

But I couldn't.

I didn't want Robert to wed me because he felt guilty about not honoring the promise he'd made my brother. I didn't want him to feel *responsible* for me. Maybe once upon a time that would have been enough, but now it seemed hollow and empty. I wanted more from a husband.

I wanted to fascinate him. Like Olivia had fascinated Robert. Like the Lantern Man fascinated me. I wanted him to be so intrigued that he couldn't stay away even if he tried. That I would be the first thing he thought of in the morning and the last thing he thought of at night. That he would be willing to perform Herculean feats just to be with me.

I would never be those things to Robert. I would be safe and comfortable, and a salve to his conscience.

Perhaps I was foolish to let such an opportunity go. After all, wasn't it better to be the mistress of my own house than a governess or unpaid companion, beholden to others for the roof over my head? The thought did give me pause. Maybe Robert didn't love me, but he did care for me, and I would have our future children to adore. I would also have Kate's affection and companionship. Elsewhere I might have no one.

I was nothing if not practical, and so the refusal stuck in my throat.

Robert must have sensed the turmoil inside me. "I know this is sudden. So don't answer me now." He smiled tightly. "After all that has passed, I deserve to wait."

I nodded once, grateful for the reprieve. But regardless of what Robert said, I knew I couldn't force him to wait indefinitely.

He offered to escort me home, but I declined. I wanted some time to think. However, as I walked slowly away from Greenlaws, I realized I needed to speak to Kate. After everything that had happened four years ago between me and Robert, and the loyalty she had shown me, it would be wrong not to tell her about Robert's proposal this afternoon. She deserved the right to express her opinion on the matter. In truth, I welcomed it. Anything to help clear the muddle in my head.

I retraced my steps and veered west of the house toward the garden where earlier the butler had told me Kate was. She might not be there now, but it was as good a place as any to begin looking.

Greenlaws' gardens were not vast, but they were lush and almost overgrown. Contrary to her mother, who had liked everything to be trim and tidy, Kate preferred them that way. She'd told me once that she wanted them to appear so wild and natural that one felt as if they'd wandered into the Garden of Eden. Although I doubted anyone would mistake this corner of Norfolk for paradise, I appreciated her sentiment.

I wandered through the gardens, past the tall ash tree at its center where Kate sometimes liked to sit, but the bench tucked under the shade of its long branches was empty. I turned my steps toward the River Yare next, knowing her preference for the sunny riverbank and the lazy warble of the water. As I neared the river I thought I could hear voices. They were definitely male, but too indistinct to make out exactly what they were saying when they called to one another periodically. They were probably just wherry men plying their barges down the river or even delivering more supplies to Greenlaws.

I strolled beneath the dappled light of the arbor stretching over the path that led down to the river. Leafy vines and creepers twined around the wooden support posts and beams, interspersed with ivory honeysuckle and pale purple clematis. Their heady scent perfumed the evening air, nearly as thick as the filmy shadows gathering beneath the greenery.

I plucked a clematis bloom, twirling it between my fingers, and I nearly dropped it when a man suddenly appeared at the other end of the arbor. He stumbled to a stop, surveying me through the arching vines. For a moment I thought he might turn back the way he'd come, but then he seemed to settle himself and moved toward me.

It was the man Kate had jestingly called Hector, the dark-haired wherry man I had first seen delivering supplies here at Greenlaws and then later at the windmill. He was dressed in working clothes—dark pants and tall boots that still dripped water. The sleeves of his shirt were rolled up to reveal strong forearms.

I assumed his reluctance in entering the arbor was because he knew he was not supposed to be here, though I wasn't about to tattle on him for approaching the house through the gardens rather than circling around to the lawn. They must be delivering supplies to the outbuildings beyond the garden. Robert had mentioned something about building a new pier there rather than always having to haul the goods down the riverbank from the dock behind the house.

He stopped a few paces away and touched his forelock. "G'day, miss."

"Good day," I replied.

"Be ye lookin' for Miss Rockland?"

"Why, yes," I answered in surprise, though I supposed it wasn't any great riddle why I was here.

He gestured toward the house. "She went this way no more than a quarter hour ago."

"Thank you." He nodded and turned to go, but I asked for him to wait. "What's your name?"

He hesitated before finally replying, "It's Jack, miss."

Even though I couldn't see his expression well where he stood beneath a thick shadow in the arbor, I could tell he was eager to be off. "Thank you, Jack."

He nodded again and walked away. I watched him go, waiting almost until he'd disappeared from my sight before swiveling to return to Greenlaws.

My thoughts were distracted as I rounded the hedgerow and nearly sauntered past Kate.

"Ella?" she called.

I turned and blinked at her. She sat on a bench angled into a corner of the shrubbery, surrounded by the bright colors of lady's slippers and bachelor's buttons. A book lay open on her lap.

"Kate. I was just looking for you."

Her gaze drifted to the clematis bloom I still held in my hands. "Down by the river?"

"Yes." I glanced behind me distractedly, and when I turned back a tight smile stretched her lips.

"I suppose you saw the wherry men, then?"

"Just one."

"And?"

I refused to take the bait. "He told me you had gone back toward the house."

But this answer seemed to satisfy her anyway, for her shoulders relaxed and she tilted her head knowingly. "Then you must have spoken to Achilles."

"Hector, actually. Well, Jack."

She arched her eyebrows as she slid over to let me sit beside her.

"That's his real name."

"I see." There was a world of speculation in those two words. "Well, Achilles isn't really Achilles, either. He had no idea what I was talking about when I told him that's what we called him. His name is Harry, and he's from Scratby."

I eyed her smile with some misgiving. "You've spoken with him."

"A few times. He's here at Greenlaws often enough delivering supplies." She gave me a nudge with her shoulder. "Oh, don't give me that look. He's harmless."

I wasn't so certain of that, but until I knew better I decided not to press the matter. "So what are you doing out here? Escaping the house?"

Her mouth twisted. "And Reynard."

I had wondered if he was still visiting. After the events he'd witnessed yesterday at the church, I had no desire to see him. I wasn't sure I could tolerate any of the sarcastic remarks he was sure to make about it.

"Do you know why he still comes here?" As impertinent as the question was, I knew Kate wouldn't take offense. "Since Olivia's passing he doesn't really have a reason to visit, so why does he continue?"

She closed her book, running her fingers along the spine. "He made some promise to Olivia to look in on us from time to time should anything happen to her."

I frowned. "That's odd."

"Yes." She scoffed. "Who knew Olivia cared."

"Or that Reynard was the type of person to take familial duty so seriously."

"True. But he did visit Olivia quite frequently. Something drew him here."

I supposed she was right. Maybe he'd cared about her more than we realized. The two of them had been remarkably alike.

But it was apparent from Kate's expression that she was thinking something else. Her eyes had narrowed and her lips had pursed. I studied her, trying to understand what it might be.

She glanced up, and upon noticing my curiosity, determinedly masked her disapproving expression with a smile. "Was there some reason in particular you sought me out? Or were you simply in need of my sparkling wit?"

I wondered what she was keeping from me, and whether it was as remarkable as my encounters with the Lantern Man.

I opened my mouth to tell her about Robert, about his proposal, but no words emerged. For I knew if I told her about that, I would need to tell her about Father, and Sergeant Watkins, and the fines. And the Lantern Man. I simply wasn't ready to do that. Not yet.

Kate deserved to know about her brother's proposal. She deserved a chance to express her opinion. But couldn't that wait until I was more certain of my own feelings on the matter? Until I knew whether there were other options open to me? And what if I didn't like her answer? What if it swayed my decision before I'd even begun to know my own mind? Would I later resent her input? Would she resent me if I chose not to listen to her?

Perhaps it was best for the time being to remain silent.

I summoned a smile of my own. "Nothing in particular."

She tilted her head quizzically, so I leaned in closer to distract her.

"What are you reading?"

Chapter 17

THAT NIGHT I STOOD MOTIONLESS in the shadow cast by my window curtains and stared out over the fens. The reeds and grasses swayed together in the wind, their pale tips catching the light of the moon like the white caps of ocean waves crashing against the shore. There was no fog to mar the landscape. The day had been too mild for it. But still I searched for any sign that someone was watching the cottage from among the tall marsh grasses. There were too many suspicions swirling around my head, as yet hazy and insubstantial but troubling nonetheless.

From time to time the light breeze passed through the window, ruffling the curtains and the hair at my temples. The cool night air felt good on my face, blunting the sharp edges of the megrim that throbbed in my temples and stabbed behind my eyes. I'd spent hours at my writing desk earlier, examining and reexamining the household accounts, shuffling numbers, trying to figure out some way to pay the fine without selling our cottage. But there simply wasn't enough money or property left to sell to yield more than a third of the total amount needed.

From where I stood, this left me with four options, the first of which I refused to entertain. As angry and disappointed as

I was with Father, I was not going to watch him be carted off to debtors' prison.

The second choice was little better. We could sell the cottage for a fraction of what it was worth, if anyone would buy it in its current state of disrepair. But that would mean we would have to find other lodgings, most likely in a city like Norwich or London, and I could only imagine how horribly Father would fare there, surrounded by dozens, if not scores, of pubs and taverns.

So in truth, I had but two viable choices. I could accept Robert's proposal of marriage. He would pay Father's fine, plus a bit more to bribe Sergeant Watkins to leave us alone. I would move to Greenlaws as Robert's wife, and Father would remain at Penleaf Cottage until his inevitable demise. My future would be secured.

I sighed and turned away from the window to sink back down in the chair before my writing desk. So why did that option twist my stomach in knots?

I had originally thought to ask Robert for the money to pay the fine, but now I couldn't very well do so without promising him my hand. I would feel too indebted to him to ever decline his proposal. But could I really marry him and pretend I wasn't just another promise kept, another duty performed? Pretend that I wouldn't always be competing with the memory of Olivia and all the passion and excitement she had brought into his life?

My hands clenched at the painful remembrance of his confession in the churchyard. I might have accepted his explanation and apology. I might have been reconciled to them. But that didn't mean I was in any way satisfied or content with the knowledge.

If I ever did decide to marry Robert, I didn't want it to be out of a sense of guilt or obligation. We were already too bogged down in a mire of duty and responsibility, and

I refused to add to it. At the least, I needed time to give his proposal serious consideration. Time to wait for a reply from my grandfather and great-aunt.

Unfortunately, time was not something Sergeant Watkins would be willing to give us much of. So it seemed I had no choice but to turn to my fourth option, though it stung my conscience to do so.

I glanced up at the meager collection of books arranged near the corner of my desk. Flanked between my mother's Bible and the three-book set of *Sense and Sensibility* Kate had given me for Christmas stood my brother's much-loved copy of *Robinson Crusoe*, one of his few possessions I still owned. He'd taken it with him when he left for Portugal, but one of his fellow officers had been kind enough to send it to me, along with Erik's last unfinished letter. It was tucked between pages 63 and 64 even now.

I reached out to carefully run my finger over the worn spine, wondering if I buried my nose in its pages, if amidst the leather and ink I could still smell the sandalwood cologne he had insisted on dousing himself with. Erik had declared the scent fashionable and Kate had agreed, insisting it was quite appealing, but I had never appreciated the aroma. Until it was no longer around.

I closed my eyes against the guilt that welled up inside me, praying he and Mother would forgive what I had to do. I could simply see no other way. Had there been any other noble or wealthy families nearby, I could have offered my services as a governess or a companion, but the closest family who might require such staff lived more than ten miles distant, and the amount of my wages would not even make a tiny dent in the fine we owed. And as for Sergeant Watkins's degrading insinuation, I would sooner drown myself in the marsh than let him touch me.

No. Here in this isolated stretch of Norfolk, there was only one reliable method for someone like myself to make money. Smuggling.

It was my only alternative. At least until I'd paid Father's fine.

I'd circled around and around the problem until my head ached, and I could see no other solution. Pushing away from my desk, I snatched up my cloak and dashed down the steps before I lost my nerve. It was better to do what needed to be done than continue to stew over it. My conscience would never be salved.

Preparations had already been made. Somehow I'd known it would come to this. Now it was only a matter of whether I had the courage, the daring—foolish though it might be—to do what needed to be done.

I paused just long enough to light the lantern sitting by the front door and then hurried around the house toward the path leading to the dock. I didn't dare look back, already struggling with my nerves and reconsidering the wisdom of my actions.

My first thought had been to go to Mr. Ingles and offer to join his local band of smugglers, but then I'd realized such a thing was impossible. Not only would I burn with mortification, but if they rejected me—as they were almost certain to do—I would have to live with that humiliation for as long as I remained in Thurlton. I would see it in their eyes, and those of their wives and neighbors every Sunday, every time I walked through town or purchased something in one of their shops. The knowledge of how far I had fallen would always be there.

No. Imprudent as it might seem, it would be easier to approach these men masking as Lantern Men, no matter how dangerous they might be, than to broach that social barrier with the locals.

In any case, the likelihood of Mr. Ingles having a large enough amount of money at hand to loan me the sum I needed to pay my father's debt in exchange for my services was extremely slim. Most of his blunt was almost certainly tied up in contraband, and much of the profits he earned likely went on to investors elsewhere, in Norwich or London. Otherwise, why weren't he and the other villagers spending it on themselves? Their belongings were few, their table spreads modest. These weren't men with an excess of money to spend, nor the wiles to conceal it so thoroughly if they had. The men of Thurlton certainly made a better wage from smuggling than they would as day laborers or other menial jobs, but their resources were still humble.

I carefully picked my way across the dock to the end, staring out over the murky, eddying waters of our channel. There was no way of knowing how long I would have to wait, or if he would even appear, but given the pattern of our other encounters I had every reason to believe he was near. Watching. Waiting.

I gripped the handle of my lantern tighter and closed my eyes, listening for any sounds beyond that of the wind in the grasses and the burble of the water. As always, I sensed him before I heard or saw him. One moment I was alone, and the next I was not. Some subtle change in the air sent tingles racing across my nerves like fire set to kindling.

I held my breath, trying to feel the reverberations of his footfalls across the wood of the dock as he approached. They were faint at first, but grew stronger with each step as he drew closer. I counted the soft thuds of his feet, hoping I'd estimated his stride correctly, praying he didn't halt too far away. My heart rose into my throat and my muscles tensed as I realized he'd passed the point of no return.

The next thump of his foot landing against the planks was followed by a resounding crack. My head reared back in shock, half-surprised my dubious scheme had worked. Prodding myself into action before he could recover himself, I swiveled around in time to see his forearms crash into the dock boards in front of him as he plummeted downward with a sharp grunt.

I rushed forward as he dangled half on and half under the dock, his right leg having punched through the boards I had tampered with. Earlier in the evening, I'd removed two of the slats of wood running across the deck and flipped them over to saw them nearly in half, leaving only the faintest sliver of wood at their top to keep them in one piece. When I replaced them with the cut side down, their damage was undetectable, save for the missing nails normally holding them in place, which I felt almost certain the Lantern Man would fail to notice in the dark of night. I'd both hoped and feared the boards would break as planned, and momentarily trap him.

While he struggled to pull his foot back through the broken boards, muttering curses that surely weren't meant for a young lady's ears, I leaned down and pulled the hood of his cloak away from his face. He reared back awkwardly as I lifted my lantern to see his face, no doubt blinding him. When I saw him clearly for the first time, I couldn't say I was surprised. After my last visit to Greenlaws my suspicions had been aroused.

"Bloody—" He bit off an oath. "Get that out of my face."

I complied, but only because I now knew his identity. "But of course, *Jack*."

He glowered up at me, and then resumed his efforts to climb out of the hole. I considered offering my assistance. After all, I hadn't meant to hurt him, just restrain him for a short time. But seeing his extreme agitation, I thought better of it.

Let him be angry. I was the one who had been deceived, and stalked, and lied to. It would do him a bit of good to suffer this indignity.

In any case, it was the work of only a few moments before he was back on his feet. He hobbled once and then lifted his right ankle, rolling it round and round.

"Are you injured?" I couldn't help asking.

He lifted his dark eyes to glare at me. "Just a slight twinge. So if your intention was to maim me, you've failed."

I scowled. "If I'd wanted to harm you, I would have bashed you on the head with my lantern while you were caught in that hole."

He slowly straightened to his full height, which I'd somehow forgotten was at least a foot taller than me. I felt a tremor of unease, but I arched my chin, determined not to be cowed.

"Why are you pretending to be a Lantern Man?" I demanded.

He considered my question for a second or two longer than was necessary, which let me know he was debating how he should respond. "How else was I to encourage foolhardy females to stay out of the marshes at night?" His mouth twisted into a wry smirk. "Little good it did."

But I was not to be deterred. "So I wouldn't stumble upon whatever you were *smuggling*?"

He didn't react. Or at least not how I expected. "What are you talking about?" he replied with a frown.

I narrowed my eyes. "I know you're a smuggler."

"No. I'm not." He spoke very slowly, as if I were stupid. "I'm a wherry man."

For a moment, I began to question my own conclusions. What if the barrels and crates I'd seen him unloading at Hardley Mill weren't contraband? What if my suspicions had grown out of proportion because of his strange behavior? He seemed so composed, so unmoved by my accusation.

But then a thought occurred to me.

"Yes, because all of the wherry men I know speak such precise English," I drawled.

He stiffened minutely, and I knew I had him. When he'd spoken to me in the garden at Greenlaws just two days before, he'd affected a rougher accent, but he'd never bothered to do

so during the times we'd met in the marsh. Just as he'd forgotten to do so now.

I pressed my point. "Besides, wherry men don't traipse
about the marshes at night in disguise. Not unless whatever
they're plying on their crafts is illegal." I arched my eyebrows,
waiting for him to reply.

"I'm not sure what you want me to say," he responded
tersely. "I'm not about to admit to anything."

"Of course not," I replied, realizing this was the opening I
needed. "Just as I won't. If…"

"If what?"

"If you take me on as part of your crew."

I waited for his reaction, but again he gave me none. Until
he crossed his arms over his chest and affected a bored stance.

"Now why would I do that?"

I furrowed my brow, irritated that he hadn't already understood my implication. "So that I don't expose you and your
entire enterprise."

"Oh, I don't think you'll do that."

I tensed. "Why not?"

He sidled a step closer, looming over me. "Because you've
never exposed the local men working as smugglers. Because
you know that if you call the revenue men's attention to the
marshes around Thurlton that you also risk revealing your
local men's illegal activities." The corner of his mouth curled
upward. "And I don't think you want to do that."

My grip tightened around the handle of my lantern.
"Then…then I'll tell Mr. Rockland that the wherry men
delivering his supplies are smugglers," I declared, hating the
betraying tremble in my voice. Especially when Jack's smirk
only grew wider.

He shrugged. "Tell him."

I frowned, wondering how he could be so certain Robert
wouldn't care. Or at least that he wouldn't do anything about

it. Did Robert already know?

I shook that thought aside to contemplate later.

I had bigger problems, for this confrontation was not going as I'd planned. How had Jack known I wouldn't actually expose them? How could he be so smug that I would remain silent? I needed something else to threaten him with, for I refused to beg. Not to a stranger who had so blithely duped me, and stolen a kiss for extra measure.

"Well, if you won't agree, I'll simply have to approach another member of your crew," I bluffed.

His face hardened. "I wouldn't do that."

"Why? They might be more reasonable."

"I wouldn't rely on it."

There was something in his voice that told me he was right. Jack might not be so willing to harm me, but I wasn't sure I could say the same for Achilles or any of the others. They could sink me in the marsh like one of the casks they hid from the revenue men and no one would ever know what happened to me. But I saw my chance to press my appeal.

"You leave me no choice," I declared as carelessly as I could and began to turn away.

His hand shot out to grab my arm. "Why? Why do you want to join a lot of ruthless smugglers?" His upper lip curled derisively. "Do you think to snag yourself a bag of pretty gems, or some bolts of French silk?"

"No," I retorted. "Do you honestly think me so vain and senseless?"

"Then why?" he demanded. "What on earth would impel you to do such a thing?"

"Why do *you* do it?" I shot back, pulling my arm from his grasp. "Are you a younger son looking for an easy way to make money? Too skeptical to join the church, and too…too cowardly to join the military?"

He stiffened and I knew I'd struck a nerve.

"My motives are of no concern. I'm not the foolish chit trying to blackmail my way into a band of smugglers. Doesn't your father give you enough pin money?"

"My father doesn't have any money," I snapped before I could stop myself. "And what he does have he drinks away."

Jack stilled, and I could see in his eyes the moment he began to grasp my implication.

"I haven't had a new gown of my own in years." I gestured toward the old frock hidden beneath my patched and worn cloak. "And the only jewelry I own is my mother's brooch. The one you required a lock of my hair in exchange for before you would return it," I added in accusation.

He didn't look at all ashamed of his actions, but he did stop looking at me as if I was a brainless twit. "So you need the money?"

Humiliation washed over me at the realization that this man now comprehended just how desperate I was. It burned across my skin and scoured my insides. I dropped my gaze to stare at our feet. "My father was caught with a bottle of French brandy. For the second time." There was no point in keeping anything from him now. "And we don't have the money to pay the fine."

"How hefty is it?"

I looked up as I told him the sum and I could tell from his tight expression that he understood.

"Then you can't ask Rockland for a loan."

I was gratified he hadn't suggested I simply ask for it out-right. "No."

He stared down at me, a frown marring his brow. I could see him running the implications through his head.

I realized I had never seen him this closely before. When we met in the marshes, he had always hidden his face, and the few times I had encountered him elsewhere he'd been careful to keep his distance. I had been correct about the shape of his eyes. They were sly and narrowed at the corners like a cat. But they weren't as dark as I'd expected, being more of a muted shade of brown, like the feathers of a nightingale.

I couldn't be certain exactly how much Jack understood, but he opened and shut his mouth several times, as if forming and then discarding questions before he could ask them. And all the while his rugged jaw clenched harder and harder.

He inhaled deeply as if to calm himself and then finally spoke. "I assume, had you any other palatable options, you would not have come to this conclusion?"

I nodded slowly. I supposed Robert's proposal could be described as unpalatable. At least under these circumstances.

Jack continued to study me through narrowed eyes, and I couldn't tell if he didn't believe me or if he simply didn't know what to say.

"This isn't a lark," I retorted. "I knew what I risked trapping you. If you won't accept my offer, I'll find someone who will."

"You truly would approach one of the other men, wouldn't you?" he asked, as if believing me for the first time.

Before, I thought I'd been lying, but now I wasn't so sure. "Miss Rockland is acquainted with Achilles. Perhaps he would be more willing to accept my services."

His eyebrows arched. "Achilles?"

I wanted to bite my tongue. "Harry," I clarified. And then seeing the flicker of amusement in his eyes, I hastened to explain. "It's what Miss Rockland called him."

"I see," he drawled. "And how did she refer to me? As Ajax, or Hector perhaps?"

I flushed. "Perhaps."

His eyes twinkled with laughter though his mouth remained firm. "Well, let's hope my fate isn't the same as my namesake's when I tell Harry we have a new member of our crew."

I blinked in surprise. "So you…you're going to let me join you?"

All the humor fled from his face, and he inched a step closer, looming over me. "That is what you wanted, isn't it?"

I was startled by this swift change in him. "I...yes."

"Then we will make use of you. In whatever way we deem best." His eyes hardened. "But know this: There is no turning back. You will not recant. You will not change your mind. And should you even consider betraying us, those will be the last thoughts that ever flit through your pretty little head."

I tried to back up a step, but his hands came up to grasp my arms just above the elbows, holding me immobile.

"Careful," he murmured silkily. "We wouldn't want you to tumble into the marsh."

I glanced behind me. Under the onslaught of his words I'd forgotten I was standing at the edge of the dock.

He squeezed my arms, recalling my attention to him. "Be here waiting for me tomorrow at sundown." His dark eyes probed mine. "Do not make me wait." Then he pressed a firm kiss to my mouth, all but stopping my breath, before turning my shoulders in the direction of my cottage. "Now, go!"

I leapt over the hole in the boards where earlier Jack had fallen through, nearly stumbling on the rough planks, and fled down the dock. It was all I could do not to break into a run. My heart pounded in my ears, urging me to move faster. Yet something made me pause at the edge of the dock and look back.

Jack stood tall and proud, a stark silhouette in the moonlight, his unruly hair lifting in the breeze. It was too dark to see his face, but I could feel his eyes on me, meeting mine across the distance.

He had intended to frighten me, and he had succeeded. Even now, shock and fear vibrated through me. But standing here at a distance looking back at his solitary figure, so removed and self-contained, I felt an impulse as strong as my desire to escape. A desire to go to him.

It was madness, but still the ache in my chest did not diminish, even when I turned to disappear through the reeds and up the path to Penleaf Cottage.

Chapter 18

THE NEXT EVENING WHEN I made my way down to the dock, Jack was there waiting for me. At the sight of him I hesitated, all too conscious of his warning the previous night to not make him wait, but how was I to know he would be there early? I'd had a difficult enough time escaping Mrs. Brittle, who had turned disapproving and surprisingly argumentative when I informed her I was going to Greenlaws. I was accustomed to her sharp glances, but not her challenging my actions outright. It was clear she suspected something. I just hoped it wasn't the truth.

I knew he was aware of my presence, but he didn't look up as I crossed the dock toward him. He sat with his legs dangling over the edge, the tips of his boots nearly grazing the water, staring out over the marshes.

"The sun__"

"Hasn't yet begun to set," he finished for me. "I know." He rose to his feet and turned to me.

It was the first time I'd faced him in such proximity in the sunlight, even the drowsy light of early evening. With the setting sun at my back, I could see all of his features quite clearly, even those that had remained hidden in shadow the night before, and he did not disappoint. I thought he must be the most attractive man I'd ever seen, even with the pale pink ridge of a scar just visible at his hairline when the wind blew the curls away from his forehead. Was that why he let his hair grow so unkempt? He didn't strike me as a vain man. Not like Reynard, anyway. But I supposed everyone must have something they felt insecure about.

I crossed my arms over my chest, the better to hide the faded print of the bodice of my mother's gown and the loose way it hung on my frame.

"Are you ready?" he asked.

I glanced down at the small boat floating in the water below. "Where are we going?"

"To meet the others," he answered vaguely.

I searched his face, wondering if climbing into a boat with him would be the most ill-advised thing I could do. He could row me far out into the marshes and push me out of the boat. The water, the boggy vegetation, and the weight of my skirts would do the rest of the work. There was little chance I would ever be found.

I clutched myself tighter at the thought.

But if he meant to kill me, why hadn't he done so last night? Why carry on this charade?

My fear and uncertainty must have shown, for Jack lifted his arm to rest it against the dock post, exposing the white shirt beneath his loose coat. "This is your last chance," he leaned toward me to say. "If you return home now, I'll forget last night's conversation ever happened. As will you," he added with a hard glint in his eyes. "But if you step into that boat…" he gestured with his head "…there will be no turning back. Your decision will be final. And I can't promise you will like the outcome."

Perhaps incongruously, his offer to let me change my mind actually quieted some of my fears and firmed my resolve. Though from the forbidding furrow between his brows, I was certain that was not his intention.

"Yes, well, I am certain that if I *don't* come, I won't like the outcome," I replied.

His shoulders stiffened. "So, I suppose, there we have it." He seemed to search my face for any sign of wavering, but I knew he would find none. "Very well," he finally muttered before climbing down into the boat.

I followed him down the ladder, and when I reached the next to last rung I felt his hands clasp my waist and lift me down into the small vessel. My feet landed unsteadily, but he held tight until I was able to right myself. As soon as he released me, I quickly turned around and sat down on the bench opposite him, struggling to control the catch in my breath.

He untied the boat from the dock and pushed us off, propelling us out into the middle of the waterway with such force that I gripped the wood beneath me. Then with a skillful flick of the oars, he directed us north toward the main channels and rivers.

I tried to ignore him, to focus on the landscape around us, but in the dying light of the sun there wasn't much to see, just the lengthening shadows of the reeds and the murky blur of vegetation beyond. The water below us faded from a cloudy brown to an oily shade of charcoal. The chorus of insects increased and the cry of a marsh harrier echoed overhead, but beyond that the only sound that could be heard was the splash and pull of the oars through the water.

So I spent the better part of our trip observing Jack out of the corner of my eye while pretending not to. He seemed disinclined to converse, and I hardly knew what to say under such peculiar circumstances. I couldn't very well ask him about the weather, or compliment his clothing. The rules of social decorum utterly failed me in this situation.

When we neared the river, Jack lifted the oars from the

water, bracing them across his lap and turned to lift a lantern from the bottom of the boat behind him. I watched as he carefully lit the lamp and then snapped the panel shut. The light was muted, as if shown through a fog, and I realized the glass panels appeared to have been deliberately smoked.

"It draws less attention when we want to pass unseen," he explained, correctly interpreting my curiosity.

"Do you use them when you're walking the fens?" I asked, thinking of all the times he'd seemed to appear out of nowhere.

"Sometimes." He dipped the oars back into the water, resuming the easy rhythm of his rowing.

I frowned in puzzlement. "Then why pretend to be Lantern Men? Wouldn't it be smarter *not* to draw attention to yourselves?"

"Perhaps. But then without the myth of the Lantern Men, there might be more people wandering the marsh paths at night, wouldn't there? We're simply putting the local lore to good use."

"Perpetuating the myth so that when you do want to pass unseen there's less chance of encountering anyone," I surmised.

His eyebrows arched. "*Most* of the time it works."

Meaning I was the exception. And all because I'd been urgent to take medicine to Kate.

"But the locals… Some of them must know who you really are," I argued before I stopped to consider this might not be known to him.

Jack's lips quirked. "Yes, we know." He held his oars down in the water to slow us, and glanced over his shoulders. "We encounter each other from time to time when making a run. There are only so many waterways leading inland from the sea. It's bound to happen."

"And you don't try to stop them?"

"Why should we?" he asked with a small grunt as he turned

the boat into the river and began rowing upstream. "They'll keep quiet, just as they know we will. So long as they don't interfere in our business."

His voice sounded forbidding, but I didn't know if it was from true hostility or if it was simply due to the effort it now took for him to row against the current. The river was swollen from the rain that had fallen late the night before and most of the day. Still, I couldn't stop from questioning him further.

"But doesn't that make you competitors? I mean, aren't you smuggling the same things?"

"In principle," he replied vaguely.

"What does *that* mean?"

"It means the Thurlton gang smuggles the usual—gin, brandy, beer, tobacco, tea, sugar—while our operation is a bit more…extravagant."

"Extravagant?" I repeated, still not understanding.

He answered slowly, his voice tightening and releasing with each pull of the oars. "Let's say you're a lady of quality and you wish for a bolt of a specific type of silk or lace. Or a gentleman with a taste for claret made at a specific distillery. Or a lord eager to gift a special woman with an exotic gem. Who would you ask to handle your request? Certainly not the likes of Mr. Ingles."

Now his involvement made more sense. These weren't just common smugglers. They were brokering contraband for the nobility, perhaps even royalty. And as such, they were likely protected by them.

I'd suspected he was more than a suspiciously well-educated wherry man, but I'd thought he was a member of the gentry, or perhaps a younger son of a minor noble. Not that he regularly socialized with members of the ton.

"So you travel to London, then? To handle these requests?" I struggled to keep my voice even.

"Not me."

This silenced me, for it was not the answer I'd been expect-ing. And when I spoke again it was not with as much sang-froid as I'd been affecting. "Who, then?"

Jack's eyes fixed on me with interest and I struggled not to squirm.

It was dark now, with only the dim light filtering through the smoked glass of his lantern to illuminate us. It sat at his feet and cast strange shadows upward over his features, mak-ing him look rather wraithlike. If I hadn't touched him, hadn't felt the warmth and solidity of his form, I might have believed he was a Lantern Man in truth. That he'd lured me into his boat and was now abducting me to wherever such creatures came from. Just the thought of it sent a trickle of unease run-ning down my spine like a drop of icy rain, and tightened the breath in my lungs.

"You'll find out in due time," he finally replied, giving a hard pull on the oars.

I openly studied his face, not caring now if he knew I was doing it, and wished I knew more members of society. The only people I'd had the opportunity to meet were friends of the Rocklands, many of whom lived nearby in Norfolk or Suffolk. But perhaps they were enough.

After all, Jack understood the Broads, possibly better than I did. He was comfortable amongst the marshes and waterways, and that was something I doubted he could have learned in a matter of months. Though, for all I knew, these men may have been smuggling through Thurlton since before I was born, but I didn't think so. Perhaps a year or two. Surely I would have noticed had it been going on for much longer. Which meant Jack must have grown up here, or in some other area of the fenlands.

I searched my memory, trying to recall if we'd ever met, or if I'd met someone he resembled, but my mind couldn't form a connection. He could be from any number of families with roots in East Anglia, and I felt fairly certain I would not have forgotten him or his kin had we chanced to meet.

But perhaps there was a more direct way of finding out who he was.

"I feel a bit forward calling you Jack," I said. "But you've never told me your surname, Mister…" I trailed away, hoping he would respond without thinking.

"Oh, I think we've far surpassed simply being forward," he drawled.

I was grateful that the darkness hid my fiery blush, but my embarrassment must have been communicated to him regardless for he smiled suddenly, a flash of white, even teeth in the relative gloom.

"Jack will do," he added gently in a voice still laced with humor.

I turned aside, wishing I hadn't attempted such a silly ploy. Something familiar about the shoreline caught my eye, and I realized we were nearing Greenlaws. We rounded another bend in the river and there it was, perched on a rise above us. Candlelight blazed in the windows and reflected off the white trim, a tidy outline against the black of night.

I wasn't surprised to see one light brighter than all the rest, perched on the balcony running across the back of the house. Kate liked to sit there and read in the evenings, until her brother or her maid chased her inside, warning her about the ill effects of night air. Then fifteen minutes later she would return, heedless of anything they said.

I smiled at the thought, imagining her there now, absorbed in one of the Gothic novels her mother had forever chided her for reading. Once upon a time she'd hidden them under her mattress to keep them from being confiscated. But now she could curl up with them wherever she pleased, even on the portico, and read for hours on end.

"You'll have to remain quiet," Jack murmured as he slowed

the rhythm of his rowing.

My smiled faded, as I began to grasp the consequences of what I was doing. Lying to my friends. Slipping past their house under the cover of night with a strange man. A man I'd kissed more than once, and yet I was still considering Robert's proposal. That realization scalded me with guilt.

When we passed the black oak tree at the edge of Greenlaws House, its gnarled roots exposed at the river bank, Jack lifted his oars from the water so that we could glide silently past the dock and the house. The boat gradually slowed as our momentum was all but lost in the current, but as we reached the border of the gardens, he slipped his oars back into the water and resumed rowing.

I had to wonder why he had not directed us toward the opposite bank of the river, away from Greenlaws. In the darkness, the far shore was nothing but a blur. But the answer was soon made apparent, for beyond the garden trellises where I had encountered Jack just a few days before, he began to steer the small boat toward the pair of docks that had been built to provide easier access to Greenlaws' outbuildings.

I stiffened at the realization that these men were operating on Robert's property, right under his nose. Did he know? Had he guessed what the wherry men delivering his supplies were involved in? Had our quiet approach been intended to hide their efforts from Robert, or to shield Kate and his servants?

I had a difficult time believing Robert was unaware of the illegal activities happening in his outbuildings. Almost as difficult a time as I had believing he knew about such a thing and let it go on. Robert was nothing if not dutiful, always following in his father's eminently proper footsteps. Except when he did not. I had never been able to predict Robert's odd whims, when he would suddenly decide the traditional route wouldn't suit. Like when he married Olivia. Was this another of those instances, or was he being willfully blind?

I pushed the thoughts aside in order to prepare myself for what was to come. I could see the silhouette of a man now, standing at the edge of the second dock. His feet were braced apart and his arms crossed over his chest. Jack seemed unimpressed by his unwelcoming pose, tossing the boat's line up to him without a word. It smacked the man in the chest, and for a moment I thought he would let the rope drop, but at the last second he caught it.

I could see now that it was Harry—the man Kate had dubbed Achilles—and he didn't look the least bit pleased to see me. His eyes narrowed in challenge, never leaving my face even when he leaned over to tie the line around one of the dock poles. The ground was higher here, and less prone to flooding, so the dock posts did not need to stand so tall.

Jack maneuvered the boat up next to a ladder. "Up ye go," he told me in the rough accent I'd heard him use the time we met in the gardens.

I flicked a glance up at Harry and then back to him.

"He won't harm ye," Jack murmured, correctly interpreting my hesitation. "'Least, not while I'm close by." He levelled a glare up at Harry.

I swallowed and pushed to my feet, hoping the men would attribute my shaky steps to the rocking of the boat. When I reached the top of the ladder, Harry didn't offer me a hand to help me up onto the dock, even though he stood just two steps away watching me balance precariously. Seeing his expression, I decided I should simply be grateful he hadn't done the opposite, tipping me off the ladder into the river. I pressed my hand against the adjacent post and fumbled to step up without tripping on my skirts.

When I finally managed to get both feet flat on the solid planks, I shook my skirts out and backed a few steps away, consciously keeping Harry in my sight as Jack climbed onto the dock with the lantern. Harry didn't wait long to interrogate his friend.

"What's she doin' here?" he demanded, thrusting a meaty thumb in my direction.

Jack's jaw hardened and he reached a hand out to grip my arm under my elbow, drawing me gently but insistently forward. "You'll find out wi' the others."

Harry drew himself up even taller, refusing to move. "She's meetin' wi' us?"

Jack shifted half a step closer, exploiting the height difference between the two men. "Yes."

However, the several inches Harry lacked in height he more than made up for in bulk. Jack was by no means scrawny, with broad shoulders and strong arms, but Harry topped him by at least two stone of solid muscle. I held my breath, worried for Jack's safety—and consequently mine—should they come to blows.

Harry's eyes closed to slits. "Does Himself know 'bout this?"

"Yes."

My eyes jerked to Jack, surprised and a bit unsettled by this bit of information. The tone of his voice brooked no argument, so I had no reason to doubt it was true. But who was "Himself"? And just what had he and Jack discussed about me?

Jack ignored me, keeping his attention firmly focused on Harry. Probably a smart decision, under the circumstances.

My shoulders tightened as Harry inhaled, his nostrils flaring. "Aye, well, this oughta be a treat," he replied, shifting his angry golden eyes to me.

Given the way he had just challenged Jack, I knew the worst thing I could do was cower under his glare. So instead I forced myself to square my shoulders and lift my chin.

"Care to step out o' the way, then?" Jack growled. "Or do ye wish to take a dip?"

Harry moved to the side, never taking his eyes off me. "After you," he declared with a twist in his voice.

Jack hesitated, but only for a second, before pulling me forward. I did my best to avoid touching Harry, but he'd afforded us little room to pass, so it was impossible to evade him completely. My elbow brushed against his lower stomach, and I was tempted to thrust it into his gut. As if sensing my inclination, Jack tightened his grip on my other elbow and hurried me past.

The hair on the back of my neck stood on end as Harry turned to follow us. I wondered how Jack could trust he wouldn't drive a dagger into our backs. A quick glance at Jack's face told me he didn't.

We turned off the dock into the shadows of the outbuildings, and followed them to the smaller wooden structure at the end. I could see light flickering through the window next to the door, and I guessed that this building must be some type of a watchman's shelter. Perhaps to guard the other storage buildings, or to shield the servants and wherry men as they waited in poor weather. It was just the sort of consideration I would expect Robert to show to the men working for him.

At the sight of it I quickened my steps, eager to be near others, whoever they might be, and away from Harry and whatever his intentions might be. But this time Jack held me back. He didn't say a word, didn't even so much as glance at me, but I could sense what he was thinking. *Keep calm. Be easy.* I obeyed, but I couldn't understand why he was so determined to keep to his pace. Perhaps for him to speed up would be seen as a sign of weakness by Harry, but at the moment it seemed more important we actually make it into the watchman's shelter alive.

I inhaled deeply as Jack opened the door to the hut and escorted me through, but my relief was short-lived. Half a dozen men stood and sat ranged around a fire crackling in the hearth. Two of them were bent over a pair of canvas sacks, sifting through something inside. They had all been chatting amicably until they'd turned to hail Jack and spotted me. Their voices fell silent and their faces turned stony.

I stumbled to a stop, unprepared for their animosity. I'd known it was likely that my involvement would not be welcomed, at least not at first. I'd expected I would need to convince them much the same way I had convinced Jack. But in my eagerness to escape Harry's hostility I'd allowed myself to think the others would react better. I was wrong.

The door slammed shut behind us, and I jumped at the sound, whirling around to find Harry glaring down at me. I backed away several steps, and then swiveled to keep the wall at my back so I could keep everyone in my sight. Harry's gaze cut to the men with the sacks, who gathered them up, clinking together whatever was inside, and lowered them into a cask nearby.

Jack sidled farther into the room, and the look he turned on me as he crossed his arms over his chest was only a fraction less chilling than that of the others. "This is Miss Winterton," he declared, as if that was all that needed to be said.

And apparently it was, for one of the men seated with his feet propped up on the fender before the fireplace grunted in agreement. His coal-black eyes gleamed in the firelight. "Aye. Now what we gonna do wi' 'er?"

Chapter 19

M Y HEART KICKED SHARPLY AGAINST my ribs, urging me to run. Except Harry stood over my shoulder, blocking the door. I knew I would never be allowed past him, so I had no choice but to stand there, waiting to hear what they decided to do. I wanted to hurl curses at Jack, furious that he had betrayed me, but I had to be satisfied with shooting him an icy glare. Which did not seem to faze him in the least. If anything, his gaze seemed to sharpen more.

"Did ye bring 'er to share wi' us?" The man with the greasy pate leered.

I stiffened.

"In a way," Jack replied.

I stifled a gasp, staring at him in alarm.

His lip curled in a sneer. "Miss Winterton is joinin' our crew."

This seemed to stun the other men for it was several moments before anyone else spoke.

The man at the fender narrowed his eyes as he swept them up and down my form. I was grateful for the folds of my summer cloak shielding me from his gaze. "Ye mean, a bit o' welcome distraction fer us?"

"No," Jack said slowly. "We need 'er to deliver the Longshore cargo."

I inhaled a shaky breath in relief, while the others glanced at each other in displeasure. The men before me still eyed me with enmity, but at least I now knew Jack didn't intend to pass me around like a common whore or sink me in the marsh. There was every chance one of the others might attempt something, but Jack appeared to be keeping his word.

"We don't need no help," a man with a thick red beard growled.

"'Specially no' from some fancy lady," the stoutest of the men added, eying me with distaste.

"Does Himself—" the coal-eyed man began.

"He does," Jack interrupted loudly. "An' he's decided her job. Not me." There was a strange look in his eyes, one I couldn't quite read. "He thinks she'll be useful."

I could feel all of their gazes on me again, appraising my worth, but I did not look away from Jack.

"If any o' ye choose to disagree," he continued, favoring all of them with a disdainful scowl, "he'll see that as yer offer to take on her role yerself. An' he's offerin' to make the necessary cuts."

My eyes widened at the threat, but it didn't seem to trouble the others beyond a few low grumbles.

"No need. Freddy's already had his cobblers nipped," the stout man cracked, and they all turned to laugh at the man who appeared to be the youngest of this motley crew.

He straightened from his slouch to glower at them all. "Oy, better 'n missin' me frock, Dibs."

My cheeks heated at this exchange, having guessed at the meaning even if I didn't quite understand their language. In any case, my reaction went unnoticed as Dibs launched himself at Freddy and the others jeered and heckled.

"Enough," Harry snapped, crossing the room in a handful of angry strides. He grabbed Dibs's shoulder in one meaty hand and pulled him away from Freddy, sending him stumbling back into Red Beard. "If ye want to flap at each other like a couple o' pigeons, do it when I don't have to watch."

Dibs frowned, but fell quiet along with the others. Only Jack seemed unaffected by Harry's outburst, watching the proceedings with almost bored indifference. Perhaps that was what ruffled Harry the most, for when he turned back to look at him, his chest still heaving with fuming breaths, he couldn't have failed to note how unintimidated Jack was. Harry was clearly a man accustomed to inspiring apprehension, if not outright fear, and Jack's apathy may have rankled.

Harry's narrowed gaze shifted to me. "If Himself wants 'er to join us, so be it." His teeth flashed in a wolfish grin. "I can think o' a few choice tasks for 'er."

The other men began to chuckle, clearly understanding what tasks he was referring to even if I didn't. I could hardly complain. I'd asked to join their crew. I couldn't refuse whatever dirty, unappealing duties they might ask of me now.

"Himself already has a plan," Jack said. There was a momentary gleam in his eyes that made me think perhaps he was quite satisfied to have delivered this bit of news, foiling Harry's ideas, but it was gone before I could be sure it wasn't just a trick of the firelight.

Whether he'd also seen it or he was just reacting to such a statement, Harry was not happy. "Does 'e, now?" he rumbled in a low, agitated voice.

"Says he's stealin' a ploy from an old friend."

I stared at Jack's profile, wondering again just who the devil Himself was. I knew that now was not the time to ask him, if he would even tell me, but I couldn't help feeling a prickle of unease. Plainly it was someone who knew me, or at least knew of me. As it was, after meeting these men I was starting to wonder just why he had accepted me onto his crew. Either they truly had needed me for some purpose, or Jack had used some strong means of persuasion to convince him.

Did it really matter? Whatever the reason, there was certainly no turning back now. No matter how my stomach churned or my chest hollowed with dread.

"So what is it?" Harry demanded.

Jack's mouth flattened. "One o' ye louts offer Miss Winterton yer chair and I'll tell ye."

A short time later, I found myself seated in the boat across from Jack again. I had yet to speak. My thoughts were too preoccupied with the plans he had shared. The plans for my first foray into the perilous and illegal world of smuggling. Plans in which I featured quite prominently. To say I was alarmed and, to be perfectly honest, terrified would be putting it mildly.

When I'd asked to join Jack's smuggling crew, I'd thought my role would be a minor one. That I would act as a lookout, or help sort and deliver the goods. Or that I would help water-down the spirits and add coloring, a process I'd overheard one of the local men discussing many months ago. Apparently, French distillers shipped brandy and other spirits over-proof so that it could be transported in smaller casks, and then the smugglers watered it down into its traditional form and added caramel to color it. At most, I'd guessed they might use me as a distraction. But this…this was a far more active and *risky* part than I'd ever thought to play.

Thus far the only advantage I could see in my taking such a crucial part in the venture was that I would be able to more quickly earn back the loan "Himself" had given me to pay off Father's fine. As Jack had spelled out the terms, more dangerous jobs would earn me more credit than the minor tasks I'd anticipated performing, allowing me to gain my freedom sooner. Potentially.

Jack must have sensed how stunned I was, for he did not try to engage me in conversation. He simply pulled rhythmically at the oars, letting the current do most of the work as we floated downstream. I appreciated his forbearance. At any point he could have reminded me of the fact that I had little choice in the matter. He could have reminded me that he'd warned me about joining their crew. I was the one who'd refused to listen. But he kept his counsel, allowing me to sort through the implications myself. Letting me grow accustomed to the realization that I was going to be actively smuggling costly fabrics and gems off a ship, and right under the noses of the revenue officers in Yarmouth.

When Jack had explained Himself's plan, the others had rubbed their chins and grunted their approval. However, I didn't know if their ready acceptance was a testament to the scheme's chance of success or relief that they would not be the ones risking their necks. I was not experienced enough to know, but the brazenness of the plot left my insides quivering.

I studied Jack through my lashes. I wanted to ask him if he believed the plan would work, but I knew I shouldn't seek or expect any reassurance from him. That even if he gave it there was no guarantee he would be speaking the truth. Nor could he foretell the future. So I bit my tongue.

Or at least I thought I had, but when he spoke I suddenly couldn't be sure.

"Yes. I think the plan will work." His eyes turned to lock with mine, and I swallowed.

"Did I…" I began faintly.

The corners of his lips quirked upward. "Your eyes spoke for your lips," he explained. But then his mouth fell. "We'll have to work on that."

I clasped my hands tighter in my lap and nodded.

"But so long as you don't act suspiciously and expose yourself, there's no reason to think the plan shouldn't work." He pulled harder on the oars, guiding us into a smaller channel. "I wouldn't have agreed to it otherwise," he added almost as an afterthought.

I studied his face in the pale light cast by the lantern, wanting to believe him but afraid to do so. I couldn't recall the last time I'd been able to rely on a man—not my father, nor Robert, nor even Erik, who had abandoned me for the army and never kept his promise to come home. I knew it was foolish to hold that against him given the fact that he'd been killed in battle, but it was yet another example of all the ways the men in my life had failed to honor their word. What made me think Jack would be any different?

I inhaled swiftly, deciding it was time to stop brooding and turn my mind to the details. "When do you think the *Longshore* will reach port?"

"Not for a few more days, at least. Perhaps a fortnight. Which gives us plenty of time to prepare."

"Good," I replied, knowing it was inane, but how else was I to respond? I was completely out of my depth.

"You understand what attire is needed?" His eyes remained steady on me, even as he rocked back and forth with his rowing. "You can manage finding appropriate clothing?"

"I'll make something work." Altering a gown to suit our purposes was the least of my worries.

His head tilted to the side. "You might also consider modifying one of your bonnets. Aren't tall crowns all the rage now?"

Perhaps they were, but I hadn't purchased a new hat in more than three years. However, I couldn't tell him that. Or I refused to, at any rate. "I'll see what I can manage," I choked out.

I turned away from his too-perceptive gaze to stare out at the night-shrouded marshes. "What sort of man is the captain of the *Longshore*?" I asked, trying to decide which dress would be best. "What type of woman would his sister be?"

"Respectable. A merchant's wife, I should guess."

I nodded.

"Although, you understand the ship is not named the *Long-shore*…"

I turned to him with a frown. "Oh. But…isn't that what you called it?"

"Yes, but it's not her name." He glanced over his shoulder, studying the reeds at the edge of the waterway. "That's what we call a ship laden with goods too delicate to be sunk in tubs in the Yarmouth Roads for us to retrieve later."

I watched as he expertly turned the boat into the channel that ran behind Penleaf Cottage. When he resumed his steady pace at the oars, I ventured a question I'd already guessed the answer to. "So am I allowed to know the name of the ship I'll be boarding?"

"Not yet."

I waited for him to elaborate.

"Himself doesn't want you to know until we're on our way to meet it."

"In case I should decide to inform the Board of Customs of these plans," I finished for him in a flat voice.

His silence was answer enough.

"I suppose that means you won't tell me who the man you refer to as Himself is either?"

"No."

His tone was not apologetic, but it wasn't without sympathy, and I felt encouraged I might be able to wheedle some more information from him eventually.

Our dilapidated dock emerged from the darkness over Jack's shoulder, a weathered pile of wood that seemed to be sinking into the marsh. I wondered how much longer before it was too dangerous to use. Would it outlast my father, or was his body already more rotted than the pocked and pitted wood and rusty nails before me?

Fortunately, Jack was not privy to these thoughts. He fastened the boat's moorings to the dock post and helped me to the ladder before following me up. I pulled the fabric of my summer cloak tighter around me and turned to face him. We had already agreed to meet under the trellis in the garden at Greenlaws tomorrow afternoon to prepare me for my role when the Longshore made port. I wasn't sure what more there was to say. Or was speaking not what he had in mind?

Jack clearly sensed my hesitancy, for he did not approach. Not immediately anyway. He waited a handful of seconds before he slowly inched forward.

"Are you worried? Do you think you were missed?" he asked after tossing a glance toward the shore.

I scoffed. "It's doubtful."

His dark eyes softened and I looked away, uncomfortable I'd revealed so much.

"Then they won't miss you a few moments more."

I lifted my gaze to meet his, awareness of his intentions spreading through every inch of me. It prickled across my skin and flooded my veins with warmth, the effect growing ever more potent because he hesitated, giving me the chance to stop him. I felt his hands lift to my waist, their heat penetrating through my clothing, and watched as his mouth descended toward mine, but in the end all I could do was close my eyes and wait for his lips to touch mine.

The kiss was over all too swiftly and I was soon staring up into his eyes again, still unable to understand my reaction to him. His proximity did something to me I'd never experienced before, not even with Robert. It was half the reason I'd believed he might actually be fae or some other superstitious being when he'd masqueraded as a Lantern Man.

But as unsettling and confusing as my reaction was to him, what baffled me more was his wish to trifle with me at all.

How could I possibly hold any appeal to someone like him? Or was I merely convenient?

"Why do you kiss me?" I murmured before I could think better of it.

His eyes gleamed in the darkness as he considered his answer. "Because I want to."

I watched as he backed down the ladder—that twinkle still in his eyes—and dropped down into the boat. With a swift tug and a push, he floated out of view. Only the splash of his oars entering the water told me where he was. I stood still, listening to the sound of his rowing recede until it was only an echo in my mind. It was a long time before I turned my feet toward shore, and the fitful night I expected.

Chapter 20

THE NEXT WEEK WAS SPENT in preparation for my first smuggling operation. Every afternoon I met with Jack and often one or more of the other smugglers to practice for the Longshore's arrival. At first I was shocked and dismayed by their crude and threatening behavior, until I realized it was all part of my training. If I was to accomplish my part of the ruse, I could not blush and stammer when faced with a sailor's rough manners, or cower under the eyes of the revenue men. The captain's sister would certainly be familiar with such conduct, even if she behaved gently herself.

As Jack had said, I was not accustomed to hiding my feelings from anyone but my father, and I knew full well he usually wasn't the keenest observer. For this to work I had to be as calm and unmoved as stone, and ready for anything. I still had my doubts about the plan, but I devoted myself to it whole-heartedly nonetheless. There simply wasn't any other option.

Most of the time we met somewhere on the grounds of Greenlaws, away from the manor house and all its prying eyes. I would visit with Robert or Kate before excusing myself and sneaking off to the outbuildings or the orchards or one of the farthest fields bordering its property. That way if I was discovered later, I would have some semblance of an excuse for being there.

However such a precaution proved unnecessary, just as my attempted visits often proved futile. As often as not, Robert and Kate were both preoccupied with other matters. Matters they seemed hesitant to share with me. I did not press them. After all, I was being quite deceitful, and to expect them to divulge their concerns when I refused to speak of mine was hypocritical. But all the same, their increasingly strange behavior bothered me.

Robert acted either warm and welcoming or cold and distant—there was no in-between—and his mood would sometimes shift quite suddenly. I'd never known him to be so mercurial, and this new inconstancy confused and startled me. Twice he had excused himself abruptly, abandoning me to the hollow stillness of the drawing room or Reynard's dubious company.

If I'd had to guess at his frustrating behavior, I suspected it had something to do with my continued silence on the matter of his proposal. He had not asked me for my answer, had not even broached the topic, but I knew he must be thinking of it. Was he angry I had not accepted him yet? Had he expected me to jump at the chance, even after all that had happened?

Though every bit as maddening as Robert's changeability, Kate's conduct was more distressing. She did not avoid me or abuse my friendship. In truth, she seemed pleased to receive me—when she was there to do so.

She'd taken to disappearing at odd times, and no one seemed to know where she'd gone. When I attempted to ask her about it, she countered that she'd merely gone for a stroll or a long ride on her horse. But I knew she generally hated to walk—she found the task too mundane—and in the past she'd always taken a groom with her on her rambling rides.

There was no doubt she was being quite secretive, and Kate had never been one to keep her thoughts to herself. In fact,

her mother had forever despaired of Kate's lack of circum-
spection. She reminded me of Marianne from the book *Sense
and Sensibility*. All passion and fire with little restraint. For her
to suddenly mince her words, especially with me, was worrying.

In contrast, little had changed at home in our solemn cottage. I returned each evening to find that Father had already
retreated to his study while Mrs. Brittle finished preparing
dinner. Sometimes there would be an empty bottle or two
sitting on the table and I would carefully sink the evidence of
my father's continued imbibing in the marsh before washing
up and joining a scowling Mrs. Brittle at the scarred kitchen
table. Father had stopped taking most of his meals altogether,
and I had finally tired of cajoling him into dining with me.
He rarely ate anything anyway, and the entire endeavor only
upset me. If he preferred to drink his supper, so be it.

Mrs. Brittle had also retreated into quiet, though in her case
I suspected this was because she knew I was not being forthright with her. Her hearing might be poor and her eyesight
failing, but she was not dull-witted or imperceptive. She had
always known when Erik and I were up to mischief, and in
many ways this was no different.

I had not asked for her help in altering one of my gowns,
preferring not to have to explain myself and suffer one of her
scolds. So instead I sat up into the wee hours of the morning
with needle and thread, straining my eyes in the candlelight
and trying not to stain the fabric with blood as I repeatedly
pricked my fingers. I'd never been particularly skilled at sew-
ing, and I knew Mrs. Brittle would have finished the task in
a quarter of the time but I stubbornly resisted involving her.

So on the sixth day of my training, I did not protest when
she shooed me out of her kitchen after the strained silence of
our meal. I thought I might even have become accustomed
to her icy glares. At least they hadn't soured my appetite for

once, but perhaps that was the result of the number of miles I'd walked that day since we'd met out at Hardley Mill instead of Greenlaws.

I was halfway up the stairs when I heard a loud thud coming from inside Father's study. Lifting my skirts, I pivoted and raced back down the steps, berating myself for not stopping to at least look in on him.

I didn't knock, but simply threw open the door and rushed inside. My eyes darted around the room. "Father! Father, where are you?"

At the sound of his groan, I dashed around the sofa. His legs were splayed out across the floor near his heavy oak desk. I was relieved to see he'd pushed his torso to a mostly upright position, but my calm quickly fled when I spied the blood trickling over the hand he pressed to his head.

"Father," I gasped, dropping to my knees beside him. "What have you done?"

"I haven't done a dashed bloody thing," he snapped. "'Tis that desk." He lifted the hand that propped him up to gesture at it and almost toppled backward.

I helped to keep him upright, and then threw a glance over my shoulder. Mrs. Brittle had rounded the sofa to observe us.

"Towels," I ordered. "And some warm water."

She hobbled away as fast as she could move, no doubt knowing better than I what was needed.

"Why don't you lie down," I turned back to tell Father.

He gritted his teeth. "I don't need to lie down. I'm no' some frippy wastlin'." His words were slurring now, but I didn't know if that was from the drink or from his head wound. The desk was old and scratched but built from solid oak. It was perhaps the only thing left in the cottage harder than my father's head. Had it not been bigger than the doorway, I would have sold it long ago.

Since he would not lie down, I helped him to shift closer to the desk so his back rested against its side. I tried to get him to move his hand so I could examine the wound to discern how serious it was, but he refused to budge, flapping his other hand at me. I sat back on my heels and studied him.

His clothes were askew, his cravat abandoned. That is if he'd even donned one that day. His skin was a pale, sickly hue—a sharp contrast to his bloodshot eyes. I didn't immediately spot the inevitable bottle of brandy, but I was sure it wasn't far away. With any luck the remainder had spilled out onto the floor when he bashed his head.

"So what happened?" I persisted. "Did you trip?"

He scowled at me. "I told ye. It was the dashed desk."

"Father, desks don't move about striking people on the head."

"Well, this'n did! It's not where it's s'posed to be. You an' that harridan musta moved it."

"Neither Mrs. Brittle nor I moved it," I replied impatiently. "It's too heavy to do so even if we wanted to."

"It moved!" he protested more loudly. "Are ye callin' me a liar?"

"No, but I *am* questioning your eyesight."

Mrs. Brittle returned then, pushing me out of the way as she slowly knelt down with her stack of supplies. I stood over them and watched as she tried to peel Father's hand away from the wound. Blood had dripped down his arm, staining his shirt sleeve.

"Move yer hand, Mr. Winterton," Mrs. Brittle ordered firmly. "Or I'll douse ye on the other side and be done wi' ye."

Father transferred his glare to her, but he was no match for her gimlet stare. He slowly lowered his hand and she pressed a towel to his head in its place. He sucked in a sharp breath through his teeth as she began to dab at it, trying to sop up the blood and get a better look at the wound. Perhaps it was wrong of me, but I felt no compassion for him. Whatever pain he was feeling he deserved, and I silently hoped Mrs. Brittle would not be gentle with him.

"Do we need to fetch a surgeon?" I asked, worried the gash might require stitches. How we would pay for it I didn't know, but if it had to be done I supposed I would find something to barter.

"Nay. Head wounds always bleed somethin' fierce. Looks worse 'n 'tis. Dinna fret. I'll fix 'im up."

"I'm right here," Father growled. "Don't speak about me like I'm a child."

"Then stop actin' like one," Mrs. Brittle retorted, pressing the towel harder to his head.

"Ow! Stop tha'!"

"I have to stop the bleedin'. Or would ye rather I let ye run dry?"

His scowl darkened, but he didn't argue. Instead, he lifted his gaze to where I stood. "I s'pose ye think this is my fault. That if I were sober this wouldn'a happened."

"I didn't say anything," I replied as calmly as I could, knowing that arguing with him when he was in this state would only make it worse. But apparently he was past placating.

"I know that! I'm not deaf *nor* stupid."

When I didn't reply, he tossed up his hands, lolling his head back against the desk. "Why can't ye all leave me in peace?" he moaned.

Mrs. Brittle took a firmer grip on his scalp, forcing him to hold still.

"Is that too much to ask? Ye don't see me pesterin' ye." He threw a sharp glance my way. "Orderin' ye to stay home 'stead o' danglin' after Rockland as ye do. Spendin' all yer time at Greenlaws. Hopin' he'll finally marry ye."

I felt sick to my stomach. Was that what he thought? That I was some weak, lovesick fool trailing after Robert, begging for a small portion of his attention? I gritted my teeth, swallowing down the hot retort that sprang to my lips. Words that were useless, because he would never understand, let alone remember come morning.

But apparently he wasn't finished.

"'Tis pathetic, that's what 'tis." His face screwed up in distaste. "Followin' him 'round. Waitin' for him to make good on his promises. If yer mother were here—"

"I wish to God she was," I snapped, at the end of my patience. "Pathetic! That's what you call *me?* I'm not the one drowning myself in brandy night after night, too weak, too pitiful to do anything else. *Pathetic?*" My voice rose to a shriek. "What right do you have to criticize me? Our house is falling down around our ears, you're in danger of being thrown into the Marshalsea, and you dare to censure me. You know *nothing!*"

Father's waxy skin had paled further and Mrs. Brittle stared up at me in shock, but I didn't care. I was sick unto death of his selfishness and her self-righteous behavior.

I inhaled sharply. "If you only knew the things I've been forced to do to keep this roof over our heads, to keep your hands from being clapped in irons." I narrowed my eyes on my father. "And you're tired of people pestering you to leave your study, to eat a decent meal? So be it!" I declared. "Do what you wish. Starve yourself. Stumble into the fire. Trip down the stairs and break your fool neck. I'm done caring."

And with that, I turned on my heel and stomped out of the room, down the hall, and out the kitchen door. I halted at the old sycamore, pressing my hand to the rough bark as I stared out at the sky painted yellow and pink with the rays of the setting sun. I breathed deep of the evening air, letting it cool my temper as it cooled my brow.

Truth be told, I was a bit shaken by my own outburst. I'd never spoken to my father like that. I would never have dared to. But his careless words and accusations had struck at me like nothing he had ever said before. For me to risk so much,

compromising my morals and jeopardizing my life, my freedom, and worst of all my integrity, and then face his cruel
criticism was simply too much.

But as freeing as it had felt to say those words to him, they
also stung my conscience. I had been bitter and spiteful. And
I had lied. I was not done caring. I never would be. He was
my father.

I watched the light drain from the sky, too ashamed to
return to the house until the last tinge of color had faded
from the horizon and the stars had begun to poke holes in
the darkness.

When I stepped across the threshold into the kitchen, Mrs.
Brittle was waiting for me, perched on her usual chair at the
table. She cradled a cup of tea between her hands, waiting for
me to join her. I didn't try to demur. I no longer wanted to.

Sinking into the chair across from her, I accepted the cup
she poured for me, though I didn't drink it. I stared into
the amber liquid, surprised by its deep color. Apparently
this night's events called for fresh tea leaves instead of the
batch from breakfast we normally reused throughout the
day to stretch our resources. I wondered momentarily what
the leaves at the bottom of my cup would foretell about my
future. Mrs. Brittle had once earned a small side income from
reading tea leaves for the local villagers as well as my family
and our guests, but since my mother's death she had refused to
indulge in any tasseography, no matter the sum offered.

"Where is Father?" I murmured into my cup.

"In his study. The pigheaded man refused to gae up to 'is
bed." She paused and I glanced up into her narrowed eyes. "At
least ye come by that trait honestly."

I didn't refute her. I was too busy trying to form the words
to ask her what I really wanted to know. In the end, words
weren't necessary.

Mrs. Brittle's jaw softened, and she reached across the table to pat my hand. "He'll live, lass."

I swallowed. "Yes, but…" Again I was at a loss. "Did I…"

"He'll no' remember, lass. Ye ken that as well as I do."

I nodded, dropping my gaze to my cup again. Such a reminder did not blunt the sting of my guilt, but it would assuage it in time.

Mrs. Brittle let me ruminate a moment longer, taking a drink of her tea before setting it aside with one last sip at the bottom, as always. I supposed she was worried what she would see. "Noo, are ye goin' to tell me what ye've been hidin'?"

I sighed. "I've joined a crew of smugglers."

I expected shock or disappointment, but she made no discernable reaction. "Ingles' crew?"

I shook my head.

She stared at me expectantly, waiting for me to explain.

"They're the men who have been masquerading through the marsh as Lantern Men."

Her mouth tightened. "The one who's been visitin' our dock?"

I stiffened. How had she known about that? "Yes," I admitted hesitantly.

She didn't speak for a long moment, and I struggled not to squirm under her sharp gaze. That a scolding was imminent there was no doubt, and yet it was a relief not to have to keep this secret to myself any longer. Little as I'd wanted to embroil her in such a sordid business, it was somehow reassuring that she now knew.

And then she surprised me again.

Her eyes hardened into dark beads. "Curse yer da! If he'd taken care o' ye as he was s'posed to, ye'd never have had to sully yersel' wi' such nonsense." She shook her head. "Yer mam would be sore ashamed o' him."

"And me?" I couldn't help but ask.

Mrs. Brittle's voice lowered. "Lass, yer mam kens well

enough ye've done all ye could. She wouldna have expected this much o' ye. But she canna condemn it, neither."

I couldn't speak past the lump in my throat, so I nodded.

"Have ye heard from yer grandda or yer great-aunt?"

I shook my head. "No. Not yet."

She sat back in her chair with a sigh. "Well, I s'pose ye canna change yer mind noo, even if ye wanted to."

"No. I'm already too entangled."

Her mouth firmed. "Then show me what changes ye've been tryin' to make to that dress upstairs. I think ye've butchered it enough."

I couldn't stop the small smile that curled my lips. I should have known better than to try to conceal anything from Mrs. Brittle. She saw all. She probably knew about Robert's marriage proposal, too. But I wasn't about to broach that subject on the chance that she didn't. In any case, I needed her help with the gown immediately if I was to have it ready in time for the Longshore's impending arrival.

"I'll just go fetch it," I told her, rising from my seat. Then on an impulse, I turned back and leaned over to peck the old woman on her leathery cheek.

She scowled and shooed me toward the door. "Gae on wi' ye noo."

I smothered a laugh as I hurried out of the kitchen.

Chapter 21

I DID NOT RETIRE THAT NIGHT until the wee hours of the morning. It had taken me and Mrs. Brittle several hours to finish the dress alterations I had quite honestly made a hash of. And as it turned out, I had needed her help even more badly than I could have realized, for I received a hastily scrawled missive from Jack at dawn. The Longshore was expected to make port that day. A quick glance at the clock told me I had only minutes to prepare before I was expected to meet him at our dock.

I scrambled to wash, dress my hair, and don the oversized gown Mrs. Brittle and I had fashioned to accommodate the hidden pockets sewn inside. It had to be roomy enough to obscure the items I would conceal, yet conform to a womanly shape. My pale blue pelisse with matching epaulet trim and buttons would help hide the loose fit of the jonquil dress fabric as I boarded the ship. So long as the day did not grow so warm that such a garment drew too much attention. My mother's brooch would have complemented the ensemble, but I left it behind, worried what would happen to it should anything go wrong.

I snatched up my best bonnet, a rather plain affair with a crown barely tall enough to accommodate my thick hair, and dashed downstairs. Father's study door was still closed, but I had no time to worry about him. With any luck he would stay hidden until I was gone.

Mrs. Brittle pressed a cloth-wrapped parcel into my hands as I hurried through the kitchen. "Some cheese and apples," she informed me. "Ye mun' have somethin' to break yer fast. I'll no' have ye faintin' from hunger and givin' yersel' away."

"Thank you."

"Aye, aye. Noo oot wi' ye." She pulled open the door for me, but then stopped me with a hand on my arm. "But tell that scoundrel should any harm come to ye, I'll track 'im doon mesel'." She squinted up at me and leaned closer. "I may be old, but I'm crafty. And I'm sure to die afore they could ever hang me."

In the face of her vehemence, all I could do was nod.

Jack leaned against one of the posts, already waiting for me when I pushed through the marsh grasses out onto the dock. I was momentarily startled by how dashing he looked dressed in the attire of a gentleman farmer. His dark green cropped riding coat and gray breeches fit him quite well. And quite comfortably.

All sorts of questions formed in my head.

He straightened when he noticed my approach, returning his hat to his head. His eyes roamed up and down my frame. I knew he was only inspecting the suitability of my attire for the task at hand, but my breath quickened anyway.

"Well done," he murmured. "Suitable, but not notable. Just as we requested. And the pockets?"

"There are six. All well-hidden."

He stared down at me in approval. "Then let's be on our way."

I pressed a hand to my stomach, hoping to calm the nerves fluttering there. I didn't pause to allow myself to contemplate the implications of what I was about to do. There had been enough of that in the past few weeks. I had set myself on this course and I would see it through. What lay at the end of it, I didn't know, but I would find out soon enough.

Jack helped me into the boat and then settled into the rhythm of rowing, the shoulders of his fitted coat straining with each motion. Hoping to divert my attention, I glanced over my shoulder at the box I'd spied when I took my seat, wondering what was inside.

"Open it."

I looked up at Jack uncertainly.

His eyes flashed with amusement. "Go on."

I set aside my breakfast and carefully lifted the package onto my lap. It was relatively light, and when I opened the lid and looked inside I saw why.

I gasped. It was a bonnet, a lovely tall-crowned bonnet covered in Maria Louisa blue satin and trimmed with crepe and bunches of white auriculas. It looked just like the hats featured in the fashion plates from one of Kate's most recent issues of *La Belle Assemblée*.

"I'm glad now I chose that blue. It should match your pelisse quite smartly," Jack said.

I couldn't speak. This was the nicest thing anyone had given me in years, and all I could do was stare down at it. I knew he hadn't gifted it to me out of the goodness of his heart, that its true purpose was to aid in the smuggling, but my hand still shook slightly as I reached in to finger the smooth satin on the crown.

I doubted the other smugglers, including Himself, had contributed to its purchase, which meant Jack had paid for the bonnet with his money. My pride smarted at the realization he had known I didn't own such a hat, even though I had not told him so after he suggested I wear one. Of course, it wouldn't have been difficult to guess. If I could afford new bonnets I wouldn't have trapped him and demanded to join his band of smugglers in the first place.

"Try it on," Jack urged, showing no sign he recognized I was struggling to control my emotions. Still, I didn't dare look at him, lest his eyes show any tenderness or sympathy. Either might undo me.

I swallowed and reached up to remove my old bonnet from my head and smoothed back my hair. Then I slowly lifted the confection from the box and placed it over my tightly upswept curls. It smelled of lavender, likely because of the few crushed stems nestled amongst the paper that had cushioned the bonnet. Which told me that this hat had not been purchased from any ordinary milliner, but from one of the best shops in Norwich, perhaps even in Bond Street in London.

I looked up at Jack. *Who exactly was he?*

He studied my features. "It suits you." Dipping his oars back in the water, he pulled hard to propel us forward again. "And it will provide you with an additional place to conceal contraband."

I nodded, grateful for the reminder that this wasn't some friendly gift. But still I thanked him, feeling it would be inconsiderate not to.

He shrugged it off.

"I'll take good care of it," I murmured, rolling a loose thread on the trim of my pelisse between my fingers. "And return it when my task is complete."

Jack shook his head. "No. It's for you to keep."

I glanced up in surprise.

"*I* have no use for it." His mouth firmed. "Besides, you might have need of it again."

For another smuggling job. Of course. After all of the unsettling things I'd experienced this week, the thought of more such operations seemed daunting. So I turned aside to stare out at the marshes, trying not to think of it. The future would keep for a little while longer.

Thin, wispy clouds trailed across the morning sky, as if drifting across the surface of a lake, too lazy to form anything
more substantial. Yellow Flag irises speckled the tall grasses to
the west, their bright blooms lending a bit of much-needed
color to the landscape. A sudden plopping sound and a cluster
of rings forming on the water told me a water vole had just
dived below the surface, disturbing the pair of white waterlil-
ies floating nearby. This early in the day, the air was still fresh
with dew and new grass. I breathed deep, trying to calm my
nerves. I had to admit, the Longshore couldn't have picked a
lovelier day to reach port.

Jack skillfully guided the boat into a larger channel, staring
over his shoulder at the waterway ahead of us a bit longer
than seemed necessary, but perhaps something was floating in
our path.

Then I saw it—the top of a wherry boat's distinctive high-
peaked sail rising up over the reeds. I tensed at the sight, even
though I should have been expecting it. Jack and I couldn't
row all the way to Yarmouth.

As we rounded the bend, I could see Harry, Freddy, Dibs,
and Red Beard—who I had since learned was called Rory—
lounging against the canvas stretched across the hold at the
center of the ship. I didn't ask what was stored underneath;
I knew better. But I was curious. Was it legitimate cargo, or
something they intended to smuggle out? Given the brazen
manner in which I was about to retrieve a load of contraband,
it seemed foolhardy to attempt to export smuggled goods as
well, but I had no way of knowing how reckless this crew
could be. Certainly they were willing to take steep risks.

I eyed the men warily as we approached, for none of them
looked happy. I learned why when Rory reached across to
help me onto the boat. The whites of his eyes were nearly
as red as his beard, and he smelled as if he'd taken a bath in
gin. Apparently, they had not been expecting the Longshore

to arrive in Yarmouth today and so had made free with the strong Geneva in their possession the night before.

I did not comment on their slovenly appearance. They were acting their part as wherry men. It mattered little how they looked. Jack and I were the ones with other roles to play.

I skirted around the edge of the deck to the bow of the boat, deciding it would be best to sit quietly out of the way while the men worked rather than risk aggravating any of their fragile tempers. Freddy stepped down into the skiff Jack had collected me in and rowed away as the wherry boat set off. For the most part they all ignored me. Jack and Harry stood near the stern, while Rory and Dibs slumped against the cargo on either side of the boat, occasionally rousing themselves when the sail needed adjusting.

Under the circumstances, I was grateful to be left to my own silent contemplation. I was finding it difficult enough to maintain my veneer of calm without having to modulate my voice and consider my words. I tried my best to pretend I was simply on my way to Yarmouth to do a bit of shopping—the story I had been ordered to tell should anyone ask while we were traveling into or out of the town. Not that I was to talk unless absolutely necessary. Instead, Jack would explain my presence, pretending to be my husband.

However, once we reached Yarmouth the story changed, and I was on my own. That was what made me nervous. No one would be accompanying me onto the Longshore, and if anything should go wrong then there would be no one to rely on but myself.

We glided silently down the river, past where it joined with the River Waveney and across the expanse where it broadened into the lake of Breydon Water. The crumbling walls of the old Roman fort at the village of Burgh Castle were visible along the south shore, as were the imposing white turrets of Waveney Hall, glimmering in the distance. Then just as quickly as the waterway had widened, it narrowed and turned sharply south. Great Yarmouth stretched along the water on both sides, but predominately to the east, between the river and the North Sea beyond.

I occupied myself with observing the buildings we passed— the shops with their windows gleaming in the sun, cozy homes built of brick and flint, and tall church spires pointing up toward Heaven as if to reach out and touch it. The people strolling the quay and sailing by on similar wherry boats paid us little heed. We were just another vessel come to town to deliver goods and collect a shipment from one of a number of large cargo ships docked offshore in the deeper water.

I strained my neck as we passed one particularly splendid row of buildings, wishing I truly had time to wander the streets of Yarmouth. Before she'd fallen ill, my mother had insisted on making biannual trips to Norwich. Oh, how I had looked forward to those excursions. We would return home, our carriage filled to the brim with boxes and packages, while I cradled some new doll or toy or book in my lap. But it had been years since I'd ventured farther than our small village. It turned out trips to town weren't all that enjoyable when you had no money to spend.

Even though my pockets were still to let, my legs physically itched with the desire to stroll Yarmouth's streets. To pretend my reticule was filled with guineas I hadn't yet decided how to spend.

I clenched my hands into fists and turned away, only to see Harry approaching. I stiffened and glanced toward the stern where Jack stood watching us. Harry and I had never warmed to each other. In fact, I suspected Jack had been keeping us apart as much as possible. However, this appeared to be one occasion where such an intervention was not forthcoming.

"Here," Harry growled, pressing in close to me. I leaned away, even as I heard the clink of something dropped onto the edge of the hold where I perched. The corner of his lips curled upward in an ugly smirk as he reached up to pretend to adjust the sail. Should anyone from shore be watching us, they would see nothing out of the ordinary.

I reached down to touch the two canvas pouches.

"The smaller one is to get ye to the ship an' back," Harry explained. "An' a bit for a bribe, if'n ye need it."

I swallowed. "And the larger one?"

"Give it to Captain Haywood on the *Reliance*." His eyes hardened. "No one else."

Something in his tone of voice made my senses sharpen. I gripped the bag tighter, feeling the crinkle of paper next to the solid bulk of coins. "What is it?"

His nostrils flared as he risked leaning closer to me. "No' yer concern."

I frowned, wanting to argue, but I knew it would be no use. Harry didn't care that I was risking my neck, quite literally. He would probably rejoice to see me caught, if it didn't mean jeopardizing the exposure of their entire crew. He didn't trust me. None of the men did, except perhaps Jack. And while I couldn't fault him for his suspicion, I did curse it. The paper inside the bag was probably something as simple as banknotes or a letter of instructions, but he would refuse to share that just to be contrary.

I slipped the bags into my reticule.

"Yer also to give 'im a message."

I tilted my head in annoyed expectation.

"Greybar twenty-three."

My brow furrowed. Clearly, that wasn't supposed to mean anything to me.

"Did ye hear?" Harry asked impatiently when I didn't respond.

"Yes. Grey—"

He held up a hand to forestall me. "Don't repeat it. To anyone."

There was a ferocity in his voice I had not heard before, and it unsettled me. All I could do was nod.

He continued to study my face, and then, as if satisfied with what he'd seen, walked away without another glance.

I sat rigidly as the boat veered toward the quay, making ready to dock so that I could disembark. Snatches of an argument at the stern of the boat periodically reached my ears, but I pretended I could not hear them.

"She's s'posed to be calm. Do ye *want* the preventives to catch 'er?"

"She needed to be warned."

"Mayhap. But not given the shakes."

I inhaled deeply and forced my shoulders and jaw to relax, just as Jack had taught me. If he could tell how upset I was merely from looking at my back, my expression must be terrified. I heard the stomp of boots approaching and prayed it was Jack. I wasn't sure I could face Harry again so soon.

Jack perched next to me, using the prevarication that we were husband and wife to sit close. He didn't speak at first, joining me in my contemplation of the ships lining the river's quay, their white sails rippling in the sea breeze. I began to wonder if he was simply offering me a bit of silent support when he finally glanced at me out of the corner of his eye.

"You remember your training?" he murmured in a low voice.

"Yes."

"Good." His foot tapped against the deck. "He gave you the ship's name?"

"The *Reliance*."

"And you recall what to do should you be detained?"

I pressed my fingers against my thumbs, channeling my distress into my hands—another technique he had taught me. I breathed evenly in and out. "Yes."

He nodded in approval before abruptly declaring, "Forget them."

This time I couldn't completely contain my shock. I jerked my head around to stare at his profile.

His eyes slid sideways to meet mine briefly before returning to the shore we inched ever closer to. "Tell them everything."

"But…my father…"

"You understand Harry's instructions?"

"I…yes," I spluttered. "But—"

"And the message you are to deliver?"

I blinked up at him. "Of course."

"Which is?" His eyebrows raised.

I inhaled in frustration. "Explain what you mean—"

"Do you recall it?"

I scowled at him. "I'm not daft. It's Greybar twenty-three." Surely Harry hadn't meant I couldn't repeat it to our own crew.

He nodded. "Good."

"But you haven't—"

"Best of luck, Ella," he murmured, rising to his feet.

But I wasn't about to let him leave. "Stop!" I hissed as I grabbed his arm. "Explain yourself. What did you mean?"

His eyes flicked toward the other members of the crew, as if to remind me of their presence. I released his arm. "Only that there comes a time when enough is enough." His gaze hardened. "You wouldn't survive transportation to New South Wales. Not among the population you're likely to be thrown in with."

This time I didn't stop him when he walked away, too stunned by his comment. I knew he was right. If I was caught I would be facing transportation to a penal colony on the opposite side of the globe, and no one's interference would halt it. Except perhaps my grandfather's, but the likelihood of the earl exerting himself in such a manner on my behalf was slim.

Jack and the other smugglers had initially instructed me to keep my mouth shut if the revenue men nabbed me. They'd promised if I held my tongue they wouldn't demand my father repay the loan I'd been given to cover his fine. But if I did talk, what then? Would they punish him for my betrayal? Would they hurt Mrs. Brittle? Either outcome seemed horrifying.

Then my only option was simply not to be caught. Squaring my shoulders, I gathered up my reticule and ordered my nerves to settle. I could not fail. I would not.

The boat glided up to the quay, knocking gently against the wood. While Rory stepped up to tie us off, I reached up to adjust my new bonnet before standing to shake out my skirts and brush off my pelisse. I gathered some confidence in knowing that if nothing else, at least I looked my best.

Jack appeared at my elbow, like the dutiful husband he played. "We'll return for you here in three hours' time," he leaned down to murmur.

I nodded coolly, taking his hand as he helped me step up onto the quay. Rory was there to offer me another hand should I falter, but my legs proved long enough for the task. Once my feet were solidly on the wooden planks, I bustled forward without a backward glance. I couldn't afford to lose my newly found composure, and I wasn't certain it could withstand the sight of the wherry boat pulling away, with Jack pretending not to watch me from the bow.

Chapter 22

THE QUAY BUSTLED WITH ACTIVITY. Wherry men loaded and unloaded goods from boats lining the docks while revenue men, their metal collar badges flashing in the sunlight, looked on. One official stood with his head bent over a stack of papers that appeared as if it had seen better days, while a wherry man tapped his foot impatiently beside him. Another pair leaned over a pile of barrels, inspecting them and murmuring together. Whatever they were saying seemed to make the man loading the casks nervous.

I did my best to ignore them all, choosing instead to focus my attention on the women who periodically strolled past, some of whom were dressed in imitations of the latest fashions from London. It seemed like the sort of thing a newly prosperous merchant's wife would do, comparing her clothing to theirs. In truth, it wasn't difficult, for I already found myself a little envious of their Polish walking pelisses and ruffed collars, styles I'd only seen in Kate's fashion plates.

I wandered after a pair of ladies in chestnut-brown and spring-green spencers with floating muslin skirts as they led me deeper into the market that edged the riverfront, and then out into the streets lined with more exclusive shops beyond. However, rather than drift inside to browse the pale blossom silk and buttery tan kid gloves displayed in one store's window as they did, I hurried on. Though I did pause outside a milliner's shop on the corner, pretending to be absorbed in the selection of new bonnets as I studied the reflection in the glass to see if anyone had followed me. Yet another trick Jack had taught me in the past week. When I felt certain I was not being trailed, I turned my steps toward the sea.

As I strolled east farther away from the river, the shops gradually gave way to homes. Some of them were quite large and beautiful, and those closest to the shore were gifted with magnificent views of the North Sea. Though I suspected this unrestricted view wasn't always welcome when the fearsome winds of a winter gale began to howl. But today I welcomed the ocean breeze as it blew cool against my cheeks heated from the exertion of my walk. I'd begun to regret the necessity of wearing my pelisse, but near the water I didn't feel so warm.

I turned south, following the road that separated the town from the beach, and from a distance I could see the short pier jutting out into the sea. It was lined with small rowboats and shallow-bottomed skiffs, bobbing merrily in the high tide. Much further out to sea the tall masts of larger ships dotted the endless horizon, their hulls too deep to risk entering the Yarmouth Roads or venturing closer to shore. My nerves began to flutter in my stomach again, so I gulped deep breaths of the salty sea air and lengthened my stride. The sooner this was completed, the better. Dawdling would not make it easier.

The fine homes and buildings lining the coast steadily deteriorated the further south I walked. The paint became more worn, the wood more weathered, and the lovingly tended gardens bordering front walks all but disappeared. The scent of fish also became stronger, overwhelming everything else, and I realized the squat buildings that dominated the area surrounding the pier must house fishmongers. A group of rough-looking men clustered in front of one such building eyed me. I clutched my reticule tighter and crossed the road toward the boats.

The pier was not as well populated as the quay on the river, but there were at least a dozen men about—mending nets or working on their boats or simply lazing in the sun. I scanned the seamen assembled before me and decided to approach an older man perched on a post, a pipe clenched between his teeth. His face was tan and weathered like leather and his beard grizzled, but he had a twinkle in his eye.

"Excuse me. Is that your boat?" I asked, nodding to the weathered but tidy skiff behind him.

He studied my face before replying. "Aye. An' who might be askin'?"

I ignored his question in favor of my own. "I wish to be rowed out to the *Reliance*. Can you assist me?"

His bushy eyebrows lowered in a leer. "Ye want to visit the *Reliance*, do ye? Now why would that be?" The tone of his voice left no doubt as to what insulting conclusion he'd come to.

I straightened in indignation. "The captain is my brother. Not that that is any of your concern." I flicked my gaze over him contemptuously. "But perhaps you're not capable of the task." I pivoted to go, but his rusty voice stopped me.

"Aye, aye. Don't work yerself into a huff." He rose to his feet, and I could have sworn I heard his bones creak. "I'll take ye out to the *Reliance*." His eyes sharpened. "For a quid."

I arched a single eyebrow. "I'll pay you a half-guinea to row me there and back, and not a pence more," I replied, knowing that was still more than the task deserved, but perhaps the little bit extra would encourage his discretion.

He tilted his head as if to consider my offer, and I raised my other eyebrow, letting him know I wasn't fooled. If he chose to turn this down, he was daft.

He flashed me a cheeky grin, revealing a mouth only half full of teeth. "'Twill be me pleasure." Then he swiveled toward the far end of the pier. "Crisp," he hollered.

I turned to see a young man with shaggy red hair, almost as dark as mine, step away from a trio of men and move towards us.

"Me boy," the old sailor explained.

I nodded, wondering if he meant his son or his grandson.

"Crisp, we've got a passenger."

The young man glanced at me with a level of disinterest only the very young are capable of. I dipped my head and held my tongue. If the old man and Crisp were both going to row me at the same cost, then so be it. The trip would be quicker.

In a matter of minutes, we set off across the sea. Father, or grandfather, and son were surprisingly even matched, and we made better time than I'd expected. Perhaps I'd overestimated the old sailor's age. It was difficult to tell with his wind-beaten skin and deep wrinkles from squinting into the sun.

All too soon the ships loomed before us, their large hulls towering above the waves. Even the *Reliance*'s, which was by no means the largest ship anchored off Yarmouth. In fact, those to its left and right seemed to dwarf it.

The old sailor, who I'd learned went by the name Mick, called up to the deck. When one of the crew leaned over the side, he raised his voice again, lifting his hand to cup his mouth so that the wind wouldn't snatch his words away. "Mrs. Warnes to see yer cap'n."

The man dipped out of sight and I twisted my hands in my lap, praying the captain recognized the false name. Jack had promised the captain was aware of the plan, but missives went awry, people grew skittish, and I could easily find myself denied the chance to board. Or cornered when I did.

I could feel Mick's eyes on me, but I ignored him, doing my

best to look calm and unruffled as I gazed across the water toward shore. It seemed so far away. Crisp frowned at the handle of his oar, rubbing his thumb back and forth across what I guessed was a rough strip in the wood.

Something swung out from the ship above and thumped against the side of the hull, startling me. It was a rope, and as it lowered toward us I could see that the end was fashioned into a loop. I glanced up at the man leaning over the side of the boat, guiding it toward me. My heart hammered against my ribs as I realized I would have to trust that man and his crew to pull me safely up to the deck. From where I was sitting, that distance seemed a long way. If their grip slipped and I plummeted into the ocean, I could be seriously injured or drown tangled in my skirts.

I tried to push those thoughts from my head as I rose shakily to my feet and reached up to take hold of the rope.

"Crisp, help the lady," Mick ordered.

The young man lurched to his feet, setting the small skiff rocking, and I was forced to latch on to his upper arms or tip over the side. Crisp dropped the rope's loop smoothly over my head and guided it past my shoulders. His eyes lifted to meet mine for the first time, and I was intrigued by how blue they were. He didn't speak, simply stared back at me, and I realized he was waiting for me to release him and pull my arms through the loop.

I flushed in embarrassment and dropped my gaze, helping him finish the task. Once the rope was resting against the back of my legs, he looked up at the man on the *Reliance*. That seemed to be signal enough, for the rope pulled taut, lifting me into the air.

Crisp's eyes met mine again as I rose out of the boat, and I began to wonder if I'd misjudged his age. The intelligence shining back at me seemed far too mature for a sixteen-year-old, as did the faint lines radiating from the corners of his eyes.

Perhaps he was closer to my age than I'd assumed.

The rope swayed, demanding all of my concentration as I gripped it between my hands and struggled to keep my seat. I tried to gauge how far I had yet to rise, but I could no longer see the man above me. The world began to spin along with the rope, and I forced myself to take slow, even breaths. If I passed out now there would be no one to catch me when I fell. I had to at least make it to the top before I could succumb to the vapors.

When finally I caught sight of the man peering over the railing at me, I was relieved to see he was almost near enough to reach his hand out to clasp mine. Two more heaves of the rope and a pair of arms pulled me over the side.

I inhaled sharply as my feet touched the boards of the deck. "Thank you," I gasped to the men standing around me, offering them a tremulous smile.

"Don't thank them yet," a voice drawled to my left.

I looked up to see a man crossing toward me, his hands clasped behind his back. This, I surmised, was the captain. Though he didn't particularly look like one. In fact, he didn't particularly look like anything.

He was handsome, I supposed, the way a vicar or a shop-keeper was pleasing to look at, but he certainly wouldn't attract many admirers. His coloring was neutral browns, his clothing unremarkable. Even his voice was of a middling tim-bre. The only thing remarkable about him was the impact he seemed to have on his crew, who all stood at the ready, if not exactly at attention. This was a trade ship after all, not a cruiser for the Royal Navy. And yet I suspected that if he'd wanted to pass unnoticed, he could have—a useful skill for a smuggler to possess. I was instantly wary, though I did my best not to let him know that.

His eyes narrowed in challenge, scrutinizing my features. "Ye're Mrs. Warnes, are ye?"

"Yes. Apparently I'm your long-lost sister."

This appeared to have been the right tack to take, for the corners of his mouth quirked upward and several of his men chuckled, making me suspect they were already aware of the ruse. "I see. Well, 'tis a shame. For I'm told it isn't proper to ogle yer own sister."

I arched an eyebrow in scolding. "It isn't proper to ogle *any* woman."

This seemed to amuse him. "And yet all us gents do it." He sidled a step closer. "And I s'pose ye found our brother well."

I knew where this comment was leading even without his raising his voice slightly at the end. "Yes. He sends his regards. And his compliments."

"Aye, then." He offered me his arm. "Let's discuss that over a bottle of Holland."

I rested my arm lightly on his and allowed him to guide me across the deck. I could only pray he would behave like a gentleman once we were alone, for I knew from glancing around at his crew that none of them would intervene should he not.

Captain Haywood's cabin was down a short flight of stairs at the stern of the ship, facing out to sea. I'd been expecting a dim and close space, and it was true the room was far from bright and airy, but it appeared quite comfortable, even cozy, save the dank smell. He led me to a table near the corner and then sat across from me.

"Gin?" he asked, reaching for a bottle at the center of the table.

"No, thank you," I replied, worried my hands might tremble if I tried to hold a cup. In truth, a drink would have been welcome, but not here or now. And not gin.

He shrugged and poured himself some of the liquid before leaning back in his chair and propping one booted heel on the table. He drained the cup in one smooth swallow before setting it back on the table with a thud. "Now, down to business." His eyes scoured my face, for weaknesses no doubt. "What do ye have for me?"

I slowly extracted the larger coin bag from my reticule and passed it to him. "This."

He hefted the bag in his hands, as if able to tell how much money was inside just by feel.

"Along with a message."

His pupils widened in alertness and I knew I had his full attention.

"Greybar twenty-three," I told him as if I knew exactly what that meant.

His lips curled in a roguish grin, and I wasn't sure if this was because he was pleased or because he found my feigned understanding humorous. Either way, I didn't like it. His smugness irritated me and I was ready to be gone.

I lifted my chin. "And what do you have for me?"

His smile slipped a fraction into something darker. "A dangerous question, lass."

My heart surged into my throat at the implication of his words. I tensed, wondering if the heft of the coins remaining in my reticule would be enough to do him any harm should I need to defend myself.

"But..." his head tilted to the side "...seeing as ye're me sister, and Saucy Jack's girl, I'll just show ye the silks."

I frowned at his back as he crossed the room, uncertain what he'd meant about my being Jack's girl. Had Jack told him that, perhaps in warning?

Captain Haywood bent over to seize a cloth covering what appeared to be a low table next to his bunk. When he whisked back the material, I could see it was actually a large trunk. He dragged it away from the corner and propped open the lid.

I moved closer, my eyes widening at the array of fabrics inside—shimmering silks in shades of blue and pink and gold; the finest Indian cotton in snowy white; and delicate lengths of French needle lace. As I knelt to examine the contents more closely, the captain moved towards the opposite corner, returning with another smaller chest. He lowered it for me to see inside and I actually gasped. There was almost a dozen gems nestled within, each one probably worth more than our cottage.

And I was supposed to line the hidden pockets sewn inside my gown with them and simply waltz past the revenue men. I was nearly sick all over the trunk full of expensive fabrics.

I inhaled a steadying breath. "Is this everything, then?"

"Aye."

"Then if you'll allow me a bit of privacy—"

"I'm afraid I can't do that."

I blinked up at him. "But…I'm to conceal these items under my clothing."

"Aye. I surmised as much."

I frowned. "Which means…well…" My cheeks began to heat, unaccustomed to saying such words in front of a man. I'd been taught that there were certain words, certain topics that a lady did not dare address in front of the opposite sex, including the act of disrobing. I swallowed. "That means I'll…I'll have to remove them." Some of my embarrassment swiftly turned to anger as I witnessed how much he was enjoying my discomfort.

"Does it? Well, that's my luck, then."

"I'm not going to undress in front of you," I snapped.

He reclined on the bench I had recently vacated, leaning to the side to prop himself up with his elbow. "And what makes ye think ye have any say in the matter?" His head sank back against the wall behind him as he watched me grapple with this bit of news.

I was tempted to turn and stomp out the door, but then what would become of the silk and jewels? I suspected the bag I'd delivered had contained at least a partial payment for the goods. If I abandoned those items here he might very well decide to resell them elsewhere. What would Jack and the others do if I returned empty-handed? What would Himself do?

Whatever it was, I suspected it would be far worse than letting Captain Haywood view me in my chemise and corset.

Suppressing the urge to shriek at him—he would only like that too much—I set my bonnet aside and began to unbutton my pelisse.

"Ye let me know if ye need any help wi' that," he murmured cheekily.

I glared at him, but that only seemed to amuse him more. After draping my pelisse over a chair, I turned my back to him and set about unfastening my dress. I pulled the ends of the ribbon sash wrapped around the high waist of my gown, just below my bosom, with a sharp tug. "I wonder what Jack will think of your refusal to give me any privacy," I muttered over my shoulder, not above using his name in such a manner since Captain Haywood had already linked us together.

"Oh, ol' Saucy Jack wouldn't begrudge me such a lovely sight. Not when he knows I've been at sea for more than a fortnight, what with the Waterguard increasin' their patrols."

I scowled, uncomfortable with the possibility that the two men knew each other so well. But what had I expected? They were both smugglers, obviously working in tandem. Perhaps they came from different backgrounds, though neither man seemed as rough as they pretended to be, but that didn't mean they weren't friends.

I paused after slipping the last button at the top of my back from its hole, feeling color begin to flood my cheeks again. No man had ever seen me in a state of undress, at least not since I was too young to remember, and the indignity of allowing such a rascal to do so now infuriated me. I latched onto that anger, anything that would help me forget some of my humiliation and discomfort. Then with one swift motion, I pulled the dress over my head.

I bent over and quickly gathered up some of the costly fabric, winding it around me. The silk was cool against my heated skin, and more slippery than I'd anticipated. It took a great deal of tugging and tucking, and the creative use of some satin ribbon I found at the bottom of the trunk to make it stay in place. After all, I couldn't have layers sliding off my body to pool at my feet as I made my way back across Yarmouth to the river.

And all the while Captain Haywood sat back watching me with a smirk on his face. I was relieved when he made no move to approach me until I pulled my gown back over my head. While I filled the pockets sewn inside my dress with lace, a few pairs of finely-worked leather gloves, and the remaining ribbon, he tucked the gems into a velvet pouch before passing them to me. Then he lifted a pair of bottles from the bottom of the small chest and wrapped them in a small handkerchief.

"The finest French perfume," he explained with a sardonic twist in his voice.

I slid the bottles into the pocket on my left side, thinking they would not shift as awkwardly if they rested against my torso above my hip. I reached for my bonnet, deciding to pack the bag of jewels in the tall crown along with the last lace-edged shawl, but the captain was not finished. He knelt to remove one last parcel from under his thin mattress. I glanced up at him in question as he passed it to me.

His eyes gleamed. "A special order."

I frowned at his vague response, pressing it between my fingers. It was flat like a book and wrapped carefully in oilskin. I'd never heard of anyone smuggling in works of literature, but I supposed if a book was rare or perhaps even banned, and someone was willing to pay the right price, anything was possible.

"Is there a problem?" Captain Haywood asked, interrupting my thoughts.

"No. I was just trying to figure out which pocket it would be best to stow it in."

He watched as I slid the packet in place, and then directed me to turn around. I hesitated, not certain of his intentions, and he huffed, grabbing me by the shoulders to spin me about himself. I stiffened as I felt his fingers deftly button up my gown, wondering if I should protest. But the truth was it had been difficult enough to unfasten my dress myself. I could only imagine how much worse it would be now that the frock was much more fitted. He tied off the ribbon at the high waist and I hastily stepped away, reaching back to be sure he had not made a hash of it.

When I was certain the bow was even, I pulled on my pelisse, which now fit quite snug around my frame. Once my bonnet and its hidden contents were secure on my head, I turned to face the captain.

He eyed me critically from head to toe. "Well, ye've gained a stone or two." His head tilted to the side. "Which wouldn't be amiss. Ye're as scrawny as a bird. But so long as no preventives were payin' ye much mind, they shouldn't notice."

I swallowed and nodded, smoothing a nervous hand down my bodice.

He offered me his arm and we exited his cabin, climbing the shadowed staircase up toward the deck. I lifted a hand to shield my eyes from the sudden glare of the sun.

"Tell Jack I says to buy ye a box of sweetmeats for once instead of whatever fripperies he's given ye," the captain leaned down to murmur in my ear.

His gruff comment surprised a smile out of me, even though I strongly suspected he'd just insinuated I was a kept woman. "Jack does not buy me things." *Except bonnets.* But that was one time, and only because it had been needed for this task.

"And he certainly doesn't feed me."

"Hmm. Well, he should."

I shook my head at the absurdity of his motherly chiding.

The crew stood in more or less the same positions as earlier when we'd gone below deck, as if waiting for us to return. From their curious expressions I could tell they wondered just what had occurred between us, but none of them dared to ask.

"Is her skiff still waitin' below?" the captain asked the man who directed my ascent.

"Aye, sir."

Captain Haywood's gaze swept up and down me again. "Make a sling for *my sister* this time." He flashed his teeth in a sly grin. "There's no need for her to risk the wind blowin' up her skirts."

And revealing everything I had concealed underneath.

"Thank you, brother dear," I told him with a strained smile as the men set to work.

"'Til next time," he declared, turning on his heel and walking away.

I didn't say I hoped there wouldn't be a next time, but I couldn't help thinking it. Though the captain seemed to divine my thoughts anyway, if the cheeky smirk he cast back over his shoulder was any indication.

Chapter 23

IN SHORT ORDER, THE CREW had me settled in a rather precarious sling fashioned out of ropes and canvas and began to lower me over the side. I grasped the rope above me tightly, uncertain this was a better option than the looped rope that had pulled me on board. Yes, my skirts didn't threaten to fly up over my face, but my body was tipped at an odd angle, making me terrified I would fall backward out of the contrivance.

When finally Crisp captured the sling and tipped me forward so that my feet touched the skiff's deck, my arms were ready to give out from the strain. I sank down on the bench and pressed my hands to my torso, anxious to feel if all the fabric had stayed in place. Mick leaned forward, puffing on his pipe much as he had when I met him at the pier barely an hour earlier.

Could that really be true? It seemed like at least half a day had passed, but when I glanced at the watch pinned to my pelisse I could see I was correct. I had more than an hour left before Jack and the others would return for me at the river quay.

"Did ye find what ye were lookin' for?" Mick asked with far too shrewd a look in his eyes.

I lifted my chin. "My brother? Yes."

"Oh, aye. Yer brother."

I decided the best course would be to disregard him, and turned to stare out over the water as Mick and Crisp began to row me toward shore. I didn't glance back at the *Reliance*, even to see if Captain Haywood was watching our departure. I didn't want to know.

As we neared land I could see the pier was busier than when we had set out. At least half a dozen more boats were docked there, and several small wherries seemed to be unloading cargo. The sight set a trickle of unease down my spine, for if there was cargo then surely there would be revenue men about to inspect it.

I spotted one or two men examining the tubs and bales being stacked on the deck. They shouldn't be a problem. The trio standing about chatting, however, were not so easily dismissed. Of course, I couldn't be sure they were customs officers. Not from this distance. But something in the way they conducted themselves, the too-casual way they watched those around them, told me they were.

I inhaled and exhaled slowly, in and out, just as Jack had taught me, and tried to show them little interest. They were just another group of men gathered on the pier, and of no concern to me. But as we bobbed closer, I saw the flash of one of their collar badges, letting me know I had been correct.

Regrettably, Mick and Crisp chose to dock their boat and tie it up just a few feet from where these men stood. Whether this had been done purposely, I didn't know, but Mick appeared particularly pleased with himself. Crisp leapt from the boat to secure the line, sending the tiny vessel rocking, and I gripped the sides to steady myself. Out of the corner of my eye, I saw the revenue men's gaze pass over us and then return. I prayed this was because I was a woman and not because I'd already given myself away. I forced myself not to hurry as I extracted

Mick's payment from my reticule.

"Pleasure doin' business with ye, *Mrs. Warnes*," Mick said, placing a bit too much emphasis on my name.

I smiled tightly and then rose to my feet to take Crisp's proffered hand. But at that moment further up the pier some cargo slipped out of the hands of one of the crews and crashed down onto the dock, rattling it. Crisp's attention wavered for only a moment, but it was long enough for me to trip and nearly stumble to my knees. Had I not been wound up tightly in silks and India cotton it might not have even happened, but my movements were so restricted I couldn't rotate or extend my limbs as far as normal. To my horror, one of the revenue men had seen my fumble and when I recovered my footing and looked up it was to find him clutching my elbow.

"Watch what ye're doin', lad," he scolded Crisp, before turning to me. "Are ye all right, miss?"

"Yes," I gasped, pulling my arm away once I'd regained my balance. I began to smooth out my pelisse, and then thought better of it. "Thank you."

The revenue man grinned, flashing a deep set of dimples, and tipped his hat. "My pleasure, miss."

I nodded and turned to go.

"Do you require any assistance?" he called after me.

I glanced back at him with a smile I hoped didn't appear forced. "No, thank you."

"Are you certain?"

I slowed my steps and turned to face him, not wanting it to appear as if I were running away.

"Maybe ye'd let me buy ye a drink at the Wrestler's Inn. It's not far." His eyebrows lifted hopefully.

I looked over his shoulder to see his fellow revenue men watching us with their heads bent together in conference. I tightened my grasp on my reticule, telling myself to remain calm. They didn't suspect anything. Not yet, anyway. This man was just interested in a pretty face under a pretty bonnet. He couldn't know there was a fortune in gems tucked up underneath.

"I'm a missus, actually," I told him in a soft voice. "I'm sorry I didn't correct you before. It just seemed...unnecessary."

His grin turned rueful. "I shoulda known. The comeliest ones are always taken."

I dipped my head coyly at his compliment, hoping that was the appropriate response.

He bobbed his head toward the sea. "I s'pose ye were visitin' yer husband on one of those ships."

"My brother, actually," I replied, following Jack's instructions to keep to the same story if at all possible, lest I get confused and be caught in a lie. Even so, I could see the curiosity blossoming behind the revenue man's eyes, and I knew that was dangerous.

"I'm afraid he's always been a bit...wayward," I confided in him, hoping it would stop him from asking the types of questions I wished to avoid. "I'm not really supposed to have any contact with him, but..." I shrugged one shoulder, appealing to him to understand "...he is my brother."

He nodded. "I've a brother much like that meself. He's a heap o' trouble, but like ye said, he's family."

I smiled gratefully, even as I felt a bead of sweat run down my back beneath all of the layers of fabric. Now that I was back on shore, the midday sun beat down warm on my skin, without the benefit of the open sea breeze to cool it. My cheeks felt a bit flushed and I began to worry that if I stood there much longer the revenue man might begin to wonder why I did not remove my pelisse.

"I should be on my way," I said, hoping he wouldn't offer to escort me or fetch a hansom cab.

"Of course," he replied, tipping his hat to me once again. "Good day, ma'am."

"Good day."

I carefully made my way down the pier before turning right on the street that led into Yarmouth. I didn't look back for fear he was watching to see if I did.

When I was certain no one was following me, I turned my steps inland, weaving my way through the streets back toward the shops and market. If anyone had noted my presence on the quay earlier I wanted them to see me return from the same direction.

Unhappily, with the exertion of my walk the heat only increased. Sweat had begun to gather in all sorts of unpleasant places, and I began to fret it would ruin the silk. I seriously considered removing my pelisse, but I knew the lumps and bumps of my dress line padded with contraband would not survive close scrutiny. So I trudged on in misery, praying my undergarments were thick enough to absorb any damaging moisture.

When at last I reached the market I noted I had another half hour to wait, but the thought of doing so seemed unbearable. Maybe Jack and the others would return early. *Please, let it be so.*

I retraced my steps from earlier in the day and emerged on the quay, sighing as I felt at least the semblance of a breeze touch my cheeks. I wandered toward the spot where Jack had let me off, but the wherry was not docked there. I glanced about me for a bench or a post to sit on, hoping I simply looked like a woman weary from shopping. A packet of parcels sat near the edge of the quay, presumably my numerous purchases made that day. Jack had told me the boxes would be there when they returned to collect me—all part of our ruse—but I didn't know what, if anything, was stored inside each package.

I'd given up on finding a place to perch, and was seriously considering turning myself in to the Customs House if they would but offer me a cool glass of water, when I spotted Jack. He stood at the prow of the wherry boat as it sliced across the river toward me. Overcome with relief, I nearly collapsed, but then I straightened my spine for fear that another revenue man might insist on rendering me assistance.

Mercifully, Jack seemed to take in the situation at one glance. He ordered Rory and Dibs to load the parcels while he offered me a hand up onto the boat, seating me under the thin slice of shade the sail provided. Before I'd even begun to recover my breath, we were pushing away from the quay.

As Harry turned the boat upriver, Jack returned with a bottle of pale liquid and a cup. I drained the glass of sweet lemonade, uncaring how unladylike I looked, and then held it out to him for more. He obliged and I settled back to sip this serving more slowly.

At first Jack did not speak, though I knew he must have dozens of questions. Instead, he sat beside me and let me savor the cool lemonade and the wind billowing the sails. When at last he did talk, it was out of concern for me.

"We're far enough from shore now if you wish to remove your pelisse."

I didn't need to be told twice. He chuckled as I thrust my cup into his hands and swiftly set to work on the buttons. The breeze felt heavenly against the skin revealed at my neckline and my forearms as I peeled the garment off. I tipped my head back, heedless of the sun shining down on my face and the way the items concealed in my bonnet shifted against my skull. I was still not comfortable wrapped in all the layers of fabric, but at least I felt some relief.

A shadow fell over my face and I blinked open my eyes to find Jack standing very close to me. My body tingled in awareness as I stared up at his chiseled jaw. Surely he didn't intend to kiss me here in full view of the crew and the other boats on the river.

His gaze cut to the side, and I followed his eyes toward a boat floating a short distance to our right.

"It's a revenue cutter," he explained in a low, conversational tone.

I quickly grasped the situation. He had moved nearer to block the customs men from getting a clear view of me and my awkwardly padded figure.

"Just try to behave normally," he instructed and I bit back a frown.

That was easy for him to say. Perhaps he was accustomed to standing so close to women that the tips of his boots disappeared under the hems of their skirts, but I was not used to handsome men touching me. I swallowed, as conscious of him as I was of the revenue cutter, which seemed to be pacing us. Perhaps I shouldn't have removed my pelisse. What if they decided to board us?

"Grape?" He offered me a small bunch of the tart white globes, and I took them almost without thinking, so surprised by his casual demeanor. "We've cheese, and apples, some cold pheasant, and crusty bread as well." He began sorting through the contents of a hamper I'd not yet noticed, though presumably the lemonade I'd drunk had come from inside it. "Aha!" He smiled, brandishing a small tin. "And some marzipan." He slid open the lid of the container to reveal the honeyed treats shaped like tiny pieces of fruit.

"I haven't eaten marzipan in years," I gasped. "Not since I was a child. Where did you get it?"

"There are advantages to my line of work," he replied with a teasing grin, still keeping his voice soft so the others could not overhear. "Would you like a piece?"

"Maybe later." I popped a grape into my mouth and glanced beyond his shoulder to see if the revenue cutter was still following us. It appeared they'd lost interest, drifting towards a ship floating near the opposite bank of the river.

Jack followed my gaze. "Once we pass Runham and the mouth of the River Bure, we should be in the clear. Occasionally revenue cutters patrol farther into the Broads, but they mostly focus on the coast. They rely on riding officers to handle matters farther inland."

I chewed another grape slowly as I glanced around at the other men positioned around the wherry. None of them looked the least bit alarmed, though Dibs seemed to be cleaning his knife with a bit too much fervor. Harry looked up to meet my gaze, his eyes hard and watchful as always.

Once I'd finished the grapes, Jack handed me a piece of salty Cheshire cheese, before pulling an apple out of the basket and beginning to cut it into wedges. He would pass me a slice and then pop the second in his mouth, alternating between us. I couldn't help grinning.

"What?" he asked, looking up at me through his eyelashes.

I swallowed the bite in my mouth. "It's just that I told Captain Haywood you didn't feed me, and here you are doing just that."

His expression turned quizzical.

"He told me to tell you to buy me a box of sweetmeats instead of fripperies. But I told him you don't buy me things, least of all food." I gestured toward him holding the apple and a knife, and the hamper resting on the canvas covering the hold. "But here you are."

Jack returned my smile. "I'm just having difficulty picturing Haywood uttering something so motherly. What did you two talk about?"

I shrugged. "He just noticed how thin I was."

His eyebrows quirked. "And how did he do that when you're wearing such a voluminous dress?"

I dropped my gaze. "He insisted he had to stay with me when I secreted away the cargo."

He sunk his knife deep into the apple with a juicy snick.

"Did he, now?"

I risked a glance at him, finding his jaw tight with displeasure.

"And what else did he insist upon?"

"That's all. I wasn't happy to have to...to..." I waved my hand "...in front of him, but he kept his distance." I rolled the last of my piece of cheese between my fingers. "He said you wouldn't mind him watching, but he knew better than to touch me."

Jack extracted his knife and skillfully resumed slicing the apple. "Well, I *do* mind."

I felt a strange thrill at his vengeful tone, knowing he was aggrieved on my behalf. I nibbled on the wedge of apple he passed me, scolding myself for being ridiculous. These men were smugglers. Jack was a smuggler. I shouldn't be feeling anything beyond mild courtesy. Even so, my private elation never ceased.

In fact, it only grew as the wherry boat passed the mouth of the River Bure and then crossed the wider expanse of Breydon Water before slipping deeper into the marshes. My smile broadened with each mile placed between us and Yarmouth, and I was even better able to tolerate the warmth created by the layers of fabric wrapped around me. Soon Rory and Dibs joined me in my good spirits, jesting with me and each other and passing a bottle of gin back and forth.

The knowledge that I'd just done something so daring and illegal, and gotten away with it, was intoxicating. Was this how it always felt? This rush of relief and then euphoria? If so, I now better understood why these smugglers risked it. It wasn't just for the money. It was exhilarating, and I could see in their eyes that they felt much the same way. Even Harry, who remained stalwart and sober at the helm. Perhaps they didn't feel it to the same extent I did, for this was my first time and I'd shouldered much of the risk, but they all sipped some of the same golden ambrosia.

As planned, we docked at the outbuildings beyond the gardens at Greenlaws. I slipped into the watchmen's shelter to remove the contraband wound about me and tucked into my pockets. As the last cloth fell away from my body, I slouched in relief. I would have liked to collapse into one of the chairs, but I knew better than to dawdle. Even with Jack guarding the door, I didn't trust Harry not to barge in whenever he wished.

As if on cue, just as I finished retying the sash of my dress someone tapped on the wooden door. "Come in," I called.

Jack peeked his head around the door, and upon seeing I was fully dressed and ready, strode into the room with Harry close behind. They examined the objects I'd smuggled off the *Reliance* while I folded the pile of fabrics I had dropped in an unceremonious heap in my eagerness to be free of them.

"Was the bonnet handy, then?" Jack asked in his rougher voice.

"Yes. I hid the jewels there."

He nodded and picked up the oilskin package. But before he could open it, Harry snatched it from his grasp.

"I'll deliver these to Himself," he said, tucking the bag of jewels in his pocket and the oilskin under his arm. He paused to look me in the eye. "I had me doubts, but ye done well. Better 'n I'd hoped, anyway."

I didn't answer, uncertain whether his words were meant to express his compliments or his disappointment. Regardless, he didn't seem to require a reply. He exited the building, leaving the door open behind him.

"Where are Rory and Dibs?" I asked Jack, thinking they and the others would want to view the spoils.

"They've gone on to the White Horse to celebrate. But I don't think you'll wish to join them."

"No," I replied, somewhat surprised to hear the two bands

of smugglers consorted so frequently. This wasn't the first time the men had gone to Thurlton for a drink. It was the closest village, and consequently the closest pub, but I was sure they were aware of the publican's other activities.

"Shall I escort you home?" Jack asked.

"Yes. I suppose that would be best." I felt dissatisfied somehow, and not ready for this exhilaration to end. I forced a bright smile, snatched up my pelisse and bonnet, and reached for his hand. "But let's walk. Through the gardens," I added, arching my eyebrows in challenge, before pulling him through the door after me. I knew such a venture was risky, but I didn't care. Besides, what were the chances that someone from Greenlaws would see us?

But Jack felt differently. "I don't think that's a good idea," he protested, though I could tell it was half-hearted at best.

"Of course it is."

He laughed. "Ella, you're excited from the thrill of escaping danger. That's understandable. But that doesn't mean you shouldn't still use your common sense."

"Oh, don't be such a wet blanket. We're just going for a stroll," I teased, tossing him a flirtatious glance over my shoulder.

I hurried us onto the path leading through the arbor where I'd encountered him that day almost a fortnight ago. But that's where Jack's good-natured cooperation ceased.

He pulled me to a stop and turned me to face him. "Ella, we can't. And you know it."

His bronzed skin was dappled with the sunlight shining through the trellis, and his dark hair curled about his head in wind-blown disarray. I wasn't sure if it was his roguish disorder, or the scent of the clematis vines above us, or my own reckless elation—perhaps it was all three—but I arched up on my toes and kissed him.

At first, Jack seemed surprised. I'd never initiated our

embraces before. But he swiftly recovered, pulling me into his arms and deepening the kiss. I smiled against his mouth, until the sweep of his fingers over the back of my neck fractured all my other thoughts, focusing them solely on his touch.

When he pulled back, I found I had one hand in his hair while the other gripped his jacket lapel. However, his gaze was fastened beyond me, and I suddenly realized we weren't alone. I turned my head slowly to see Robert standing at the opposite end of the arbor.

I released Jack and stepped back, but I knew it was too late. Robert had seen us. I had no way of knowing how long he'd been standing there, but he had certainly witnessed at least part of our kiss. Hot shame flooded me, filling my cheeks. I glanced at Jack, who stood still, watching me as if already certain of my next action. I opened my mouth, but no words emerged, until I saw Robert pivot and begin to walk away.

"Robert," I cried, knowing I had to say something.

He didn't stop.

"I'm sorry," I stammered to Jack. "I…" But words were useless. I shook my head and stooped to pick up my bonnet where I must have dropped it—the bonnet Jack had given me—before chasing after Robert. I would address whatever was between me and Jack later. First I needed to speak with Robert, to try to explain.

I emerged from the arbor to see the back of Robert disappearing through the archway trimmed into the hedges on the opposite side of the ash tree terrace. Lifting my skirts, I darted through another opening to the left, hoping I could catch him up by cutting through the rose garden. I weaved around the thorny bushes, their buds already clipped for the season, and hurried toward the ivory trellis spanning over the other entrance. However, the sound of giggling brought me up short. I swiveled to my right to encounter my second shock of the afternoon.

Kate leaned against the latticed wall of a small gazebo built into the corner of the garden, laughing as Harry leaned over to murmur something in her ear. I must have gasped or made some sort of sound, for they both looked up as one. I expected them to jump apart guiltily, as Jack and I had, but they didn't seem to care that I'd seen them. If anything, Harry appeared indifferent, but then I'd grown accustomed to his lack of concern for me or my good opinion. It was Kate's expression that cut me to the quick.

Her brow furrowed and her mouth tightened in displeasure. "Ella. Did you need something?"

"No." I shifted uncomfortably as they continued to stare at me in thinly veiled annoyance. "Actually, I was following Robert."

"Well, as you can see, he's not here."

"Yes. I know. I thought to catch him up by slipping through here." I fell silent, glancing awkwardly between them. I wanted to say something to Kate, to ask what she was doing with this wherry man, but how could I do so with him standing beside her? I didn't wish to embarrass her, but could she truly be consorting with such a man?

Then again, wasn't that exactly what I was doing with Jack? I flushed at the implication. No matter his birth and his education, he was now a smuggler. I should not be kissing him. And Kate should not be kissing Harry.

I tried to find the words to say this to her, but she cut me off before they came.

"Then you'd better hurry," she declared, turning her back to me in obvious dismissal.

A sour taste flooded my mouth at her cold demeanor, and I hurried to comply, as eager now to be away from her as she was to be rid of me. I glanced behind me just once as I passed beneath the trellis, to find Kate and Harry still watching me, their heads close together in whispered conversation.

I couldn't help but wonder if Kate knew what Harry was. Was she more knowledgeable of the activities transpiring in the outbuildings at Greenlaws than I'd assumed? I'd dismissed the possibility she was involved before, but now I wasn't so certain.

A weight settled in my chest, heavier than any that had fallen there before. Kate had always been my one true friend, the one person I knew I could rely on through thick and thin. But perhaps I'd been wrong. Perhaps I was a bigger fool than I'd realized.

I hastened away, knowing I was too late to intercept Robert before he exited the gardens. At the edge of the lawn, I stopped to look about me, uncertain where he'd gone. If he'd returned to the house I wasn't sure I wished to follow. It seemed wise to keep our argument away from the curious ears of servants.

I glanced toward the river, wondering where he'd been headed when he happened upon me and Jack under the arbor. Had he been on his way to the outbuildings? To inspect the cache of items I'd smuggled?

Not for the first time I considered whether Robert could be "Himself." I found it difficult to believe his presence so near the outbuildings so soon after our return from Yarmouth was just a coincidence. But then again, Greenlaws was his property. He didn't need an excuse to stroll through his own gardens.

I pressed a hand to my forehead, suddenly overcome with weariness. All the elation I'd felt such a short time ago had drained away, leaving me with an aching back from the tight restraint of the fabrics when they were wrapped about me and the beginnings of a megrim. It was time to return home. My conversation with Robert could wait. Maybe by then I would have a better idea of what I wanted to say to him.

Or at least a better idea of what I *didn't*.

Chapter 24

UNFORTUNATELY, ROBERT SEEMED TO HAVE changed his mind. I'd no sooner returned to Penleaf Cottage and settled into a chair at the kitchen table while Mrs. Brittle brewed tea, than through the open windows we heard a horse cantering down the road from Thurlton. Fearful that it was Watkins or one of the other riding officers, we scrambled to our feet. Mrs. Brittle shuffled to the front door while I dashed into Father's study to retrieve any bottles left behind from the night before. Fortunately, Father was closeted in his bedchamber upstairs.

When I returned to the hall, Mrs. Brittle shook her head. "It's no' that devil, but Mr. Rockland."

I stumbled to a halt.

"He looks fair worked up." She squinted. "Would ye ken why?"

The sounds of his heavy footfalls crossing the porch spurred me into action. I pressed the empty brandy bottle I'd found into Mrs. Brittle's hands as Robert's fist pounded on the door. I cringed, praying his banging wouldn't wake Father.

I pulled open the door to see Robert's scowling visage made red with either anger or exertion. "Ella, I must speak with you," he proclaimed loud enough for the people a mile away in Thurlton to hear.

"Yes, yes," I snapped, forcing him to step backward as I exited the cottage and shut the door behind me. "But not here." Before he could protest, I pushed past him, leaving the porch to circle around the house. I trusted he would follow.

"Where are we going?" he demanded. "Ella?"

I didn't answer until we'd put a decent amount of distance between us and the house. "Away from the cottage."

"Why? Because of your father? Maybe he should hear this."

I turned to glare at him.

"I won't mince words, Ella. Perhaps if he took more of an interest in your comings and goings this conversation wouldn't be necessary."

"Yes, well, if he cared to take an interest *many* things would be unnecessary," I snapped back. Having reached the edge of our lawn where it met the marshes and the path leading down to our dock, I pivoted to face him. "But things are as they are. Neither of us can change that now." I crossed my arms, frowning forlornly at Penleaf Cottage behind him. From this angle I could see that more roof shingles had fallen off the eaves over my bedchamber window, probably in the rainstorm a few nights past.

Robert smacked his riding crop against his thigh in agitation, reclaiming my attention. "Ella, I'm furious with you."

"I know," I replied in a more subdued voice.

"Why were you embracing that wherry man? How long has this been going on?"

I didn't reply immediately, not wanting to admit exactly how long I'd been meeting Jack, even when he'd only been the Lantern Man to me. But my silence spoke for itself, and Robert whirled away with an angry scoff of disbelief.

"I'm sorry, Robert. It wasn't something I planned."

"I respectfully offered you marriage. And I didn't argue when you said you needed time to consider. I didn't even press you for your answer, though I couldn't understand why you would need longer than a few days. I told myself you were just punishing me for what had happened when we were younger, to give you just a little more time. But *this*," he hissed, rounding on me. His lip curled in disgust. "What has become of you?"

"You couldn't understand why I would need more time?" I retorted, my growing outrage overriding any contrition I felt. "I can't believe you would think I would leap at the chance to marry you, as if I was still seventeen. As if you hadn't already trampled on my heart and my affection once before. I blindly adored you then, Robert, but I'm certainly awakened to your faults now. *You* did that. *You* were the one who opened my eyes. You can't expect me to blindfold myself now that you've changed your mind."

His cheeks crested with color. "Well, that doesn't excuse your kissing that wherry man."

"I never said it did."

He stepped toward me, pointing at the ground. "Do you know what a fool you've made me feel?"

Guilt flooded me at the pain I heard in his voice masked by his anger. Or was it simply wounded pride?

He turned to stare out over the marshes, his jaw working furiously.

"I'm sorry, Robert. I never intended to hurt you." I sighed, staring down at the tips of my boots where they emerged from beneath the oversized hem of my dress. "The truth is I needed the extra time to decide because I'm unsure of my feelings for you. We so recently reconciled. And with everything with Father…well, I thought you deserved a wife who wasn't marrying you out of necessity."

Robert's expression softened, though a furrow still marred his brow. "I thought we were friends again. Maybe not like before. Maybe not like when we were more than just friendly.

But I thought we were on our way to being so."

"Maybe," I answered vaguely. "But there are some things I must do first. Matters I must address before I can give you my answer."

Robert lifted his chin. "And the wherry man?"

I smiled tightly. "Has been a good friend." I opened my mouth to try to explain further, but then decided against it. Instead, I shook my head. "There's nothing more." There couldn't be.

His eyes searched my face, looking for something I wasn't sure I could give him.

The cry of a marsh harrier broke the silence of the fens, and I turned to watch its flight over the reeds. The sun had begun to set, casting long shadows across the overgrown lawn. Soon the crickets and other insects living among the fens would begin their nightly chorus, but for now the air was hushed and hollow, trailing its fingers lightly over the tips of the marsh grass.

"I'm going away for a few days," Robert said.

I looked at him, feeling something akin to alarm. The memory of what had happened the last time we were almost engaged and he had gone away still gripped me.

"When I return, I would like your answer." He spoke calmly, but there was an edge to his voice I'd not often heard him use. "I do not think that is too much to ask."

He was right, but that didn't stop the panic from surging through my veins, reminding me I didn't know what I wanted. I didn't tell him that, however. I merely nodded. "I understand."

Robert moved forward another step, and I fought the urge to stiffen when he lifted a finger to tilt my chin up. He stared down into my eyes, almost goading me, before pressing a kiss to my lips. It was brief, though not chaste, and it made me feel nothing. Not even the tingles I recalled his kisses inspiring when we were younger. But perhaps even more telling was the fact that the sight of him walking away did not fill me with either longing or regret. Just cold uncertainty.

I watched until he disappeared around the corner of the cottage without a backward glance, wishing I understood him. There had been a time when I thought I knew him as well as I knew myself, but I had been proven terribly wrong. I wasn't about to make that mistake again.

I heaved a heavy sigh and tipped my head back to look up at the deepening sky.

That's when I sensed him.

I turned my head as he emerged from the trail leading to the dock, and I tensed. "How long how you been hiding down that path?"

Jack wisely kept his distance. "Long enough."

"And you didn't think to announce yourself?" I demanded.

His eyebrows lifted. "Given the nature of the conversation and what Rockland witnessed earlier, I thought it best to remain concealed. It seemed revealing my presence would only hurt matters further."

I flushed. He was right. Any apologies and assurances I had made would have been futile had Jack suddenly appeared at my home. But, of course, if Robert *was* Himself, he must already know Jack was well acquainted with my home. It also meant his witnessing our embrace might very well have endangered Jack, and yet he didn't seem particularly concerned.

I crossed my arms over my chest in frustration. "Why *are* you here?"

He sidled a few steps closer. "I came to be certain you were well. To be sure you'd made it home without incident."

I studied him through my lashes, uncertain how to respond. He'd escorted me home numerous times before with the pretense he was seeing to my safety, but we both knew he was truly keeping an eye on me, making sure I didn't share information with anyone. This time seemed different.

When I'd pulled away from him in embarrassment at being caught kissing him and then chased after Robert I thought Jack would wish to avoid me. Instead, he'd followed me to my home and was now gazing down at me without the least bit of rancor to mar his expression. It all left me confounded. I didn't know what to think.

"Well, I have. Made it home safely," I clarified. "I was about to drink a cup of tea and retire when Mr. Rockland decided to pay his unexpected visit."

"I suppose you can't blame him."

"No," I admitted, though I wanted to point out that Robert could have spoken to me at Greenlaws had he not run away.

Jack turned to glance back in the direction he'd come. "So…we're friends?" His gaze locked with mine and I realized he was referring to what he'd overheard me tell Robert.

"Yes, I suppose so. What else would you call us?"

His eyes dipped to my lips and the air between us suddenly seemed thick with unspoken things. "We could be something more," he proposed in a deep tone that made my insides flutter.

But this time I kept my head about me, suspecting that what he was suggesting was not entirely honorable. And even if it was, we both already knew the answer.

"No, we can't."

Jack's expression shuttered and he nodded. "Get some rest," he instructed, shifting his feet toward the marsh path. "I'll contact you in a few days after I receive word of when you will be needed next."

To smuggle more goods.

Somehow in the tumult of Robert stumbling upon me kissing Jack I'd almost forgotten everything else that had happened that day. The realization was enough to make my head spin.

I pressed a hand to my temple and nodded, but Jack had already begun to retreat down the path to the dock, the reeds swaying in his wake. I didn't try to stop him, but I felt a twinge in my chest at his departure all the same.

Chapter 25

IN SPITE OF THE HEAVY worries weighing on my conscience, or perhaps because of them, I tumbled into sleep easily that night, too exhausted to resist. The morning was already half gone when I awoke and another half hour passed before I finally descended the stairs in search of some sustenance. As I did so, I noticed the door to my father's study stood open and I moved forward to greet Mrs. Brittle, expecting to find her straightening up after my father.

"Good morning," I began before stumbling to a stop upon seeing my father seated before his desk. Mrs. Brittle was nowhere to be found.

His face was wan and haggard, which in and of itself was not surprising after a night spent drinking, but there was something different this time. Normally his face exhibited at least some trace of color across the crests of his cheeks or about his mouth, but today even that was washed away. His red-rimmed eyes stared unseeing down at the papers strewn across the surface of his desk. He'd yet to lift his eyes to acknowledge my presence, and I thought to leave before he did, uncertain what this new development meant. But before I could take more than a step, he surprised me by speaking.

"Elinore, might I have a word," he murmured in a voice

ravaged by too many years of strong drink.

I stiffened. Father never called me by my given name. It was always Ella. Not unless something was very wrong or I was about to receive a strongly-worded scolding. Of the two alternatives, I thought I preferred the latter, given that the last two times he'd delivered news to me when something had been very wrong was to tell me of Mother's and then Erik's death.

"Yes, Father?" I inquired, approaching his desk.

He still did not lift his gaze, and I began to wonder if this was about my outburst two nights prior. That is, until I saw that he was clutching a letter. I leaned closer to see, wondering if Robert had followed through on his threat to inform Father of my recent activities. If he had, so help me, I would give him a tongue-lashing he wouldn't soon forget. Or perhaps I would send Father after him when he was in one of his more sullen moods. Maybe Robert would feel a bit more sympathy if he had to suffer one of my father's drunken, rambling rants.

But even at such an awkward angle I could tell the handwriting was not Robert's. It was too neat, too precise. Likely the work of a clerk or a secretary.

Father's hand shook, rattling the paper as he lifted it. "You wrote to the earl, your grandfather?"

My gaze darted to the letter and then back up to meet Father's eyes as he finally looked at me. Grandfather had replied?

"You told them about me."

It was an accusation, even softly spoken, and a slow trickle of guilt began inside me. "I told them you were ill and dying." Which was essentially the truth, and far easier to admit than the fact that my father was a drunkard who cared little what happened to me.

The letter fell from his grasp as shock radiated across his

face. Did he not realize he was drinking himself into an early grave?

I frowned. "When you're gone, your stipend will stop, and I won't have the income to house or even feed myself." I crossed my arms over my chest, gripping my elbows against the chill of that prospect. "I cannot afford to wait until then to fathom what I should do."

Father stared up at me and I could tell he was grappling with these thoughts for the first time. That realization snapped something inside me. How could he be so oblivious to everything around him? How could he be so selfish that he hadn't given any consideration to his daughter's future?

I bit my tongue against the hot words I wanted to say to him, but I did not try to mask the fury I felt, and Father saw it. His brow furrowed in answering anger.

"Well, the earl has responded true to form. The heartless wretch has offered to find you a position as some thankless dowager's companion, an unpaid drudge. But, here…" he thrust the letter at me "…you can read it for yourself."

I snatched up the crisp vellum, feeling my heart sink at his pronouncement. I'd been prepared for such an eventuality, or at least I'd told myself I was. But it was evident now I'd been holding out hope that my grandfather might be eager to see me, and offer to take me into his home. I folded the paper carefully and stuffed it into my pocket, choosing to read it later when I was alone, especially after seeing the almost smug expression on Father's face at this confirmation he'd been right about the earl. I wanted to wipe it away.

"Well, at least he's offered me something," I told him. "That's better than starvation. And in this position I assume I won't be forced to hide brandy bottles from the revenue men."

I didn't stay to see his reaction, turning on my heel to march out the door. I hoped he choked on the knowledge that it might be the father-in-law he so loathed who secured his daughter's future and not himself. If he even thought of me at all.

I spent the next few days helping Mrs. Brittle about the cottage, doing my best to ignore the doubts and worries swirling inside me. I'd yet to reply to my grandfather or make a decision about Robert, and I was avoiding Greenlaws. Even though Robert was currently away, Kate was still home, and after her callous behavior during our last encounter I wasn't eager to see her.

So it came as some surprise when I looked up from the patch of carrots I was tending in the garden one morning to see her standing on the opposite side of the gate. I didn't know how long she'd been watching me, but I suspected it wasn't long. Patience had never been one of Kate's virtues.

She shook her head. "Really, Ella. That bonnet is atrocious. I much prefer the one you were carrying the other day."

Her comment startled a smile out of me because it was so typically Kate. I pushed to my feet, dusting dirt off my apron and the front of my dress.

"Yes, well, not everyone dresses smartly for gardening. After all, someone must do the dirty work."

She smiled. "True."

I regarded her across the distance between us, making no move to inch closer. Surely she didn't think matters between us could be made better by a simple quip. It was reassuring to hear her familiar banter, but the awkwardness between us over the past week and more couldn't be ignored.

Kate seemed to sense this, for her smile faded. She reached out to run an elegantly gloved finger over the chipped paint of the fence. "Do you have a moment for us to speak?"

I studied her face beneath the pale pink blossom-colored

brim of her bonnet, undoubtedly crafted to match her sarsenet gown trimmed with tufted Chinese silk fringe. Another special order procured by Captain Haywood, perhaps?

"Of course."

I removed my apron and gardening gloves and draped them over the fence before joining Kate on the other side. We strolled silently toward our lone bench tucked between two rose bushes on the far end of the fence line opposite the sycamore tree. Like Greenlaws' bushes, the buds had already been clipped, but the perfume of Mrs. Brittle's oxlips still scented the air.

The prospect from the bench was nothing to admire, most of it being blocked by the untrimmed reeds and marsh grasses behind our house, but at least we weren't facing the weathered boards of the cottage. It had been one of my mother's favorite places to sit and read, and many a night from my window I had spied her and my father seated there, their heads tilted toward each other. Therefore I usually avoided it, not wanting to dredge up those memories, but today I wished to avoid the sparse rooms of the house more.

We sat side by side, Kate in her fashionable frock and me in my drab, dirt-smeared hand-me-down, and at first neither of us spoke. In the years since my mother's death, as my situation deteriorated, I had rarely let the differences in my and Kate's circumstances bother me. The truth was she had always cared more about clothing and the latest fashion plates than I did. Of course, I had enjoyed beautiful dresses and hats and shoes, but I'd never needed to impress anyone. Robert had always liked me just as well romping through the marsh in an old, tattered dress as in my fanciest gown, and my mother had loved me the same in any light. She saved her scolds and disappointment for poor behavior, not for my appearance.

I knew Kate's life had not been so fortunate in that regard. Her mother, so beloved by everyone else for her sweet nature, had been impossible to please. No matter how Kate tried, nothing was good enough. Her naturally exuberant, fun-loving disposition seemed to be the opposite of the meek, compliant daughter Mrs. Rockland wanted. Somehow the only thing they'd been able to agree upon was clothes. Her mother might fault her figure or her posture, and her conversation and demeanor were never genteel enough, but her wardrobe was always impeccable.

Because of this I never begrudged her beautiful gowns, even if I did envy them from time to time as mine were patched and mended to last another season. That is, until this past week, for now I strongly suspected most of Kate's wardrobe was fashioned from smuggled goods. Did Kate know where the fabric that made her dresses came from? Did she care? And what of her bonnets, and gloves, and stockings? Before, I'd always thought she sent for items from London to supplement the items she purchased on trips to Norwich. Now, I strongly doubted it. Had I been more interested in such things I probably would have noticed sooner.

I was trying to think of a way to ask her without accusing her outright when she spoke.

"Why didn't you tell me about Robert's marriage proposal?" She turned to look down her nose at me in that annoying manner of hers, but I knew her well enough to realize that this display of indignation was meant to mask the hurt she truly felt.

"I meant to," I replied calmly. "That day I went looking for you in the garden."

Her eyes narrowed shrewdly. "When you met Jack?"

I didn't react to her goading comment. We would discuss that later. "Yes. Your brother had just asked me, and after everything that happened before, I believed you deserved the right to express your opinion."

"But you *didn't* tell me."

I frowned, staring at the amber tips of the reeds where they met the azure sky. "I didn't know how I felt about his proposal. I didn't know whether I was pleased or not. If I even wanted to say yes. It seemed like I should at least have some idea what *I* wanted before I spoke to you. And I *did* plan to speak to you before I gave Robert any sort of answer."

Kate's brow did not clear, but her shoulders did relax. "But that was over a fortnight ago. You still don't know what you want?"

I brushed at a stubborn streak of dirt on my gray serge skirt. "It's complicated."

Kate did not try to argue. She knew as well as anyone how fraught my and Robert's past was.

"Did Robert tell you?" I asked, curious if he'd been more astute and considerate of his sister than I'd given him credit for.

"No." She seemed reluctant to say more, though I wasn't sure why.

"Did you overhear us discussing it?"

"Not you." Her lips pursed as if she'd bitten into something particularly sour. "Robert and *Mister* Reynard."

A tingle of unease started at the base of my neck. "Robert discussed me with Reynard?"

"Yes."

I waited, sensing there was more.

Kate plucked at the fringe on her dress. "Because Reynard has been trying to convince Robert to wed his cousin Sophie. He has been for months."

I felt as if someone had punched me in the stomach. "The girl whom he bragged played the pianoforte so well?" I asked, recalling Reynard's comments.

"Yes."

I nodded. "And is Robert interested?"

Kate hesitated. "I don't know. I didn't think so, but…"

But I had made him wait for my answer, likely wounding his pride and exposing him to Reynard's venomous barbs.

She sighed. "I don't know."

I couldn't help but wonder where Robert was now. Where had he gone on this sudden trip? Would he return with a bride like he had four years ago? I supposed it depended on whether she fascinated him like Olivia had.

I shook away the bitter thought. I could contemplate Robert and the possibility that he was meeting this Sophie later. Kate didn't need to be torn between her brother and me yet again. But still…

"Thank you for telling me," I said, doing my best to mask my emotions from her. This would normally have been more difficult, but she didn't seem interested in analyzing my feelings. I watched her out of the corner of my eye, trying to understand her guarded demeanor. "Is that why you were so unfriendly when I caught you with Harry in the rose garden?" I had chosen my words deliberately to provoke a reaction, and she obliged.

"You did not *catch* us." She scowled. "There was nothing sordid in our meeting. We were merely talking."

"Oh, come, Kate. I saw the two of you together. There was more than conversation between you."

"And what of you and Jack?" she retorted. I thought I'd controlled my response quite well, but she laughed mirthlessly. "Oh, yes. Harry told me. So Robert isn't the only one exploring his options."

Just what had Harry seen? Jack had limited his more engaging comments and attentions to the times when we were alone, and I'd been careful to keep my distance otherwise. Had Harry seen through my efforts to remain indifferent? Or had he followed us? The thought unsettled me.

"I admit Jack is attractive," I hedged. "But he's a wherry man. There can be nothing between us."

Kate looked away with a mutinous expression on her face.

"You do know that, don't you, Kate?" I leaned forward, trying to catch her eye. "There could never be anything lasting between you and Harry."

"Do you think me simple? Of course I know." She surged to her feet. "But you know nothing of the matter." Her eyes sharpened to glare into mine. "So leave it be."

I sat mutely, watching as she stalked off. The very fact that she had actually warned me away told me there was much more going on than a simple flirtation. Just what had Kate gotten herself into?

Chapter 26

AFTER MY UNPLEASANT ALTERCATION WITH Father over my grandfather's letter, I made certain to rise early enough each morning to collect the mail. I was rewarded for these efforts one misty dawn when a post-boy from the White Horse trotted up to the cottage. I took the letter and paid him the coin he was due from my dwindling supply.

Flipping it over, I noted Mr. Fulton's precise handwriting and crossed the drawing room to the small writing desk in the corner. For days now, I had been expecting a missive from our solicitor to confirm that the funds the smugglers had advanced me had been received and my father's latest fine had been paid. So it was with some relief that I slit open the seal on the letter and settled down to read.

However, the contents were not all that I expected. My directions and the money from the smugglers had been received and the fine taken care of, but Mr. Fulton had more to tell.

Another bank draft was also delivered to my office, in an amount slightly larger than that of the funds you had forwarded me with your directive to pay Mr. Winterton's fine. This draft also included instructions that I utilize much of the money to pay said fine. As I have not received notice from you or Mr. Winterton regarding any additional expected income, I thought it best to inform you of this discrepancy and request clarification on how you wish these funds to be allocated.

I sank back in my chair in shock. A bank draft? But from whom? And why?

I turned to stare blindly at a bright square of wallpaper where a landscape painting had once hung. Evidently, the draft must be from someone who both knew of our predicament and possessed the resources to pay Father's fine, but I had informed so few people, and no one who could afford such a thing.

My brow furrowed. But Robert was not stupid, and he certainly had more connections than I had. It wouldn't have been difficult for him to find out about the second fine, either by chance or because his suspicions were aroused. I readily admitted my behavior over the past few weeks had not been normal. As to whether he'd then taken steps to assist me anonymously I supposed remained to be proven, but I knew no one else who had both the means and the wherewithal to interfere.

I folded the note and stuffed it into my pocket before pulling my light cloak from the hook by the door and draping it around my shoulders. Mrs. Brittle looked up as I came striding angrily through the kitchen.

"Where are ye goin' in all this damp?"

"To confront an intrusive meddler."

I didn't give her time to respond, slamming the door in my

wake and not worrying for once if it woke my father.

I knew that Robert was still away on his trip, but I expected Kate would have some answers for me. There was very little that her brother did that she didn't know about. Olivia had been the ultimate exception. Kate might hem and haw at first, but eventually she would tell me the truth.

Despite the recent strain between us, I knew she would understand my indignation. After all, she had been the one who held me as I'd wept bitter tears and later raged when Robert returned to Greenlaws with Olivia as his bride. She had been the one to hold my hand through the long days following my mother's and then my brother's deaths when my father had been too consumed by his own grief to notice me. And she had vented her own share of resentments and vexations over the years—of how impossible it was to please her mother, of how her brother never took her side, of how her father merely patted her on the head and sent her off to play as if her concerns were silly and she was a brainless ninny. Whether she agreed with her brother's decision to intervene or not, I knew I could count on her as an ally at least in uncovering the truth.

By the time I reached Greenlaws House, my thin cloak was nearly soaked through from the cool mist while my temper was as hot as ever. I was certain I looked a bedraggled mess, but the Rocklands' butler didn't so much as blink.

"Is Miss Rockland at home?" I demanded.

"Yes. I believe she's with Mr. Rockland and Monsieur Reynard in the drawing room."

I hesitated at this pronouncement, unprepared to face Robert, who had apparently returned from his journey. I'd not forgotten his ultimatum. I scowled. Well, that would simply have to wait. If Robert was home, then so much better I confront him directly.

The staff at Greenlaws rarely stood on ceremony where I

was concerned, and the butler did not do so now as I charged past him. I halted in the open doorway to take in the scene before me. It wouldn't do for me to start shouting if Reynard's beautiful cousin was present. Not that I'd ever seen her, but I was certain she must be lovely. And accomplished. And perfectly poised.

But I was relieved to discover she was not there, as I'd half-expected her to be. What did that say about the amount of trust I placed in Robert?

Kate and her brother stood across the room near the hearth. From the sharpness of their gestures and the harsh, hushed tones of their voices it was clear they were having a disagreement. One they didn't want Reynard, who was lounging in a chair near the door making no effort to feign disinterest in what was being said, to hear. He lifted his gaze as I entered the room, skewering me with the same sardonic amusement.

I ignored him and marched across the room to confront the Rocklands. Kate noticed me first, sparing me but a brief glance, and then a lengthier one as the fury in my expression must have communicated itself to her. Robert took longer to note my presence, as he was in the midst of pleading some impassioned point, caught up in his own heightened self-consequence, no doubt.

"Did you think I wouldn't find out?" I snapped. "Did you think I wouldn't know it was you?"

Robert's eyes widened and he glanced at his sister, who merely continued to scowl, albeit less ferociously. "Find out what?" he replied, pretending ignorance.

"Who told you about my father's second fine? Who relayed that choice tidbit?"

Robert's expression turned sheepish. "I…well…"

"Don't try to tell me you didn't know. Save me that insult at least."

He straightened as if I'd slapped him. "Yes. I knew."

I wasn't sure how or why my face began to heat, but it did. Evidently, I was still capable of feeling shame even in the midst of my rage. "And so you decided to pay it. There wasn't a pianoforte or a necklace for you to furtively purchase, so you decided to just send Mr. Fulton the funds outright. Well, I didn't ask you to do that!"

I could hear how ridiculous I sounded, how hysterical and ungrateful, but if I'd needed any confirmation, the looks on Kate's and Robert's faces would have done it. There was no need to glance at Reynard to know it would be the same, but I couldn't contain my outrage. Here I had been struggling to find a way to pay the fine and keep my father out of debtors' prison, even sinking so low as to resort to smuggling to earn the money, and all of this was at least partially done because I didn't want to be beholden to anyone, particularly Robert. So that I could consider his proposal without that impediment between us. But then he'd gone and done the very thing I'd wished to avoid. If I didn't scream I was afraid I would weep, and I much preferred anger to tears.

"I don't want your money, Robert! I never have."

Inexplicably, his expression softened and he stepped toward me, extending his hand. "Ella."

I backed away from him, not wanting to be placated.

He stopped, looking at me like he might a spooked horse. "I didn't send Mr. Fulton any money."

I stared at him, not knowing whether to believe him. "You didn't?"

Robert offered me a tentative smile. "No."

I frowned at him skeptically, beginning to feel doubt for the first time. I'd been so certain, because who else would have done such a thing?

I glanced at Kate, but she shook her head. "Don't look at me."

I didn't bother to suspect Reynard, which he seemed to

find humorous. "Aren't you going to ask me, Miss Winterton?" he mocked.

I glared at him over my shoulder.

"Mr. Fulton didn't say who the money was from?" Robert asked, recalling my attention.

"No." I stood stiffly in the middle of the room, feeling incredibly puerile after the scene I'd caused. "I'm sorry," I told them. "But after the pianoforte..."

Pressing a hand to my brow, I turned toward the window. Their denial had left me completely bewildered, and more than a little unsure of myself and my perceptions. Were they lying? But if so, why? Not so long ago, I would have thought it impossible for me not to be able to tell if they were being untruthful, but so much had happened since. So much that I couldn't help but wonder if I could really trust them to be honest.

"Ella," Robert said gently.

I looked up, surprised to find him standing so near.

He gestured toward one of the settees. "Perhaps you should sit down. We can ring for some tea." He nodded to Kate who was watching me with her arms crossed over her chest. I could read the concern in her eyes, and something else I couldn't immediately define.

She made to ring the bell to summon a servant, but I stopped her.

"No. I...I should go." I hurried towards the door, anxious to escape.

My hand was already on the front door when Robert caught up with me in the entry. "Ella, please stay. We need to talk. I..."

"Robert, please," I pleaded without turning to look at him. "Don't press me now. I can't. I just can't."

I heard him exhale, and when he didn't argue I pulled open the door and slipped out before he could change his mind and demand my answer to his proposal.

The late morning sun had burned off most of the mist on the higher ground where the house stood, but as I plunged downward into the marsh, the wispy vapors closed in around me again. Though not as substantial or disorienting as it was at dawn and dusk, or in the deep of night, it was still a nuisance, forcing me to move slower than I would have liked. I squinted against the brightness of the sunlight reflected off the white haze, passing in and out of patches of fog. One second it would be bright and clear and the next I would feel the mist condensing on my face, momentarily blinding me to much of my surroundings.

Now that I knew the Lantern Men were simply Jack and his fellow smugglers in costume, it seemed that I should be more comfortable passing through the fog. But apparently memory was long. I found my eyes scanning the haze and my shoulders inching upward whenever a small sound penetrated the silence. No matter how much I tried to convince myself there was nothing to be concerned about, just frogs and insects, my mind simply would not listen.

So when a faint light appeared in the distance beyond one of the fog banks, I stumbled to a halt. My heart had risen into my throat, and it took me several seconds to collect my wits. When I did, it was to scold myself for such foolishness.

"Jack," I called out crossly. "Is that you?"

But no one responded.

"Who's there?" I demanded. "Harry? Freddy? Is this some sort of jest?"

Still there was no reply, and the hair at the base of my neck began to stand on end.

"Stop it!"

The light seemed to move toward me all at once, and my breath caught. Why weren't they answering me? My feet began to scramble backward as I tried to decide whether to stand and face whoever this was or turn and run.

Just when I was about to shout at them again, the light suddenly vanished. I blinked hard, wondering if my eyes were playing tricks, and then a hand landed on my shoulder.

Chapter 27

I SHRIEKED AND WHIRLED AROUND TO face whatever was behind me.

"Ella! It's only me," Jack exclaimed, clasping his hands around my arms to keep me upright before I fell backward in my haste to escape.

My knees nearly crumpled beneath me in relief.

"Must you scream?" He pressed a hand to one of his ears and cringed.

"Must you sneak up on a person?" I snapped back.

He glowered in accusation. "You called my name."

"Why didn't you answer?" I pointed toward the path, now behind me. "And who's prowling around with a lantern?"

"It's daylight. Why would someone need a lantern?"

"I don't know. But I just saw one through the mist, over there." I gestured again, before standing taller to glare at him. When he didn't reply, I paused to consider what he'd just said. "You didn't see it?"

His glower turned puzzled. "When?"

"Just now. When you were *sneaking* up on me."

He arched his eyebrows at my testy tone. "I didn't see any lights."

I turned back around to stare at the spot I'd last seen it. Had

I imagined the whole thing? I discarded that possibility with a firm shake of my head. "No. I know I saw something."

"Probably a light from a passing boat," Jack offered in explanation. "Maybe the river is choked with fog."

I nodded, but I hadn't heard any boats or barges.

"What are you doing out here?" he asked, linking my arm through his and pulling me down the path toward Penleaf Cottage.

I pushed a damp lock of hair back from my cheek. "I was at Greenlaws."

"Ah," he replied in comprehension. His voice was tight. "Giving Rockland your answer."

I'd forgotten he'd overheard much of my and Robert's previous conversation. "No."

Jack looked at me in question and I sighed.

"As it happens, accusing him of rendering me aid," I replied in chagrin. "Probably falsely." As I'd suspected, it sounded as ridiculous as I'd thought it would.

His eyebrows arched again.

"Someone sent my solicitor money to pay my father's fine. Someone other than, or to be more precise, in addition to whoever Himself is. I thought it must be Robert." I frowned, still finding it difficult to believe it wasn't him. "I don't know anyone else who would have the motive or the means to do such a thing."

"But I take it he denied it."

"Yes."

"What of your relatives? Could one of them have rendered you aid?" he suggested, borrowing my phrase.

I glared up at him through my eyelashes. "Don't you think if that were even an option I would have asked them for the money first instead of getting involved with the lot of you?"

"I would have hoped so." His brow furrowed in thought. "But sometimes family are the most difficult to be beholden to, lest every favor, every mistake, every sin be tallied against you."

I watched him out of the corner of my eye, suspecting he was talking more about himself now than me. I shook my head. "It's not them."

He fell silent, though it was obvious he was still considering the matter, the same as I was. When he spoke, it was to voice the very question I was asking myself. "There truly isn't anyone else?"

I scoffed. "Not unless I have a heretofore unknown fairy godmother."

"Then it sounds like it truly must be Rockland."

I glanced at him, confused by the hesitancy of his pronouncement. "It does, doesn't it?"

Jack fell behind me, allowing me to cross a narrow section of the marsh path in front of him. Then as the trail widened again, he lengthened his stride to rejoin me.

As he did so, I exhaled a breath of pent-up frustration, making a decision. "In the end, I guess it doesn't really matter who sent it. It will still have to be returned."

"Why?"

I repaid his scowl with one of my own. "Because I'm not keeping money given to me by Robert or anyone else. I'll not be beholden to them, especially when I don't know whether accepting the gift will later prove to have strings attached."

"Don't be stupid, Ella."

I stumbled to a stop, shocked by his derisive words.

He glared down at me. "This is your chance to repay part of the loan Himself gave you, to extricate yourself from this entire sordid affair and move on with your life. Why would you pass that up?"

I didn't know how to reply. Part of me recognized that what he was saying made some sense. If I kept the money, I would no longer feel this gripping fear about how we would survive another year. Father's fine would be paid and I would have a bit of money set aside to settle a few more debts and replenish our larder. Though it was still unclear at what cost.

But another part of me only heard that he was ready to be rid of me, to wash his hands of my annoying interference and be on his way. It was silly and absurd, and yet I felt his careless words squeeze my heart like a vise.

"It…it's a matter of principle," I replied, stumbling over my words.

"Principle," he scoffed, "will not save you from transportation—or worse, the noose—should you be caught." He moved a step closer to loom over me. "It will not keep you safe from the smugglers you've chosen to associate with."

My fury rekindled at his blatant attempt to intimidate me. "Do you think I don't know that? Do you think I haven't considered keeping the money even though I know it would place me right where I didn't want to be—in Robert's debt?" I turned away, incensed that he didn't seem to understand, and disturbed that he seemed so anxious to be done with me.

"Besides…" I whirled back to face him, cutting off whatever he was about to chide me with next. "The chances of Himself allowing me to pay back my loan and leave his crew are minuscule. *You* told me yourself there was no turning back."

"Except you're not even going to try," he snapped back. "He could be reasonable."

But I could tell from the look in Jack's eyes that even he doubted that assertion.

"And if I anger him?" I demanded. "Can you guarantee Himself won't retaliate?"

His mouth clamped into a tight line, giving me all the answer I needed.

I crossed my arms over my chest and began to move off into the haze still surrounding us. He didn't try to follow me,

merely allowed me to disappear into the mist to face whatever was beyond it on my own. I clutched my arms tighter
around me, trying to squash the hollow ache inside me.

Upon returning to Penleaf Cottage, I sat down to write
Mr. Fulton to tell him to return the second bank draft, just
as I'd told Jack I would. Perhaps my refusing the money was
the height of foolishness when we needed it so desperately,
but I simply couldn't stomach the alternative. However, I
didn't reject the money without also attempting to uncover
the benefactor's name, if our solicitor even knew it. I appreciated Mr. Fulton's courtesy in trying to shield me from any
unpleasantness that might arise from my knowing such a fact,
but I needed to know the full truth, no matter how much it
might wound me.

I didn't venture out into the marshes or to Greenlaws the
next day, not yet ready to confront Jack after our argument,
and too confused and frustrated to face either Kate or Robert after my behavior the day before. I still suspected Robert
was the one who had sent the second bank draft, despite his
denials. Which meant any interaction between us would be
strained and awkward until I uncovered the truth of the matter.

So the following morning when a servant from Greenlaws
arrived with a letter, my first thought was that it might be
an explanation. Robert never had been very good at making
apologies, preferring to issue them by letter. However, when
I turned the letter over to examine the handwriting, I could
see it was written in Kate's elegant script, not Robert's messy
scrawl. Perhaps she was writing with the answers I sought
instead.

Unfolding the paper, I crossed the drawing room to sit at

the writing desk. Sunshine streamed through the windows to spill across the floor, making the room feel a little less stark.

But rather than an explanation, I discovered the letter was an invitation to dine that evening, several hours later than usual. It seemed an odd departure for Robert to make from his normal schedule, but perhaps this was Reynard's influence at work. He did perpetually complain about Robert's insistence on keeping country hours.

However, that wasn't the only thing that seemed peculiar about the note. Its wording was also rather adamant. In fact, it read more like a summons than a request. After reading through the short note a second time, I realized why it sounded so jarring. These weren't Kate's words—her lyrical, exuberant commentary. The contents had clearly been dictated to her by someone. Robert, no doubt.

A disquieting feeling settled over me. Why hadn't Robert penned this invitation himself? Or why hadn't he trusted his sister to invite me in her own way, as was usually done? It didn't make sense.

My gaze fell on the bare spot across the room where my mother's pianoforte had once stood. Maybe Robert was as cross with me as I was him, tired of waiting for my answer to his marriage proposal. After all, I had fled without giving him an answer. Though how I was supposed to give him one when I presumed he wasn't being truthful about that second bank draft, I didn't know. Perhaps this was my chance to broach the matter again, more gently this time. Maybe then he would admit his part.

I read through the letter one last time and nodded. Yes, that seemed sensible. Regardless of whether I was satisfied with his response to my questions or not, I recognized that Robert deserved to have my answer. He had waited long enough. But that did not mean I knew exactly what I was going to say.

I was preparing to set out across the marsh in my lavender sprig gown with my mother's brooch affixed firmly to the bodice when the Rockland carriage suddenly appeared at our door. Having not expected such a courtesy, the sight of the conveyance gave me pause. But then I realized how silly I was being. The hour was growing late. It was only right that Robert should send his carriage for me. I climbed inside and settled back against the plush squabs.

The ride was blessedly short, and I breathed deep of the cooler evening air as the footman assisted me down from the carriage, trying to settle the nerves that had suddenly begun to flutter in my stomach. The summer sun now hung low in the west. It had been a day of piercing blue skies, the type that heralded a brilliant twilight to come. There would be no drowsy fade from day into night, not in this part of Norfolk, but a swift bleed of light and color into crisp darkness, as if a knife had been sliced across the sky to drain the heavens. I had witnessed many such sunsets here among the Broads, and they were rarely a portent of anything good.

The butler nodded his head in greeting. "Good evening, Miss Winterton."

I replied in kind as I preceded him through the door where I then paused, glancing toward the drawing room. After the formality of being procured in the carriage it seemed wrong somehow to proceed without being announced, or at the least directed to. In any case, it appeared my hosts had different plans.

"Mr. Rockland asked that I show you into the billiard room," the butler informed me. "If you would please follow me."

I hesitated, somewhat unsettled by this second departure from routine. Clearly sensing it, the butler smiled encouragingly, as he'd done when at age seventeen I had arrived at Greenlaws for my first dinner party with nerves fluttering in my stomach. I returned his smile with a grateful one of my own and forced my feet into motion. If Robert's design for this evening was to press his suit and ask for my answer—and the billiard room was as private a place to do it as any—then the staff must have suspected something of his intentions. Whether this pleased them or not I didn't know, but after the unhappy uproar Olivia's presence had wrought, I guessed they would welcome someone familiar. Someone who was not likely to ask them to change their ways, or threaten to replace half the staff with outsiders from London, of all places.

We crossed the hall toward Robert's study, passing beneath the large glass chandelier, its crystals tinkling lightly together in a stray cross breeze. My eyes lifted toward the merry sound, only to catch sight of Kate standing in the shadows at the top of the wide staircase. Her expression was pensive as she watched me, and it stirred up all the anxieties I'd only recently quieted. She did not call out a greeting, so I remained silent as well, wondering why she did not approach.

We passed through the study to the door standing open on the opposite side of the room. This led directly into the billiard room positioned in the back corner of the house. In truth, the chamber acted as more of a masculine parlor, where the men had often gathered to smoke and drink port when they did not wish for female company. The billiard table for which the room was named only took up half of the space, while the other side boasted a rather unattractive collection of furnishings in various shades of brown. They had clearly been chosen for comfort rather than style, as had everything else. Though I couldn't understand how the atrocious painting of a hunting scene—complete with dead geese and rifles—that graced the wall above the hearth could be termed comfortable.

I expected to find Robert waiting for me there alone. But once again I was mistaken.

Robert stood staring out through a pair of open French doors at the lawn and river beyond, and next to him slouched Reynard, his elbow propped negligently against the door he leaned against. Did the man never sit or stand with proper posture?

When the butler announced me, Robert whirled around guiltily, as if he'd been caught doing something he shouldn't, while Reynard merely glanced over his shoulder. His lack of concern was nothing new, but the avid gleam in his eyes made me wary.

"Ella," Robert murmured as the butler retreated. He shuffled toward me, as if he wasn't certain whether I would welcome his approach. "You received Kate's note."

"Yes," I replied, wondering at his inane comment and his breathless tone.

"Good, good," Robert answered, awkwardly taking my hand and bowing over it.

My gaze returned to Reynard, who was now smiling his smug little smirk. I narrowed my eyes in dislike even as I allowed Robert to draw me farther into the room.

"Miss Winterton." Reynard lowered his arm and turned to greet me with a nod of his head.

"Mr. Reynard." I refused to address him correctly. Not when he was so clearly relishing whatever was about to come.

I stood between the two men, looking back and forth between Reynard's annoying sneer and Robert's wide-eyed fidgeting, waiting for one of them to end this dreadful anticipation.

"I suppose you're wondering why I asked you here," Robert finally said.

Stifling a huff of growing irritation, I voiced my first suspicion. "Is this about Sophie?"

Robert's face crinkled in momentary confusion, while Reynard chuckled softly.

"My cousin? No, Miss Winterton." Reynard's voice was almost mocking, and I soon learned why. "This has nothing to do with any romantic entanglements." His gaze flicked toward Robert. "Or at least no current ones."

Robert's mouth flattened into a thin line.

I frowned in confusion, but before I could voice any of the questions forming in my head, Reynard abruptly turned away.

"Come," he ordered, moving out through the French doors onto the lawn.

I stared after him, slowly comprehending he actually expected me to follow. And from the way Robert was looking at me, he did also.

"Truly?" I asked Robert in appalled amusement.

The corner of his eye twitched as he nodded. "Yes."

Any humor I felt at the absurdity of the situation quickly fled, and my brow furrowed in affront and bewilderment. I couldn't believe what I was witnessing. Robert was actually going to allow his late wife's cousin to order me about like a lap dog, directing me out into the lengthening shadows of dusk. I opened my mouth to protest, but my words faltered upon examining the look on Robert's face more closely.

He was terrified, or at the very least thoroughly intimidated. But from the rounded shape of his eyes and the tightness about his mouth, it looked much more like fear to me.

The trickles of unease I had felt running through me since receiving Kate's dictated invitation suddenly merged into something much more malevolent. I stared at Reynard's back, for he'd yet to turn to look at us, and wondered what power he could possibly hold over Robert that would cause such dread, such obedience. What influence could he have?

And then I knew.

Somewhere in the back of my mind the thoughts and impressions I had been gathering began to coalesce, forming a horrifying picture. One I should have seen sooner. One I should have guessed.

I jumped when I felt Robert's hand wrap around my arm, gently but insistently urging me forward. "Come."

I knew I had no choice. Should I choose to resist, Reynard would force me, and Robert would stand by and do nothing. I glanced around us at the fading daylight. If I tried to run, I had no doubt I would be stopped, perhaps by some of the other smugglers, maybe even Jack, probably now hiding just out of sight. Disillusionment and dismay flooded my mouth with their bitter taste.

Falling into begrudging step with the two men, I allowed them to lead me through the gardens and down to the river. It was evident now that Reynard had been the one to force Kate to write that invitation. He was the one truly in charge at Greenlaws, not Robert. But for how long? And why hadn't I noticed it before?

For most of our trek, Reynard ignored me, but once the watchmen's shelter came into view, I felt his eyes settle on my face, prodding me with his sharp delight. I refused to give him the reaction I knew he was looking for. I would not squirm for him like a worm on a hook. He would just have to search for his malicious gratification elsewhere.

It wasn't until Robert opened the door to the shelter and Reynard ushered me inside with a swift shove to my back that I realized inciting him had perhaps not been the wisest thing to do.

The other smugglers were all gathered there around the firelight in the hearth much as they had been the first time I'd met them, save that Harry perched on the edge of a table while Jack leaned against the wall beside him. Their rough voices fell silent as they took in the sight of first me, and then Reynard and Robert following close behind.

Jack's gaze met mine, and he slowly straightened to his full height. There was a question in his eyes, one that could not be so easily answered with a simple shake of the head. I didn't move toward him as I wished to, sensing that to do so would only show a fatal weakness. Instead, I shuffled through the dust and dirt scattered across the wooden floor toward the opposite side of the room, as far away from Reynard as I could manage, while the other smugglers muttered to one another in curious speculation.

"It appears Miss Winterton has a mysterious benefactor," Reynard began, his voice ringing with disdain. "One who desires to pay her father's fine."

I stiffened, wishing I had kept my suspicions about the second bank draft to myself. Wishing I had not charged into the Greenlaws drawing room two days ago and flung my accusations at Robert, especially in front of Reynard. If only I'd known, if only I'd had the foresight to see this knowledge would be used against me.

As a weapon, it proved quite effective. Reynard's words dropped into the silence of the room like a pebble pitched into a well, and I could see their effect rippling across the smugglers' faces, first in shock, then in suspicion. One by one their features turned to stone.

Reynard's eyes sparkled with malice. "And have you uncovered who this benefactor is? Has he bought your loyalty…" his gaze drifted insultingly down my body "…as perhaps he's bought the rest of you?"

Lifting my chin, I stared at him defiantly, even though inside I was quaking, desperate not to reveal my fear. For I'd fully grasped just how much danger I was in. And just how little chance I had of escaping. "No. I don't know who it is," I replied, doubtful that any of them would believe me. "I still thought it was Robert."

My eyes flicked to Robert, who would not meet my gaze, and then to Jack, in challenge. How much more hostile would Reynard be if I'd listened to Jack and written to "Himself" asking to repay my loan?

As if reading my thoughts, Reynard began to stalk toward me. "Let me guess. Did you think to use this…*unexpected* windfall to your benefit? Did you think to repay *my* loan and end our association?" His face hardened with anger. "You do recognize who I am?"

I scowled at his implication that I might be an idiot. "You're the man they call Himself," I bit out. My accusatory gaze slid beyond his shoulder to the figure still cowering in the shadows behind him.

"Very good," Reynard jeered, casting a glance back over his shoulder at Robert. "Though I am a bit dismayed you might have thought Himself could actually be Rockland." He smiled as if such an idea was preposterous.

I didn't correct him. I refused to. For though I had never seriously believed Robert capable of orchestrating such a thing, I had questioned how all of this could be happening on his property without his knowing. He was already wealthy. He had no need to indulge in such illegal activity. And yet here he was, smuggling with the French, the same nation who had killed his best friend, my brother.

I felt tears of anger and hurt and futility suddenly begin to gather in my eyes, and I turned my head to the side, blinking furiously.

"Ella," Robert murmured, speaking up for the first time. He moved across the room toward me.

I held up a staying hand. "How long has this been happening?"

Robert's mouth pursed like a petulant child. "Olivia started it."

Reynard's smile turned conceited. "Hmm, yes. My delightful cousin found her husband, or rather his land, extremely useful." His eyes flicked up and down Robert in distaste. "The rest of him, not so much."

"You put her up to it. You're the one who convinced her to marry me in order to run your little smuggling operation from my home."

Suddenly so much seemed clear. The reason for the rift between Robert and Olivia. Reynard's frequent continued visits even after her death. The rumors that Olivia had been unfaithful. Part of me wanted to feel sorry for Robert, to pity him for his wife's perfidy, but an even stronger part of me refused to. Not after he'd betrayed me and my brother so cruelly. Wasn't this what he deserved?

"But why didn't you stop it?" I asked him, trying to understand why he had let this go on for four years. He had even built these outbuildings to hide the activity.

Robert turned his head aside and clenched his fists, as if unwilling to face me or my questions.

Reynard moved closer, almost taunting him. "Because once he realized he'd committed treason he really had little choice."

My neck snapped around to stare at Reynard, and I realized too late this was exactly what he'd been waiting for.

"As have you, Miss Winterton."

My skin flushed warm and then cold. "I hardly think a few bolts of silk and a handful of gems will be given much notice," I bluffed, all the while knowing he had more to reveal.

Reynard's smile turned wolfish. "Ah, but those gems were bribes from French families for services rendered. And that special package wasn't just a book. It was coded messages from the French to their spies here in Britain."

I thought I might be sick all over his shoes as the full implication of his words hit me. "And the papers in the bag I passed to Captain Haywood? They weren't simple bank notes, were they?"

"No, Miss Winterton." The look in his eyes told me how much he was relishing every second of my shock and horror, drinking it in like it was the finest wine. He clucked his tongue. "I suspect the British government would be eager to hear about such traitorous activity." He dangled the threat before me, and then moved one step closer, reaching up to grasp my chin roughly between his thumb and forefinger. "But lucky for you, you are useful. *Very* useful. For who suspects a quiet little mouse like you of being capable of such treacherous things."

I stared into his dark eyes, seeing the bleak, soul-shriveling future he planned for me. However unwittingly, I had crawled straight into his web, and now he pounced, spinning his silken threats around me, securing my silence and compliance so later he could use me as he wished.

Was this what Jack had been trying to warn me of? Was this why he had been so frustrated when I wouldn't listen? Did Reynard hold something over him as well? Was he blackmailing all these men?

I dismissed that possibility as soon as I thought of it. Most of these men would sooner kill Reynard than give in to any demands that did not benefit them. I wished I was ruthless enough to do so—to stick a knife between his ribs—but I knew I was incapable of such an act. And he knew it, too. He counted on it.

That realization filled me with rage. Why hadn't Robert resisted? Why hadn't Jack? Every ounce of me rebelled at letting Reynard have his way.

"You're bluffing. If you inform the government about me you risk exposing your entire operation." I pulled my chin from his grasp, though it hurt to do so. "Questions will be asked, and I won't remain silent."

If possible, Reynard's eyes only glittered brighter in the firelight, clearly appreciating the challenge I was offering. "Will they?" His eyebrows lifted. "Or will you be thrown into a dark hole to rot until your trial? If you're ever given one. After all, traitors are rarely shown consideration. Even an earl's granddaughter. And I doubt even your benefactor, whoever he is, would care to save you after he's learned what you've done."

I had no way of knowing if what he said was true, but even if that was not enough to sway me, what he said next was.

"And your father, well, he might have escaped justice this time, but what will he do when his daughter is no longer there to save him? When casks of his favorite French brandy are found on his property? That would be rather more condemning than that single bottle he was swilling at the church's anniversary dinner."

"You rotten blackguard," I spat back at him, knowing now who had been responsible for giving my father that bottle of brandy, even if he hadn't been the person to hand it to him. He had found my weakness and he knew it. Unable to face him a moment longer, I pushed past him, headed toward the door.

"Let her go," I heard him say. "She'll be back."

The words were like claws being raked across my soul.

Chapter 28

I THREW OPEN THE DOOR AND charged down the dock into the deepening twilight. I heard Robert calling my name, an odd turnabout to the scene that had played out just a few short days ago.

"Ella, wait!"

I darted into the orchard rather than the garden, hoping he wouldn't follow me, but I was not so fortunate.

"Ella," he gasped, grabbing my arm and pulling me about to face him under the dark branches of one of the apple trees. The sickeningly sweet perfume of their ripening fruit filled the air. "Let me explain," he pleaded.

"What is there to explain?" I snapped. "Your wife and her cousin blackmailed you into letting their treasonous smuggling ring operate on your property, and you weren't brave enough to stop them."

Robert's head reared back at hearing me state the truth so bluntly. Why spare his feelings? He hadn't spared mine.

"I had no choice," he argued. "If Reynard told the government what was happening at Greenlaws I would lose everything."

"Including your head."

He scowled. "Kate would lose everything. My servants and

tenants would lose their livelihoods."

"Does Kate know?"

I could tell he was growing angry at my lack of sympathy. "I suspect so. But we don't discuss it."

"I can't believe this has been going on for *four years*. That you asked me to *marry* you, intending to drag me into this tragedy without informing me of it." Then a thought occurred to me. "Why haven't you turned the tables on Reynard and reported him? Surely you have some contacts in London you could go to? Some legitimate business associates?"

"It's happening on *my land*, Ella. And as you said, for four long years. Who is going to believe me now?"

I realized then what I suspected I'd known for a long time: Robert was forever ruled by others. His father, his mother, Erik, Reynard, even Olivia—whom he thought he had wed in a fit of impassioned rebellion, but in all likelihood she had been in control of their relationship from the start, manipulating him to do what she wished. I even guessed that Robert had initially been drawn to me because I followed his lead. I did as he wanted. But in the end that had also been what had torn us apart. With his parents dead and Erik gone off to war, he had looked to me to guide him, but I couldn't, especially in my still grief-stricken state over my mother's death. Olivia and Reynard had seen that weakness in him and used it to their advantage.

He would never be able to free himself of Reynard. How could I expect him to offer me help in doing so? It was simply beyond him, and this both infuriated and saddened me. No assistance would come from him. At least, none that I would want.

I shook my head in frustration. "I don't have time for this. I must go."

"But Ella…" he protested.

I paused to glance back at him, knowing there was one way

to make him stop following me. "Robert, I cannot marry you. I will not," I stated more firmly and then hurried off into the darkness with only the moon and the orchard's neat rows of trees to guide me.

I sensed swiftly that I was not alone, but as I knew almost certainly who it was, I was less concerned and more agitated. At the far end of the orchard, I grew tired of waiting for him to catch me up, if in fact he even intended to do so rather than shadow me the entire way home, and paused to stare out across the road at the blur of fields and the lights of Greenlaws House in the distance. He took longer to approach than I expected, but eventually I heard the soft sweep of his feet through the grass behind me as he came forward to stand beside me.

"Just doing your job, I suppose. At Reynard's bidding?" I muttered in a brittle voice, wondering if he'd been tasked to follow me.

"No," Jack replied quietly. "Only mine."

I turned to look at him, wishing I could see his face in the darkness, wishing I knew whether he meant now or always. Though I didn't know why I thought seeing his expression would help. I suspected I might have seen him more clearly even before he'd ever allowed me to see his face.

"I suppose Reynard was only too thrilled when you informed him I wished to join his smugglers." I hated the sullenness that filled me, knowing I only had myself to blame for falling into his trap. I might not have created the circumstances that had necessitated it, but I had been the one to latch onto it as a solution.

Jack's head turned so that his dark eyes could meet mine, glistening in the moonlight. "I tried to warn you," he replied with more empathy than I would have been able to manage had our situations been reversed. The regret in his eyes was all that kept me from snapping back at him.

I sighed heavily. "Is there any more I should know?"

"There's always more," was his quiet response.

Weary and overwhelmed from the night's revelations, I shook my head. "I suppose it doesn't matter now."

"Don't say that." His voice was suddenly fervent. "It always matters."

I watched as the wind combed through his hair. "So how is Reynard extorting you? Or are you just motivated by greed?"

He glanced down at his feet, shifting his stance wider. "When I was a young man, I was careless, reckless."

"You aren't now?"

I could see the faint outline of the scowl he leveled at me.

"I believed that I and everyone I cared for were invincible. But…I discovered I was wrong." He paused and I could feel him gathering himself, weighing his words, trying to form them on his lips. "It was the evening before Bonfire Night. I had imbibed too much and so I decided it would be great fun to light the bonfire laid for the next evening a day early. But first I thought the kindling needed to be built up a bit higher."

I pressed a hand to my mouth, afraid I already knew where this story was leading.

"As you can guess, in my sorry state I did a rather slapdash job of it. It collapsed on top of me. After I'd already set it ablaze."

I gasped.

"Fortunately for me, my brother was there and he was able to pull me out. But then another section of the bonfire collapsed, trapping him underneath, and I was too inebriated to do a dashed thing." His voice grew sharper with each word he spoke. "By the time help arrived…and they were able to free him…" He swallowed audibly. "It was too late. He was…"

"Oh, Jack," I cried, wrapping my arms around him, trying to spare him from having to say the words. He remained stiff in my embrace, as if denying himself the comfort I offered. "How old were you?"

"Old enough to know better. Young enough to learn it's best to never take anything for granted." His arms slowly lifted to return my embrace.

"I'm sorry," I whispered into his chest.

"You shouldn't feel sorry for me. My brother is the one who deserves your sympathy, not me."

"Yes, but it obviously affected you greatly." I pulled back to look up at him. "We all make mistakes, Jack. All we can do is hope to learn from them."

His hand lifted to my jaw, brushing the tips of his fingers through the short tendrils of hair along my neck behind my ear. "Which is why I'm telling you. So you can learn from my mistakes."

I furrowed my brow, standing a bit straighter.

"You cannot go on shielding your father from the consequences of his actions."

I tried to back away, but he wouldn't let me.

"I understand that he's your father. I understand how that makes everything more difficult. But you are not obligated to sacrifice your life for his."

Finally managing to pull away, I whirled around, not wanting to hear this, not wanting to acknowledge his words or the deadly earnest tone in which they were spoken. Because I knew he spoke the truth. And sometimes the truth could wound. I supposed that was why we so often lied to ourselves.

"You've done all you can, all anyone could ask of you," he continued on relentlessly. "But now it's time to let him stand or fall on his own. You cannot allow Reynard to control you with this. You must escape while you can."

I reached up to swipe at the wetness on my cheeks, realizing I was weeping. "But the charges of treason?" I whispered.

Jack turned me gently to face him. "Was a bluff," he pronounced with such certainty. "He knows he risks too much by exposing you."

I wanted to believe him, but my insides still quavered at the thought of facing possible arrest, of leaving my father open to Reynard's wrath.

Jack gripped my shoulders. "You need to get away from here."

"But I have nowhere to go."

His eyes studied my face as I clung to his upper arms, feeling as if I might suddenly fall apart if he released me.

"What if I found you a place?"

I began to shake my head. "Jack—"

"If it were safe. If it were secure. Would you go?"

I stared up at him in astonishment. What was he saying? What did he mean? "I don't know," I admitted honestly.

He inhaled as if shouldering a heavy burden. "Then we shall just have to address that when it becomes necessary."

It was so autocratic, so like something my father or his friends would have said when they visited us before my mother's death. I felt my curiosity awaken. I searched his face, studying him as I sifted through memories and impressions. "Who are you?" I couldn't help asking, thinking maybe this time he would trust me.

At first he didn't respond, and I waited patiently, hoping the fact that he hadn't immediately dismissed me was an encouraging sign. But when he spoke it was only in more riddles. "People are not always who they wish they could be."

I frowned. "I don't understand."

His lips curled into a wistful smile. "I know."

I opened my mouth to ask more, but he stopped me with a kiss. This time I didn't fight it or spare a thought for Robert or anyone else. I simply gave myself over to it, letting it overwhelm me. He was strong and warm, and his mouth tasted like whiskey. My knees went weak, and I could almost feel my bones dissolving under the ministrations of his tender touch.

I knew it was dangerous to let myself rely on him in any way, but I couldn't seem to help myself. I was already too much on my own, and his words, his presence were a heady comfort I couldn't seem to resist. He made me feel for the first time in many long months that I wasn't quite so alone. And that was more alluring than any kiss.

During the next few days I avoided Greenlaws, which was beginning to become something of a habit. Though this time, I also largely stayed away from the village, worried I would encounter one of the smugglers, or Robert, or worst of all Reynard, and be forced to accept what increasingly seemed to be inevitable. Would Jack find a safe place for me and Mrs. Brittle, who I refused to leave behind after all her care and loyalty? Would I be able to abandon my father to his fate?

Those questions weighed heavily on my heart, and I spent long hours contemplating them as I sat on Mother's bench, staring out at the marsh. I knew what Jack and Mrs. Brittle had both counseled was correct, but the heart doesn't always accept reason, no matter how many times it's been wounded.

It was there that Mrs. Brittle approached me one midday, hobbling around the kitchen fence. "Yer father is callin' for ye. Shall I tell him ye've gone?"

I sighed and rose to my feet. "No. I'll see what he wants." More brandy, I suspected, as I'd dumped out the remains of his bottle from the night before.

Mrs. Brittle harrumphed in disapproval, but walked with me back to the cottage. At the kitchen door we heard my father bellow and shared a look.

"Dinna forget I tried to spare ye," she declared.

I followed the sound of Father's grumbling into his study,

where he was pacing back and forth behind his desk, working himself into an indignant fury. Before I entered I braced myself for whatever petty grievances he had decided to air today.

"Yes, Father. Here I am."

He rounded on me, brandishing a piece of paper. "What is the meaning of this?"

I frowned upon seeing the folds in the foolscap, reasoning it was a letter. Not this again. "Where did you get that?" I demanded. Since he had intercepted my grandfather's letter, I had been so careful to personally accept the delivery of all our mail, little as there usually was. Had the post-boy come late today?

Father's eyes narrowed in suspicion. "Ingles gave it to me yesterday evening."

I bit back a curse, wishing Thurlton's postmaster was not also its publican.

"Not that that should be any of your concern. Why is Mr. Fulton writing to you again? And who is Viscount Waveney?" He bit off the last two words.

I pressed a hand to my abdomen, attempting to quiet the apprehension gathering there. I wished I could read the letter. Just what exactly did it reveal? How much did its contents require I tell my father? "We were attempting to find a way to pay your second fine," I hedged. "As for Lord Waveney…" My brow furrowed as I tried to recall whether I'd ever met the lord who bore that title. "I have no idea why you mention his name."

The muscles along Father's jaw flexed and I realized he did not believe me, and that he was very angry. "Then why is he paying you such an exorbitant amount of money?"

I glanced at the letter, swiftly deducing that this Lord Waveney must have been the second person to send Mr. Fulton funds to pay the fine. But why?

I shook my head. "I don't know."

Father slammed his fist into his desk, making me jump. "Do not lie to me! What have you done?"

Shaken by his outburst, I couldn't find words. "I...I don't..."

His expression tightened as if in pain. "My own daughter." He scowled fiercely. "How could you sell yourself so cheaply?" His eyes flicked down to the letter. "Or not so cheaply, as it is."

It suddenly dawned on me what he thought the money had been paid for, what he believed me capable of, and I was momentarily stunned. Fury raced through my veins. "I'm not his mistress! I would never... I couldn't..." I spluttered. "How could you accuse me of such a thing?"

"Then why is he paying you? What else am I to believe after reading this?" He flung the letter at me and I fumbled to catch it.

While Father continued to glower at me, I quickly scanned the contents. Mr. Fulton had given no explanation for Lord Waveney's generosity, though he did inform me that the viscount had requested the solicitor keep his identity confidential. However, Mr. Fulton had felt his allegiance was to us, his clients, not this lord.

I looked up at my father, feeling his cruel allegations wrap around my heart like a cold fist. "I don't know Lord Waveney. I've never met the man, that I can recall. And I should have hoped you knew me better than to accuse me of such a thing."

Father didn't even react to my rebuke. "The viscount owns a large swath of land on the other side of the marsh, as well as Waveney Hall. It would have been easy for him to arrange to meet you."

"But he didn't," I snapped.

"Then why is he sending you money?"

"I don't know!" My voice strained with hurt and frustration. "But he knew about *your* fine. He designated that the money be used to pay that. So someone must have told him.

Someone *you* know."

Father sank down in the chair behind his desk. His expression was stony, and I realized he still didn't believe me, at least not completely. That insult drove the air from my lungs. After everything I'd done, after all my sacrifices… Just when I thought he couldn't injure me further I was proven horribly wrong. Again.

"Perhaps it's my fault. I shouldn't have let you roam so freely, with no need to account for your time. I should have found you a husband, so you wouldn't have grasped onto whatever you could." He squinted and nodded. "It's my fault."

"O' course it is," Mrs. Brittle proclaimed.

I turned to find her standing in the doorway. Her black eyes glittered with rage.

Father glared at her. "This is none of your concern."

"It is when ye slander yer ain daughter." She shambled into the room, favoring her left hip as always. "Drink has finally addled yer wits, 'cause that can be the only excuse for it."

"Old woman…" he warned, but Mrs. Brittle ignored his threat.

"Yer daughter has sacrificed everythin' for you." She stabbed her finger at him. "While ye sit around feelin' sorry for yersel', drinkin' yersel' barmy, she's scrounged and bartered and rationed to keep this roof o'er our heads and food on our table. And wi' no thanks from ye, only more grief." She flicked a disgusted look over him. "But 'tis no' enough. Ye have to drink that cursed French brandy and get fined no' once, but *twice*. And does that make ye even take pause? Nay! Ye heap it all on yer daughter."

Father's mouth was tight with irritation, but Mrs. Brittle ignored it, moving closer to stand over him.

"Do ye ken what yer daughter's been forced to do to keep yer sorry hide oot o' debtors' prison? Do ye have any notion o' what yer careless, selfish behavior has cost her?"

I touched her arm. "Mrs. Brittle, don't. He doesn't need to know."

She rounded on me, though her voice gentled. "Nay, lass. He does."

"Know what?" Father demanded. "What has she done?"

"She's joined up wi' them smugglers. And no' Ingles and his lackeys, but a band o' real scoundrels. Ones that'll gut a man and no' think twice."

His face paled and his eyes widened as he glanced at me, but I turned away, unable to face him and whatever thoughtless thing he might say next.

"Yer daughter is consortin' wi' the lowliest o' men and riskin' her neck to pay *yer* fines. So, *aye*! 'Tis yer fault. And ye can be sure Mrs. Winterton is heartbroken lookin' doon on what ye've done to her bairn."

Before Father could form a reply, Mrs. Brittle took hold of my elbow. "Come, lass. I'm sure yer father has some *drinkin'* to do."

I willingly allowed myself to be escorted out, but couldn't help looking over my shoulder to see how Mrs. Brittle's words had affected him. His face was turned toward the wall, his eyes wide and unseeing. It was an expression I'd seen many times before and I knew Mrs. Brittle was right. It would end in another bottle.

I wasn't going to wait around to watch it happen yet again. Mrs. Brittle didn't try to stop me as I headed toward the door, simply reminded me to take my bonnet.

I marched up the dusty road to Thurlton, veering right before I entered the village proper to follow the dirt path that led behind the shops and buildings that lined the main street. This way, hopefully, I could enter the churchyard through the back gate without being seen. The graveyard was silent, save for the faint sounds of Mrs. Clark practicing the organ inside the church and the wind rustling the leaves overhead.

I knelt before my mother's and brother's graves, clearing away the debris and trimming the grass growing in front of their gravestones by hand. When I had finished I sank back on my heels, wondering if I would ever have a home that was more comforting to return to than these two markers.

I bowed my head in despair, crinkling the paper in my pocket. I'd forgotten I'd stuffed the letter from Mr. Fulton there after Father threw it at me. Unfolding it, I read over the contents more closely, but I still didn't understand why this Viscount Waveney had sent me money. Was it a mistake?

No, that didn't make sense, for he'd specified how much of the amount was to be spent in the payment of my father's fine. I searched my memory for any recollection of him, but I still didn't think I knew him.

Perhaps my grandfather did. Perhaps the earl had contacted Lord Waveney, knowing he owned property nearby, and asked him to gather information about us. That made some sort of sense. If Lord Waveney had found out about my father's fines then maybe Grandfather had asked him to send me money on his behalf, hoping I would never realize it was from him.

But why? If my grandfather was as uncaring and spiteful a man as my father claimed, wouldn't he want us to know? And why hadn't he sent the money directly to the Collector of Customs and addressed a simple note to our solicitor explaining what he'd done? Wouldn't that be more logical?

I sighed, feeling the beginnings of a megrim gathering behind my eyes. The organist had stopped playing, leaving an odd hollow space at the end of each gust of wind. It was during one of these lulls that some sort of sound alerted me to the fact that I was no longer alone. I glanced over my shoulder to find Kate standing before her parents' elaborate gravestone several rows away. I was tempted to ignore her, but she was my dearest friend, and I was tired of this tension between us. It had gone on long enough.

Rising to my feet, I dusted off the knees of my faded lavender sprig dress and began meandering through the gravestones toward her. Her Pomona-green gown and spencer looked new, for I'd not seen them before, as did her tan gloves. Courtesy of the last smuggling run? I felt an uncomfortable stab of envy, suspecting the color of her ensemble would have complimented my green eyes and auburn hair, and that the slightly gathered sleeves and flared skirt might have given some sort of shape to my rather slight figure.

As I rounded the last gravestone between me and her parents' large monument topped with an ornamental cross, Kate turned to meet me with her hands clasped tightly in front of her. As I drew closer, I realized she was physically shaking with a fury that glittered in her eyes.

"How could you be so foolish?" she snapped. "How could *you* fall prey to him?"

Chapter 29

I STARED AT HER, DUMBFOUNDED. "YOU mean Robert?" I finally asked.

"No, you lummox. Reynard."

I studied her, trying to understand the source of all her rage. "So you know."

"Yes!"

"About the smuggling?" I clarified. "About *my* smuggling?"

She glared at me and then hissed, "Yes."

I scowled. "Then don't you think I should be the one who's angry, seeing as your brother, and apparently you yourself, have been complicit in Reynard's illegal undertakings for years?"

"Complicit?" She laughed humorlessly. "If you can call blackmail complicit."

"What did he threaten you with? Your brother?"

She turned her face to the side, glowering at her parents' marker. "Did you know that the first time Reynard visited I thought he might be interested in me?"

"You never told me that."

She inhaled a shaky breath. "It was soon after Robert jilted you, and somehow it seemed wrong to talk of potential suitors when you'd been so cruelly used. I thought maybe you'd be even more hurt."

I remained silent, knowing she was right. If I'd suspected for even a moment that I might also lose Kate to Olivia's family, I'm quite sure I would not have handled it well. Not when I thought she was all I had. What a poor friend I'd been for her to have to shield me from her excitement. And her pain, for it was obvious what was to come.

"He mocked and flirted, and I thought it so charming." She sneered, deriding herself. "I convinced myself he visited so often to see me, when in actuality he was there to oversee his…business venture. And tup Olivia."

I must have gasped for she looked up at me with a world-weary gaze.

"I saw them. And Reynard knew it. He actually *smiled*."

"Oh, Kate."

"He knew how I felt. I'd invited his attentions. And he'd continued to trifle with me for his own amusement." She shook her head. "How stupid I was."

"Did Robert know?" I asked quietly.

"About Olivia and Reynard? Yes. I went to tell him, but when he dismissed me so readily I realized he already knew. He just didn't want to admit it, let alone discuss it."

I nodded in sympathy, but I was still confused. "So Reynard threatened to make his affair with Olivia public?"

"No. He could have tarnished Olivia's and Robert's names irreparably for all I cared. My brother made the hasty decision to marry her while you were at home patiently waiting for him. His problems in his marriage were his own concern."

She began to pace in a tight circle. "No. Reynard is much more cunning than that. He had been listening to my chatter during those months I thought he was courting me, and he set his sights on the one person he knew I cared for most, the one person he hadn't yet tainted." Her eyes lifted to meet mine and I felt my stomach pitch.

"Me?" I guessed.

Her eyes gleamed. "He saw how I loved you. How Robert idealized you, especially as his marriage continued to sour. Reynard wanted you under his sway. But you weren't interested. I don't know if it was because your heart was still broken or you simply recognized him for what he was faster than I did, than all of us did. Either way, it infuriated him. So he sought to ensnare you another way."

"But you stopped him?" I guessed.

She nodded, her jaw set. "If I remained silent about the smuggling, about the spying, he would leave you alone."

I was astounded by her devotion, by her willingness to protect me even though she risked being charged with treason because of her silence.

"Which is why I'm such a fool," I murmured softly, finally understanding her fury.

"Yes." Angry tears streaked down her cheeks. "Why did you get involved with Jack? Why did you let him pull you into this?"

"He didn't. Actually, he tried to keep me out of it, but I...I forced him. I didn't think there was any other way."

"To pay your father's fine," she guessed.

"Yes."

"Why didn't you ask Robert for the money? He would have paid it."

I closed my eyes. Her raw emotion was simply too much to bear alongside my own. "I was going to. But then he asked me to marry him, and I just couldn't take his money unless I was certain I would say yes."

Kate sniffed on a brittle laugh. "What a noble pair we are."

I opened my eyes. She was right. And yet Reynard had found a way to use that nobility against us. It was sickening and terrifying all at once.

"I'm sorry, Kate. If I'd known..."

"If only I could have told you."

I reached out my hand to her, wanting to offer her comfort, but afraid she would reject me. I should have known better. She took my hand and pulled me into her shoulder, hugging me tightly. Her hair smelled of lilacs warmed in the sun, just as it always did, and it eased some of the ache inside of me.

We both sniffed as we released each other, and Kate reached up to push an unruly strand of hair back under my bonnet. Her eyes were still troubled, but gone was the uncomfortable rage and despair. However, I had one more question and I hesitated to ask it, afraid of upsetting her again. But if not now, when would I broach it?

"Kate, may I ask you one more thing?"

She met my gaze, clearly hearing the uncertainty in my voice, and then nodded.

"What of Harry?"

"Ah." Her lips curled in a tight smile. "He shares a mutual loathing for Reynard, and when I was forbidden from speaking to you about the smuggling, I found I still needed someone to confide in." She inhaled. "He became that person."

My heart pinched in jealousy. "But there's more."

She nodded slowly. "Yes. Or there was. We've been nothing but friends for some time."

I tried not to feel hurt. "Why didn't you tell me?"

Her eyebrows arched. "Why didn't you tell me about Jack?"

I glanced to the side, at a bundle of wild roses someone had left before a gravestone. She was right. I was just as guilty of subterfuge. "At first, I wasn't even sure he was real," I found myself admitting. "And then, I guess I didn't want to share him. I was worried…" I frowned and my voice trailed away.

"That someone would make you see reason?" she finished for me when I couldn't find the words. "That the joy and excitement and thrill would shatter and you'd be forced to give him up?"

I looked up at her, realizing she did understand. "Yes."

Kate looped her arm through mine and we turned to stroll through the churchyard toward the lychgate. The summer sun was high in the sky, falling warmly on our necks.

"Has he been worth the secrecy?" Kate suddenly asked, dabbing the corners of her eyes with a handkerchief she pulled from her sleeve.

"I think so," I replied cautiously, and then with more certainty, "Yes. Yes, he has."

Her mouth curled into a tentative smile. "Well, at least that's something."

But was it? I admitted I cared for Jack, and perhaps even more surprising I trusted him, but what did that mean? Our relationship was hardly leading toward marriage. He was trapped as a smuggler, and I was facing a terrible choice: give in to Reynard's threats and join his crew, or flee Thurlton and leave my father to face the consequences. It was an impossible decision.

I pressed closer to Kate's side as we veered around a rosebush, trying to keep the thorns from catching on the worn fabric of my skirts. As I did so, I felt the letter in my pocket crinkle again and a thought occurred to me.

"Kate, are you acquainted with a Lord Waveney?"

"Not personally. Though I've seen his name mentioned in the newspapers from time to time. He's a commissioner or a Lord of the Treasury or some such thing." Seeing my surprise, her smile brightened. "What? I do read things other than fashion plates. Though admittedly I'm usually searching for the gossip column."

I narrowed my eyes at her flippant excuse. I suspected there was more to it than that if she'd gleaned that Lord Waveney was a Lord of the Treasury, but I didn't press her.

"Why do you ask?"

I explained about the payments my solicitor had received

on my behalf to cover the expense of Father's fine, the first from Reynard and the second from Lord Waveney.

"That is puzzling." Her brow furrowed in thought. "You're sure you haven't met?"

I shook my head.

"What of your father?"

I thought of his crude accusations. "He's not acquainted with him either. I'm sure of it."

We paused on the other side of the lychgate, preparing to go our separate ways.

"Well, I shall think on it." She released my arm. "If he's truly taken an interest in you, with his position perhaps he can help you."

"More likely he'll deny any association," I jested wryly.

"Yes, well, not every gentleman is as ignoble as experience has led us to believe." She frowned. "Or at least let us hope not."

Another day passed without incident, but I knew I could not go on ignoring Reynard's threats and demands indefinitely. It had been three days since I'd fled Greenlaws, and even though he might have given me time to accept everything he'd told me, he would not be patient forever.

Jack had not contacted me. I tried not to think about what that meant. After all, plans took time, particularly if they were secretive. His silence did not mean he had lied or changed his mind. But the fact had to be acknowledged—I had no immediate alternative other than to obey Reynard's orders. Even running to my grandfather, if I could manage to escape unnoticed, was risky. For if Reynard found some way to inform the earl of my part in the smuggling ring there was no telling how my grandfather would react.

Still, every inch of my being rebelled at the idea of giving in to Reynard's commands. I wanted to scream at the unfairness of it all, to lash out at God for letting this happen to me. Was no one listening to my prayers?

That afternoon, my time ran out. I emerged from the kitchen door into the garden and looked up to find Rory standing at the edge of the marsh. I wasn't certain how long he'd been waiting, but he leveled a hard glare at me and then turned to leave. It was clear I'd been summoned, though at least he gave me the courtesy of allowing me to follow behind him rather than escorting me to Greenlaws like a prisoner.

I glanced back at the door, wishing I could step back inside and pretend I hadn't seen him, but I knew that if Reynard was forced to send someone after me again I would not like the consequences. I exhaled in frustration and discouragement and followed Rory out into the marsh paths. Though he'd disappeared into the fen only a minute before, I never caught sight of the back of his scruffy red head, even when I emerged on the lawn before Greenlaws.

The butler led me through Robert's study to the billiard room in the back corner of the house, just as he had a few short days prior. I gritted my teeth as he opened the door, prepared to meet Reynard's smug visage, but his was not the first face I saw. Instead, I met the jaded gaze of a man I didn't know, who relaxed in a mahogany leather wing chair with one ankle resting across his opposite knee. In his hand, he cradled a glass of warm amber liquid, which he lifted to sip as he took in my appearance through narrowed eyes. His clothes appeared rumpled and travel-stained, as did those of Jack and Harry, who stood immediately to his right in front of the open French doors. Neither Jack nor Harry looked particularly pleased, and I felt a stab of apprehension upon seeing Jack's fierce scowl.

It was obvious I had interrupted some sort of discussion. Reynard sat at one end of the settee across from the stranger, smiling his sly, self-satisfied smile, while Robert sulked at the opposite end. Robert looked up at my entrance and glowered. Apparently, he'd not taken my rejection well. It was all I could do not to roll my eyes.

"Ah, Miss Winterton," Reynard drawled. "I see you've finally come to your senses. With impeccable timing as always."

I arched a single eyebrow at his statement, uncertain whether he was needling me or attempting to make a joke. None of the men seated rose to their feet or offered me a chair, so I clasped my hands in front of me and stood straight. It appeared I was being made to understand my place.

"Are you resigned to your fate?" Reynard asked me. Belying his lazy demeanor, there was a sharp glint in his eye that told me to tread carefully. He would not be fobbed off again by a display of shock and anger. The blackguard was determined to have his victory.

I could feel Jack's eyes on me, but I refused to look at him, not with the others looking on. He'd said that Reynard was bluffing about informing on me to the authorities, but facing Reynard's hard stare I trusted that assertion even less. In any case, Jack had not contacted me. So it appeared I had no choice.

I glared daggers at Reynard and swallowed the hot retorts that burned on my tongue so I could speak in as calm a voice as I could manage. "Until the loan is paid off. Until my debt is settled."

I could see in his eyes that we both knew it was a lie. Reynard would never let me stop. But my pride would not let me agree to anything else. I had to believe there was some way out, an ending to this terrible farce.

"Agreed," he replied with a nod that said he could afford to be magnanimous in this since he was getting his way in everything else.

The man in the chair beside him lowered his leg, recalling

our attention. "*This* is Miss Winterton?"

I stiffened upon hearing his thick French accent.

"*Oui, monsieur.*" Then Reynard turned to me with mock courtesy. "Allow me to introduce Colonel Junot." He paused for effect. "Lately of *la Grand Armée.*"

I studied the officer more closely. He was perhaps thirty and sported a thick head of hair and a well-trimmed mustache. Even lounging in ill-fitting commoner's clothes, he held himself with the haughty condescension of the privileged. His sneer fairly dripped with the disdain I perhaps unfairly attributed to the French, but the only frog-eaters I had ever met were Olivia and Reynard. The fact that their country-men had slain my brother, and their liquor was slowly killing my father, only made me more predisposed to dislike any French man or woman I met.

"I am beginning to doubt your proposed plan of action," the colonel told Reynard.

"Don't let her drab appearance deceive you." Reynard's eyes traveled up and down my form, making me want to cross my arms over my chest to hide from him what I could. "Once she's properly attired, our little sparrow will play the part admirably. Miss Rockland should own something more suitable she can wear."

I glanced around at the others, wishing someone would tell me what he was talking about. Robert and Harry would not meet my eyes, and Jack's mouth was clamped into a thin line. His gaze cut to the side and I felt the rebuff like the slice of a knife.

I scowled. "What plan?" I snapped, wishing I could tell Reynard, tell all of them, to go to the devil instead.

His lips curled. "It seems you've acquired a new lady's maid for your upcoming voyage, my dear."

I nearly snarled at his deliberately vague response. "Stop talking in riddles, Reynard."

He leaned back into the settee, crossing one leg over the other, and then gestured to his fellow Frenchman. "Colonel Junot needs to return to France. Post haste. And *you* are going to escort him there."

Chapter 30

ISTIFFENED IN SHOCK, BUT REFUSED to acknowledge the insidious trickle of fear spreading through me. Reynard couldn't possibly be serious. He wanted me to travel to France, to actually board a ship and leave England, with this strange man posing as my lady's maid?

I flicked a glance at the scowling colonel. "But he's…"

"A prisoner of war? Yes." Reynard tilted his head in satisfaction. "But not for long."

I'd heard the British government often granted parole to captured enemy officers, while the regular soldiers remained locked up in prisons and aboard floating hulks, but I'd never actually encountered any of those men. Thurlton was not a parole town, and one of the stipulations of an officer's conditional release was that he remain in the village he was assigned to. His sense of gentlemanly honor was supposed to keep him in place.

It was ridiculous.

How could anyone expect these men to not try to escape? To not attempt to return home to their loved ones? If, rather than dying, my brother had been taken as prisoner and then granted parole somewhere in France, I would have expected him to make every effort to return to England. I would have anticipated that he place his obligations to king and country and family above honoring a promise made to some foreign government.

So the fact that Colonel Junot was attempting to return to France did not surprise or unsettle me so much as the implication that I was being ordered to help him do so.

"Escort him...?"

"Yes, Miss Winterton," Reynard replied very slowly, clearly savoring my horrified expression. "Some of those gems you delivered. They were payment from Colonel Junot's family for services to be rendered. He is going to pose as your lady's maid and accompany you on your voyage to visit a sick family member in Amsterdam."

I paused to consider his words. "But we won't be going to Amsterdam," I guessed.

"Perhaps a storm blows your ship off course." He arched his eyebrows. "Perhaps you find yourself forced to land a little further west."

In France. In the company of smugglers and a prisoner of war. It was beyond scandalous. It was blatant treason.

My mind whirled with all of the implications. Maybe I'd known about the letters I'd passed to Captain Haywood; maybe I hadn't. Maybe I'd been threatened or manipulated by rogues and blackguards. But in this instance, there could be no doubt: I would be aiding an enemy of the British government to flee the country and return to France, where he would undoubtedly resume his command in their army and take up arms again, to kill and command others to kill British soldiers. Soldiers like my brother Erik.

That realization made my body go cold.

How could I possibly do such a thing? How could I even consider it? I looked to the other men in the room. Why didn't one of them put a stop to this? Why did they remain silent?

Robert had closed his eyes and pressed a hand to his temple, as if to block me from his sight. Harry at least met my gaze, standing sullenly with his arms crossed as he watched my struggle. But it was to Jack that my eyes looked longest, hoping for some assistance, some sign that at least he sympathized, but even he seemed determined not to interfere. He clamped his mouth shut and stared at me as if I was no one.

I tightened my hands into fists and fumbled for some excuse to stop this awful plot. "Colonel Junot will never pass for a woman," I protested. "He's much too tall. And his facial hair…"

"Can be shaved." Reynard glanced at the Frenchman. "He will slouch. And once we drown him in a shapeless garment with some strategic padding… " His gaze returned to me, scouring my figure once again. "And provide those revenue mongrels with a worthy distraction, he shall waltz right past."

"I don't think it'll be tha' easy," Jack murmured, finally speaking up.

Reynard shrugged one shoulder carelessly, unimpressed with his opinion. "It will suffice. You will *make* it suffice."

"But how will I return?" I persisted. "On the same boat? What if the revenue men notice my lady's maid is no longer with me?"

"Do not worry. Arrangements have been made."

"What arrangements?"

"For a lady's maid."

I blinked. "But who…"

He yawned aloud and flicked his hand as if to shoo a gnat. "Those details shall be discussed later."

I scowled, wanting to address them now. Who would be accompanying me back to England? Not a real lady's maid, surely? A smuggler in disguise? A French spy?

Or perhaps it would be a British prisoner of war? Maybe Reynard wasn't taking any sides in this contest. Maybe he was only interested in the profits.

It would clarify some of my confusion. After all, much of the Comte de Reynard's family had been killed during the revolution, and the wealth and property that could not be carried with them as they fled France had been either confiscated or destroyed. They had been left with their limited holdings here in England and a hollow title. If the *ancien régime* was restored and a king returned to the throne of France, he had some chance of regaining at least a portion of his former inheritance. So why would Reynard help the revolutionaries who had taken so much from him by smuggling information back and forth across the channel and assisting prisoners of war to escape?

Unless he was only motivated by greed. That would fit my assessment of his character thus far more than some hidden devotion to home and country. Reynard seemed loyal only to himself. The rest of us were pawns to be manipulated and moved around his chessboard.

And I'd unwittingly stumbled into his game. The only question that remained was whether I was yet another piece…or an opponent. Would I allow myself to be pushed about like Jack and Robert, or push back when the time was right?

Reynard rose languidly to his feet. "Before we discuss anything further, we have a more pressing matter to deal with." He straightened his cuffs as he crossed the room toward where I still stood near the door. His eyes fixed on the mirror hanging on the wall beyond my shoulder as he shrugged his shoulders in his fashionably close-fitting deep blue frockcoat, preening like a bird. "A matter of discretion. Of…reliance."

When his hand shot out to wrap around my throat, I barely had time to react. He yanked me closer, cutting off some of my breath, and turned his head to stare angrily into my eyes. "Now, Miss Winterton. Did you tell anyone about Greybar twenty-three?"

My heart pounded in my chest and my gaze flicked unbidden toward Jack.

Reynard squeezed harder and I gasped, trying to draw breath.

"Do not even think of lying," he bit out.

My mouth worked, but I could not make a sound until he slowly eased the pressure around my throat. I inhaled as deeply as I could, trying to calm the fear and panic rampaging through me, threatening to block all rational thought.

As I struggled to form words, Reynard's eyes flicked to the mirror on the wall behind me. "Do not even think it," he told one of the men in the reflection.

Out of the corner of my eye, I could see Jack retreat back a step to resume his position beside Harry.

Reynard fastened his hard gaze on me again. "Who?" he snapped, shaking me.

"Captain Haywood. And…" My mind raced. What if I shouldn't have shared it with Jack? What would happen to him?

Should I lie? Would Reynard know?

But I could tell that Reynard expected me to utter another name, and if I didn't the results would not be kind. Ultimately there was no other name I could give him.

"And Jack," I admitted softly, praying I had not just placed him in further danger.

Reynard's hand eased another fraction, and I realized he'd been anticipating that very name.

"He was part of the crew. I thought he already knew," I added, trying to rationalize my telling him.

He didn't respond to that comment, but continued to search my face. His thumb ran back and forth over the vein at the side of my neck. He must have been able to feel how fast my pulse was pounding. "No one else?"

I tried to shake my head, but his hand prevented me from

making such a movement. "No one."

His eyes narrowed as if weighing the truth of my words, and then his mouth curled into a vicious smile. "Good," he leaned closer to murmur, never taking his eyes off me, even when he pressed a swift, hard kiss to my lips.

Then just as quickly, he pushed me away, making me stumble back into the wood of the door. I lifted my hand to my throat, feeling the rise and fall of my chest as Reynard returned to his seat on the settee. Still dazed by what had just happened, my gaze lifted to the men standing across the room. I knew better than to look to Robert for any comfort, and Harry had never liked me, but I sought some reassurance from Jack. Instead, his eyes remained trained on the wood above my head, never wavering. My heart squeezed in my chest, and the pain was worse than anything Reynard had inflicted.

"You may go, Miss Winterton," Reynard declared without even looking at me. "We'll expect your return tomorrow after midday."

His cold dismissal barely penetrated the shock still holding me almost immobile, but somehow I managed to twist the door handle and turn to go. I closed the door carefully behind me and crossed Robert's study. Then without conscious thought, my feet led me out of the house and down the hill into the marsh. All I knew was that I had to get far, far away from what had just happened to me. Away from Robert's cowardice. Away from Jack's cold stare.

I don't know how long I walked that way, unmindful of my surroundings, but somewhere in the midst of the fens a voice calling my name suddenly penetrated the haze of my thoughts. I stumbled to a halt and turned to see Kate hurrying after me, her skirts fisted in her hands. She panted for breath as she opened her mouth to speak, but then her gaze dipped to my throat and her eyes widened. I lifted my hand to touch the marks that Reynard must have left behind, wondering almost idly if they were pink and red or black and blue.

"Oh, Ella," Kate murmured, reaching her hand out as if to touch them herself, but then she grasped my shoulder instead.

I let her pull me into her arms, reluctantly at first, and then more eagerly as I began to tremble and a whimper escaped my throat. I clung to her and wept as the waves of remembered terror at Reynard's actions and the heartache of Jack's callousness swept over me.

I'd never been treated in such a way, never been so violently handled or threatened, and it shook me to my core, especially knowing none of the other men in the room had done anything to stop it. It seemed Jack had started to, but then he'd backed away, cowed by Reynard's rebuke. What if Reynard had done more? What if he'd truly begun to strangle me in earnest? Would they have stood by and let him murder me?

I had trusted Jack. Had confided in him what I couldn't confide in others, had leaned on him when I couldn't stand on my own. But today there had been no warmth in his gaze when he looked at me, no defiance when he witnessed how Reynard had treated me. How could I care for such a man? How could I rely on him when he would not protect me from such ill treatment?

I'd wanted to believe he was honorable in his own way. I'd wanted to see the good in him. But the truth was that he was just as much of a coward as Robert or any of the other men, blackmailed and ordered about by Reynard, happy to line their pockets for their crimes. It was one thing when I thought they were merely smuggling silk and brandy and perfume. Those actions were illegal, but relatively harmless. However, passing sensitive information to the enemy and trafficking in prisoners of war were entirely different matters that were not only disgraceful, but also treasonous. The fact that Jack had not spoken up or put a stop to it said much about his character, much that I had not wanted to believe. But when faced with Colonel Junot and the plan they proposed I take part in, I could no longer pretend. Jack was as much a criminal and a scoundrel as the rest of them.

There was also the matter of Greybar twenty-three. What did it mean? And what had so upset Reynard about it that he had lashed out at me, demanding to know who I had shared that information with? Or had it simply been a test, an excuse to intimidate me?

When I felt I had myself more in hand and I could stand without Kate's assistance, I stepped back from her embrace. Her hands loosely clasped my upper arms, offering me comfort as I dabbed my eyes with a handkerchief I'd pulled from my sleeve. She didn't say anything. She didn't have to. She must have guessed what had happened.

Her eyes crinkled with a lassitude I'd never seen in her before, and it tore at something inside me to see her that way, to know that her brother had perhaps failed her in ways that cut deeper than even my own betrayals. My father had been devoured by his grief and his need for the forgetfulness contained in a bottle. What was Robert's excuse?

As for Jack and Harry, I supposed they'd been happy to take whatever they could get from us. And though I knew Jack had only stolen kisses from me, I suspected Harry may have taken a bit more from Kate. I didn't ask her. If she wanted to share that with me she would. But I felt indignant on her behalf all the same.

I crushed my sodden handkerchief in my fist, welcoming the anger that began to fill me as it pushed the fear and pain aside. "We cannot let him do this," I told Kate.

Her hands fell away from my arms. "But how can we stop him? If we say anything, we'll be charged with treason."

"Maybe," I murmured. An idea had begun to form in my mind, as yet insubstantial.

"There's no maybe about it. We will go to prison, Ella. Or

worse. Dance the hempen jig."

Her words startled a smile out of me. "The hempen jig?"

"Yes. Be turned-off." She huffed when I didn't respond. "We'll be *hanged.*"

"I understood what you meant. I'm just surprised to hear you using the smugglers' slang."

She frowned. "Yes, well. It does have a certain ring to it."

"That it does."

"Be serious, Ella." She inhaled a shaky breath. "I'm not ready to die. Not yet. I've barely left Norfolk."

I reached out to take hold of her hand. "I'm not ready to die either."

She studied my face as if to be sure I was somber again and then nodded.

"But do you truly wish to live the rest of your life this way, under Reynard's thumb? Always looking over your shoulder, always worried what he'll ask of you next, and whether your conscience can bear it? Wouldn't it be worth the risk to at least try?"

Kate considered my words. "I suppose that's not much of a life, is it?"

"Neither of us will ever be able to leave Thurlton, or marry, or have children, unless it's at Reynard's bidding." I grimaced. "Personally, I think I'd rather be transported to a penal colony on the other side of the world than face such a fate."

Kate's gaze drifted past my shoulder, staring out over the tall beds of reeds that surrounded us. "He's so cruel." The anguish in her voice made my breath catch.

"He quite possibly may be mad."

Her eyes flew to mine. "Do you think so?"

"How else do you explain his quicksilver changes of mood, or his merciless behavior?" I shook my head. "He feels no shame."

"But I don't know that that makes him mad. Evil, perhaps."

"Either way, I'm not remaining under his thrall." I paused, wondering how I could convince her that we needed to do something to stop him, because none of the men were going to. Blackmail or not, they were content to reap the financial benefits of working in Reynard's business. Kate had been living with this far longer than I had. She had been trapped into silence by her devotion to me. Maybe it was time I proved worthy of that dedication.

I squeezed her hand where I still held it. "Do you trust me?"

"Yes," she replied, and the fact that she did not even hesitate nearly brought tears back into my eyes.

Instead, I lifted my other hand to press her palm between my own. "Then continue on as if I've said nothing. Do as you're instructed. I will send word if your help is required. But rely on me to find us a way out of this tangle." I tightened my grip. "I will not fail you."

She closed her eyes against a wave of emotion that washed over her face only to escape through her mouth in a short gasp. She inhaled swiftly and nodded. "I'm not sure I deserve you."

"Of course you do. We deserve each other."

Chapter 31

OVER THE NEXT FEW DAYS, I followed the same advice I'd given Kate. I appeared when and where I was told. I listened to the proposed plan to smuggle Colonel Junot out of England and I learned my part. I helped design our wardrobes—when they would allow my input—and endured Reynard's barbed comments and insufferably arrogant demeanor. In short, I did exactly as I was told, and nothing more. However, I was careful not to seem too complacent. I suspected that would only draw unwanted attention, something I wished to avoid at all costs.

When my tasks each day were finished, I returned home to Penleaf Cottage, refusing to dawdle either at Greenlaws or in the marshes, where Jack might find me. I was not yet ready to face him alone. I was still hurt by his behavior the day I had met the colonel, and too afraid he would somehow make me forget that pain. I was well aware of his effect on me, and how easily I seemed to abandon my good sense where he was concerned.

I also had other reasons for lingering near the cottage whenever I could, but as the days passed and no visitors or letters appeared, I began to suspect something had gone awry. The letter I had sent Mr. Fulton immediately upon my return home after my conversation with Kate in the marsh should have reached its intended destination days ago. Our conscientious solicitor would not have failed to follow my instructions or at least send me a reply if he found he could not carry them out. Of course, there was every possibility that one of our missives had been intercepted. After all, Mr. Ingles acted as the local postmaster, and it was clear he was intimidated by Reynard's gang of smugglers. If they had instructed him to seize my correspondence, he would have complied.

I chafed at the thought I was already being isolated from outside assistance. My note to Mr. Fulton had been deliberately vague, but that did not mean Reynard would not suspect my intentions to expose him should it fall into his hands. Thus far he had not indicated he suspected anything, but that didn't mean he wasn't biding his time, allowing me to think my deception had gone undetected as he considered how best to punish me. Whatever the consequences, I knew I would not like them. His threatening to strangle me had been horrifying enough, and as easily as it had been done it was clear Reynard was capable of worse.

Regardless, as the week stretched on, so did my nerves, until I spent much of the night pacing around my room or sorting useless clutter in the drafty attic by candlelight. Only once had I ventured downstairs. I'd found my father standing in the middle of the drawing room, surveying the mostly bare walls with unseeing eyes. The furrows on his brow and the lines of discomfort radiating from the corners of his mouth told me he must not yet be inebriated, but I did not allow myself to wonder why. It was certain to be temporary. Not eager to converse, I'd backed away before he saw me, and closed my heart to the suffering etched across his features.

After his appalling accusations about my playing mistress to Lord Waveney, I had been avoiding Father even more than usual. So when one evening sought me out, I expected more complaints. I placed my marker in the book I had been unsuccessfully attempting to read, spending more time staring at the walls than the pages, and steeled myself to confront whatever charges he would lay at my feet.

"Come in," I called after reaching up to adjust the silk scarf borrowed from Kate I'd taken to draping around my neck to hide the fading bruises left by Reynard.

Father opened the door, but at first he did not enter. He simply stood gripping the door handle, his gaze fastened on the floor several feet in front of him. He looked horrible, with sunken cheeks and eyes, and a waxy pallor to his skin. I wondered when he'd last taken a drink of his beloved brandy. It was true I hadn't found any empty bottles in the cottage for nearly a week, but I'd assumed Mrs. Brittle had disposed of them. I hadn't wanted to note Father's level of soberness. Doing so only made me sad, or angry, or gave me false hope. I couldn't afford to be distracted by it. Not now.

But seeing him like this, so terribly pale and weak, I couldn't help but feel alarmed. Especially when he remained silent for so long, as if he'd forgotten where he was and what he was doing.

"Father," I murmured, rising to go to him. "Perhaps you should sit down."

He nodded almost dazedly and allowed me to escort him to the chair I'd vacated. I could feel now that he was shaking, but was it from cold or weakness or want of brandy?

I poured him a glass of water from the chipped ewer on my washstand and pressed it into his hands, urging him to drink. The cool liquid seemed to revive him somewhat, for his eyes lifted to mine as he set the glass aside.

"I'm sorry. I…" He shook his head, as if discarding what he was about to say. "I suppose I've had a bit of a shock."

I pulled my dressing table stool closer and perched on the edge of it. "What happened?"

Had he left the cottage? Or had someone paid us a visit? Someone I would rather stay far away from my father?

He swallowed and lifted his gaze to meet mine again. "I went to Thurlton." He licked his lips. "To the White Horse."

I nodded slowly, understanding what that meant. Perhaps Father *had* been sober. Perhaps he *had* been trying to stop drinking. But tonight the cravings had been too much for him and he'd given in, seeking succor.

I searched his bright but lucid eyes. Apparently, he had not found it.

"When I got there, that Watkins fellow was yelling and kicking up quite a fuss."

I stiffened. "What did he say?"

"Something about someone snitching on him." He shook his head again. "I don't know. I'd only just arrived, was but standing in the doorway watching, when a scraggly, stout fellow pulled out a pistol and…shot him. Right there. In the middle of the pub."

I pressed a hand to my mouth, feeling ill. I probably knew the man Father was describing. It was most likely Dibs, part of Reynard's gang of smugglers.

What had Watkins been doing there? Was it my fault? I'd written to tell Mr. Fulton to contact the Customs House in Yarmouth and tell them what we knew about the bribes their riding officers were taking. Not in those exact words, but the solicitor should have understood what I hinted at. In any case, it was clear Watkins had been confronted with his corruption. But why had he been allowed to return here? Why hadn't they sent a different group of riding officers in his place, as I'd hoped?

"He started bleeding all over the floor and cursing us all."

I looked up to find Father staring into nothingness again. His face was contorted, clearly remembering the sight of the wounded revenue man.

"Little flecks of blood-tinted spittle kept flying out of his mouth onto his lips. And then he crumpled to his knees, and to the floor, and then he was quiet."

I shivered at the image he'd painted of the dying man. "What did they do with him?"

"I don't know. They said something about him being too corpulent to sink in the marshes. That he would never stay submerged. But I didn't wait around to find out what they decided."

"They just let you leave?" I asked in some surprise.

I didn't think it possible, but his face paled even further.

"After telling us they would do the same thing to us that they'd done to Watkins if we breathed a word of this to anyone."

I pressed my hands to my abdomen, stunned by their audacity. To kill a revenue man in the middle of a pub at the White Horse's busiest time of day, and then brush it off as nothing but an inconvenience... Reynard and his crew truly would have no qualms about killing me if I crossed them.

Jack had tried to warn me. He'd insisted I didn't know what I was getting myself into, and at every step of the way he'd been proven right. I felt my heart soften toward him, remembering his frustration when I wouldn't listen.

Suddenly realizing what I was doing, I scowled, shaking aside those tender emotions. Just because he possessed a sliver of a conscience did not mean he was a good man. Nor did it mean I was any safer with him. He was still a member of Reynard's crew, and if he could work for a man like that, blackmail or not, then he was not to be trusted.

Father's large hand stole onto mine, surprising me with his gentle touch. I couldn't remember the last time he'd touched me so. Certainly as a girl I'd spent hours curled up on his lap, and even as a young woman he'd easily offered me hugs or quick kisses against my brow. But that seemed so very long ago.

"I'm sorry." His voice was broken and raspy, but this time I knew it wasn't because of drink. "I have been the worst of fathers. Not only have I abandoned you to care for everything, I've also failed to protect you." His Adam's apple bobbed in his throat as he swallowed. "I've done nothing a father should have. And I can't even promise things will change in the future." He hiccuped a short pained breath. "Look at me. I can't even last a week before running off to the White Horse for more of that cursed brandy."

"But you didn't drink any," I replied weakly, unable to help myself.

His eyes saddened further at my inane attempt to encourage him. "Only because a man was killed right in front of me!" He squeezed my hand. "You don't have to make excuses for me anymore. You never should have needed to in the first place." He sat straighter, inhaling and then exhaling. "The truth is, I am a drunkard."

Hearing him admit those words after so long made my heart ache, but it also felt oddly like a release. This dark secret I'd helped him hide from himself and everyone else was now out in the open, exposed to the light and the air, and consequently it no longer seemed to press down on me with so much weight. I knew there was no miraculous cure for this need that consumed my father. I'd seen and experienced too much to ever believe it would simply vanish. But hearing him admit his weakness and apologize for it in such a considered manner was more than I'd ever expected to witness.

"I don't like these smugglers. I don't like them one bit. And I hate knowing it's my fault you were forced to get involved with them." His grip on my hand tightened as he pleaded. "What can I do to get you out? How can I extricate you from them?"

"It's not that simple."

His eyes shone with earnestness. "I will go to prison if that is what is necessary. I will find a way to pay my debt."

"But how, Father? Once inside the Marshalsea, you'll have no way to obtain money. And what about me? What am I to do while you're locked away?"

His features tightened as if finally comprehending how impossible, how untenable a situation he'd forced us into. He slowly reached into the inner pocket of his frockcoat and pulled out what appeared to be a letter. "This might help."

I looked at him in question before lifting my hand to take it from him. I didn't recognize the seal pressed into the wax, but the graceful handwriting on the inside left no doubt it was from a woman.

Dear Miss Winterton,

I received your letter and I cannot tell you how pleased I am that you took the initiative to write to me. I have been scolding your grandfather for years that his ridiculous edict and his insistence on your family's estrangement has gone on long enough. Because he could not move beyond his wounded pride he never had the opportunity to reconcile with his daughter before she passed.

You must forgive me for being a foolish old woman. I loved your mother like she was my own. But although we kept up a correspondence, I was never brave enough to defy my brother completely and travel to Norfolk to visit her. I regret that now with all my heart.

Your mother wrote of you often in her letters, and I've longed to meet the lovely young woman she was so proud you had become. I would be delighted to accept you into my home and introduce you to society. Perhaps I can even do what your father should have done long ago, and help you   nd a husband.

I know I can never change what is past, just as I can never bring your mother back from the grave, no matter how much I might wish it. But I hope you will allow me the opportunity to know you in the present. I think it might be the greatest gift I could give your mother now that she is passed, and I so long to offer it.

I am certain you have also written to your grandfather, and I urge you to forget whatever nonsense he has written you in return. He is not a bad man, just an intractable one. I should have used my prerogative as a meddling older sister to defy him long ago.

I impatiently await your response.

With affection,
Laura, Lady Bramford

I stared at the signature for a long time before I was able to speak. "How long have you had this?"

"A little over a week. I…I told Ingles to hold all of our mail for me."

Which explained why I'd not received a response from Mr. Fulton since Father had been avoiding the White Horse Inn until tonight. I didn't know what to say. After so much time had passed, and Grandfather's less than warm reply, I'd expected animosity or dismissal. My great-aunt's kindness and her admission of guilt quite honestly astounded me.

But it seemed Father assumed my silence indicated anger. "I know I should have given it to you sooner," he hastened to explain. "But I couldn't bear the thought of your leaving.

Like your mother. Like your brother. Though it seems I've done everything possible to make you want to go." He raked a trembling hand though his unkempt hair. "I was going to prove to you I could be a good father again. I was going to make you want to stay." He inhaled a shaky breath. "But then that smuggler shot Watkins and I knew I was being selfish. Foolishly so."

I didn't ask how he'd known Dibs was a smuggler. I supposed it had been obvious.

He reached out to clutch both of my hands. "You need to leave here. It's too dangerous. Too...lonely. I should have seen that long ago." His thumbs rubbed anxiously across the backs of my hands. "Your mother tried to warn me. When she knew she..." He choked on the words. "She told me you needed to spend a few weeks in London before I let you marry Rockland. To see something of the world beyond the marshes and Norwich."

I sat very still, afraid that if I moved or spoke he would fall silent again, as he'd been these past four years. But inside I was a swirling pit of remembered suffering and loss. My mind churned with unanswered questions, with shock and frustration.

"I know you must be wondering why I never told you any of this."

That was an understatement.

"Whether I ever intended to do as she'd asked. And the answer is I don't know." His face was weighed down by a sorrow I'd never been able to comprehend, even loving my mother as much as I had. "I..." He turned his face to the side. "I don't remember much about the weeks following your mother's death. I suspect I was largely absent."

I didn't think he wanted me to reply, to tell him about the way he'd taken to his bed, refusing to see Erik or me. Or how he'd locked himself in his study with carafes of wine and whiskey and brandy. How Erik and I had felt abandoned. How we'd worried we'd lost both of our parents, not just our mother.

"But I do remember seeing you and Rockland together one evening after your brother left to take up his commission in the army."

I frowned at the change in his tone of voice. "You saw us? Where?"

"At Wilkie Point."

My cheeks flushed with heat. Wilkie Point was an old dock located in an isolated stretch of marsh that used to be attached to a farm nearby before the waters had encroached too far inland. Robert and I had only met there twice, and neither time had we done much talking. I could see that knowledge now in Father's eyes.

"I knew then that I needed to honor your mother's wishes. Before it was too late."

I pressed my lips together, fighting the burning wave of embarrassment. "Father, I never…"

"I know," he replied calmly, not making me say the words. "Your mother taught you better than that."

I exhaled, relieved to hear him say so after last week's horrible accusations.

His face hardened. "But that didn't mean I trusted Rockland."

And he'd been proven right, because Robert had essentially jilted me. At least now I better understood his fury when Robert returned to Greenlaws with a different bride. Father had known just how dishonorably Robert had behaved toward me. He must have simmered with indignation when he realized the futility of his being able to do anything about it. It was no surprise he'd lashed out after drinking too much.

"But you never took me to London," I pointed out.

"No." His voice was hollow. "Because we received word of

Erik's death a few days later."

And Father had retreated back into his study with his preferred brandy.

I turned towards my window, watching our candlelit reflections flicker across the glass like ripples on water. There had been so much I hadn't known. So much I hadn't understood. I wondered now whether I should have pushed harder for answers, but a person can only be ignored and rejected so many times before they stop asking.

The chair creaked as Father sat taller. "You must leave here." He tapped the letter he'd given me where I'd set it on my writing desk. "You must go to Lady Bramford. Tonight."

My eyebrows arched in surprise at his insistence. "How?"

"Surely Rockland would loan you a carriage. I will come with you to ask."

Oh, if he only knew.

I shook my head. "I can't just leave. It's not that simple."

"Yes, you can."

I strengthened my voice. "No, I can't."

Something of my certainty must have finally been communicated to him, for he paused to study me. His hands in his lap tightened into fists. "Rockland is involved too, isn't he?"

I didn't confirm it. I didn't need to.

His face turned to the side as his jaw worked. He slammed his fist down onto my desk, making me jump. "It's bad enough the scoundrel had to trifle with you and break your heart, but now this! This has gone too far."

He rose to his feet, but I grabbed hold of his hand, pulling him back. "Sit down," I ordered, ignoring the angry glint in his eyes as he dropped back into the chair with a thud. He truly was weakened by his craving for brandy.

"What do you think you're going to do? March over to Greenlaws and confront him?" I snapped. "Don't be a fool. The others will shoot you and not think twice. Or have you already forgotten what happened to Mr. Watkins?"

His face visibly paled, but his eyes remained defiant.

I inhaled and pressed a hand to my brow, trying to think. "You are going to have to let me handle this my way." I glared him into silence when he would have protested. "I cannot simply flee, if indeed I could. It's doubtful they would even allow me to travel farther than a mile away from Thurlton before they stopped me. Not only would they see you thrown into prison, they would have me arrested as well, and possibly tried for treason."

He stiffened in alarm.

"They're not just smuggling silk and brandy, Father," I replied in a hushed voice, as if even now someone might overhear us. "And I have to stop them. For Erik. For Kate. And for me."

Father clearly had questions, but he did not force me to elaborate. Instead, he held to what was most important. "What do you intend to do?"

I rose from my stool and crossed toward my window, rubbing the tense muscles at the back of my neck. "I don't know," I admitted. A flare of light at the edge of the marsh caught my eye and I sighed. "But it will have to be done soon."

Chapter 32

SOMEHOW I MANAGED TO EXTRICATE myself from my Father by convincing him I wished to go to bed, and he should seek his, too. He must have been exhausted, for he barely voiced a protest as I rose and pretended to ready myself for sleep. After the events at the White Horse, I thought he was going to lock me in my room, so anxious was he suddenly for my safely. Though it was nice to be cared about for once, it could not have happened at a worse time.

I was careful not to make a sound as I crept out of the cottage and followed the path down to where I knew Jack would be waiting. He stood in the middle of the dock with the special lantern he had used to signal me sitting at his feet. The night air was warm, and yet he still wore his black cloak. The better to perpetuate the myth of the Lantern Men for unsuspecting outsiders, I supposed.

I crossed my arms over my chest and slowly moved toward him. He did not glance up at me until I stopped several feet away. From such a distance I could not see his features as clearly as I would have liked, but I decided it was safer this way.

I didn't speak, wanting him to speak first. Unfortunately, he seemed to find our silence comfortable, for he made no immediate effort to dispel it with words. His eyes trailed over my features and down my body, lingering on my neck. I'd forgotten to rewrap the scarf around my neck and almost lifted my hand to cover the fading bruises from his sight, but I didn't want to reveal even that little bit of discomfort.

We had been in each other's company since the incident with Reynard, but always in a group, and never in a setting where we could easily converse. In truth, Reynard seemed to be keeping him busy elsewhere much of the time. Because he recognized Jack felt some sympathy for me, or because Reynard wanted me to believe I still had an ally in Jack? I couldn't be sure, so I was wary.

"You are well?" he finally said.

"As well as can be," I replied vaguely.

He continued to stare at me, as if waiting for me to say more. When I didn't, he grunted. "Your ship sails tomorrow."

I straightened, unable to hide my reaction. My heart surged in my chest. "When?"

"With the midday tide. But Reynard wants you to board before midmorning."

Which meant we would need to set out for Yarmouth in only a few hours' time. "And you're just informing me of this *now*?"

Jack's voice was tight. "Yes, well, he didn't want to give you the chance to run."

I narrowed my eyes in suspicion. "Are you sure it doesn't have to do with a certain riding officer being shot tonight?"

He didn't even attempt to deny it. "I'm certain that has something to do with it, but the ship also made port today."

"Captain Haywood again," I sneered.

"No. At least, not the Captain Haywood you're thinking of."

I tilted my head in question.

"They're all known as Captain Haywood. It's…safer that

way."

I had no idea exactly what he meant by that, and I decided I didn't care to. "When should I expect you?" I asked instead.

His eyes scrutinized my face, and I looked away, trying to ignore the sensations his proximity always evoked. Did he know just being near him made every inch of my skin come alive? That my breath seemed to catch in my chest? That my words would suddenly dry on my tongue? Did he feel any of those things too? Or was he as calm and unaffected as he always looked?

"I can still take you somewhere safe."

He spoke so softly I wasn't certain I'd heard him correctly.

He must have seen my confusion for he moved a step closer. "There is a place close by I can take you. Somewhere Reynard will never look."

"Yes, but for how long?" Anger flashed inside me. "And what of Mrs. Brittle, and my father, and Kate? What will become of them?" I shook my head. "It's too late for any of that. If you'd truly wished to help, you should have done so before now."

"I warned you to stay out of this," he snapped back, moving closer to tower over me. "I told you that you had no idea what you were getting yourself into. But you wouldn't listen."

I could see now that he wasn't unaffected. He was furious. Almost as furious as I was.

He inhaled deeply. "Reynard sent me after Colonel Junot. I couldn't say no."

"I understand," I bit out, not wanting to hear his excuses. Not wanting to allow even a sliver of doubt to creep beneath my anger and make me soften toward him. I couldn't afford such weakness.

But he was relentless. "Well, you shouldn't." His brow furrowed in displeasure. "I told you I would help you, that I would find a way to extricate you from this plot, and I failed to do that. I'm sorry."

His apology was so genuine, I felt the walls I'd built up against him begin to crumble. I clutched myself tighter, trying to shore them up.

"I wish…" Jack began but then stopped, sighing heavily as he shook his head, forbidding himself from finishing that thought. Instead he turned to question me. "Why did you give in to Reynard's threats? Why didn't you wait for word from me?"

Even though his accusations were gently queried, my shoulders stiffened. "I had no choice. He summoned me, and at the time I had no alternative. How was I to know if you meant to follow through on your promise? What indication was there that you could truly help me when you can't even save yourself?" I glowered at him. "Or don't you want to?"

He shook his head. "It's too late for me. And it's…complicated."

I stared up into his too-handsome face, feeling that traitorous tug. "Isn't everything?" I mused, bone-weary of all these games and secrets.

He didn't respond, and I took that as his agreement.

Conscious of the lateness of the hour and the short amount of time before I had to meet him here to set out for Yarmouth, I turned towards home. But Jack stopped me with a light touch to my elbow. His expression was still troubled, but now there was also a glint of determination in his eyes. One I didn't understand.

"Do you remember what I told you before your last engagement?"

I frowned. He'd told me many things, but somehow I knew he was referring to what he'd said to me on the boat at Yarmouth. To forget my orders to stay silent. To tell the authorities everything.

I nodded.

"It still applies."

When he didn't elaborate, I tried to ask for clarification. "But what if—"

His hand lifted to my cheek, cutting off my words as his callused thumb ran along the sensitive skin of my jaw. "You'll know what to do."

His eyes dipped to my mouth, and I realized that as much as I didn't want to want him to kiss me, the fact was I did. Whether he knew that or he simply didn't care, he captured my mouth in a searing kiss. One I knew I would spend the rest of my life trying to forget.

I turned blindly away when he released me, cursing myself for being such a fool. For letting him get close enough to touch my heart when I should never have even known his name.

A few short hours later, before the sun had even hinted at making an appearance, I stole out of the cottage. But not before making a quick stop in my father's study to retrieve something from the locked drawer in his desk. I slipped the item I sought into my reticule and tiptoed through the kitchen, carrying the pair of leather half-boots Kate had loaned me. Luckily, our feet were almost of a size. In any case, I couldn't complain. I'd been wearing my mother's too large shoes for months now since my last pair had worn through the soles.

I gritted my teeth when the door creaked in protest as I pulled it shut. Holding my breath, I waited to hear if the noise had woken Mrs. Brittle or my father, but the cottage remained dark and silent. I exhaled in relief, having wanted to avoid any confrontation, especially one requiring a lengthy explanation I wasn't sure I could fully account for. It was anybody's guess how the day would unfold, but I prayed that at least it would end with everyone I loved alive and whole, regardless of whether that was safe at home or locked in a prison cell somewhere.

I sat down on the threshold and laced up my boots before hurrying down to our dock. I did my best to save the fabric of Kate's Pomona-green ensemble from dragging in the dirt and dew, but even though it had been hastily altered to fit my figure, it was still a bit too long. I knew Kate wouldn't care, but I did. I rarely had the opportunity to wear something so beautiful, and I didn't want to damage it in the first five minutes I'd worn it.

When I arrived, Jack was not yet there, so I stood very still with my hands clasped before my waist, looking out over the marsh. It was that curious hour that seemed to fall between night and day, when the world hushed in anticipation. The creatures who scurried about in the night had found their beds and fallen silent, while the rest of the world had yet to awaken. The sky was still dark, but the stars one by one had slowly begun to fade. My eyes strained to see that first wash of blue on the eastern horizon, eager for light to chase away the shadows.

But before the sun could make its presence known, a flicker of light to my left caught my eye and then it disappeared. I turned to search for it, and just as I began to wonder if I'd imagined it, the dim light reappeared a bit further to the right, slowly drifting toward me. Had I not known about Jack and his special lantern the sight would have terrified me, for even knowing what I did, the glow of his lamp was still unsettling. It truly did look like an eerie ball of flame, a will-o'-the-wisp hovering over the marsh, just as the myth of the Lantern Men claimed. I breathed deeply, reminding myself it was merely a trick, but I knew I wouldn't relax until I'd seen Jack with my own eyes.

As the light drew closer, I could hear the slice of oars through the water. Then the boat emerged from the gloom, along with one human silhouette and then another. Both were draped in dark garments from head to toe. My heartbeat pounded in my ears as I strained to see whether either of the figures was Jack. I bit down on the urge to call out, to demand they reveal themselves, and when the first figure pulled back his hood, I was glad I'd resisted.

"Miss Winterton," Reynard drawled, looking up at me from the boat as it pulled even with the dock.

I stared down into his unwelcome visage, frantically trying to determine what this meant for me and my plans, especially if he intended to accompany us to Yarmouth and aboard the ship to France. I had not anticipated Reynard's presence because he had never impressed me as the type of man who would exert himself enough to become directly involved, but I supposed if the mission were important enough even he might make an exception.

I tore my gaze away from him as the second figure stood to grip the wooden rail of the ladder, securing the skiff for my decent. Jack's steady gaze met mine, and though he didn't speak I could hear his instructions from that week of training before my first smuggling engagement echoing through my head.

I turned around to carefully climb down the ladder in my unwieldy skirts, taking advantage of those few moments when I did not have to face either man to compose myself. By the time I'd reached the bottom I'd calmed some of my nerves in preparation for what was to come. Jack pressed a hand to my back as I stepped into the boat, steadying me as we rocked in the water. I realized I would have to sit beside Reynard on the bench, and though I thought I'd successfully masked my dismay at this he seemed to sense it anyway. His lips curled into a leering grin as I wobbled toward him.

I plopped down on the bench perhaps a bit too hard, for he had not offered me his hand in assistance, and ended up pressed against his side in order to keep myself from toppling backward off of the seat. I pulled away as quickly as I could, but there was still no escaping the fact that our hips remained touching. The gentlemanly thing for him to do would have been to slide over those last few inches on his side of the bench to give me more room, but it had become apparent long ago that Reynard was no gentleman. I gritted my teeth, refusing to squirm. That would only add to his enjoyment of my discomfort.

I stared across the boat at Jack's averted eyes. He seemed determined not to look at us as he maneuvered the skiff out into the waterway, so I resolved to do the same. I gazed out into the darkness that still masked much of the marsh from our eyes. A small bit of blue had spread upward in the eastern sky, but it was difficult to see through the reeds and grasses blocking the horizon. Daylight would come swiftly now. There was no stopping it.

"Your promptness does not disappoint," Reynard said, breaking the silence. "However, your loyalty seems to be somewhat lacking."

My muscles tightened even as I struggled not show him that his words had affected me. The hairs on the back of my neck stood on end as his hand lifted to rest on the edge of the sensitive skin revealed between my spencer's collar and my bonnet.

"I know it was you who revealed that Watkins was being bribed." His words gusted against my ear as he leaned closer, his mouth hovering next to the brim of my bonnet. "I know it was you who caused him to charge into Thurlton demanding to know who'd tattled on him. You know what that means, don't you?"

I didn't answer. I couldn't without admitting he was right. My eyes flicked to Jack, who was now watching us. Or more accurately, watching Reynard. The fierceness of his features gave me some hope that he would not let Reynard kill me. If he could prevent it in time.

"Because of you," Reynard continued, "one of my men had to kill Watkins. He'd been relieved of his position, you see, and was raving about revenge, threatening to reveal all. It had to be done. And I'm afraid *that*, my dear Miss Winterton, is on your head."

His words pinched in my chest as guilt washed over me. I knew that was exactly what he wanted me to feel, just as I knew I hadn't been the one to kill Watkins. I hadn't pulled the trigger. But I had set in motion the events that caused his death. I could not dismiss that fact.

Watkins had been a despicable man who deserved to lose his position as a riding officer, but he hadn't deserved to be murdered, and his body dumped in the marshes or some isolated shallow grave where no one could mourn him. I'd wondered why Dibs would shoot a riding officer and risk bringing more revenue men to Thurlton looking for him, but now it was clear no one would be searching for Watkins. No one of consequence anyway.

Reynard's fingers brushed a trail across the back of my neck that was at once a caress and a threat. "I thought I made myself clear, but you seem to delight in defying me. Not that I don't appreciate your spirit." His voice dropped even lower. "But your efforts are best channeled elsewhere. Olivia was much the same."

My breathing hitched upon hearing Olivia's name.

"Fortunately, she proved to be an able pupil."

I wanted to squirm at the lecherous tone of his voice, but then it abruptly changed.

"Until she discovered she was carrying Rockland's—or my—brat. Then she developed a rather inconvenient conscience." He sighed. "So unpleasant how she had to die, especially when she was still young and beautiful."

My empty stomach turned over at the implication of his words. I stared wide-eyed across the boat at Jack. Even if he could not hear Reynard's words, he must have recognized how terrible they were simply from the look on my face. His brow creased in concern, but he continued to row, never breaking his rhythm.

Did Robert know? Had he guessed that his wife had been murdered? That the carriage accident that killed Olivia and her unborn child had somehow been intentional? Had he known…and done nothing about it?

The thought further sickened me. That the man I had known and loved since he was a boy could be capable of such cold indifference… I didn't want to even think it was possible, but Robert had already done so many terrible things I'd never imagined he could do that nothing seemed unbelievable anymore.

Reynard pressed his lips against my ear, shifting my bonnet back on my head, the silk ribbon pulling against the faded bruises on my neck. "You would do well to learn from her example."

His teeth clamped down on my earlobe and I jumped. He didn't bite hard enough to draw blood, but I felt the scrape of his teeth regardless. It made my insides crawl. I closed my eyes, fighting my fear and revulsion for this man.

When he finally pulled away, I couldn't look at him, not without either striking him or breaking down in tears. I couldn't face Jack either. So I sat stiffly, waiting for the prickling sensation along my skin to subside and the fear choking me to sink back into my stomach. It was a long time before they did.

Chapter 33

IN THE END, I WAS proven correct. Reynard did not board the wherry boat. He didn't even deign to row the small skiff back to Greenlaws himself, but waited for Freddy to take Jack's place at the oars. He wouldn't risk being apprehended. He would let the rest of us face that possibility.

I turned away from him the moment I boarded the boat to join the others, including Colonel Junot now dressed as an exceedingly unattractive and lumpy-figured lady's maid. However, Reynard was not finished with me.

"Harry, search her reticule."

I whirled about in surprise. "Why?"

He didn't answer, merely stared at his henchman waiting for him to do his bidding. Harry scowled and stomped forward to take my bag. Knowing resistance was futile, I removed it from my wrist with a frown.

Fortunately, Harry was kind enough not to remove most of the more personal items for Reynard's inspection, though I suspected that was less out of sympathy and more because he'd already found what he was looking for. He extracted the pistol I'd taken from my father's desk that morning and held it out for all to see.

Reynard tsked.

"The others carry weapons," I argued. "I've seen them." Assorted knives and daggers, and even a pistol or two. "I thought it only prudent to possess one as well. To discourage the crew of the ship carrying us to France from becoming too friendly, if nothing else."

Reynard shook his head and Harry passed me back my reticule while keeping the gun. I wanted to howl in frustration, but I knew my reaction would only elicit amusement from the others.

"Do ye even know how to use this?" Harry asked, examining the weapon as Reynard's skiff finally began to pull away.

"Not really," I lied, hoping he would pass the loaded pistol back to me. All I needed was that single shot.

He rolled his eyes and moved away. I swallowed my irritation and followed him toward the stern of the boat. I was forced to stop short when Harry suddenly swiveled around, arched a single eyebrow, and pointed toward the bow. Sighing loudly, I did as I was told, though it chafed to do so.

I skirted past Jack, who was shrugging into a livery jacket, the better to portray a footman accompanying me and my maid abroad. No family of quality would allow a young female to travel without a male escort, even if he was merely a servant. I couldn't help but note how dignified he looked in his uniform. With his height, broad shoulders, and good looks, he could have been the footman of a duke, or possibly even royalty.

Colonel Junot leaned against the canvas stretched across the cargo hold, looking decidedly masculine despite his mauve dress with puffed sleeves and white poke bonnet wrapped in pale pink ribbon. I started to tell him that no one would believe he was a female if he stood like that, but then stopped. I was required to play my part, but that didn't mean I had to instruct the Frenchman in how to play his. The likelihood of him listening to me was slim anyway. He and Reynard had ignored me when I expressed concern that dressing him in overly feminine attire would only draw more attention to his masculinity.

Dismissing the tiresome Frenchman from my mind, I perched on the edge of the hold several feet away and considered my options now that my pistol had been confiscated. I clenched my fists as renewed fury swept through my veins. It was true Reynard had unnerved me with his threats and intimation that he'd arranged Olivia's early demise, but if he thought this new information would convince me to cooperate he was sorely mistaken. It only made me more determined to see him captured and punished, even if it meant my own imprisonment as well.

I glanced up as Jack moved forward to stand next to the mast. He wrapped his hand around the pole, staring out over the marsh as we drew closer to Breydon Water and the ruins of the Roman fort. Colonel Junot shifted a step closer to look beyond me at the crumbled stone walls. He did not speak at first, but I could sense his interest, and assumed it was the normal curiosity many held in the remnants of Rome's once great empire.

But then he scoffed. "Is that the gammy viscount's manor?"

If I had not been watching Jack, I probably would have missed how his hand tightened around the wooden pole, his knuckles turning white. I frowned in confusion. "Do you mean Lord Waveney?" I asked, feeling my own interest pique. The man who had sent us money through my father's solicitor was crippled?

Colonel Junot turned his derisive glare on me, though it lost some of its bite coming beneath the flared brim of his bonnet. "My apologies. Did I injure your genteel sensibilities?"

Ignoring his nasty behavior for the moment, I arched my eyebrows in disbelief. "How do *you* know him?"

"I don't. But Monsieur Reynard said he has been trying to

halt his trade with France."

And by trade, I knew he meant smuggling.

"He said that because the viscount is too lame to hold a commission in your army, he's playing soldier at home, inventing his own battles."

I lifted my chin, glaring down my nose at him. "You do know, such insolence from a lady's maid would see you sacked. Have a care you mind your tongue."

He narrowed his eyes, but I turned a cold shoulder to him, as any haughty mistress would do to a servant she had chastised. Correcting him broke my vow to remain silent, but I secretly hoped my reproach would have the opposite effect.

I fully expected the Frenchman to make some snide retort, but incredibly he held his tongue. I realized why when I saw the wherry boat approaching us from the direction of Yarmouth. It was nothing more than a coal barge returning inland, but it passed closer to us than I would have guessed the others felt comfortable with. I considered calling out to them, but swiftly recognized how foolhardy that would be. The wherry men on the other boat could do nothing to aid me, and my drawing attention to our enterprise would only place them in danger.

So I remained silent, though that didn't stop me from eyeing the other wherry longingly. Which was how I noticed that our boat was sitting rather low in the water by comparison. Lower than I recalled it sitting on our last sojourn to Yarmouth.

Out of the corner of my eye, I studied the canvas covering the hold. I knew my traveling trunks were stored beneath for appearances' sake, but not what other cargo we carried. The sharp stench of coal—a wherry boat's traditional cargo—lingered from previous hauls, but it was not strong enough to suggest any was stored on board now. I knew better than to ask the others about it, but I began to suspect we were hauling something more than a prisoner of war to Yarmouth and further on to France. And it was something heavy.

I gritted my teeth and thought harder, but by the time we sailed into Yarmouth inspiration had still not come to me. Everyone was playing their roles well now. Jack stood tall and at attention—but of course he always did that—while Colonel Junot slumped his shoulders to disguise his height. Having the simplest tasks of all, Dibs and Rory lounged against the sides of the hold, and Harry steered us through the busy river port.

For this task, the wherry boat would be delivering me and Colonel Junot directly to the ship anchored out in the North Sea. Why they could not have done the same thing the last time I'd smuggled, I didn't know, except that perhaps they'd been testing me and my resourcefulness and acting skills. Maybe Reynard had already been thinking ahead to this operation.

Or maybe they had worried my presence would draw unnecessary attention to the other smugglers' activities. I still didn't know what they'd done that day while I was visiting the *Reliance*. To be honest, I hadn't given it much thought. Now I wondered if that was a mistake.

The quay bustled with early morning activity, and I could see numerous revenue men milling about, completing their assigned tasks or watching the river. Their distinctive collar badges made them easy to pick out amongst the mass of men. Up ahead, I could see the Customs House near the end of the quay, and I knew once we passed it my chances of alerting anyone to our cargo grew slim. I had to draw their attention now. But how?

Harry had taken my pistol. I'd thought to fire it into the air or at a harmless object, drawing the revenue men's gaze and eventually a boarding party, but that option was no longer open to me. He'd also directed me away from the back of the boat, where the smallest items of cargo were stowed. Tossing items overboard would surely have captured the customs officials' notice.

I realized the simplest thing to do, of course, would be to wave my arms and shout, but the quay was too far away for my voice to travel over the noise of the busy port, and the smugglers were much too close. They would be next to me before I could do much more than flap my arms once.

I briefly considered jumping from the wherry, but that would be suicide. The heavy skirts of my gown would wrap around my legs and pull me under the water to drown, if another passing boat didn't strike me in the head first.

Panic inched along my skin, making it more difficult for me to think, knowing that with each heartbeat I was moving closer to failure. I glanced about me, searching for something, anything, until my eyes landed on the Frenchman. If I could remove his bonnet or provoke him to behave strangely, perhaps that would be enough. Perhaps that would draw the revenue men down on us.

Without allowing myself time to reconsider, I sauntered over to stare up into his face. I started to form a harsh insult to his manhood, but from the sharp look in his eye, I knew that would never work. So I latched on to the only thing I could think of.

I kissed him.

Lurching forward, I pressed my lips to his, pushing both our bonnets askew. At the same time, I reached up and tried to rip the hat from his head. The ribbon under his chin held fast, preventing me from completely removing it before he shoved me backward, but the damage had been done, and he knew it. Before I could blink, he backhanded me across the face with a stinging blow, knocking me to my knees.

The pain stunned me, but I also felt a quiet elation, knowing that if the sight of two apparent women kissing each other didn't capture the customs men's attention, then a servant striking her mistress so violently would. I could already hear shouts from the shore, and the thud of footfalls as the men scrambled about the wherry. I attempted to stagger to my feet, knowing I was too vulnerable in this position at the edge of the deck, but a rush of movement nearby brought my head up just in time to see Dibs cock a pistol and point it in my face.

My breath seized as I stared directly into the barrel, wondering idly if this might be the same gun that had killed Watkins. Was this the end for me as well?

I had no time to react, other than to squeeze my eyes shut as he pulled the trigger.

The shot rang out so close to me I inhaled the sharp odor of the gunpowder, and felt its heat on my face. My ears rang from the repercussion, but somehow I never felt the impact of a bullet. I blinked open my eyes to find Jack wrestling with Dibs for control of the pistol.

"You fool," he exclaimed, towering over the shorter man as he punched him and then yanked the gun from his grasp. "Do you want to be charged with murder as well?" I noticed his lower class accent had slipped.

"Wha' does it matter?" Dibs pressed a hand over the eye Jack had struck and glared down at me with the good one. "We're all gonna be hanged for treason."

"Not if ye keep yer gob shut." Jack shoved him further down the deck, back to his post, and flung the weapon into the river. Still scowling, he turned to offer me his hand to help me up. "Stay close," he murmured next to my ear as I gained my feet.

I didn't know whether he was instructing me to do so because he meant to salvage what seemed irreparable, or because he was worried someone else would attempt to harm me. At any rate, I remained close to his side as I noted a revenue cutter drawing up along our flank. The men lining the ship had their rifles aimed at us, and the gun ports holding their cannons were open.

I felt the other smugglers' eyes cutting toward me in fury, but I did not dare look at them. Only Jack seemed oddly unperturbed, but was that simply because he was calm under pressure or because he was glad I'd scuttled their plan?

An officer with graying hair at the temples and a bicorne hat ordered his men to secure lines to our boat. Then he followed a trio of men aboard, pivoting left and then right to study each of us with a hard look. He stared between me and Colonel Junot the longest.

"Remove your bonnets," he ordered.

I complied swiftly, tugging the ribbons beneath my chin and pulling the confection from my head. A few strands of my auburn hair fell loose, trailing around my face.

The Frenchman took his time, as if postponing the inevitable. It was obvious from the customs official's expression that he already suspected he was not a woman. When Colonel Junot finally succeeded in taking off his bonnet, the official's scowl turned black.

"Why are you *attempting* to impersonate a female?"

Colonel Junot set his mouth into a stubborn line. When he refused to answer, the official turned to me. His gaze narrowed on the side of my face that still smarted from the colonel's strike. I could only guess it was discolored.

"Answer me. Why is he playing the part of a woman?"

I could almost hear the other smugglers cursing under their breath.

"Because he's a captured officer of the French army, and he's attempting to flee the country."

The colonel did curse aloud then, loudly and savagely in French. Words that made me wish I was not quite so fluent in the language.

The customs official apparently concurred, snapping at the

man in French to hold his tongue. Then he commanded two of his men to bind the colonel's wrists and detain him aboard the cutter. He paced a small circle on the deck as we waited for his men to follow his orders and two other revenue men boarded to take their places. As he pivoted to march in my direction again, I pushed the hair back from my face, trying to capture his eye. Once I had his attention I cut my gaze toward the hold, trying to communicate to him without words.

He paused and his eyes narrowed. "Search the cargo."

The canvas was removed to reveal my traveling trunks, a few kegs of produce, and half a dozen crates filled with what appeared to be foodstuffs. The weight of all of it combined could not have accounted for the depth the boat sat down in the water. One glance at the customs official's face told me he had also noted this discrepancy.

"You and you." He pointed to Rory and Dibs. "Move those crates."

The two men grumbled, but did as they were instructed. The official had them rotate the cargo about the hold, as if searching for something. But Rory's and Dibs's movements seemed odd. Rather than shift the barrels and trunks in a logical manner to maintain an even weight distribution, they kept leaving cargo over a portion of decking near the right back corner.

The official was not a stupid man. He noticed this, too, and sent one of his men down to inspect that piece of flooring. It didn't take long for him to locate a pair of loose boards cut into the deck. He pulled the planks up and reached inside.

I gasped as he opened his hand to reveal a pile of gold coins. They glimmered in the morning sun.

"'Tis a false bottom," the man called up to his officer. "There's more than two dozen sacks o' these guineas down here."

I turned to Jack, searching his face for the answers to the

dozens of questions forming in my mind. The sale or transport of gold out of the country was illegal. It had been for years. Even I knew that. And they were planning to transport all of this to France? I was too shocked to even speak.

However, the customs official was not. "Seize the boat, and detain everyone aboard." His gaze swung to me, but I couldn't tell what he was thinking. Whether I would be given special consideration or be lumped in with the other smugglers remained to be seen.

Chapter 34

UPON OUR ARRIVAL AT THE Customs House, the men were herded down a dank flight of stairs while I was taken to a small, windowless room above. I wasn't certain whether the officer was showing me consideration as a lady, or if he had witnessed Dibs' attempt to kill me and was worried someone would try again, and this time succeed before he got his answers. Either way, I was grateful to be segregated from the men. Their animosity had been unsettling enough on the short trip here, the hatred burning in their eyes burrowing into my skin. Only Jack seemed undaunted by our situation. I couldn't help but wonder if he was already familiar with being detained by customs officials, or if he knew something the rest of us didn't.

The room was empty save for two lit wall sconces, a small table, and an exceedingly hard ladder-back chair. Or at least it felt so after sitting on it for hours while I waited for someone to question me. At first, I'd welcomed the reprieve to gather my thoughts and organize my words so that I might explain myself in the best way possible. But as the minutes stretched into hours, I started to grow uneasy. Why had no one returned?

I rose from my chair to pace the room, even trying the

door to confirm it truly was locked. It seemed morning had turned into afternoon, and yet still no one came. I began to contemplate the possibility that they'd forgotten about me when a scrawny man entered carrying a glass of water and part of a loaf of bread. He plunked both down on the table and turned to leave, barely acknowledging my presence, let alone responding to my queries.

I sat down to devour the modest repast, and considered the possibility that perhaps they would not give me the chance to explain. Perhaps they meant to keep me here indefinitely.

I tried to push the frightening thought from my mind. After all, there was no bed or straw to sleep on. I hadn't even been given a bucket to relieve myself in. And the candles in their wall sconces were slowly burning down to nubs. Surely, they must return.

I buried my head in my arms on the table, trying to block the room from my sight and imagine I was somewhere else. Somewhere safe and cared for, with the sun shining warm on my cheeks.

It was then that a key turned in the lock and the door finally opened, but instead of the revenue officer who had arrested us, a balding man wearing spectacles entered, followed by Jack. I stared at him in confusion, trying to understand why he would be with this man. He had changed out of his borrowed livery into gentleman's riding clothes, including tall Hessians and buff trousers.

"Ask her whatever you wish, sir," he began, being the first to speak. "But as I already explained, I enlisted her and her father's help to flush out the culprits. And as you have seen, it worked." His gaze bored into mine as he addressed the balding man. I wasn't certain exactly what he was trying to communicate, but I was smart enough to ascertain he wished me to keep my mouth shut.

"I heard you the first time," the man responded crossly, glaring down at me. "Though I still do not understand why I was not forewarned of such activities occurring in my jurisdiction."

"I understand your frustration," Jack replied, clasping his hands behind his back. "But as a Lord of the Treasury, Lord Waveney charged me to keep this operation as secret as possible, and to involve only those I deemed absolutely necessary. I could not disregard his orders."

"Yes, well, Lord of the Treasury or not, your dashed brother is going to hear from me." He huffed. "I knew you both when you were but pups. I should think you both could have shown me a bit more consideration."

"Again, I apologize, sir. No offense was intended."

Both men turned to look at me then, and I was sure my eyes were as round as saucers. I thought I might bite a hole in my tongue trying to keep quiet after all of these revelations.

The balding man skewered me with what I assumed he thought was an intimidating stare, but after hearing the petulant tone of voice he'd used when speaking with Jack it only looked like he was sulking. "And you say she was assisting you?"

"Yes. Mr. and Miss Winterton were both indispensable in drawing the Comte de Reynard out. He never involved himself so overtly in the enterprise until he was enticed by the prospect of ensnaring them."

I felt a little sick hearing him explain the matter so succinctly. Clearly, I had been the bait, even if I had entered into the trap willingly.

The balding man leaned over the table, speaking to me directly for the first time. "So your father's excessive consumption of French brandy was all part of this plan as well, hmm?"

"It was," Jack answered for me.

"Well, then, I suppose I have no reason to continue holding her." He almost sounded disgruntled about that. "But I'm afraid we won't be able to reimburse the fines they paid. After all, Mr. Winterton did purchase illegal goods."

So *this* was the main source of his contention. I wondered how much of the revenue from those fines he had directly pocketed, and it was obvious Jack wondered that, too, but he chose not to argue. "I understand. I'm sure Lord Waveney will be willing to reimburse them himself."

"Hmm. Quite right." The customs official clapped his hands together, now content. "Well, then, I'll see that Miss Winterton's paperwork is completed and she is free to go."

We watched as he trundled happily out the door, closing it behind him, leaving me alone with Jack.

I stared up into his dark eyes, wondering if I knew him at all. This man I'd believed to be a smuggler, a member of the gentry, or a well-educated merchant's son fallen on hard times, was actually a viscount's brother working covertly to uncover all the players in a dangerous smuggling ring. Everything about him had been a masquerade, not just his act as a Lantern Man.

"I suppose I owe you a lengthy explanation," he began, though I could already hear the addendum to that statement coming. He glanced significantly at the door. "But we haven't the time."

I crossed my arms and scowled up at him.

"Suffice it to say, I'm not a smuggler, or a wherry man, or anything of the sort."

"You're Viscount Waveney's brother," I stated flatly.

"Yes." He scrutinized my face, as if trying to decipher what I was thinking. "I was an officer in the light infantry until my brother requested I return to Britain to assist him with a matter of delicacy. I left home at a young age, you see, because of the incident I described to you. So few people would recognize me, even here among the Broads where we spent much of our childhood."

I arched a single eyebrow. "So everything you told me wasn't a *complete* lie," I bit out. "Even if you did lead me to believe your brother was *dead*, not injured."

He didn't appear the least bit contrite. "Yes, well, you leapt to that conclusion, and I decided it would be best not to correct you.

"In case I made the connection?"

"Precisely."

I clenched my hands into fists in my lap. "I guess you fooled us all then," I remarked bitterly.

His brow lowered, the first indication that he felt any regret about what he'd done. "Yes, well, it wasn't easy. With my ready knowledge of the local waterways, it was simple enough to worm my way onto the smuggling crew. More difficult to convince them to trust me. But you… You were a different matter." He fell silent, studying me with a furrowed brow as if I were some riddle he hadn't yet solved. "I'd ferreted out some time ago that Reynard was the ringleader, but was never able to directly connect him or his venturers—his financial backers—until very recently."

"Because of me?"

"Partly. I already had some of the evidence I needed, but I admit your involvement made Reynard a bit reckless somehow." He shook his head. "I'm not sure I understand it."

I wasn't sure I did either. Not entirely.

"Why didn't you tell me any of this before?" I demanded furiously.

"I didn't know if I could trust you." He pressed his hands flat on the table and leaned toward me. "I couldn't risk the months of work I'd done simply because my conscience smarted at not telling you the truth."

I pointed my finger accusingly at his chest, not wanting to hear his excuses. "Do you know what I've been through? Do you know how agonized I've been? How much I've despised myself?"

Abruptly he stood taller. "You were the one who pushed to join us, who gave me no choice but to accept your demands."

"You could have done more to stop me. You could have warned me. I was desperate! I saw no other way." I sat back, glaring up at him. "You saw that, and you used it to your advantage."

He pressed his lips together tightly, but he didn't deny it.

I turned to stare at the wall, choking on the hurt and betrayal filling me. "All those times you met me on the dock, all those times you—" I broke off, unable to say the words. "What was that? Were you just doing your due diligence?"

"No. As I told you before, I simply wanted to." He paused. "I still do."

I felt my pulse quicken at the low timbre of his voice, and I glanced up at him sideways. The way he looked at me made my skin tingle and my breath catch, but I fought against it, refusing to give in to the fascination I felt for him. "So what happens now?"

He crossed his arms over his chest and glowered down at me. "Well, after the exploit you pulled this morning, I had to advance my plans a bit quicker than I'd intended."

"What was I supposed to do?" I argued. "Board that ship to France? Allow Colonel Junot to escape?"

"Yes. And no."

I scowled at him in confusion.

"I had a ship waiting to intercept us once we rounded Lowestoft Ness. Our ship never would have made it twenty miles out to sea, let alone to France."

I sank back in vexed disbelief. "And how was I to know that? Perhaps you should have thought to inform me."

His lips actually quirked. "Had I known you were going to kiss Colonel Junot so soundly while he was in his disguise as a lady's maid, I would have altered my orders." Then another thought seemed to occur to him, for his eyes hardened. "But I would have reacted more swiftly when it happened and broken Junot's knees before he could strike you."

His gaze fell on the side of my face where I had been struck. I had not yet had the opportunity to view the damage, but I was conscious of how tender it was to the touch.

"You might be happy to know he won't be striking anyone again, not for a very long time. Nor will Dibs be capable of wrapping his finger around any triggers." The sharp glint in his eye made me suspect the men's time at the Customs House had not been peaceful.

Seeming to recall the press of the clock, Jack glanced at the door. "But there's no time for this," he snapped in sudden annoyance, moving around the table to stand next to me. He pulled me up from my chair. "What you need to know now is that we raided Greenlaws."

I gasped.

"Everyone has been taken into custody—"

"Kate!"

He squeezed my arms. "*Except* Miss Rockland."

I sagged in relief.

"I instructed her to go to Penleaf Cottage. That you would return soon and she should remain there with you for the time being."

I nodded in gratitude. "And Robert?"

Jack searched my eyes before replying. "Is weak and cowardly, but not dangerous. I've offered him a proposition. If he testifies against Reynard and the other venturers, if he reveals all he knows, the government will allow him to relocate to India, permanently, instead of being tried for treason."

I knew without having to ask that Jack was doing this for me. He didn't like Robert. I couldn't blame him. But because of my friendship with the Rocklands he was sparing me the grief of seeing him hanged.

"Thank you," I murmured, trying to convey in those two small words how much his leniency meant to me.

He nodded once curtly before continuing. "But unfortunately, Reynard has evaded us." He grimaced. "I don't know if he knew somehow that you were going to cause problems for him, even after his blatant threats this morning."

I shuddered at the memory of his teeth scraping along my earlobe.

"Or if he planned all along to leave today. No matter, somehow he had already fled. So I must go after him." Jack pulled me closer, lowering his head so that he could see directly into my eyes. "However, I want you to promise me that you will wait for me at your cottage."

I stared up at him, the pain of his betrayal still too fresh for me to speak.

"I don't want you rushing off to visit your great-aunt."

I stiffened.

"Or haring off to places unknown."

I opened my mouth to demand how he'd known about my great-aunt when the door suddenly opened behind him. Jack swiveled to tell the man who had entered to give him a moment before leaning even closer to me.

"I want to be able to find you when I return. And then…" He sighed. "Then I'll answer your questions," he added almost resignedly. "But it may be a few days or possibly weeks before I can do so. It all depends on how elusive Reynard proves to be. I've suspected for some time that this operation isn't the only smuggling ring he controls, so he may go into hiding." His eyes and his voice were insistent. "Will you wait?"

I stared up at him, wishing I could deny him, wishing I could tell him to go to the devil. But I knew I couldn't. Not when his request was so simple. Not when he looked at me like that. "Yes," I murmured.

He exhaled in what sounded like relief and nodded. "Then I must go." He swiveled to include the man standing in the doorway. "But Crisp will see you safely home, and remain close by to be certain you come to no harm before I return."

I blinked in surprise, and a cheeky grin spread across the other man's face, lighting his bright blue eyes. "You! You're one of the men who rowed me out to the *Reliance*."

"Aye. One and the same."

I glanced at Jack, trying to understand.

"Did you truly think I would let you embark on that mission alone?" The glimmer in his eyes said he knew I'd believed just that. "I had people watching you the whole time."

And before I could find my tongue to ask him how, he was gone.

I stared after him for longer than was probably proper, but Crisp didn't seem to mind. When I finally gathered up my bonnet and joined him in the doorway, he offered me his arm, which I accepted with a weary smile.

"Did I mention ye're in for a treat?" he said, guiding me down the corridor. His eyes twinkled. "Grandda insisted on joinin' us."

Chapter 35

THAT NIGHT KATE AND I lay awake side by side in my bed, staring up into the dark shadows of my bed curtains. We hadn't had the chance to talk earlier, what with Mrs. Brittle hovering over us, plying us with tea and biscuits just as she'd done when we were children and we'd fallen and scraped our knees. Then later I'd left Kate in the comfort of the kitchen and gone in search of Father.

He had looked even more haggard than the night before, proving he hadn't yet indulged in his brandy. When I sat down to explain what Jack had done, how he'd lied to clear our names, his eyes had stared bleakly back at me, as if in shock. Then his Adam's apple bobbed in his throat once as he swallowed and nodded.

I had expected nothing more from him, but he had surprised me when he stopped me and Kate on the stairs before we retired, telling us to sleep easy. He would make certain we were safe. And with a kiss on my forehead, like he'd done when I was young, he sent us off to bed.

Kate had remained quiet as we moved slowly about my bedchamber to ready ourselves for bed, sensing that I'd needed the time to think after Father's uncustomary display of affection. She could have slept in any of the three vacant bedrooms in the cottage, but she stayed with me, like always. There was a comfort in knowing we were not alone, in feeling the solid weight of another human being lying beside us on the mattress, in hearing the rhythmic inhale and exhale of their breathing. Particularly on a night like this.

"Do you know what you'll do now?" I finally ventured to inquire, speaking into the darkness. Kate hadn't moved for some time, but I knew she was awake. I could feel her worrying.

She sighed. "No."

"Will you go to India with Robert?" I murmured, pushing the real question I wanted to ask past my lips.

"I don't know." Her voice was tentative. "I don't think I want to."

I could understand that. India was half a world away. The journey alone would require weeks if not months of travel, and unless she married a man who planned to return to Britain, she might never set foot on English soil ever again.

I found it difficult enough to accept that Robert was essentially banished, even though I knew he deserved such a punishment, or worse. But the thought of Kate being forced to join him in exile made my chest ache. If she went, I might never see her again.

"Do you have any relatives who might welcome you?"

"*Welcome* might be too strong a word," she replied with a sardonic twist to her voice. "But yes. An aunt and uncle in Bedfordshire with four exasperating children and approximately twenty dogs, and a widowed aunt in Westmorland who constantly writes to tell us how lonely she is."

"I think I would choose the lonely aunt."

Kate's hair rustled against her pillow as she turned her head. "She does seem like the obvious choice, doesn't she? She may only require companionship, while my Bedfordshire relatives are constantly in want of a proper governess." She scrunched up her nose in distaste and I smiled as I tried and failed to imagine Kate caring for four small children.

"Although Mother did always say my widowed aunt was a bit balmy. But then again she claimed the same thing of about half of her acquaintances. So either my mother made a habit of visiting Bedlam or she declared that about anyone who didn't meet her impossible standards."

"What happened to your aunt's husband?"

Kate began to play with the ends of her braid. "I don't know. She was wed and widowed very young. Before they were able to have children, I guess."

"So maybe she *is* just lonely." Then another thought occurred to me. "Westmorland is awfully far away."

"It is," she conceded. "But not nearly as far as India."

"True."

We fell silent, each of our minds busy with our own thoughts. Kate's hand slid under the covers to grip mine where it laid by my side, and I could feel her misery and uncertainty.

"I'm sorry, Kate," I said, wishing there was something I could do.

She tightened her grasp. "There's no need to apologize. This is a better outcome than I could have ever hoped for. If you hadn't been so brave, if Jack didn't care for you so, I suspect I would be facing destitution and the scandal of the century, if not my own trial for treason." Her voice hardened. "Robert is lucky to be granted exile and a hefty fine. He could have been made to forfeit everything, including his life."

"I know. But I still hate the fact that you now have to choose whether to join him in that exile or go live with some distant relative you barely know. If only you could live on your own at Greenlaws." I huffed. "It's ridiculous. If you were a widow like your aunt no one would think anything of it."

Kate surprised me by laughing. "Don't worry about me, Ella. This is probably more than I deserve. And in all likelihood, I would probably get into serious trouble if I lived on my own. Scandalize the village."

A reluctant grin escaped my lips. "I would keep you from disgrace."

"You'd try," she scoffed. "But you never have been good at saying no to me."

She was right. I was abominable at it. When he was alive, my brother had forever been berating me for it. He'd sworn that someday Kate was going to drag me into some sort of trouble I couldn't extricate us from. Not entirely, at least.

And he'd been right.

"You must promise to write," I told her, knowing just how abysmal she was at keeping up with her correspondence.

"I'll try," she answered honestly.

"You'd better. Or I'll hunt you down just to scold you."

Her voice softened. "I'll hold you to that."

I felt a lump forming in my throat, but somehow I was able to push my voice past it. "Good."

She released my hand then and we both closed our eyes, but it was a long time before either of us slept.

Two days later, Robert was released. I heard from Kate that he had been given one week to put his affairs in order and book passage on a ship to India. Even though he tried to convince his sister to accompany him, Kate had made up her mind to stay in England, a decision I knew had not been easy for her. Despite all of his flaws and mistakes, he was still her brother. I could see how much it broke her heart to say good-bye knowing she might very well never see him again.

I shed no small amount of tears as we said our farewells and she climbed into the carriage that would whisk her off to the north. Robert was conspicuously absent, and though Kate tried not to show how much this bothered her, I could tell from the tightness around her mouth and the way she continued to glance at the house that it did.

"He just can't face us," she murmured when I asked where he was. "All this time, I think he still wanted to believe he was being noble, wanted us to believe it. That he had wed Olivia with good intentions, even though it hurt us. That he hadn't stopped the smuggling the moment he found out about it because he was protecting his wife and then me and his servants from destitution. That he'd been cruelly used and forced into all of this." Her brow furrowed. "But now that it's all come out, now that he's realized that you were able to do in a matter of weeks what he couldn't do in four years—free us from Reynard—he simply can't face us." Her gaze shifted to meet mine. "Especially knowing it was your influence that saved him from the noose."

I recognized the truth in what she said, but nevertheless I was irritated by his absence, as much for Kate's sake as my own.

With a coachman, a footman, and her eminently capable lady's maid in tow, I knew Kate was as protected as she could be as I watched her carriage roll down the drive to the road, but I still fretted. It would be a long time before I stopped doing so. Kate was lovely, spirited, and loyal, but she was also rash, overly-romantic, and possessed of a quick temper. There was no telling what sort of trouble she would encounter.

As for Robert, I wasn't sure words could adequately express how angry and disappointed I was in him. Not only had he refused to see his sister off—the sister he had failed to protect—but he also could not be bothered to tender me an apology in person. He took the coward's way out, sending me a short, almost terse note along with my mother's pianoforte. While I was grateful to have the instrument back, I was incredibly hurt he hadn't cared enough to see me one last time before he sailed for India. No matter how upset I was with him, I still would have liked to say a proper goodbye.

Several weeks passed and there still had been no word of Reynard's capture or any sign that Jack had returned. I began to wonder if I'd made a foolish promise agreeing to wait for him. He'd warned me it could take some time, but I supposed I expected the matter to be concluded rather swiftly. After all, how far could Reynard have run? Was he truly that elusive or had he been apprehended in secret and Jack had merely forgotten about me?

It had taken many days, but my temper had finally cooled enough that I could view things more objectively. I was still hurt that he had lied to me for so long, especially after I'd given him my tentative trust, but I also recognized he'd been placed in a difficult situation. He'd made promises to his brother and to his country, and he could not have easily broken them. I still believed he should have confided in me the truth, but I better appreciated his predicament.

Had I been in his shoes I'm not sure I wouldn't have made the very same choices he had. And he did clear my and my father's names, and spare my friends from a worse fate for their crimes. In truth, beyond that Jack owed me nothing, not even an explanation, no matter how I longed to hear it. No matter how much I wanted to believe there was more to our association than expedience.

At least one good thing came of my weeks of waiting: I was able to spend time with my father while he was sober, more time than we'd spent together in years. He truly was trying his best this time. His haggard appearance began to improve with each passing day, helped along by our long walks in the countryside and Mrs. Brittle's cooking.

The money Lord Waveney had given us—which he'd refused to have returned, stating it was payment for services to the Crown—had allowed us to pay off the remainder of our debts and restock our larder, with a tidy sum still left over. I even made a new agreement with Mr. Ingles. I wouldn't reveal to the authorities just what had happened to Mr. Watkins in his establishment so long as he stopped bribing my father with brandy.

As for Watkins's body, it had never been located. Though in truth the revenue men did not seem to be searching for it since no one had come forward to report him missing. I found it somewhat suspicious that a portion of the flooring at the White Horse had been newly replaced and the pub smelled strongly of turpentine, but I didn't ask why. I didn't want to know.

Crisp, on the other hand, seemed to be doing his best to make the innkeeper and the rest of Thurlton sweat over his presence at the White Horse. True to Jack's word, Crisp had remained nearby to watch over me and Kate to be certain Reynard didn't return to Norfolk to cause trouble. Though I was quite certain Crisp hadn't gone so far as to introduce himself as a revenue man, the villagers seemed to have sniffed him out anyway. It was evident that Crisp didn't mind. In fact, from the twinkle in his eye, he seemed to rather enjoy the effect he was having on the villagers, and I could only assume he knew why. However, I didn't expect him to do anything about it. Not for the moment anyway.

I knew better than to believe Father's craving for French brandy and the forgetfulness it could bring would ever completely end. It would always be there, beneath the surface, a sneaking thing waiting to take him away from me again. I even found him standing at the front window on some evenings, staring out at nothing, his fists clenched as if fighting against something. The urge to visit the White Horse? But he continued to resist, and I had hope he would keep doing so, because he seemed to have found a reason stronger than his desire to give in.

However, Father and I had both agreed I should visit my great-aunt. After reading the few letters she had written my mother that my father had not destroyed long ago in a fit of drunken rage, I was intensely curious about her and all of my mother's family, even my grandfather. If all went well, I had hopes that perhaps some arrangement could be made where I split my time between Lady Bramford and her homes in London and Suffolk, and my father at Penleaf Cottage. Whether she could help me find a husband, I didn't know, but it was simply enough to know I had someone else who cared. If Father began to drink heavily again, if he lost our cottage, I would have someone to turn to, somewhere to go. I wouldn't be left all alone, as I'd so desperately feared.

And so all there was left for me to do was wait.

Until one morning when Mrs. Brittle returned from the village to tell us how Thurlton was humming with the news that Waveney Hall was being opened up across the marsh. Orders had been given to augment the skeleton staff who maintained the property in the viscount's absence with people from the local villages.

"Sounds like it's to be more than temporary," Mrs. Brittle explained. "And 'twill do the folks here a lot o' good. 'Specially those who lost their positions at Greenlaws when the house was closed up."

I nodded absently, only partially listening as she prattled on. I was too busy wondering exactly what this meant. Was Lord Waveney merely attempting to make up for the loss of the surrounding villages' main legal employer? Or was he actually taking up residence again here in the Broads? And would his brother be joining him?

Chapter 36

THE DAY HAD BEEN WARM and damp, so when the sun set and the temperature rapidly began to drop, the fog rolled up from the marshes like storm clouds piling up on the horizon. It was an evening much like the night I had first encountered Jack masquerading as a Lantern Man while on my way to deliver that much-needed medicine to Kate.

Staring around me at the swirling fog I could almost believe it had all been a strange dream, except too much had changed. I was no longer that hesitant girl, hiding from the past, running from the pain, waiting for my life to change. Waiting for someone or something to intercede on my behalf, to save me. I had lamented that my prayers were not being answered, that I'd been abandoned, when in truth the options had already been laid before me, waiting for me to take action.

I pressed my hand to my mother's brooch pinned to my chest and crossed toward the end of our dock. The boards I had removed to trap Jack had since been repaired—their pale, smooth finish glaringly bright next to the weathered wood of the rest of the dock. The water trickled softly beneath me, swishing about the pilings as it made its way toward the river. Its sound was the only accompaniment to my breathing, as the insects and other night creatures hid from the fog. Occasionally I would hear the burble of a fish passing by or a bubble of marsh gas escaping to the surface, but the rest of the night was still, silent, waiting.

As I was.

Perhaps it was silly to think he would appear here tonight. Perhaps I was reading too much into the news Mrs. Brittle had shared about Waveney Hall being reopened, and was deluding myself to believe it was a sign. There could be any number of reasons the viscount had decided to return to the Broads after such a long absence, and most of them had nothing to do with me, or his brother Jack, for that matter. But somehow this felt right. Even the mist seemed like a portent, though I hoped this time it was of something good.

Setting my lantern at my feet, I closed my eyes and began to hum a song my mother had sung to me as a child, something soft and sweet and soothing. I could still hear her voice in my head as she cradled me close, smell the perfume on her skin, and this time the memory brought me no pain, only peace.

As I paused to draw breath between verses, I suddenly realized I wasn't alone. My heart quickened, but this time not in alarm, but anticipation.

I knew he was standing behind me, however I didn't want to face him yet. I didn't want to be drawn into his gaze, so I simply turned my head to the side so that he could better hear me. "You returned."

His footsteps moved closer, until he was standing almost directly at my back. I could feel the warmth of him through my clothes. "Yes." His voice was cello-deep, as it had been that first night we met on this dock and it resonated in me as it had before. "You worried I wouldn't."

"I didn't know what to think," I admitted, though his statement had not been a question. I lowered my chin, pulling a deep breath into my lungs past the tightness in my chest. My scalp and the fine hairs down my neck, back, and all along my arms had come alive, tingling at his nearness. "Did you capture Reynard?"

Out of the corner of my eye, I saw him nod. "Just as he was boarding a ship in Romney Marsh."

"In Sussex?"

"Apparently he thought to take his chances directing his enterprise from across the channel in France."

I inhaled again, this time in relief. "So it is finished?"

"For now."

I turned to look at him then, noticing he wore no hat. He never had, unless his role required it. And just like always his still too-long dark hair was carelessly tousled by the wind, as if he couldn't be bothered with it. It was reassuring somehow. So much about the man I had known had been a charade, from his garments down to his occupation, but there were still parts of him that remained unchanged. Like his eyes the color of nightingale wings, which stared intensely into mine now.

"There are other smuggling rings. Other men out to undermine the British currency and the British government for their own gain. Reynard was just one of the most cunning."

I pulled my cloak tighter about me and swiveled to face him fully. "Tell me." I had no way of knowing if he would confide in me or not, but I stood patiently, waiting for him to decide.

He studied me with a puckered brow. "All right. Have you heard of the guinea run?"

"No."

"It's what we call the smuggling of gold from Britain to France. You know it's illegal?"

I nodded.

"The runs are mostly made along the coasts of Kent and Sussex, where the channel is narrowest. But my brother discovered that an operation was also working among the Broads of Norfolk or Suffolk, somewhere near our childhood home.

This one was a better kept secret than most, with higher rank-ing venturers. Rockland was able to divulge some of their names, and we're hoping Reynard will prove cooperative enough to tell us the rest." He scowled. "But I'm not opti-mistic."

"So that gold in the false bottom of the wherry boat…"

"Was not the first they'd smuggled out," he finished for me. "Nor was Colonel Junot the first French prisoner they'd helped to escape. This was a clever, furtive, well-run opera-tion. Hence the difficulty in catching more than the lowest rung of men—those who did all the work and shouldered most of the risk, and were consequently easiest to replace."

He tilted his head. "Do you remember the code Harry asked you to relay to Captain Haywood? The one Reynard was so furious you might have shared?"

"How could I forget? Greybar twenty-three."

"The words mean nothing to most people, but Haywood would have recognized it immediately. It told him at which point along the coast to look for the gold that had already been stashed there for him to retrieve. And it let him know how many casks holding the gold had been sunk in the shal-low water at that location."

"Is that what you all were doing while I paid my visit to the *Reliance*?" I asked in some shock.

"No. The work of sinking contraband is almost always done at night. And I had not been part of that particular crew." His mouth twisted wryly. "That day we were actually plying an honest trade."

I arched my eyebrows. "Except for the part I had to play."

"Yes. Except for that."

"So I guess I wasn't supposed to reveal the code to you when you asked me?"

"No. And I had to make a quick explanation as to why you'd told me when Reynard began to rant about how you had betrayed us after their twenty-three casks of gold were confiscated by the revenue service." He flashed me a grin.

"What did you say?" I gasped.

"That you had been acting jittery and I was afraid you would forget the message or relay it wrong."

"And he believed you?" I asked doubtfully.

He shrugged. "He didn't have me killed."

Hearing him state it so bluntly made me realize just how much danger he'd been in. At any point, if Reynard or any of the others had realized who he really was, or had even begun to suspect his true reason for joining their crew, they would have murdered him and sunk his body in the marsh. "How long have you been working to entrap Reynard?"

"The better part of a year."

And all that time I'd never known it. But, of course, I'd also never apprehended that a smuggling ring was centered at Greenlaws for the past four years, or that Robert was involved. Clearly I was not as perceptive as I'd believed.

The direction of my thoughts must have been evident, for Jack reached out to brush a stray hair back from where it curled against my jaw. "Remember, I said they were more furtive than most. And I haven't been here in the fens the whole time. I did spend my fair share of nights crossing the channel, dodging naval vessels manning the blockade, and secluded at the special compound Napoleon has built near Gravelines to accommodate and encourage British smugglers."

I stared at him wide-eyed. It was almost too much. "Truly?"

He nodded. "Napoleon recognizes that if he wants to win this war his best chance is to weaken the British economy. And his best chance of doing that is by encouraging the guinea run."

It was dastardly, and seemingly occurring without most people knowing about it. But perhaps that was by design. Perhaps the government didn't trust this information not to cause panic, or inspire further smuggling. But something Jack had said earlier troubled me. "And you said it's happening elsewhere?"

"Yes." His eyes were serious, as if he already anticipated my next question.

"And you've been given the task of stopping them?"

"Given and willingly accepted. But it's not all I do. And most of the time it does not require me to work in disguise."

What he wasn't saying, what I knew he meant, was that it *did* require him to travel extensively, to place himself in danger, and sometimes to embark upon jobs such as this one, where he concealed his true identity to work alongside the smugglers. I could read it all in his eyes, and it settled over me like a heavy blanket, smothering the foolish hopes I had been harboring in my heart.

I swallowed past the lump that had formed in my throat and nodded, hoping he could not sense my disappointment. I tried to gather my thoughts, to voice my thanks for vouching for me and my father so I could then escape with my dignity still intact. But before I could find the words, Jack found his.

"I have something for you," he declared.

I didn't know what to expect, so I watched with some misgiving as he leaned over to pull something from inside his boot. It wasn't until he raised it to his head that I realized it was a knife. I pressed a hand to my throat in alarm as with a swift slice he severed several strands of his hair.

Then he held out his palm to me, showing me the dark hairs nestled within. I glanced up into his eyes to find him staring at me intently. Still uncertain, I reached up to accept what he offered.

"Now you also have power over me," he murmured. "Though in truth, you always did."

The impact of his words pushed the breath from my lungs, so that all I could do was exhale a startled puff of air as I wrapped my fingers tightly around his gift. But he must have understood anyway, for he gathered me in his arms to steal the rest of my breath.

Sometime later when he pulled away, I discovered I was trapped between his warm body and the rough dock post, and not in the least averse to such a position. I rested my head against his chest, listening to the steady drum of his heartbeat, and the rumble of his voice when he next spoke.

"I told my brother I require several weeks of leave, so we shall be able to have the banns read here in Thurlton and across the marsh in my home parish beginning this Sunday."

I lifted my head to look up at him in astonishment. "The banns."

"Yes," he replied as if he'd just declared something entirely reasonable. "Unless you wish for me to procure a special license. I'm sure my brother could arrange it."

"Of marriage?" I asked, still trying to comprehend.

"Yes." His eyebrows lifted. "Unless you object."

"No. But…" I gazed up into his face at the sly slant of his eyes, the scar near his hairline, the amused quirk of his lips, and realized it was senseless to argue. Not when my answer to his unasked proposal was yes.

So instead I smiled and kissed him.

Later, when the candle in the lantern had begun to burn low, we still stood in each other's arms, whispering things to one another that had yet to be said. And when our words were through, I rested my head against his strong shoulder, marveling at the turn my life had taken, wondering at the twists that awaited me. I should have been tired, but the joy still thrumming along my nerves kept my eyes open, staring into the swirling mist that seemed to wrap around us like a cocoon, sheltering us from the rest of the world.

It was then that I noticed the light. It was faint, just a tiny orb shining in the distance, but it sent a chill racing down my back. I blinked once, then twice, trying to clear it from my vision, to dismiss it as a part of my imagination. But there it remained, if possible seeming to glow brighter.

I opened my mouth to tell Jack, but then stopped. Would he chase after it? Would he insist on discovering what it was? I wasn't sure I wanted to know.

So I held my tongue, and seemed to be rewarded when the light slowly began to fade, until there was nothing but fog and beyond that the dark of night. But it was a long time before I closed my eyes.

Titles by Anna Lee Huber

Anna Lee Huber is the Daphne award-winning author of the national bestselling Lady Darby Mysteries, as well as the forthcoming Verity Kent Mysteries and the anthology *The Jacobite's Watch*. She is a summa cum laude graduate of Lipscomb University in Nashville, Tennessee, where she majored in music and minored in psychology. She currently resides in Indiana with her family and is hard at work on her next novel. Visit her online at www.annaleehuber.com.

CPSIA information can be obtained
at www.ICGtesting.com
Printed in the USA
LVOW03s1659270917
550098LV00001B/2/P

9 780997 939620